UNDERSEA ATROPHIA

GEOFFREY MORRISON

Cover Design by Clara Moon
Edited by Karen Finer
Proofread by Jeffrey Ricker

This is a work of fiction. Names, characters, places, brands, media, and incidents are either the product of the author's imagination or are used fictitiously. Any resemblance to similarly named places or to persons living or deceased is unintentional.

PRINT ISBN 978-0-9847779-4-5
EPUB ISBN 978-0-9847779-3-8

1st Edition

UNDERSEA
ATROPHIA

INTERSTITIAL

We fled under the seas out of protection. Out of necessity. Our broken world had driven us here, unprepared, cowering.

But we endured, two city-sized submarines our new home. Over time, we spread to the watery sea floor, stretching our tentative tendrils, eking out life using what we had, and what we could find.

But resources were limited, and tensions erupted. The two subs, the Universalis *and the* Population, *battled for years, deciding eventually that avoidance was the only path to peace.*

Time passed. Life evolved. The ships aged. Lasting far longer than their designers could have hoped, the Uni *and* Pop *couldn't avoid the relentless grind of entropy.*

A plan was conceived, an attempt by the Universalis *to assist a slowly healing planet. A giant tower, the Fountain, taller than the ships were long, anchored at the top of the world. Hopes were high for a return to the surface, before the submarines fell.*

Those on the Population *perceived this as an attempt to disrupt their way of life, and a new battle raged. With pure offensive might, the* Pop *subdued the* Uni *and nearly destroyed the tower in the process. Countless died, more would soon follow.*

But there were survivors...

PART 1

GERAN LO braced his bulk against the dripping white wall and allowed himself a moment. He felt exhaustion descend like the weight of the ocean above him, so he keyed his mic.

"Go on pump one," he spoke for the countless time. Water churned around his waist in the partially flooded corridor. His armored pressure suit had been a second skin for two days. Two days without respite. Two days without sleep. Fatigue blurred anything that came before. There was just the suit. The crash, and the suit. Protective armor that kept the world out, but the tired in.

Had it been more than two days? Geran's mind drifted, sluggishly, from event to event as he tried to piece together the past few days. Event to event to... He pushed off the wall, realizing he'd lost consciousness for a moment. His bulky frame swayed under its own weight. He made his way down the inclined corridor, submerging under the water as he went.

It was easier to hear the banging under the water. It was slower now, as if the sound itself was tiring. This was definitely the corridor, though. But then, he'd thought that before. He pushed his way along, the water fighting him with every step, warning him to turn back.

The citysub *Universalis,* mortally wounded, had embedded itself into the seafloor at a shallow downward angle, crushing the entire bow and, Lo assumed, most of the Yard. Not that the Yard hadn't flooded long before the crash. The *Population* had seen to that. The Garden, the biggest open space on the ship, was also open to the sea beyond. How they were ever going to have enough food again was something Lo chose not to think about. Tried not to, anyway. He just didn't have the energy.

Not that he had the energy for search and rescue either, but here he was. Most of his team from the *Reappropriation,* the rugged attack sub that'd been their home for months, had survived. This was largely due to the armored drysuits they had been, and he still was, wearing. He'd floated, powerless, watching his battered ship, depleted of ammunition, embed itself into the bow of the juggernaut citysub *Population...* to no effect. A boulder rolling over a pebble.

So his team had followed the *Uni* down, horrified at the inevitable carnage as it slammed into the seafloor. Getting aboard was the easy part, the hull rent and torn. There were survivors. Lo, a sergeant in whatever still existed as military, had taken command of a small group and tasked them with helping whoever they could. Emergency bulkheads had done their job, sparing many but trapping others. So Lo and his team struggled on, clearing section by section, shoring up leaks where they could, freeing trapped survivors when possible. As his mind drifted to the *Reap,* he realized the last time he'd slept had been aboard that ship, and now that he focused on it, it had definitely been more than two days ago.

He opened his eyes with a start, only then realizing he'd passed out again. It hadn't been too long, but the pumps had dropped the water level in the corridor to eye level. A few minutes, maybe? This had revealed a high-pressure leak in the bulkhead, the water rushing out of a thin crack with enough force to sever an unarmored hand.

The engineers called the tool a fusor, but to Lo it was the best kind of magic. He held it near the leak and pulled the trigger, walking it along the gash. The intense stream of water vaporized instantly as it struck the fusor's heat but, more importantly, the bulkhead began melting together, closing the tear tiny bit by tiny bit, until fully sealed. It took a few minutes, more for larger breaches, but it worked, it held, and it was progress. The water was by his ankles by the time he was finished, revealing the top of a lock farther down the corridor. It was faint, but he could definitely hear the banging in the air now. Through the exhaustion, his heart jumped; this *was* the right corridor. All of a sudden, he was awake, and excited. He sloshed quickly toward the lock. Enough of the water had cleared by the time he got to the door that he could brace himself before it and pound hard with his armored fist.

The response was immediate and rapid. He could hear the shouts through the door and his helmet. The door had automatically sealed, sensing water, but staring at the control panel, Lo realized he had no idea how to override it. This was something he'd need to discuss with the engineers before the next section. For now, he did what he normally did in situations like this: He punched it. The control panel disintegrated from the impact of his huge gauntleted hand, revealing a mass of wires and relays no less confusing.

Nothing happened. With a weary shrug, Lo leaned his bulk against the door and used the reinforced gloves to wedge into the seam between the door halves. Little by little, the doors slid apart. The light from his helmet cast an eerie glow through the slit, illuminating several pale and excited, but clearly exhausted, faces. The water rushed out around his feet, barely noticed in the excitement. Finally, he got his fingers around the edge of the door and, with one mighty shove, forced the doors fully open.

The scene beyond churned the big man's stomach. Two corpses lay on tables against the far wall of what appeared to be an office. The water level was at least knee high on the bow side of the room, and still calf high on the stern side. Over a dozen people, soaked and shivering, pushed forward toward the door and escape. He was glad to be breathing recirculated air, as he could only imagine the smell. After checking that the doors wouldn't seal shut if he let go, Lo stepped back and let them escape. Each, in their own way, thanked him as they passed. Some with a mere nod, others a smile, others, a brief hug.

Lo hesitated entering the room, a prison of darkness and terror, not cleansed by the meager light from the corridor. He forced himself inside. These poor people, he thought, trapped and expecting to die in the dark. Some had. Three more bodies floated in the corner, bloated and discolored. He turned away.

Something caught his eye. In the far corner of the room, farthest from the door, farthest from the bodies, a tiny girl sat balled up in an office chair. Knees to her chest, arms wrapped around her legs, she looked alive to Lo, as he figured a corpse couldn't remain that way. He maneuvered around the tables, chairs, and other detritus and loomed over the girl. No, he realized; woman. Though her face was partially buried against her knees, she looked only a few years younger than him. Her hair was the color of copper pipe, her skin so white it looked almost transparent under the lights from his helmet. Oh, crap, the helmet, he thought. No wonder she's shaking.

Lo knelt before her, knowing that even so posed, his frame was still taller than this tiny woman would be standing on her toes. He touched his gloved hand to the side of his helmet, and the visor slid back, revealing his face. While his body was huge in size, Lo prided himself that it was largely muscle, but his face still held all the fat of his youth: soft and rounded. He was told he looked friendly, unless he was scowling. Then he looked terrifying. It felt foreign as he did it, but he managed to flash a smile.

"My name is Geran Lo. Are you injured?" he asked. The room smelled worse than he'd imagined, almost making him gag.

"Dija Yunner." Her voice was as small as she was. Almost so quiet he didn't hear it, muffled, as it was, by her legs. "Dija Yunner. Technician, 1st Class. Dome F511. Dija Yunner. Technician. Dija Yunner." She began rocking back and forth, causing little waves to radiate outwards from the chair.

"Ms. Yunner, are you injured? Can you walk?"

Lo watched as she continued silently rocking. He shifted uncomfortably.

"Uh, Ms. Yunner, I'm going to pick you up now. Please don't be alarmed. We can get you some help."

Lo reached out slowly, and as gently as he could, put one arm under her knees, and the other behind her back. Even without the suit's assistance, he would have been able to lift her with little effort. It amused his weary mind briefly that in his last workout, so many days — weeks? — before, he'd used weights heavier than this woman. For each arm.

There it went again, his mind wandering off. He needed to be careful. That could be dangerous in these conditions.

But in the light of the hallway, he got a better look at the woman and couldn't look away. This time he let his mind wander.

II

"THIS IS Ralla Gattley, requesting assistance. Please respond. This is Ralla Gattley, transmitting from the bridge of the *Population*. Anyone… please respond."

Countless holes in the hull let in streams of sunlight and a sharp, frigid wind that hissed through the ruined bridge. Ralla shivered. Slumping into a chair, she clicked the radio off. The chair was cold. The console was cold. She was cold. Moving helped, so she stood, jumped in place a few times, then made her way forward. The impact with the ice had shattered the ship's bow, rendering the structure an unrecognizable maze of torn bulkheads, snapped girders, and dangling wire. It had also opened access to the outside.

Outside. The thought hadn't gotten old in the day or so they'd been stranded. Here she was, carefully making her way through a passage that, dangerous as it may be, led *outside*. She could see it at the end of the jagged tunnel: a bright white expanse. Ducking through the last part, the exterior hull, she emerged into the sunshine. It offered little warmth, but that was hardly the point. Before her, in its painfully bright brilliance, lay the slowly growing, artificially created ice cap. In the center, far in the distance, the proud gray-blue tower of the Fountain stood majestically above it all. From its improbable height erupted a steady stream of tiny ice particles upwards and outwards, to fall and help grow the berg cap below. The sunlight caught these in flight, sparkling. Beyond these, and all the way to the horizon — the *horizon* — was a sky a shade of pure blue she'd never seen before. She couldn't stop marveling at it. It made her feel small, yet calm.

The wind had already created random hills and drifts, lapping against the black hull of the former citysub *Population*. The wreck spread out below her, beside her, and behind her, lying like a beached, crushed, and decaying carcass. Pieces scattered by the impact were already disappearing beneath the snow. Massive gashes split the hull support beams jutting outward at disturbing angles. Whatever happens in the future, Ralla thought, this will be the final resting place of this once-mighty vessel.

The sun had remained rather rigidly overhead. It had been years since she had studied it in school, but she was pretty sure it was supposed to disappear over the horizon at some point. It had barely moved since she first stepped outside with Thom the day before.

Had it been a day? Hours? She couldn't tell. They'd done so much since the crash, it was all a blur. Or maybe that was just her. Her brain was fuzzy from all the painkillers. Ralla looked down at her ruined right hand. The new bandage didn't show any signs of blood, largely thanks to the emergency sutures Thom had found in a medkit shortly after the crash. She wasn't going to bleed to death today, so there's that, she thought. However, she wasn't going to be counting higher than seven any time soon, either. She was surprised how little she cared about her missing fingers. Maybe that was the drugs too, or maybe not. If three fingers was the price she paid for saving the Fountain, and the world, so be it.

The sun hadn't warmed her up, like she knew it wouldn't, so she made her way back inside. Thom, bent at the waist, poked his head into the bridge opening of her tunnel. He looked beat up, with his scraggly beard, unwashed hair, blood-caked ears. Although she couldn't see it as she crouch-walked down the passage, she knew his right arm was coated in dried blood. But he was alive and he was here. And so was she. That was enough, for now.

_—-__

Thom looked down the passageway at Ralla. She looked beat up, with her overly bandaged hand, closely cropped hair, and emaciated frame. Not that it mattered in the least. It had only been an hour or so since he'd seen her last, but the excitement at seeing her again still overwhelmed the fear and anxiety of their current situation. She stood as she exited the passageway, and they kissed. He knew they both smelled terrible, looked terrible, *tasted* terrible, but for the moment they were safe, and together. Sunlight filtered in from thousands of tiny holes in the hull around them.

"Any luck?" he asked, ending the kiss but still holding her tight. She shook her head and kissed him again. It had taken hours to scavenge enough parts to rig the transmitter to the ship's remaining battery power. Whether it was actually broadcasting, they had no way of knowing. Whether anyone was alive to hear it, even if it was transmitting, they chose not to think about. Around them, ominous echoing creaks and groans seemed to portend imminent collapse, or a catastrophic slip into the sea below.

Ralla shivered again.

"I found three escape subs; two were crushed, but the third seems intact," Thom said. After shivering their way through an apparently endless day, they'd gotten each other patched up the best they could and gotten the ship broadcasting... maybe. While Ralla tried to make contact, Thom had set out to explore the deserted remains of the *Population*.

Ralla nodded as she buried her face in his chest. His arm, thankfully sans bullet, ached from holding her. It was easily ignorable given the circumstances. Taking it out hadn't been fun, especially with

Ralla only able to use one hand. The sutures were holding, though, and the bleeding had slowed to a trickle, so he counted it as a win.

As much as he didn't want to move, however, he was sure he was about to pass out. Counting back, he couldn't remember the last full night's sleep he'd had. Couldn't even estimate. He remembered sleeping in his command chair on the *Reap*, but that was before they engaged the *Pop*, before the crash, before, before, before. It had seemed they had been on the surface for days, but it was still light outside. He wondered if it was always light on the surface.

"Come on," he said quietly in her ear. She followed sluggishly. The hull was at a slight angle, bow up, giving the pair a downhill journey away from the bridge. Oppai's cabin directly across from the bridge was trashed but intact. Ralla refused to enter it, and Thom had no desire to ask why, in case the former *Pop* leader had done worse to Ralla than Thom already imagined. Beyond, past its balcony, snow and ice partially filled the massive shipyard, thanks to its open bay doors and cracks in the ceiling far above.

Shapes of light were visible, decorating the far walls in myriad shapes, the result of random holes all over the bulkheads. It was as desolate as it was beautiful. In his search for supplies, Thom had found the ship's back broken, snapping behind the aft bulkhead of the shipyard. The rest of the ship remained tenuously attached though, dangling lifelessly from the bow section by steel and carbon-composite tendrils. He was sure enough aft compartments had remained watertight to give some buoyancy, otherwise the hanging bulk would have dragged them into the sea hours ago. It still might, he realized, but there was nothing he could do about that now, or probably ever.

Thom and Ralla descended a flight of stairs, then backtracked forward, a level below the bridge. Deserted, empty cabins made up the inward side. Once living spaces, then storage for the war machinations of Governor Oppai, they were now dark foyers to the snowy courtyard that was once the shipyard. There was enough light to follow the meandering passage. They finally turned left, toward the exterior hull. As they neared the end of that passage, Ralla eyed three pairs of jumpseats, arranged too neatly against the bulkhead.

Thom opened a circular hatch in the wall. Beyond, amber lighting illuminated a small escape sub, slightly longer than a typical transport sub. Seating for ten ran lengthwise, with a one-man cockpit at the far end. The viewscreen was dark, the view outside blocked by something. In the center, where Ralla assumed the jumpseats had been, lay a thick blanket. In the center of that a small storage cube acted as a table, holding two plastic glasses of water and what looked like a flower made from the bowl ends of colored spoons.

Thom couldn't help but be pleased with himself as he stood in the hatchway, displaying his creation. Ralla was speechless. It was the most beautiful, and romantic, thing she had ever seen.

"You know, it's like our first night together in the transport," Thom said with a smile.

"Really? *That's* what you want me to remember right now," she replied with mock annoyance. The night in question, spent in angry silence aboard a crashed sub, was an inauspicious start to their eventual relationship. She reached up and held his head in both her hands, and kissed him. It took her a moment to remember her bandage, but as she let it drop, he held it gently against his chest. Thom closed the hatch behind them.

III

THOM AWOKE, every muscle sore, Ralla asleep on his chest. Nothing could have forced him to move from that spot. Well, almost nothing. He slid from under her, tucked the blanket around her, and left to find a bathroom or a suitable substitute. The nearest cabin, just down the hall, its balcony open to the shipyard, sufficed.

He should have taken one of the blankets, he realized as he stood at the edge of the cabin, relieving himself out into the shipyard. The cold was going to be a real problem. They'd been moving around too much the first day to be much bothered by it. But if they were stuck here for any length of time...

Thom stared at the spots of light and dusting of snow that gave the massive space the appearance of being long deserted. The sub could have been here for decades, not days. He leaned forward and looked down, and immediately wished he hadn't. The snow-and-ice-covered floor was at least nine stories below.

Thom made his way back toward the escape sub, their new little home. For a moment, he let himself imagine this was it. That they'd stay here forever, make a life for themselves in the creaking, desolate hulk of the *Population*. He looked down the corridor, shadowy darkness in each direction, and shuddered. There was no denying how creepy this place had become.

He reached the escape sub and paused at the hatch to enjoy the quiet moment. They'd have a lot of work to do today. They'd need to find more food, something more than the sub's limited supply of stale rations. They'd have to try again to raise someone on comms. There had to be someone else alive, and there was little chance anyone would be searching the surface. Maybe in one of the cabins they'd find some warmer clothes and actually be able to walk outside. Now that would be amazing. She would probably love that, he thought. But for now, Thom stepped inside and enjoyed the quiet and the peace of the sleeping Ralla.

That was odd, he thought, she sure was breathing fast. Was she dreaming? He knelt beside her and gently rubbed her arm.

"Hey, wake up. It's morning... I think," he said quietly, noting as if for the first time he felt rested, but had no way to tell the actual time. "Ralla?" He moved his hand to brush the hair from her face and had to force himself not to panic. Her face was dripping with sweat, yet held the pallor of death. He tossed back the blanket, taking a sharp breath as he saw her arm. Tendrils of black and red reached out from the bandage on her wounded hand, working their way under the skin up her arm. "*Ralla*," he spoke loudly.

Nothing.

Thom stood, breathing quickly himself. He looked around the cabin, panic now setting in. He didn't need medical training to know some kind of infection was rapidly moving up her arm. They had only found one medkit, which held only painkillers and bandages. He cursed himself for letting her have so many painkillers.

He put on his clothes and wrapped himself in one of the extra blankets. He kissed her forehead and left the escape sub. Once outside, in the dark of the hallway, he realized there was no place to go. He had searched the ship the day before. The areas he could reach had been stripped bare. There was nothing else. The Medbay, if it was even in the same place as its counterpart on the *Uni*, would be deep underwater in the stern of the ship. Thom realized he needed help, and fast. There was only one thing he could think to do, and it terrified him.

_-_--

Geran Lo knew he was in trouble. In the darkness, he had bumped one of the hanging, now floating, planters in the flooded Garden. In his surprise, he'd twisted around too fast and gotten tangled in the cabling. Worse, the soil had mixed with the surrounding water in the struggle, and now he was knotted up somewhere in the middle of the Garden, in opaque water. Sub drivers spoke of this, unsettling the silt, then not being able to tell up from down. You didn't believe your instruments, and like that, you drilled yourself into the seafloor.

Lo wasn't worried about hitting the seafloor, he wasn't even moving. He forced himself to relax. The suit was set for neutral buoyancy, so he wasn't going to sink or float. The silt would clear in a few minutes. All he had to do was relax.

He thought of the woman he'd rescued, Dija. She had been in rough shape, but the medics couldn't see any signs of physical injury. Then he thought of Commander Vargas. Thom, he'd insisted on being called, at least when off duty. They'd spent months together on their commandeered warship, the *Reappropriation*. He was a natural leader, and a good man. In a different situation, they'd probably have been friends. Lo wondered if he'd found Ralla. The way he'd talked about her... His heart sank as he realized they were both probably dead. If the *Population* had succeeded in its mission, the Fountain was probably gone, which meant they were all dead.

But instead of being weighed down by the fatalism, the thought actually gave Lo energy. He knew there were survivors. He and his team were finding more each day. They'd all find a way to survive another day. And then another.

They had to. He had to.

He suddenly felt an intense need to be free of the wires, not out of a feeling of being trapped, but out of an intense desire to get on with his work. No more wasting time. He could rest later.

Lo mentally retraced his movements. He'd entered the flooded Garden from a maintenance lock connecting this space and the still pressurized, and thankfully dry, Basket. His helmet light had done nothing but light up the particles in the water, so he'd shut it off. A tiny bit of light filtered down from the surface at this depth, which he'd used to move around. It was dark, but he'd thought it was enough. It wasn't.

However, he could start to see again, an early sign the silt was clearing. He looked where it was a little brighter — up, he knew, because of the gaping maw ripped open along the Spine by the impact with the *Pop*. He could start to make it out now, as a shaft of light in the darkness.

Much of the loose destruction had settled, but it was obvious the room was a total loss, even if they were able to pump out the water. He'd used his suit's integral impeller to maneuver toward the bow, intent on his mission. That had been stupid, floating through the center of the Garden. He hadn't even seen the cables that caught him like a fish in a net.

Lo felt the adrenaline fading, drawing his energy with it. He pictured the space as he'd known it his entire life. The major hanging planters had two main horizontal wires port and starboard, two more attached near the ceiling on each wall, and two more diagonally fore and aft, like an "X." He must have snapped at least one of those, which was now wrapped around him and pinning his left arm. He tested his range of motion. There was pressure on his left leg and right arm. He keyed the impeller control on his glove's finger with his thumb. He felt the thrust pull him backwards slightly. The wire around his chest tugged on him, but his right arm seemed to free a little. A few more tugs and it was free of its captor. He used this to trace the other wires and was quickly able to free himself.

He added some buoyancy to his suit and powered cautiously toward the ceiling and away from any remaining wires. Seeing the Garden from above in the bluish darkness seemed like a bizarre nightmare. What had been the brightest area on the ship, teeming with life, was now just shadows and death.

He made his way along the ceiling until he reached the scar, the jagged opening to the sea beyond. It was enormous; a pair of transport subs could pass each other with room to spare. Lo pulled himself up around the edge and marveled at the sight before him.

He had seen the exterior of the *Uni* many times, but not like this. Not so eviscerated. Aft of the scar, the ship was relatively intact. Turning the other way, it was as they all assumed. The bow had taken the brunt of the impact, with both the *Pop* and then the seafloor. Debris littered the area around the ship. The sight of the remains of the bow, crumpled and torn, broke his heart.

The ruin extended far enough aft, nearly to the scar itself, that it was clear the primary and secondary transceivers had been destroyed. No way to get a message out, no way to get one in. That had been his main purpose coming up here, and he was going to have to return to his team with the bad news. They'd have to rig something else if they ever wanted to find other survivors. Geran Lo descended back into the darkness of the ship, exhausted to his soul.

—-̇--

Thom lifted the clear safety cover, closed his eyes, and pressed the button.

Decades-old explosive charges and rusting high-tension springs catapulted the escape sub out of its holding crèche. Designed to counter the pressure of water at depth, the air offered little resistance as the sub burst from the side of the *Population*. Its trajectory, though, was acute. Gravity pressed its mighty hand, rapidly knocking the first flying object in generations out of the sky and toward the ice. A slight rearward weight bias caused the sub's stern to drop slightly, hitting the ice first. The top surface layers, not as compressed as the older snow and ice below, absorbed some of the impact and transferred some of the energy forward. The sub's sturdy structure took the rest, slamming hard and skidding some distance before coming to a rest. The long channel, dug into the surface, started filling with fresh snow from the Fountain almost immediately.

Inside, Ralla remained unconscious, though multiple contusions from the hard seat edges added to her already extensive injury list. Thom slumped in his seat. There was blood on the console.

IV

THOM COULDN'T open his right eye. When he touched it gingerly, his hand came away sticky.

Ralla.

He twisted in his seat, pains spiking down his left side. Ralla remained where he'd strapped her in, more or less. Turning back, carefully, he noticed the viewscreen for the first time. It was a wall of white, and the coating of blood on the console gave him an idea what'd happened.

Well, Thom thought, exactly what I expected to happen. He tried to convince himself this had been the least bad option. The *Pop* lacked the necessary medical resources — not to mention Thom's own total lack of knowledge of what was needed — and there had been no response on the radio, if it had even been working. The escape sub was the only working submarine, dry and high as it had been. He touched his face again and, wincing, found the gash. Not too deep, it seemed. That, at least, he could fix.

Clean and bandaged, Thom checked on Ralla before opening the rear hatch. Sun and snowfall and quiet, like nothing had happened. The dark, partially crushed hull of the *Population* loomed large, what looked no more than a few minutes' walk. Far up the hulk, a black circle was the only indication of where they'd been. Then Thom, despite all that was going on, despite all that had happened, couldn't help but smile to himself, at the historic moment, as he stepped out onto the surface of the planet for the first time.

Terror flashed through him as he flailed and fell into the snow, sinking to his waist. It took a long moment to calm down as the snow gripped him, securely holding his weight. It had looked so solid, but it very much wasn't. He ran his hand through it. It was a powder, at least on the surface.

Thom had seen the plans and had a rudimentary understanding of how the Fountain worked. The very top of its dark, stalky shape was still visible in the far distance, beyond the landscape of snowdrifts and despite his position half-buried in snow, deep in the sharply cut half-circle wake of the escape sub. Thom grabbed a handful of the cold white powder and sniffed it. He watched as the crystals melted in his hand. This was supposed to be seawater, he thought, wasn't it? Touching it to his tongue, he was surprised that it was sharp, cold, and... clean. It tasted better than any water he'd ever tasted. He put the handful in his mouth, enjoying it as it melted. More snow fell on his face, there thanks to the Fountain. His smile faded, along with the excitement and newness of the moment, as he thought how much Ralla would love this. He had a job to do.

Laboriously, he extricated himself from the snow and climbed onto the roof of the escape sub for a better view. As he looked back the way they'd come, the towering hulk of the *Pop* blocked his view, its collapsing carapace a blight on the otherwise pristine landscape. To the escape sub's right was nothing but pure white snow. To the left, and even closer to the front, was the sea.

It was tantalizingly close, no more than a few sub lengths, and it filled him with a longing for home. The edge of the artificial iceberg sloped slightly downward toward the... Thom lost himself for a moment staring at the waves as they crashed against the ice. He'd never thought he'd see them, *hear* them like this. He wasn't sure if it was his recent head trauma that kept distracting him, or just the incredible surroundings. Once again thoughts of Ralla focused him to the task at hand. The bow of the sub, little more than a few thruster vents and the curved viewscreen, had dug itself into the soft snow. It probably wouldn't take long to dig it out, he realized, but what then? There was no way he'd be able to push the sub down to the sea.

The panic he'd felt on the *Population* started to creep back in. His best plan was not much of a plan. He swung back down into the sub and closed the hatch. The circs kicked on, blowing warm air into the cabin. Ralla's face was contorted in pain, but she refused to wake up. Maybe that was a good thing, he thought. He took his seat at the front console again and surveyed the controls at his disposal. It was an older design compared to the *Uni*'s subs he'd piloted. Even older than those he and Ralla had stolen from the *Pop* so many months before. There were traditional ballast controls, not much good on the surface; individual thruster adjustments, ostensibly for setting trim or docking; and of course the main throttle and a yoke. He activated the thrusters, firing down. The snow wasn't dense enough to actually allow the motors to create thrust, but there seemed little else to do. He heard their dull whine radiate through the cabin; it was odd to hear them working and not feel any movement.

There was no radio and no sensors, just the gaping holes where the equipment had been ripped out long before. Were those pieces in some attack sub Thom had destroyed, he wondered. Or had they been removed years, or even decades, earlier as the *Population* dealt with the atrophy that had led, inexorably, to the eventual final war between it and the *Universalis*? It didn't matter.

Thom leaned back in the chair, took a slow breath, and forced his mind to stop bouncing from random topics. He tried to focus on the problem at hand, cycling through ideas and dismissing them. There was nothing on the *Pop* of use, there was nothing on this sub that could help

Ralla. For that matter, he wasn't sure there was anyone left alive who could help them anyway. His one last gamble had failed. He had freed them of the *Population*, as he had once before. This time, however, it hadn't led them home. A fatalistic calm washed over him. He and Ralla had shared one night together. It was not enough, but it would do.

Red warning lights began to flash, preceding an ominous and gritty pitch change in the thruster motors. He had forgotten he'd left them on, and according to the board, they were overheating. Well, that made sense. Normally, the water that rushed through them was used to cool the motors. They weren't designed to move air.

They were overheating. Thom reversed direction on the thrusters, now sucking air from above the sub, past the motors, and into the snow in front of and below the sub. He half rose out of his chair, pressing his head against the viewscreen to peer down the bow of the sub. It was only a matter of moments before the white snow started to turn clear as it melted, just like it had in his hand. Thom shouted in triumph. He had no idea what good it did, but it was *something*. The sub suddenly lurched down and forward, knocking him off balance and back into the seat. He lifted his hands and leaned away from the console, not wanting to mess up whatever was happening. After a few moments, it happened again, angling the sub further downward, and sliding even closer to the water.

The warning lights increased their frequency, and were soon joined by an alarm. Thom grabbed the bottom of the seat and tried to shuffle it forward, as if his tiny amount of momentum could help. Thom reached forward and throttled up the main engines. They were at the top of the hull and presumably still above the snow line, but perhaps their tiny bit of thrust added by pushing air could help. Another lurch down, and Thom had to brace himself against the ceiling, the angle was so sharp. He looked back at Ralla. She had slid some, but was still buckled in.

They started moving with a little more speed as the bow thruster melted snow in front of them and the weight of the sub carried them forward on a slide of liquid water. Thom reduced the speed on the vertical thruster. Slide, slide, slide, he thought. The lights flashed even faster. The thrusters had taken on a horrifying mechanical squeal as the remaining lubricant boiled away and metal scraped against metal. They weren't going to last long.

They didn't have to. With one final long slide, the bow of the sub touched the ocean. Thom reversed direction on the bow thrusters, sucking the vessel into the water and down into the deep. Thom raised his arms in quiet triumph.

Home, he thought.

———

Lo wanted nothing more than to sleep, even more than food. His team had located another group of survivors, and this time the pumps had been enough to reach them without his assistance. He and his team had set up their base camp at the forward most portion of the Basket. It was an otherwise unremarkable open space of aging deck plates surrounded by wreckage and detritus haphazardly tossed in piles. The wall to the adjoining Garden loomed above them, a constant reminder of the water and sea close beyond. The other direction was only slightly less disturbing.

What once was a proud open space, lined with aging-but-intact ships and submarines, had taken on the chaos of destruction. In the battle and crash, multiple ships had dislodged from the walls, crashing into the deck; shipwrecks within a shipwreck. Debris lay everywhere, pushed aside to allow movement in makeshift corridors, lacking, as they did, any place for proper disposal. Hundreds of people sat in groups and clusters all around the floor, refugees in their own home, their cabins destroyed or flooded.

The *Uni* had partial power. A pair of emergency generators survived undamaged from the attack. So the circs were going and the survivors were breathing. There was even some food from the few restaurants and many personal kitchens around the Basket.

Lo's heavy armored boots dragged and scraped along the deck as he made his way from the starboard fore stairwell, nestled in the corner against the forward wall. There were so many people. Thousands of people, he slowly realized. Lo looked down the length of the Basket. While it appeared a disaster, and it was, it was remarkably orderly. Everyone had entered crisis mode, and it warmed his heart to see how much people were helping each other. Those whose cabins had survived opened their doors to homeless friends and strangers. From the debris, people had already started to cobble together small shelters as a way of creating a space to call home. His eyes moistened at the sight. For the moment, they were alive. Alive and trying to make what they had, work.

That wouldn't last long, though. He knew it. They knew it. But one problem at a time. Many more corridors, blocked by collapsed bulkheads or water or both, still needed clearing. All along the length of the ship where the outer hull had buckled, stores of food, supplies, and equipment could still be salvaged. The Garden may have flooded, but plenty of compartments alongside it hadn't.

Lo's pace slowed as the vastness of the problem weighed on him. It was a big ship, and there were only a few suits left capable of venturing into the flooded compartments. His suit was too big to fit anyone else. He approached his team's small camp, little more than a few blankets and a tarp hung from the wall. His blanket, and his disintegrating pillow, beckoned.

He'd given up his cabin when he'd accepted the position on the *Reap*, many months earlier. It hadn't been a hard decision. He'd be gone for months at a time, if not forever. It was war, after all. He'd given it to the family that lived across the hall. His cabin was marginally bigger, and they needed the space more than he did. Their old apartment went into the lottery. Both cabins were probably underwater now. He couldn't remember their names. He could remember their faces.

Lo didn't remember sitting down, or getting a package of dry rations. He wanted to lie back, willing to sleep in his suit if he had to. But he couldn't shake the faces from his mind.

Swallowing the dry rations, Lo forced himself to his feet and made his way back toward the corridor where his team was working. At the edge of camp, he saw the woman he'd rescued earlier. She was so small, he hadn't noticed her when he'd arrived. She didn't seem any better, still rocking back and forth, clutching her knees. He understood the inclination. He paused, returning to camp and retrieving his blanket. Wrapping it around her, he was slightly disappointed when she didn't seem to notice. Then, ever so slowly, she reached out with her fingers and pulled the blanket tighter. Another time in another place, he thought, before returning to his team.

—˙--

His eyes hurt. That was the weirdest part. Also, everything seemed louder, somehow. The fatigue in his muscles was annoying, but he was used to that. Lo learned in his teenage years that if he didn't work out every day, weight would overwhelm him. Running, lifting weights, combat training, these were all part of the routine. So even as he dragged his leaden feet down the corridor, he knew the soreness in his muscles was just part of a long day. The mental fatigue, that was the problem. It took longer to react, and he'd already made some stupid mistakes.

In the latest of an increasing number of instances where his mind drifted, he wondered how long the mind itself could go without sleep. What would happen? He was pretty sure he was going to find out.

Lo rounded the corner and saw the latest makeshift lock his team had engineered. Most of the corridors in this section of the ship had never been designed for air-to-water transitions. Too... residential. Carpets, wall paneling, this was clearly the *inside* of one of the former ships that made up most of the interior of the *Uni*, or at least had. Sure, emergency hatches were everywhere, but the designers hadn't seemed to consider the possibility that people would be trapped in pockets of non-flooded areas, surrounded by crushing water, and need to get out.

Silently, his four-man team nodded as he approached, his armored boots thudding and squishing on the still damp corridor. In their tired faces, he saw his own. Like himself, any order he'd try to give for rest would be met by quiet, and forceful, disobedience. No words were spoken here, or needed. Lo stepped into the lock, hardly larger than him, and had a brief moment of respite as the door shut behind him, and water began its replacement of air.

"Sergeant Lo, please respond. Sergeant?"

"I'm fine. I must have... I'm fine. Open the hatch."

The water transmitted the scrape of metal on metal. Lo didn't remember closing his eyes, but clearly he'd fallen asleep. No, *passed out*, he realized.

Ahead, another corridor, just like the others. Litter and debris floated eerily. The lights from the front of his helmet illuminated dirt particles like a pointedly specular fog. There was no banging, or any other sound apart from his breathing. Lo stopped, mid-corridor, his helmet lights spreading like cones in the darkness. Why was he here? Was anyone left alive? Had he asked? There was no point in trying to remember; he knew his brain was shot. Lo keyed his comm.

"What's my destination?" he asked, hiding his fatigue.

"There's access to S Street at the end of the corridor."

"Got it. Start your pumps."

The unique hum of the high-powered axial flow pumps entered his helmet, followed by the familiar gurgle of air being forced in to replace the water. The meeting came back to him now. Someone had suggested they try for S Street, since they'd been working on the starboard side of the ship anyway, and if any of the compartments along the outer ring of ships inside the main hull of the *Universalis* had remained dry, they could access them from S Street. The longest continuously open spaces on the ship, S Street, and its mirror on the opposite side, Port Street, ran the length of the ship. Once major thoroughfares of people and goods, Lo hoped the extensive lock system had sealed in time to keep the sea at bay. Damage and flooding in the engine rooms had cut off access to the Streets as far forward as the Basket. He knew other crews were working on shoring that up. With the bow crushed, they'd all hoped the middle remained clear, not least as a safe haven for survivors, but also to access the manufacturing and industrial equipment in the outer ring.

Lo neared the end of the corridor. To minimize drainage times, they'd concentrated on the smaller pedestrian corridors. That is, except in the cases where they could hear survivors like they had earlier that day. The final lock was shiny metal, an anachronistic addition to the carpeted and wallpapered hallway. The pumps had cleared some space above his head, and a mirrored ceiling of air-above-water rippled as it descended. He pounded on the lock hatch. He hadn't expected a response, but the fatigue had made him overly emotional, and he was disappointed.

It didn't take long for the water to drop below his waist, and he pounded again. Still no response. Looking back the way he'd come, there seemed to be no additional leaks. The hatch panel was offline, but the red override handle was adjacent. He smashed the glass, ignoring the long-memorized warnings about flooding, damage, and death, and gave the handle a solid tug. Nothing.

Lo tried to slide the hatch itself, but it wouldn't budge. He tried the handle again, this time gripping it underhand and jolting it hard in annoyance.

The wall of water hit him like an explosion.

_-_--

Lo lay on his back, not wanting to move. The hallway was full of water again. S Street was flooded, though how badly he didn't know. He arduously got to his feet, surprised at the effort. The wall of water from the hatch's abrupt opening had knocked him good, but it was more than that. He put the thought out of his head. Instead, he let his mind go back to the woman he'd rescued earlier that day. Yesterday? She was just one of a few dozen, of course, but something about her stuck in his mind. Another time and another place, Sergeant, he reminded himself yet again. The hatch to S Street was still open, a dark maw to the space beyond.

No, not quite dark. Emergency lights, embedded in the floor every few paces, each with its own power supply, dimly lit the center of the street. He stepped toward the closest one, cautious for any hazards.

Stepping onto it, the light lit him from below and ignited his armor in an amber glow. Lo turned to look down the length of the ship. He could see the lights continue into the distance. He turned the other way and saw the same. His heart sank, and only with effort, his knees didn't.

"None of the locks activated," he said into his comm. "S Street is gone."

V

THE THRUSTERS had ground themselves nearly to pieces and were only capable of an ailing partial thrust. It didn't matter; they were making progress, painstakingly slow as it might have been. Thom controlled their descent with the ballast tanks. He had no idea how far the *Population* had traveled after its impact with the *Uni*, but he figured if he followed the line of the *Pop*'s hull and descended toward the bottom, he'd find home. The real question: Was there anyone left to greet them? He realized now how much Ralla's incessant optimism had rubbed off on him. He was sure there were people alive. Somehow.

Traces of light trickled down at this shallow depth. He needn't have worried about finding the *Uni*. The *Pop* had shed a trail of debris that led the way. Sure enough, less than a hour later, the jagged remains of a bow emerged from the seabed like a terrifying and decaying flower. The gash along the spine looked worse than he remembered, a mortal wound sure to have killed thousands. His eye followed the line of the ship as more came into view. The rest of the hull was wrinkled, no doubt from the final impact, but it seemed intact. Being half buried in the silt meant all the major locks were obscured.

"There!" he shouted as if anyone could hear him. A submarine. No, two. As he neared the stern, Thom's heart pounded with excitement. More. Submarines, as far as he could see. A veritable swarm of survivors, their running lights little stars of radiance, and hope, in the darkness.

—·--

There seemed to be organization to the confusion. One by one, a sub would dock with the *Uni*, presumably discharge its cargo, then return to the swarm. The emergency landing platform at the rear of the ship was intact, and seemingly the only lock in use.

They must have comms, though why they hadn't answered his distress call from the *Pop* Thom wasn't sure. He figured that would wait for later. Without a radio, he was going to have to cut in line. They could yell at him later.

He made no effort to hide it. As soon as the next sub in line docked, a long and wide cargo hauler, Thom started his approach. The hauler rose away from the platform and Thom nestled in, backing toward the lock's universal collar. He could hear the seal and the water drain from the connection. The door opened as he was unstrapping Ralla. The ensign who stood in the doorway looked annoyed and opened his mouth to chastise. Thom cut him off.

"Ensign," he said in a loud, official tone, "this is Councilwoman Ralla Gattley, and she is in immediate need of medical attention. I need you to clear a path for us to Medbay. *Now.*"

It took a moment for the ensign to register what had been said, but he nodded and beckoned toward the interior of the citysub. The small waiting area just inside from the platform, normally cramped, was crammed with people. Men, women, children, all packed together. Some struggled to stay together, others jockeyed for position closer to an officer with a clipboard. The ensign shouted for people to clear a space, which they did begrudgingly until they saw Thom, caked in dried blood, with a dirty, ratty beard and carrying a lifeless, pallid body. Without her trademark curls and missing a third of her body weight, it was doubtful even her friends would have recognized Ralla.

The ensign pushed people aside, opening a space for Thom to move through that closed up quickly behind, people straining to catch a glimpse. Someone recognized them, and he heard their names echo through the crowd. If you only knew, he thought.

Along the Spine they went, dodging freshly welded beams supporting damaged areas of the superstructure and pushing past people standing and sitting in the narrow corridor. It occurred to Thom this was the now the main entry to the *Uni*, and it was ill-suited for the task. The ensign shouted well, though, and within minutes they were headed down some stairs and into the ship itself. It was going to be a long descent, he knew. If they were going to the main Medbay, and he hoped they were, it was below the Basket.

The corridors passed in a blur as they moved from one stairwell to another. He knew there were better routes, but said nothing, not knowing how much damage this part of the ship had taken.

They finally reached the Medbay level, Thom's arms and legs burning from the effort. The hallways were packed with sick and the injured. Bandaged faces looked up from the floor, prostrate bodies wheezed and coughed. He rounded the corner of the wide entrance of Medbay.

Even with the preamble of the hallway, he was unprepared for the sight. The normally white floor was smeared with blood and gore. Doctors and nurses, caked in carnage, hurried from one table to another. Sheets covered what were clearly bodies in one corner. Every one of the fifty beds he could see was full, with even more patients in chairs and on the floor. And this, he knew, was just the entrance to the sprawling Medbay complex, which spread out nearly the entire width of the Basket and down four more floors. Thom had no doubt all of it was full.

A nurse approached, appearing to Thom even more weary than he felt. Given all that was going on, the shouts and the screams and the pain, Thom half expected to be turned away. He braced himself for a fight. He wasn't going to give up now, not as far as he'd come. The nurse said nothing, didn't seem to possess the energy to say anything. Instead, she pulled back the bandage on Ralla's hand. Blood had soaked through where the fingers had been. Turning her attention to Ralla's face, the nurse pushed open the sickly eyelids with abruptness and adroitness of a professional in a rush.

"Fingers?" she asked.

"Three," Thom replied.

"When?"

"A few days ago, I think. She just..." Thom stopped in mid-sentence as it was clear the nurse was no longer listening. "This is Ralla Gattley," Thom said, as if this explained something. The nurse showed no signs it meant anything.

"You?" she asked. It took Thom a moment to understand what she was asking, eventually having to follow her gaze to his own bandaged arm.

"No, I'm fine." Looking at the bandage awakened some previously suppressed pain, and it started to throb intensely. "I think."

"Stay here," the nurse said, walking away. Thom noticed that in the few moments he had been standing there, several more people had entered the Medbay behind him. All were in some state of disrepair.

The nurse returned with a syringe and some bandage. The syringe went into Ralla's arm like it was going into a piece of fruit, the bandage went in a pile on her stomach. It suddenly seemed weird to him he was still holding her. His arm started to shake, partly from the wound, partly from fatigue. Maybe he should get checked out too, he thought. His head had taken quite a beating. This realization, plus the adrenaline wearing off, caused his head to pulse in pain with the same beat as his arm. Looking around dispelled him of the idea quickly. He didn't have anything some sleep and food couldn't cure.

"Take her to B wing, level 3. Tell them... do I need to write this down?"

Thom shook his head.

"Tell them I gave her a double dose of BSA. She needs fluids and further treatment. Got that?"

Thom nodded.

"Go."

He nodded again. Thom looked back to thank the ensign who'd led him here, but he was gone, replaced by a sea of damaged people.

Careful not to slip, Thom weaved his way around the scrambling doctors and nurses, and followed the signs to B wing. He tipped Ralla up toward his face and kissed her forehead gently, very, very conscious of the horror around them.

— ¯--

Lo stumbled back into base camp physically, mentally, and now emotionally exhausted. The flooding of S Street had snapped something inside him. Throughout the entire rescue — no, before that even, all the way back to the first attack on the *Universalis* months earlier —he had somehow maintained an optimistic outlook. That somehow he and his shipmates would make it through. That was just his personality.

Was. It was as if everything around him had gone dark. He had left this camp seeing the people around him as intrepid survivors. Now, they were helpless remainders, the last vestiges of a dead civilization.

He stripped off his armor piece by piece, dumping it in a pile. Then he sat, arms on his knees, and stared at the floor. He was vaguely aware of people around him, but it wasn't until a frail-looking old woman placed a bowl in front of him that he looked up and around. Members of his team had found a huge pot, a portable stove, and had somehow put enough materials together for a soup. He stared at the brown, lumpy liquid in the bowl before him. Thin shards of vegetables poked out like sinking ships. The smell worked its way slowly through his brain, and he recognized it as delicious. He smiled at the old woman, and she nodded back. In her other hand was an identical bowl, which he watched her place near the coiled form of Dija Yunner. She was in a ball on the floor, pressed against the wall, enveloped by his blanket.

Lo tipped the bowl back and drank the warm soup like it was water. The vegetables occasionally required a bite or two, but most went down whole. More than anything, he hoped it would act as some sort of restorative. But as he looked up, his depression returned. A line had formed, leading to the vat of soup. It extended out of the camp and wove between the rows of makeshift huts starting to dot the Basket floor. There wasn't going to be enough soup tonight.

Or ever again.

Lo closed his eyes and leaned back against his armor, defeated.

—˙--

Whispers woke him. Had they been speaking in normal tones, his subconscious would have likely ignored it. As it was, Lo emerged from a restless sleep to listen. Two men were arguing nearby in hushed tones. He opened his eyes a slit, to see what was going on. The picosuns far above had dimmed, since he'd fallen asleep, casting a bluish gloom instead of their normal warm glow. The two men, dressed in dingy one-piece uniforms, hovered near Dija. She hadn't moved, still curled up on the floor. One of the men tried to egg the other on. He succeeded, and the first man stepped over and scooped up the still-full bowl of soup left there hours earlier.

It was a simple act. A simple theft. In a way, there was little to blame. Who knows how many hours that soup had sat there, cooling, congealing. Who knows how many hours, or days, it had been since these men had eaten.

It didn't matter. Lo pushed himself off the floor, muscles screaming, and was at the two men in four strides.

"Put it back," he said flatly. He was a full head taller than either man, and probably outweighed them both combined. His fatigued brain didn't register that neither man seemed intimidated.

"Look buddy, she wasn't eating it. She's in a coma or something. We haven't eaten. We saw it first. Now why don't you go back and sit down. It looks like you've eaten enough lately."

Lo punched him hard enough in the face that the man toppled backward and slid on the deck. A knife appeared in the other man's hand

and he lashed out, slicing open Lo's right forearm. The big man didn't feel it, swatting away at a follow-up strike and slamming his open left palm into the man's chest. The man stumbled back and tripped on his own feet, going down with a thump. Lo stepped on the man's wrist, pinning the hand with the knife. Now there was fear in the face before him. Breath gone, he wordlessly tried to say something. For his trouble, Lo slugged him hard in the face. Dead or unconscious, Lo didn't know and didn't care. He took the knife, wiped his own blood from it, and returned to the camp in search of a medkit.

He didn't think he could have felt worse than when he had fallen asleep, but as the adrenaline from the fight abated, he felt a new level of misery now mixed with self-loathing. His temper had returned. That wasn't good.

Before his eyes closed, he saw the upended bowl of soup on the deck nearby, its former contents flowing slowly toward the motionless bodies.

VI

THOM AWOKE in a chair, unsure of where he was or how he got there. It was quiet, and dark. As his eyes focused, he saw a hospital bed, and Ralla's poorly cut hair resting on a pillow. Her breathing looked normal. Her hand was wrapped in a clean bandage, and the arm had returned to some normal shade. An IV hung from a stand above her. The bed was small, but he didn't care. He climbed on, careful not to touch her hand, and lay beside her. His forehead touched the side of her head, and for the first time in months, he felt truly safe. He wanted to cry, out of exhaustion, out of happiness. Instead, he slept.

— ¯--

The nurse woke him with a gentle hand on his shoulder. Had he not been half awake, listening to the bustle of the hospital, he probably would have lashed out in surprise. The nurse's round face was kind, but tired. He figured she was middle age, but looked older. A privacy curtain, half drawn, gave the bed its own space.

"How long have we been here?" he said, trying to simultaneously stretch and not disturb Ralla. She looked peaceful, and healthier. Thom's every joint ached, whether from being wrapped around Ralla for hours, or the wear from the previous days, he wasn't sure. His mouth contained flavors and texture noticeably unpleasant.

"Her chart says you were admitted early last night."

"Is it morning?"

"No," she said, almost laughing. "It's almost dinner. None of us wanted to wake you. You two were..." She looked away. For a moment Thom thought she was blushing, but as she turned back, he saw tears. "You two were this amazing island of calm around here. I don't want to embarrass you, but the way you held her all night helped a lot of people make it through the... It's been... ugly upstairs."

Thom nodded, not sure how to respond. He had been asleep for the better part of a day, a realization his bladder took as an opportunity to make itself known. He stood up, shakily. He'd need some food, too. But first things first.

"Head?"

She pointed down the hallway. He felt the urge to run, but something was weighing on him, more than his bladder.

"She looks better, but is she? Is she going to wake up?" The words caught in his throat, which he hadn't expected.

"Yes, oh dear, yes," the nurse said, placing her hand back on his shoulder. "We're keeping her sedated for now, until the doctor can assess the extent of the damage and infection. She's responding well to the antibiotics, so she should be just fine."

The moment of panic abated, in its place he felt his knees weaken, and a lump form in his throat.

"Thank you," he said, the words not nearly adequate, but the best he could manage.

"You should have that cut looked at, now that you're up."

"I'm gonna make a mess," he said, pointing in the direction she had moments before. The nurse seemed to find this far funnier than he expected.

Stepping from behind the privacy curtain, Thom was surprised at the size of the room. He hadn't noticed much the night before. There were probably a hundred beds, not just along the walls, but spread all over the rectangular room. Each had an opaque privacy curtain. The white-on-white decor and floor thankfully lacked the red gore from the emergency room nightmare. There weren't any cries of agony or death, either. Whatever this area was, it wasn't for the doomed.

Once in the toilet, he had to brace himself using one of the hospital-standard grab-bars. He just didn't have the strength to remain standing for what was, by far, the longest pee of his life. Finished, he stood before the mirror and marveled at his appearance. Cuts, dried blood, ratty beard... if it weren't for the fact that he actually *felt* fine, he would have been a little terrified. Hungry, for sure, sore, and a little groggy, but his body had used its downtime well. Not being under constant stress was certainly a part of that. And that Ralla was alive, and was going to be "just fine." That thought actually made him feel *good*.

At the entrance to the big room he found the nurse's station. Ralla's nurse was filling out some paperwork, and for the first time Thom noticed her name badge: Kera. She looked up as he approached.

"Better?"

"You have no idea."

"Want me to patch you up?"

"I do. You wouldn't happen to have a razor I could use?"

"I'll do you one better." Kera reached into a low drawer and came up with a tiny clear plastic bag with a sliver of soap, a miniature bottle of shampoo, a razor, a toothbrush, and tiny tube of toothpaste. "There are showers down the corridor. The ship's running at partial power, but the desalinators are all running fine."

Thom turned the package over in his hands, like it was some weird lifeform. She seemed to understand his hesitation.

"Look, we've got boxes full of those, but if you want, when you're all cleaned up and the doctor says it's all right, you can give some blood. That would be the biggest help you could offer right now."

"Thank you," Thom said reverently, the words still not carrying enough weight. His blood seemed more than a fair enough trade for the moment. It was the oddest thing, he realized as he walked toward the shower. No one here had any idea what he had done. What he and Ralla had done. They had literally saved the planet, and here he was feeling guilty for taking some soap and a shower.

As his mind played back through all the faces he had seen as he carried Ralla to the Medbay, played back all the injured people who had probably died since he'd been asleep, he expected and wanted no recognition. What did it matter if the planet was safe, when this world had suffered such shattering devastation?

The shower room was empty; beige tiles covered the floors and walls. Each of the dozen tiny shower stalls had hooks for clothes and a brown plastic bench. Thom peeled off the grimy layers of his uniform, offending himself with their smell, and stood under the high-pressure hot water like it was the greatest place in the universe.

_ _ - _ _

They had tried to make a scene. Their faces showing the blood and injuries Lo had inflicted the night before. A few people gathered to their plight, but whether it was the abundance of bigger problems, Lo's size and nearby armor, or the fact that most in the immediate area had actually been rescued by him or his team, nothing came of it.

Sleep and soup had done some good; Lo felt a little more optimistic. At least enough to put on his armor and head toward where his team was working for the day. There had been reports of faint banging a few tiers up along the starboard side, and just forward of the Basket. It was going to be dangerous. Most of the ships on that wall were unstable. Before he left camp, Lo asked the soup woman to watch over Dija and try to get her to eat something.

The stairwell was tight in his suit; he brushed against both walls as he ascended. At the appropriate level, he exited and stepped into the corridor. It was one of the many interstitial hallways between the exterior of a wall ship and one of the many structural bulkheads of the *Uni*. Before him was the green and white hull of a ship he could see from his camp half a dozen stories below. Alarmingly, he could see gaps of light between the corridor floor and the ship's hull. Lo hoped it had just shifted position, not that it was loose. If that ship fell, it would kill hundreds of people in the Basket below.

There was nothing his team could do about that, and the few repair crews were busy with more immediate problems. Not for the first time, he wished his fusor would work with the carbon composite that half the *Uni* seemed to be made.

The four men of his team had already set up a temp lock, just past the bow of the wall ship. It was a bulky white contraption of metal and plastic slightly larger and much deeper than an average door. They'd attached the large diameter hoses to each side. These connected to the portable pumps placed nearby, which themselves were hooked to more hoses that serpentined their way along the corridor walls, finally connecting to this level's bilge tubes. At least those still worked, he thought to himself.

Lo nodded to his crew, and they nodded back. Having done this so many times, there was little to say. Lo stepped into the lock, and they sealed it behind him. The brackish water flushed into the lock, pooling at his feet before rising rapidly to the ceiling. His helmet lights clicked on automatically.

As he waited, his mind flashed to the two men from the night before. The anger washed over him, not at them, but at himself. His arm jerked out from his side, impacting the hatch directly in front of him, denting it. The feeling faded as the thud stopped reverberating in the tiny space. He sighed. Maybe it was just from being tired. Or the stress. Or both. He thought he'd gotten this under control a long time ago.

"That was me," he said into his comm, staving off any questions.

The pumps ceased and the door started to open, jamming halfway because of the dent. He took a moment to look at his handiwork, embarrassed and ashamed. Lo squeezed through sideways into the watery darkness.

This level had been mostly restaurants, Lo remembered, at the end of the now flooded Garden, closest to the Basket. What were people doing trapped up here? They should have returned to their cabins during the battle. In the silence, Lo heard the faint knocking of trapped people. The corridor wall to his right was unbroken as far as he could see in the dark distance. To his left, the outside hull of a ship that faced the Garden. It was a small ship, for such a prime location this close to the barrier to the Basket. It must have just been what fit. The haphazard build methodology of the citysub was taught at an early age, but the details, if Lo had ever really learned them, didn't readily come to his fatigued mind. The wall ship, or at least the long sliver he could see, looked like a fairly sizeable yacht. The exterior was either blue or black, it was hard to tell in the low light. The interior had doubtless been converted to some lavish restaurant he'd never been able to afford.

"Start the pumps," he ordered over the comm, and soon heard their hum and gurgle. After a few moments, he could see the pockets of air dance along the ceiling of the corridor. The mirrored surfaces flowed like liquid metal in his helmet lights, joining, pulling apart, joining again. It wasn't long before they'd all merged and begun to descend as one as the pumps successfully replaced flood with air. His head emerged above the descending surface, and Lo clicked open his faceplate so he could hear better. As the water level dropped below his waist, he knocked on the entrance door to the restaurant, a highly decorated, antique-looking hatch cut into the ship's hull.

As so many times before, the response was immediate and energetic. He could hear shouts from inside. Lots of shouts.

"Stand away from the door," Lo shouted. He looked down to find footing to brace himself, and saw a problem. Like the ship he'd passed in the hallway earlier, this one had separated from its mounts and pulled away from the *Universalis*'s supporting structure. Through the gaps water gushed, creating long, small fountains along the length of the restaurant's hull. The pumps were keeping up, but barely. The water was at his shins as he grabbed the hatch's carved metal handle latch and tugged it open. Dozens of faces peered back at him, ghostly in the cool white of his helmet lights. Water from the hallway rushed in, snaking around their legs, causing many to jump as if it bit them.

Everyone rushed the door at once, pushing past him into the hallway. The first escapees paused, unsure where to go in the apparently sealed corridor. Those behind continued pushing forward. More water poured over the threshold, wetting ankles. Lo could see the hull of the ship wobble, and with each oscillation, more water spurted from the crease fountains.

"Open the hatch. Survivors headed your way," he said into the comm. "That way!" he shouted, pointing in the direction of the temp lock. As he looked, he remembered his damage, and how much that was going to slow everything down.

"Sergeant, there's water coming in," one of his team said over the comm with more surprise than anxiety. Lo didn't bother to respond.

Everyone heard it: A low groan from the forward end of the yacht. The little fountains doubled in size as the restaurant further separated from the *Uni*. Rapidly, the water level started rising. The flow into the restaurant door jumped to knee level, slowing progress as the trapped sloshed and struggled against the current. He peered around the edge of the door and was shocked at what he saw. There seemed the same number of people when he first looked in. Another groan, another increase in water.

"Sergeant, the water's getting pretty bad here. It's already spreading down the corridor."

"I know that," he snarled.

"I'm just saying that if the water level gets much higher, we're going to have trouble closing the lock." Now there was fear in the voice. If they couldn't get the door closed, and the water level got much worse, the next compartment would flood, killing his team and all these new survivors.

No, he realized, *they were going to lose the Universalis*. His mind focused in total clarity on the slices of light he'd passed on his way here. Already, he was sure, water was cascading though those gaps into the Basket. If this yacht went, and the temp lock was still open, that would be it. There would be no way to stop the flooding. There would be no way to save everyone in the Basket. Tens of thousands would be killed.

It was simple math. Heart racing, he grabbed hold of the ornate restaurant hatch. Still people jostled and pushed their way forward, fear setting in. The rate of the flooding easily outpaced the weight lost from the escaping people.

Another groan. The water was rushing through the hatch, past dozens of legs, and was likely pooling against the far wall. It always ran the lowest point, Lo knew. Everyone knew.

Another groan, this one was long and loud, the yacht visibly shuddering. Gaps had opened along the ceiling, and water cascaded into the corridor. The water level was up to Lo's waist, chest high for most of the evacuees. It was nearly impossible for them to get out of the door against the rushing influx of water. Lo shouted at them to move. Pleaded with them to push harder. As they neared the door, he reached out with his free hand and started yanking them out.

Rapid popping sounds. More water flushed in from the edges.

"SERGEANT!" his comm screamed.

A young woman was in the doorway now, trying in vain to escape. Her long blond hair trailed behind her in the water. Those behind her pushed, Lo grabbed her arm and pulled. She lost her footing, and instantly she was flailing in the current. The water grabbed at her, pulled at her. Through her open, screaming mouth it poured. She locked eyes with Lo, full of a terror he'd never seen before. Convulsing in a cough, she was suddenly gone, slipping from Lo's grip and disappearing under the surface. Her body knocked all behind her underwater. Still others took this as their chance to push forward, screaming at Lo for help. Another groan and surge of water from behind nearly knocked him off his feet. No one inside was close enough to grab. Lo closed his eyes and slammed the hatch shut.

He turned away from the yacht and opened his eyes. The corridor still had twenty-some people in it, fighting through the chest-high water toward the still-open temp lock. A dozen more piled against the half-open lock, not able to get through quickly. This was his fault. Lo could see now the water was pouring through there, flooding the corridor beyond. That was his fault, too.

He waded toward the exit as quickly as he could. There was still air in the restaurant. He could come back for them, he tried to justify to himself. He reached the nearest survivor and pushed her along.

There was no groan this time, just a screech and a whoosh. He screamed into his comm as he turned.

"NOW! NOW! CLOSE THE LOCK NOW!"

The yacht finally succumbed gravity and lack of buoyancy, the bow pulling away from its mounting fully, allowing water from the flooded Garden to rush inwards unimpeded. Lo snapped his faceplate shut just as the wall of water hit him. He tumbled with the force, then stopped. There was no more push. In the back of his mind, he knew this meant his team had sealed the lock in time. The *Uni* was safe.

But didn't make what was in front of him any better. The woman he'd tried to help clawed at his faceplate as she, and everyone else still in the corridor, slowly drowned. He'd killed them as much as the water had. But there was nothing he could do. He turned away and watched as the yacht restaurant finally freed itself from its unnatural moorings and began a slow and silent tumble to the floor of the Garden four stories below.

VII

THOM STEPPED out onto the floor of the Basket in time to see the panic start. The screams started in the distance and radiated aft at a pace even faster than the water. High up on the starboard wall, near the divide with the Garden, water burst outwards from between two ships, in a waterfall that under any other circumstance would have been rather beautiful.

Without hesitation, Thom sprinted forward. His brain only partially registered how much the Basket had changed since he last saw it. Overturned ships littered the deck. Hovels built from debris filled every open space. A weaving corridor down the center was the only major thoroughfare. Ahead he could see a wave of people fleeing from the water. Thom had no idea what he would do when he got there, but there had to be something. His pace dropped to a crawl as he slammed headlong into the oncoming, terrorized swarm. It was chaos. There had to be additional locks or hatches, something up there he could get to, he thought rapidly. This was madness. Who was in charge?

The world seemed to slow around him. He'd seen the crushed bow, the destroyed Garden and Yard. That's where the command officers and staff would have been. That's where the Council would have been. They must all be dead, otherwise there'd be some order to the anarchy he saw around him. That left one person. He was ranking officer. He was in charge.

He dropped to the deck as if hit. People jostled to get around him as he struggled to get his breath. He could feel his heart beat arrhythmically, sometimes seeming to stop altogether, causing him to cough to start it again. Sweat poured out of him as flashes of heat radiated from his chest. He couldn't focus, couldn't think, as if some part of his brain knew what had caused this and wouldn't let him cause it again.

He forced his breath to slow down, forced himself to breathe normally, even as more people's knees hit his head and shoulders. It wasn't the water, it wasn't the people, it was... It was him. If no one was in charge, *he* was in charge. Thom instantly started gasping for air again, his chest burning from the inside. He buried his face in the coarse metal deck plating.

Part of him wanted to help, wanted to rush forward and do what he could to stop the flooding. But he physically couldn't. He couldn't even sit up from the shaking ball in the middle of a stampede. He felt as if something inside of him had cracked. All he could do was gasp at the air.

Around him, he felt the turmoil subside. He wasn't sure how much time had passed. People spoke in normal voices. The background hiss of falling water had disappeared. Thom was able to tilt his head up, and in between the legs that surrounded him, he caught a brief glimpse of the far end of the Basket, and sure enough the water had stopped. The crisis, this crisis anyway, was over. Someone had taken charge and solved the problem.

Thom slowly rose to his feet, swaying a little. His legs felt weak, his good mood and energy from earlier swept away. The people around him started back toward the bow end of the Basket, and he moved with the flow. Now he took notice of the huge fallen vessels around him. Once a forgotten part of the walls of the Basket, they were now embedded at odd angles in its deck. They rose above him, rusting hulks of the past creating a canyon of wreckage.

Maybe they'd be cut up for scrap, he wondered. Or maybe they'd make them livable spaces again. No matter what, they'd never be able to return them to their former berths. A passing thought of putting someone in charge of the cleanup caused a wave of panic to flash through his body. He put the thought out of his mind.

In the spaces around, on, and under the overhangs of these huge vessels, people, refugees really, had set up camps. Families and individuals staked claims to an area with whatever they could find: tarps, loose plating, shards of bulkheads, even pieces of furniture. At the edges of the ships, adjacent to the open areas, rudimentary multi-story structures had already emerged. Deck plating supported by bulkhead shards reinforced by support beams, all welded or tied together. It looked dangerously unsafe, yet what didn't in this postwar *Universalis*.

In the open spaces, makeshift tents of sheets, blankets, and tarps spread from wall to wall. Everywhere, there were people. He regretted shaving his beard, but for the moment everyone seemed preoccupied enough that they didn't recognize him. He walked to a small crowded rise that had once been one of the Basket's few green "parks," and saw the extent of the recent damage. The water had been contained in the front starboard corner, roughly where it had fallen. A dozen or so men and women struggled with portable pumps, getting ready to rid the deck of its unwelcome invader.

From one of the stairwells next to this saltwater pond, a massive armored figure stepped into the Basket's light. Thom almost shouted for joy as he started down the hill.

—-–

Sergeant Lo stepped into the Basket and saw the mess he'd made. The water was knee deep but hadn't seemed to have caused any major damage. Even luckier, it hadn't spread far enough to dampen anyone's tent "home." There had been enough harm today. Enough death on his hands. Six decks above, five people awaited medical attention. That's all he'd been able to rescue after the corridor flooded. Five people had been able to hold their breath and were close enough to the temp lock that he'd been able to stuff them in together and seal the outer hatch. The rest in the hallway had stopped moving, likely caught with their mouths open or knocked too hard into the bulkhead or any of the other countless ways to die in the deep.

He reached camp and began the process of removing his armored suit. Dija hadn't moved, but an empty ration packet nearby told him at least she'd eaten something.

It occurred to him, at that moment, he was probably in shock. Everything around him seemed too normal, or at least as normal as the world was right now. He felt in a sort of daze, and realized he couldn't remember actually getting into the temp lock himself, or the walk down here. He remembered the coughing and sputtering people, but not much else since the flood. Had he died, too?

Dija was staring at him through her matted copper hair. Her eyes were so pale, they barely seemed to have any color. This he could focus on, though it gave him no joy. It was just a person staring at him. People had stared at him in the corridor above. Corpses. He removed the rest of his suit. His T-shirt and shorts, once white, now had a dingy yellow hue that mirrored almost everything within eyesight.

Someone else was staring at him. A man, fairly tall, though still much shorter than himself. He was oddly well shaven, and his hair even seemed clean. Then the man smiled, a smile that Lo was sure would normally put people at ease and could get women to take pause. Lo wished he had a smile like that. In fact, he remembered knowing someone who had a smile like...

"Commander?" Lo asked, not sure his brain truly accepted the concept. This caused an odd reaction from the smiling man, who frowned as he stepped closer.

"Thom. Geran, it's Thom!"

The wave of emotion was too much for Lo, and as he strongly embraced his former commander, he sobbed. His huge arms enveloped Thom, the latter's barely reaching around Lo's back.

Thom couldn't help it and welled up himself. They'd been through so much together, from combat to training, to escaping the *Population*. That bond, through time and events, gave them a closeness Thom wasn't sure he'd had with anyone since his old drinking buddies. He hoped they were safe too, of course, but right now there were few people he'd rather have seen than Lo.

Finally, they patted each other's backs as they separated, and looked away as they wiped their eyes.

They shifted uncomfortably, not sure what to say next. Lo's gaze drifted to the soup woman, who approached with some bowls of steaming goodness. Both accepted graciously and greedily. They sat on the deck and ate in silence. It was one of the greatest meals Thom had ever had. As he waited for Lo to finish, he surveyed the little camp.

A heating plate had been set up in the center of a small circle of benches and folding seats. Some mattresses, torn and soiled, seemed to make up the sleeping area between the circle and the ships that made up the Garden divide. Lo's area consisted of the pile of his armor, and little else. Nearby, a child eyed him with curiosity through dirty, matted copper hair. No, not a child; a petite and rather emaciated-looking young woman. She looked vaguely familiar.

Lo finished his stew, and Thom motioned for him to start.

"My team and I were one of the last ones off the *Reap*, I think. We stuffed ourselves and a few of the crew into the pair of escape pods nearest our stations. I was directing some damage control parties when you gave the order to abandon ship."

Thom nodded, feeling his heart rate quicken at the memory.

"Once out of the ship, we had a good view of the last moments of the *Reap*. We all figured you drove her in."

"I made it out the back in one of the scout subs."

"Wow, and I thought we were close."

"Yeah, it was..."

Lo noticed Thom's change in facial expression, and figured he'd keep going with his story to distract him.

"The *Pop* passed over us, knocking us around in its wake. That's when we got separated. I'm not sure why the comms didn't work, but it's not like there were a lot of places to go. So we headed back along the *Pop*'s route, and found her," Lo said, motioning to the citysub around them. "She was just settling, and there was an incredible cloud of silt. I remembered the lock on the Spine, and I figured that was the best place get in. After we'd docked, we set the pod on automatic. It's probably still sitting outside somewhere. Inside was... madness."

"I can imagine."

"Don't. My team and I just started doing what we could. We found some damage control gear, some pumps, a portable lock, and just went. It's been..." Lo's voice faded out, and he looked upwards as if gravity would keep the tears back.

"Lo," Thom said, saving the big man from explaining further. "I've been on *the surface*."

"What?"

"No joke," Thom said, smiling despite himself. "We beached the damn *Pop* on the Fountain's iceberg!"

"I don't believe you," Lo said, leaning forward, clearly believing him and visibly relieved at the change of topic.

"We did. After I got on board through the *Pop*'s shipyard I found Ralla..."

"Ralla?" interrupted a voice. Both Lo and Thom turned toward the source. The tiny young woman was sitting up, staring at them with an incongruous, burning intensity. "Is Ralla *here*?"

"Yeah, in Medbay."

Before Thom could say anything further, the woman bolted to her feet and sprinted barefoot down the Basket.

VIII

LO FIDGETED uncomfortably in his filthy undershirt and shorts. Thom's assurances that no one would notice seemed to offer little consolation, and even littler truth. The elevator doors opened to a hallway full of injured waiting to get into the hospital. All who could, paused to look at the dirty giant and his oddly clean companion. Thom realized they would need a pit stop.

Kera was at the nurses' station, and was glad to supply some pastel blue scrubs that looked just large enough to fit Lo. Thom pointed him toward the showers and told him which shower had the shampoo and soap he hadn't finished. He could hear Ralla's voice as he approached the curtain and his heart rate doubled. Pulling it aside, their eyes locked and hers welled up. She reached out with both arms, one still heavily bandaged. He stepped over and accepted her hug.

"Thank you," she whispered in his ear, holding him tighter. "You're amazing."

Thom tensed, but didn't let go. It was some time before they released

"Thom, this is my friend Dija. We met when we were captives on the *Population*. She's amazing. I couldn't have done it without her."

Dija immediately looked at the floor and blushed.

"I didn't... I, you were..."

Thom reached across the bed to shake her hand, which she did. Her hand felt fragile. As if understanding Thom's thoughts, Ralla spoke. "She has promised me that she's going to get checked out by the doctors and" — Ralla turned to Dija — "actually *eat something.*" Ralla was smiling, but she clearly meant it. Dija nodded. "Now... the nurses told me what they saw," she said coyly. "But I do have a question for you, Thom. This looks an awful lot like the Medbay on the *Universalis*. I *distinctly* remember falling asleep on the *Population.*" She squinted in a failed attempt to look angry. "Thom Vargas, did you kidnap me?"

Thom couldn't help but smile. Dija giggled.

"And before you explain," she continued, "I need you to know that they've got me on some *amazing* drugs right now, so I can't promise I won't laugh at inappropriate parts, um... inappropriately?"

"There was snow, Ralla. I walked in the snow," Thom said, beaming. Ralla nodded a jealous smile, but Dija's face held nothing short of shock.

"You were... up there?" she said, pointing to the ceiling. Thom took a second to figure out where to begin, then sat at the end of Ralla's bed and filled them in on what had happened after he couldn't wake Ralla. As he described the view from the top of the snowbound escape sub, Ralla took his hand, and neither bothered to let go. By the time he got to the part of the story where they docked with the *Uni*, Dija asked him to back up and explain how he had gotten on the *Population* in the first place. By the end of the story, she had sat down on the other side of the bed and was listening intently.

"Thank you, Thom. Thank you so much," Ralla said, squeezing his hand.

"You would have done the same for me," he said, looking at an imaginary spot on the bedsheet. She nodded, her eyes tearing up slightly.

"What about you, Dija? What happened after you got back to the *Uni?*"

Dija transformed, seeming to shrink as she slid off the bed and stepped away, fixating on the floor. She shook her head jerkily.

"Dija, Dija, it's fine." Ralla motioned for her to sit back down with her bandaged hand. "Look, this has been more horrible than anyone could have imagined. We're all badly shook up. I bet even Thom,"

"Yep."

"Me too," Lo said quietly, though his bass voice carried. They hadn't noticed his arrival. The loose-fitting scrubs made a box of his shape.

"Geran, this is Dija and Ralla."

"Um... It's a pleasure, Ralla. We weren't introduced, but I was part of the, uh, 'rescue' team on the *Pop*."

"I thought you looked familiar. Thank you."

"Dija and I have met already, sort of," Lo said, offering his hand, and then enveloping Dija's with it. Thom marveled how gently he held her hand, and caught an odd look between them.

"I hate to cut to business, but apparently I've been out of it for a few days, and Dija says it's crazy upstairs. Who's in charge?"

They all looked at Lo, who shrugged.

"No one that I can tell. The damage crews seem to be working as fast as they can, and everyone else just seems to be taking care of themselves. Down here seems to be the most organized part of the ship, but then, I guess it'd have to be."

"What about other survivors?"

"My team and I have been getting who we can, but it's slow going. We have to clear entire sections before we can even get near where we think people are."

"What about coming around from the other side?"

"Like the bow? It's in pretty bad shape."

"My father and the other Council members will be high up in the Yard. Their offices might still be intact. Those areas were heavily reinforced after the last war... What? Why are you looking at Thom?"

Thom found the imaginary spot again, and flicked it with his free hand. He took a deep breath, squeezed her hand, and looked in her eyes.

"I'm sorry, what with everything... Your father died. His last words were to order me to find you on the *Population*." Thom braced himself for the effect of the pain he just inflicted, but other than a nod, Ralla seemed unaffected.

"I don't know if it's the drugs or the state of everything, but that's not really hitting me. Watch, I'll randomly break down into a blubbering mess in a few days, but right now... I don't know. There's too much to take in. I like that he ordered you to find me. He must have really liked you, Thom."

"I guess..."

"I need to focus on what we can do. I still think there could be some Council members, and maybe others, trapped up in their chambers and cabins. Lo, what do you need to start a rescue?"

"Are there any external locks up there?"

"Possibly, but if there aren't?"

"Not sure. I'll have to ask my team. We might have to cut through the hull, then shore up a hallway as a makeshift lock. It's going to take some time. I'll need a sub with a decent lock in it."

Thom swung his arm around the end of the bed and tapped Lo on the leg, out of Ralla's sight.

"I could use Thom's help on that," he said after a moment's pause.

"You up for that?" she asked.

"Yes. There are tons of ships all trying to dock with the *Uni* using the Spine lock, I'm sure one of them will have what we need."

She pulled him close enough to kiss, and then did. "Go see what you can do. I know you guys have been going for days, but I have some catching up to do. And if no one else is in charge, it's going to be me."

"Yes ma'am," Lo said, standing up straight. Thom squeezed Ralla's hand one more time, then the two men left.

"Do I want to ask?" Lo said as they exited Medbay.

"No," Thom replied.

———

"Di, if more people are arriving, we need to find them a place to stay. Remember how we did it on the *Pop*?"

Dija nodded, sitting down on the hospital bed.

"I've been thinking about that," Di said. "The structural integrity of the cabins and ships around the Basket have all been compromised. So there's the danger for the people on the deck, but also the potential loss of that additional cabin space."

"So we're running out of room, and it could get even worse. It's really that bad up there?"

"It's scary."

"What do you suggest?"

"I don't know. I fix machines."

"And I used to be a fast typer," Ralla said, holding up her hand. "But we're going to have to learn some new skills." Dija nodded and smiled mostly out of politeness, not entirely comfortable making light of Ralla's hand, even if it was Ralla herself doing it.

It didn't help that Dija was fidgeting with her own hands, but she couldn't help it, she was so happy to see Ralla. She was barely able to stop herself from hugging her and not letting go. They had gotten so close during their time as captives on the *Population*. Not once had Ralla made fun of her, or ever second-guessed that she could do something. Ralla was so confident, so *capable*, and she so effortlessly imparted those same traits on others. Just being in her presence again, Dija found the courage to speak out loud what she'd been thinking about all day.

"OK, I don't know if it will work. I'm not an engineer."

"I don't care that you're not."

Dija smiled on the outside, and beamed on the inside.

"I think, if I could see the plans and layout of the ship, I could figure out where we'd need to reinforce to stabilize the interior. Then we could concentrate on finding a place for everyone, or at least making sure we've optimized the space we have."

"Sounds good. You're in charge of that. Congratulations on your promotion. Now you're, um, Council Deputy of Restructuring. How many people will you need, Council Deputy Yunner?"

Dija froze. That happened so quickly, she thought. One moment Ralla had talked her into sharing ideas, now she was in charge of something? Before she'd been captured by the *Pop*'s troops, she been an invisible and lowly mechanic at a farming dome. She fixed tractors and combines, and avoided people.

"Dija, look at me," Ralla said softly. Dija looked, the fear clear in her face. "Dija, I know you can do this." Dija shook her head, unable to get any words out. "Dija, I know you can do this, I need you to do this… but I will offer you something first."

Dija looked up, hoping for a commuting of the terrible sentence.

"Right now I don't have the authority to get out of this bed to pee, so for the time being, we can wait here and sketch out what the Basket will look like when we're done. See if the nurse has something to write on, and a pen."

IX

FINDING A SUB turned out to be the easiest part. The officer in charge of the Spine lock had kept extensive notes on what subs were left where, and any special attributes. A short shuttle ride to a sub parked just off the stern got Lo and Thom exactly what they needed: a medium-sized transport sub with a universal soft-lock and a wetroom. The inside had been stripped clean by the previous owners: a dozen or so refugees from a failing farming dome, or so said the notes.

It was another three hours before the sub was up and running, and Lo's team was on board with their pumping equipment. One of the team carried a waterproof hardcopy of the schematic of the *Uni*, and they studied it, debating possible entry points, while Thom piloted the transport down the length of the demolished citysub. Lo stepped into the cockpit, crouching to avoid hitting his head on the viewscreen.

"All the obvious spots along the exterior hull, for the entire length of the Yard, were sealed and reinforced after the last war," Lo said.

"Makes sense," Thom replied.

"Then, maybe. Not so much now. It wouldn't be hard to find a flooded area, cut in, seal it, and drain."

"Except that leaves a hole. Another hole, that is."

"Right. So what the boys were thinking…" Lo let a wry but weary smile slide onto his face. "How are your driving skills, Commander?"

"As in?" Thom asked cautiously.

"One of the guys has an idea that we get in from the other side."

"The *Yard* side? That has to be all flooded."

"Exactly. If we can find a small enough cabin, we can shore it up quickly and get into the interior without making any new holes in the hull."

Thom flashed back to the moment he watched helplessly as the *Pop* slashed open the top of the *Uni*, flooding the Yard and the Garden, sinking his home. A chill flashed though him.

"Have you seen the gash up close? Will we fit?"

Lo nodded. Thom shrugged, pulling back on the stick and bringing the transport over the top of the *Uni*. Even at this distance, the jagged laceration stood out from the smooth curve of the hull. As they approached, Thom toggled the exterior lights, illuminating the black carbon-composite hull plating, but not inside the black wound. There was indeed enough space to fit. Plenty.

Thom descended perpendicular to the scar, the lights now eerily illuminating the yachts that once housed the elite of the *Universalis* population. Thom expected to see bodies, though not the one he knew to be dead. He didn't know where, but he was certain the body of Mrakas Gattley had been moved from his cabin in the Yard. He hadn't known the man well, but Thom felt the pang of loss remembering him now. No one had done as much for Thom's life and had such unquestioning faith in him. He wished he'd been able to have a more involved relationship with the man, not questioning for an instant this was an attempt to have a functional relationship with a father-type person.

As they expected, the lavish cabins and yachts of the Yard hadn't handled the water and pressure well. Shattered windows, cracked hulls, floating furniture, all made for a sorry and eerie scene. Over Thom's shoulder, the five others crowded around to see out the viewscreen. The novelty wore off quickly.

One of the team reached over Thom's shoulder and pointed. "There, down on the left. There's a balcony or something."

Thom descended further. The sub's lighting extended four cones of bluish-white through the dirty, churning water. Between two of the yachts was a small overlook balcony, with a two-person bench, presumably for lovers to bask in the light of the Yard and take in the green sights. Now, it was a shadowy hollow. More importantly, it was a *narrow* shadowy hollow.

Thom rotated the sub as the team got ready. Thanks to a camera on the stern, he was able to line up with the platform without bumping it. In the aft compartment, Lo slid on his armored suit while the rest of the team stacked plating and other supplies in the now-cramped wetroom. Thom turned to nod at Lo as the interior door slid shut. They all listened to the wetroom fill with water.

—_-_--

The doctor peeled Ralla's bandage off layer by layer, each one seeming to physically push Dija further away from the bed. Ralla wasn't bothered by the response; she wasn't eager to see her mangled hand again, either. The last layers were a little bloody, but not nearly as soaked as the first few days. They had kept her hand numb with local anesthetic, so she had no idea what to expect.

As the last bandage came off, Ralla couldn't help but recoil in horror. She hadn't gotten a good look at her injury when it first happened, not with the excitement of the moment and Thom's chivalrous, and adorable, attempt to shield her from the carnage by wrapping and suturing her hand as soon as they'd been able. Here, under the bright Medbay lights and the clinical eye of her doctor, there was nothing to do but stare at her deformity. The bottom three fingers were gone, leaving mangled stubs in their place. She was able to wiggle them in some sort of long-distance nightmare of painful vestigial movement.

It didn't seem like her hand, an effect made worse by the chemically induced numbness. It was a foreign body, held by her doctor, attached to her arm. In an instant, she was overcome with rage. First, oddly, at Thom. Why, she thought, hadn't he done a better job cleaning and suturing the wounds. But as soon as the thought appeared fully formed in her brain, she realized how ridiculous it was. He was a pilot, with minimal medic training. That she was alive at all was thanks to him, of that she had no doubt.

As she pressed back into her pillow, trying to distance herself from the doctor's exam on the partial appendage at the end of her arm, she noticed Dija moving closer. There was a look of fascination on her face, like Ralla was a damaged machine in need of a new part.

"Is there anything you can do?" Ralla asked before letting out a slow breath in an attempt to reduce a wave of nausea. The doctor paused, mid-exam, and looked at her warily. It was clear in his eyes he hadn't slept in days. Ralla felt guilt and depression overwhelm her. This was such a minor issue compared to the hundreds, maybe thousands, elsewhere that needed this man's help.

"I'm sorry. Never mind. It's not important."

"Ms. Gattley, I think it is important you realize you nearly died from the infection that resulted from these wounds."

"I know, I'm sorry."

"There was nerve damage, but the fact that you've retained some movement means you can be fitted with prosthetics and perhaps regain some functionality, or at least a modicum of aesthetic normalcy."

Dija had leaned in, at this point, trying to get a better view around the doctor's arm. He looked down at her as if she were a bothersome child but said nothing. He took a fresh bandage and a clear ointment from a pack on his belt and started dressing the wounded fingers.

"I want to keep you on antibiotics for a least another week, less if our supply runs low. You're doing well enough that I don't see any reason to keep you here. The nurses will show you how to bandage..." He looked down at what he was doing and stopped. "...your wound. If you have any trouble, please feel free to come back."

After scratching a few words on a piece of paper, which he left on her bed, the doctor left.

"Well, Di, looks like I'm sprung. What do you say about taking a walk around?" Ralla swung her legs over the side of the bed and tried to stand. Her legs buckled, and Dija stepped in to support her. "A slow walk, it seems."

—-—

Lo worked fast, placing the panels and using his fusor to seal them together. The hulls of the adjacent ships that formed the walls of the overlook offered a perfect surface to secure the plating. Within an hour he had the important parts fortified and returned to the wetroom for the umbilical that would connect his newly made wall to the back of the transport. The business end of the tube was a ring, which on Lo's command inflated to seal against the frame of his new wall. The pumps started, emptying the wetroom, the umbilical, and the newly enclosed balcony area.

It wasn't long before the team sloshed out onto the balcony area to shore up the new walls and build a temp lock at either end of the space. Lo returned to the transport and, after removing his helmet, sat on the floor. Thom twisted halfway around in the command chair and let his left arm dangle over the back.

"You look tired," Thom said. Lo just nodded, then let his head tilt back to rest on the back of his armor.

"Once we get inside, do you want to take command?" Lo asked, eyes closed. Thom shook his head. Lo didn't need to open his eyes to understand the answer. "Should I still call you Commander?"

"How about you call me Thom."

Lo nodded slowly.

The pair sat in silence as the team clanged paneling together and soldered seams at the far end of the umbilical. Thom looked over his shoulder to check the transport's main panel, but in the dead space of the Yard, the water was still.

"How long do you think they'll take?" Thom asked. Lo opened his eyes, and with the barest possible movement, looked down the ship and umbilical at his team.

"A while, yet."

"Got any good stories?"

Lo turned back and stared at Thom.

"If you're not my commander, then as a friend please let me sleep."

Thom rose his hands to signify surrender.

"Sleep , big guy, sounds like an excellent idea."

Lo was unconscious in seconds but Thom, as much as he tried, couldn't slow his mind enough to do the same. He was going to have to talk to someone. Whatever was causing this debilitating anxiety when faced with being in command had pushed him from Ralla, albeit temporarily, and clearly was too powerful even to lead these few people to rescue some Council members. He wondered, not for the first time, if any of his old friends had survived. Not that any of them would understand, but they'd at least listen and offer him a drink.

A drink, now that was a good idea.

— -̄--

Weak and sore, Ralla did her best to smile as she passed survivors on her way to the elevators. She figured it wouldn't offset her gaunt appearance, but she hoped it helped. Her time captive on the *Pop* had thinned her so much she looked beyond emaciated. Her poorly shaven head made her look like a mental patient. There would be time for a shower and haircut later, she thought as the elevator doors opened to the Basket. The thought instantly vanished, and she couldn't help but gasp at the sight before her.

Ralla had never spent much time in the Basket, and thought it had always looked rather unclean and industrial. Now, however, it was practically a disaster area. No, she realized, it *was* a disaster area. Two huge ships had fallen from their berths high on the walls and now made curved islands of metal, their keels at odd angles to the floor. People were everywhere, gathered together in huddled groups. It made the poor conditions trapped on the *Pop* a party by comparison. There were few she could see who didn't have some visible injury or bandage. Clothes were tattered and dirty.

Dija, at Ralla's side, said nothing. Both knew more people were arriving every moment. They'd have to find places for everyone and anyone who needed or wanted a home. Instead of being overwhelmed by the impossibility of it all, Ralla's mind went into management mode, seeing blueprints of the ship in her head, picturing where they'd be able to direct people.

"The first thing we need to do is create some sort of placement commission," Ralla said as authoritatively as she could. "A dozen or so people who direct the incoming traffic and can keep track of where to put people." Dija nodded, making a note on an extensively used piece of paper and stained clipboard, both borrowed from Medbay. "Then we need to start pooling resources. I'm sure people have already started hoarding what they've got, but I'm guessing most people have nothing but the clothes on their backs."

"There's been a lot of sharing."

"That's good, but food is going to be really scarce really soon. There are emergency food stores in the outer ring, but I have no idea if they're accessible. They should be in watertight compartments, so if we can get to them…"

"Got it."

"Any ideas how we can find people to help us?"

"Ummm, ask?"

— --

One of Lo's team gently shook Thom awake. He didn't remember falling asleep, and couldn't remember the guy's name. It didn't seem to matter, as he seemed as interested in knowing Thom as Thom seemed in him. As soon as Thom's eyes had focused, the guy had started back down the transport toward the umbilical. Lo looked groggy, but awake.

"He said the passage on the other side of the hatch was dry," Lo informed Thom. "Shall we see who we can find?"

"Lead on."

Lo filled the umbilical with his girth. Thom informed a different member of the team that he'd left the sub on autopilot, and that there likely wasn't going to be any issue given their secluded location. The team member said nothing, and sealed off the sub end of the umbilical anyway.

The corridor beyond the balcony was like any other in this section of the ship: carpeted, with tasteful wall decorations and an occasional painting or fancy wall sconce. None of it fazed either men, and they set off in opposite directions. Thom headed toward the bridge, knocking on every hatch he passed.

As this area had been upgraded continuously since the *Uni*'s launch decades before, all the hatches were watertight and were attached to sensors that gave pressure readings and water detection for those on either side. Each hatch showed no water on the inward rooms, but all were locked. Thom made a mental note to mention to Lo that someone should come back up here and search for supplies. At the end of the corridor, a few levels directly below the entrance to the bridge, the damage from the battle made itself known. Emergency watertight doors blocked the passage. Remembering how the damage looked when he passed over it in the escape sub, Thom figured it was only going to be worse as they ascended.

Lo met him at the closest stairwell, and neither bothered to ask the obvious. The next level up was also empty, so they continued up to the administration level. As they passed the sealed door to the Council chambers, they heard signs of life. Further ahead, Thom could see access to the bridge and Command Center was blocked off. This meant the captain and senior staff were almost certainly dead, as they wouldn't have been anywhere else. That left junior-level Council members who might have fled to their cabins when the battle started. For a moment, Thom branded them cowards in his mind, but shook this thought away. They would have been in the way on the bridge or in the Command Center. So where else would they have gone?

After a few minutes' walk, they passed Mrakas Gattley's cabin. Inward facing, Thom didn't need to check if it was flooded. He wondered if Ralla's mother Awbee had been inside. Probably. Too many people missing, he thought, and forced himself to put it out of his mind for now.

Thom and Lo neared the source of the noise they'd heard from the stairwell. It sounded like arguing, and it was emanating from an open hatch. Lo stepped into the opening, and the sound silenced. Thom looked in around a big bicep. Inside were a dozen well-dressed people. Thom presumed Council members, or something close. They were gathered around a low table covered with schematics. They stared at the shadow in the door for what seemed to Thom an exceptionally long time. Finally, the oldest of the bunch stood up and strode towards them.

"It's about time someone sent a rescue. I'm Tenncy Hennorr, and you'll want to take me to whomever is in charge immediately."

—⁻--

The signup sheets had been Dija's idea. The nurses had been able to scrounge up some pens and enough spare paper to suit their needs. That only left the problem of actually getting people to sign up. Ralla had confidence that she could handle this part without problem. She was already writing her speech in her head as they rode the elevator up to the Basket. The nurses had insisted Ralla take a cane, and as she stood woozily in the elevator, she was grateful for it. Her hand ached, but it was clear the drain on her body from the days without food or water, and the remains of the massive infection, were much more of an issue.

The elevator doors opened, and the sight was no less shocking than when she'd first seen it just a few hours earlier. She did her best to wrap her head around what was, in effect, a dangerously overcrowded, multi-ship disaster area.

The bank of elevators, and a matching set far on the opposite side of the Basket, were nestled into the aft corners of the long rectangle of the

Basket. The area between them, a wide open space of bare, rusty deck plating, was bustling with people. Most were either filing to, or exiting from, the elevators. Others seemed to mill around, lacking any place else to be.

Forward of this area were the two dislodged ships. The one on the port side, almost perfectly upside-down, formed a mountain of curved, rusted metal. The ship from the starboard side wall had fallen on its port side and looked to have rolled even a little further over. Even at distance, Ralla saw people sitting and lying on these overturned hulls, not boding well, in her mind, for the crowded nature of what lay elsewhere.

The rear wall, to Ralla's left, was a looming cliff face of passenger ship hulls and repurposed tankers. At deck level, a single ultra-long tanker created a sort of uninterrupted wall from starboard edge to port. As people started to crowd into the elevator, Ralla hobbled out, Dija carrying the plastic crate they intend to use as a podium.

Dija gripped the bottom of Ralla's white tunic with her free hand as they pushed through the crowd. The Medbay staff had donated some clean clothes, wonderfully devoid of style or size considerations. They finally arrived at roughly the middle of the tanker and set up shop. The crate went down, and Ralla began explaining what they were about to do to the people in the immediate vicinity. As she expected, most ignored her, but enough nodded in agreement. Some recognized her and gave condolences for her father. She thanked them, but did her best not to think about it.

And now, she thought, the hard part. Stepping up on the crate, requiring Dija's help and literal support to stand on it, she waved and shouted for attention.

Her weak voice didn't carry far, a stark difference from her time on the *Pop*. It was enough, though, and people started to slowly cease their conversations and turn her way. As more people turned to look, more noticed and did the same. From her perch, just above the heads of the taller men in the crowd, she could see far in the distance, clear down the other end of the Basket. The crowd density didn't seem to abate. When it seemed her audience wasn't going to get any larger, she spoke as loudly as she could. It had quieted down enough that people seemed to be able to hear her.

"Hello, everyone! I'm Councilwoman Ralla Gattley. Thank you for taking a moment to listen to me." She beamed as big a smile as she could force. "I don't know what you've heard, but I want to tell you the Fountain is safe, I have seen it myself. It's working!" This didn't get the response she expected. In fact, no one seemed to have any idea what she was talking about. One problem at a time. Focus! "The *Population* has been destroyed. We are safe!" There were scattered cheers. She realized three things in rapid succession: Safe was a relative term, many of the people here probably already knew about the *Population*, and some of the people here might be *from* the *Population*. She wasn't sure if that last part was worth worrying about. She continued, her throat already hurting from the strain. "Right now we need to work together, as we always have. Right now I'm here to organize teams to secure food, assist in housing and placement..." the crowd erupted, audibly displeased.

Ralla looked in the faces of the people around her and realized her mistake. These people were terrified, desperate. These had been the wrong people to ask for help. They had no place to go. They were refugees, homeless. She waved for silence, and eventually got it.

"I know you're hungry and need a place to stay. I'm going to help, I promise. But right now *I* need help. I need *your* help. I need people to help me organize, to find out what we have, what we need, and most of all, how we're going to do it."

"Where's the captain?" someone shouted.

"Where's Jills?" another barked. These names and their faces, they hadn't been at the front of Ralla's mind, but they rushed there now in a painful surge. She didn't know, but knew absolutely, they were dead. They would have to be, otherwise they'd be here now, trying to do what she was doing. She'd known Captain Sarras her whole life, a kind, stately man. Jills, for all his brusque exterior, was a good man. She could feel herself tearing up, and whether it was the drugs or the fatigue, she couldn't stop it.

"Rescue operations are still underway. I sent a team to search the Council chambers, they'll be back soon."

No one seemed to mind this non-answer answer. She took the opportunity of the lull in noise to wrap up. "I know you're all hurting. What we've gone through has been the worst disaster, by far, since our ancestors built this ship. But we *will* get through this. We will get through this if we work together, help each other out, and act like we always have..." she raised her hands triumphantly. "As citizens of the great ship *Universalis!*"

She didn't get the rousing response that she'd hoped, but a few people cheered and a few others clapped. Ralla stood steadfast, arms still raised, blood fleeing her wounded hand and causing it to throb. The sporadic clapping continued, and slowly seemed to spread. Bit by bit, more people clapped, either out of reluctant enthusiasm, because others were, or out of the sheer will of this small woman, arms raised, bandaged hand and all. The clapping seemed to reach a critical mass, catching and spreading like a fire.

Of the faces she could see, even those unmoved or unconvinced by her speech were clapping. It was as if they just needed something to cheer for, even if it was this little woman with the... Ralla's heart stopped, and then she had to laugh. She was practically bald. Her blond curls, with all the superficial comfort they'd given her since childhood, were in a pile in a random bathroom far away on the dying hulk of the citysub *Population*. She basked in the clapping and cheers.

_-_--

Thom watched the annoyance build on Lo's face, a violent anger clearly welling up inside, which should have been obvious to anyone. Not only had Tenncy Hennorr not noticed, he was the reason, seemingly moments away from getting his neck snapped. Thom figured he should attempt to defuse the situation, but his nerves tensed at the thought of exerting control, and he kind of hoped Lo would just hit the bastard.

After discovering the dozen refugees, Lo had suggested they do a thorough search of the dry compartments for supplies and other survivors. Thom agreed, against the vocal complaints of Hennorr and his compatriots. They insisted there was no one else alive, and claimed there was nothing of use. Lo countered that he had a better idea what was needed, and searching now was easier than coming back later. Most of the group had begrudgingly agreed, setting off for the transport sub to wait. On closer inspection, Thom didn't recognize any as an actual Council member, but they looked familiar enough to have been aides or something else official. None paid him any mind, so he didn't give it further thought.

Hennorr, however, refused to let it go. He followed them from room to room as they forced entry. Waiting impatiently at the door while they searched, he would snort in triumph when they found nothing of use. At first, they ignored him. When he got frustrated at their indifference, he started asking repetitious questions.

"How much longer do you think this will take?" he asked as they neared the end of the corridor.

"As long as it does," Lo replied.

"This is pointless. You know that, don't you?" Hennorr asked a few cabins later. Thom saw the family resemblance, and same entitled attitude and condescension, in Tenncy as his son, Ralla's former boyfriend, Cern. The last time Thom had seen Cern he was brooding in Mrakas Gattley's cabin, the night the old man died. The night everyone thought Ralla had been killed. Well, everyone except for Thom and Gattley, that is.

With every inane question, and every ungracious sigh or huff, Thom became more resolved not to talk to Tenncy Hennorr at all. The man's close-cropped blond hair was a near-match for his son's, with the exception of some gray at the temples. The tall, lithe frame and taut skin over toned muscles implied this man knew either difficult labor, or extensive time in a gym. Thom knew it wasn't the former. With no need to connect to this man, no need to share experiences about his son or anything else, Thom successfully and completely tuned him out.

Lo had been less successful. They'd been at it for an hour and a half, and had made it about halfway through the dry area, when Hennorr snapped. He blocked access to the next cabin and began shouting up at Lo.

"Listen, you imbecile, I don't care what you think you're doing, but you've wasted enough of *my* time. I demand you get me to the rest of the survivors. I demand you bring me to the person in charge. I will not be left sitting around while you two wastes of air blunder from cabin to cabin that *I've already told you are all empty.*" He started poking Lo in the chest, an amusing visual to Thom as the hard carbonweave armor could take a large-caliber projectile blast and the wearer would barely notice. Except, Lo did notice this. "You and your worthless buddy here will not keep me waiting any longer. We leave *now*. Why aren't you saying anything? Are you deaf as well as stupid?"

Lo's gloved hand curled into a fist.

"No, you're useless. I'm sure you can't do anything right."

Lo's arm went back, this was it. But something came over Thom, and he grabbed the enormous limb. Lo tensed, but didn't strike. Hennorr looked defiant, feeling he had won by getting an emotional reaction from his prey. Tenncy watched as Thom stepped between him and Lo.

"Tenncy Hennorr, my name is Thom Vargas, former Commander in the *Universalis* Navy, captain of the frigate *Reappropriation*, and quite likely the ranking military officer on this ship." Thom leaned in, now looking slightly down at Hennorr, and his voice dropped to a whisper. "I have killed hundreds of men whose only mistake was being born in a different place. All I want right now is to be left alone, do what I can for the reconstruction effort, and live a quiet life with the woman I love. Am I clear? *Quiet.* So hear me loud when I tell you I know who you are, I know who you were, and I... *don't... care.* Now go down and sit on the transport with the rest of your rich, faceless friends, and leave us *alone.*"

Hennorr stood in shock as Lo and Thom stepped around him, and walked calmly toward the next cabin door.

X

THE SIGNUPS weren't quite what Ralla had hoped for, but considering these people were giving something when they had nothing, she was humbled. Dija had picked up the podium crate and followed Ralla through the crowd. Most people said nothing, or gave a small nod. A few wanted to talk. She thanked them, but insisted she needed to press on. The crowd opened slightly at the edge of the deck plating, where the two upturned ships now dominated the space.

The rudderless and propeller-less forms seemed like naked corpses littering a busy landscape. Neither was perfectly upright. The ship from the port wall, a tanker from what Ralla could see, had its upturned bottom littered with small clusters of people. Most had set up little platforms to create a flat surface to sit and sleep.

The ship from the starboard wall had been a cruise ship. It was roughly flat on its side, and as they approached, she saw for the first time its back had broken before or during the fall. It was bent slightly in half. The superstructure had been removed before its placement in the wall, so now there was a just flat-ish wall, with a bend in the middle, of patchwork composite paneling that had been the other side of the ceiling of many cabins.

Ralla and Dija headed along that space, a sort of canyon thoroughfare that was busy, narrow, and 20 or so arm lengths across. Dija tensed, eyes darting toward the ships towering above them. Once inside the corridor, the only way out was the way you came, or all the way down the far end. Using the angles of the hulls and scavenged sheeting, people had set up small camps in the shadows. The distance, the dense flow of people, and Ralla's hobble made for slow going.

As they exited the far end, Ralla sighed, but wasn't surprised. Makeshift tents and lean-tos littered the landscape. She readied herself for another speech. Another plea to those who had lost everything. Then she realized something, and it caused her to stop short.

She had nothing, too. She had her name, sure, but her family's privilege and wealth was gone. She let the thought settle into her brain. In a way, she realized, it was rather freeing. She couldn't help but smile. Dija looked at her with a mixture of concern and query. Ralla pointed to a high point in the tent-covered park, and they set off.

— ¯--

The transport docked with a thud, and Hennorr was off before the hatch had fully opened. Lo and Thom stepped into the crowded entry room at the back of the *Uni*. Officers were still trying to direct traffic, shouting over the din. Other than a few stares, everyone left them alone.

"Lo, I've got something I need to do. Can I meet you somewhere?"

"I'm going to head back to camp. Maybe get some food. More to do later, I'm sure."

"Yeah, I have no doubt. I'll see you in a bit."

With only one way out of the room, they awkwardly walked in the same direction until they reached one of the main passageways, then split in opposite directions: Lo toward the bow, or at least as far as that end of the Basket. Thom descended several levels from the Spine, weaving his way around clusters of people sitting along the walls, passing countless open doors revealing overcrowded cabins, finally down to a nondescript hatch on a quiet corridor.

Thom entered his cabin, half surprised it looked exactly as he'd left it. Bunk along one wall, barely an arm's length to the opposite wall, clothes strewn on the floor. It was its usual mess, but in that, it was comforting. There was a decided "dirty laundry" smell. The sheets from the unmade bed looked like they'd been tossed aside the previous morning, even though he hadn't slept there in months.

First things first, he thought. Digging through the pile of clothes in the far corner, he found a fat black marker he'd used to mark... Thom paused, bent over the pile. He couldn't remember what he'd used the marker for. He just remembered that was where he'd seen it last. It was something to do with his fishing job. It was one of those things he'd done day after day, rote without thought. And now, looking at the marker, what felt like a lifetime away, he couldn't remember what he'd used it for. Not that it mattered now, he finally realized.

Thom stepped out into the hallway, closing the hatch behind him. In big letters he wrote "ALIVE" on the rust-covered surface. He stared at the letters, the word echoing in his mind.

—⁻--

Dija watched with awe as Ralla spoke to the crowd. If anything, there were even more people here than there were at the elevators. Ralla transformed when she was speaking, as if it were her natural state, being in front of so many people. But if that was Ralla's natural state, it was about as far from Dija's as she could imagine. Even now, she realized, she was trying to disappear behind Ralla to avoid all the eyes.

These people, all of them, were so weird. Most of the time they didn't understand what Dija said. All the time they looked at her like *she* was the alien. Maybe she was. It had been so much easier back home. She could go out into the fields of the dome, tinker with some gear, be alone with what she was good at. Ralla didn't let that happen. From that first day on the *Pop* Ralla had just assumed Dija could do things. Somehow, Ralla brought out in her something she hadn't even known existed. And for that, Dija knew, she would follow her to the ends of the world.

Ralla was wrapping up the speech, and naturally, the crowd was applauding. Not quite the enthusiasm from earlier, but then these people had things. Things like a place to stay, little homes made of carbonweave paneling, shards of deck plates, plastic sheeting, all the makings of a decent hovel. Dija's mind wandered to how she would design such a domicile. She looked around and saw all the people on top of the overturned cruise ship. That's where she'd pick. Build a flat platform high up on the middle, maybe nestled in against a wall. Brace it internally with some support beams so she could add a second story, if she wanted. No, even better, she would leave the top open with a low wall, so she could sit and see out across the whole Basket, yet still have some privacy. Inside it would be cozy, with lots of warm colors.

Movement drew her from her reverie. She had already secured the signup sheet to a light post near where Ralla spoke, and she stepped away from it, back toward Ralla, when people started for it. Dija picked up the crate, and followed Ralla back down the hill toward where it was less crowded.

"That went pretty well, don't you think?" Ralla said, smiling proudly.

"Yeah, yes. Maybe when we get back to the elevators, there will be a bunch of names already?"

"I hope so. I guess we'll find out tonight if people show up."

"Where do you want to go next?"

"Any ideas about food?"

"Not really. At the camp where I was for a while, they had food. We can try there."

"Lead on."

It was a short walk to the camp, located under the bow-side wall of the Basket. It was largely deserted, though the friendly old woman was cleaning and tidying up. When she saw Dija, her face broke into a huge smile.

"Hello, little one! I was so worried!"

Dija's pace stuttered as the old woman, arms wide, headed directly for her. She allowed the hug to happen.

"Who is your friend?"

Dija stepped back from the woman, though Ralla was already stretching out a hand.

"Ralla Gattley.'"

"That *is* you. You're so skinny. And your curls!" Ralla's hand went to her tattered hair absently. There was something in the older woman's demeanor that put her at ease. "I was such a big fan of your father's."

"Thank you. He passed."

"I heard. I'm so sorry. Can I get you two something to eat? The tiny one here ate so little I was afraid she'd disappear. Then you did!" she said with a raspy laugh. Dija nodded uncomfortably, but Ralla smiled, liking the old woman even more.

"If you have some spare food, we'd be most grateful."

"I do, I do. The soldiers who rescued me bring a few bits of food from their adventures, so I put together what I can for them. They saved my life."

Ralla and Dija took seats on the benches circling the hotplate. Ralla tipped up their podium crate with her good hand, giving them a small table. Two bowls appeared with a thin broth, some noodles, and small vegetables. The old woman looked rather embarrassed, but Ralla dug in immediately.

"It's delicious, thank you," Ralla said between slurps. The old woman beamed. "I don't believe I caught your name."

"Ioa Kelin," she said with a sigh, as if it reminded her of something. Ralla recognized the name instantly. "My husband was on the Council with you. He... died in the attack."

"I'm sorry to hear that, Mrs. Kelin." Councilman Kelin had been a quiet man, with a small business or restaurant in the Garden, if Ralla remembered correctly.

"Ioa, please, and thank you," she said with her grandmotherly smile. Her eyes drifted over Ralla's head. "Ah, Mr. Lo. Please have some soup."

Lo stepped into the camp, making everything seem smaller. He nodded at Ralla and Dija as he removed his armor and stacked it in a pile near his bare mattress. He thanked Ioa and ate the soup hungrily.

"Where's Thom?" Ralla asked.

"Said he had something to do. He'll meet us here."

The smell of the soup and the sight of people eating had drawn a small audience. Dija slouched, Ralla stood, and Lo watched as she worked the crowd.

_ ¯ _ _

By the time Thom reached the camp, Dija, Ralla, and Lo were all napping: Ralla sprawled out on one of the benches, Dija curled up in busted chair, and Lo on his thin mattress. Thom didn't wake them, but took some soup and the weary smile offered by the older woman who seemed to be the cook. Dija's hair draped forward like a copper-colored cascade. Lo snored quietly, but restlessly.

"I saved some for you. The others told me you were coming," the woman said in a whisper. He thanked her and sat on the floor with his back on the end of the bench nearest Ralla's head. She looked peaceful, with her injured hand tucked against her chest. He finished the soup, its warmth a welcome change. Ralla stirred, seeming to notice unconsciously he was there. She pressed her forehead into his back.

_ ¯ _ _

In different ways, both of them were happy with the 150 or so people who showed up. It seemed a good number, and easy enough to work with. Ralla stepped up on her crate podium and looked out over the crowd. They had gathered, per instructions on each signup form, at the stern of the toppled cruise ship.

"Hello, everyone! Thank you for coming!" Ralla said, her voice filled with honest cheer. "I won't lie to you, we need to act as quickly as possible. More people are always arriving, and there are still areas of damage we need to shore up. We've looked over the skills and professions you listed on the sheets, and we're going to break a few of you out for special jobs. The rest of you will be helping me."

Dija handed Ralla the list, with symbols next to each name indicating for which group they were intended. Ralla called out a dozen names, and as she did, those people moved toward the front.

"You're going to be with Council Deputy Yunner here," Ralla said, pointing at Dija, who waved sheepishly. Then Ralla called out more names and pointed at Lo. There was a noticeable difference between the two groups. Dija's group had smaller, bookish types. They had listed their professions as researchers, designers, a few engineers, all suited for their task of organizing the Basket to fit the largest amount of people in the most efficient way. Dija led them to the elevators, headed toward a quiet space she'd found where they could get to work.

Lo's group, a hardy bunch of mechanics, dockworkers, and some more engineers, were all seemingly ready and able for damage control, search and rescue, and whatever retrofit or rebuild tasks were needed throughout the ship. Lo immediately started further organizing them into smaller groups and assigning them tasks.

That left Ralla a group of almost a hundred. She gathered them closer together so she wouldn't have to shout and thanked them all again. She had everyone pair off and gave each group paper, stubby pencils, and a section of ship. Their task was counting: people, things, supplies, open space, bunk space, anything useful, anything dangerous. They were going to get an inventory on what was what, where, and how bad, one piece of recycled paper at a time. Ralla hoped they'd find a few spare tablets to compile the data, but she knew that worst case, the Medbay would allow them temporary usage of their terminals. The group dispersed, with the explicit instruction to *be friendly*.

Ralla watched them go, energized by their enthusiasm. Lo and Dija's groups had showed a cautious excitement too that brightened the otherwise dismal morale in the faces of the other survivors. She could do this, Ralla thought. She *was* doing this. She was in charge. She was going to lead these people, with Thom and Dija and Lo's help, past this disaster and into the next stage of their history. With a pang in her heart, she wished her father could see her now. She forced the thought aside. There would be time for mourning later.

Thom. He had set off already. There had been something about how he'd responded to her request for help that troubled Ralla. There would be time for that later, too. And for the first time, she was sure of that.

_-__--

Far above, looking down at the tiny-looking people, Tenncy Hennorr stepped back from the balcony of the private yacht/cabin nestled at the top of the Basket's starboard wall. Turning, he faced the assembled group. Four were loyal employees, sticking with him even though his business ventures were certainly gone. Two were Council members and personal friends of many decades. Another was the leader of the Dockworkers' union. Two more were the second in command of the Fishermans' and Engineers' union respectively. Until their bosses were found — not likely, Hennorr noted grimly — their bylaws put them in charge. One was the husband of a Councilwoman killed in the battle. He and his wife had been friends of the Gattleys, though Hennorr knew them only from official functions.

It wasn't the group he'd have wanted, but it was the group he had. They would suffice.

He joined them on a long, curved, white couch, while they sipped drinks and enjoyed some rations. The owner of the cabin, a mid-level employee of Hennorr Industries, was a twit and an incompetent annoyance. He'd inherited the cabin from his far more successful and useful father, though he'd at least been smart enough to store food when the fighting started. Hennorr had tasked him with running down all the next of kin of the remaining Council members. Most had lived in their districts, and possibly survived the destruction of the *Uni.* Better to let this fool knock on cabin doors all over the ship than be here and try to contribute.

Hennorr had to admire the yacht itself. There was lots of wood, uncommon for a cabin this far from the Yard. He swirled the ice around in his glass, and took the last sip of the particularly vicious liquid. Even watered down, whatever the clear alcohol was, it wouldn't pass for floor cleaner in one of his restaurants. Honestly, he sneered, it was little better than straight disinfectant.

Former restaurants, he thought with an audible grunt. Over the top of his glass, he saw his entrance had been noticed, and other conversations had ceased. As good a time to start as any.

"Gentlemen, we represent the surviving aristocracy of the *Universalis.* As decreed by law, and sanctioned by the Emergency Powers of War Act, you are now members of the 43rd Representative Council of Concord. Rules of Succession dictate that a Council seat goes first to the spouse," Hennorr said with a nod in the widower's direction. "After that, seats needing emergency replacement would be given to the heads of the Unions, in order of size. You gentlemen are in charge of the first, third, and sixth largest Unions, and are now official, though temporary, members of the Council." The three men nodded, having already accepted the role in private hours earlier. "Quorum rules dictate a minimum of five must be present to convene. We have six, and I don't believe we can waste any more time searching for other survivors. Do you gentlemen accept the role as Council members, with all the obligations, duties, and responsibilities bestowed by such a title?" All nodded. "I need your verbal commitment."

"Yes, I do," each said in turn.

"Thank you. The Council now has the power to appoint a Proctor Pro Tem, as defined by Article 3, Section 3 of the *Universalis* Charter."

"I nominate Tenncy Hennorr, President of Hennorr Industries," spoke Hennorr's Councilmember friend.

"Seconded," said the other.

"Whoa, wait a second," the widower said, leaning forward and looking at each man in the room suspiciously.

"The floor recognizes Councilmember Appet," Hennorr said calmly.

"You're not even a member of the Council. I mean, I'm not either, really. But my wife was, at least."

"The Charter doesn't specify the Proctor Pro Tem must be a Councilmember," Hennorr's friend replied. "Only that the person is qualified as situations dictate, and approved by a majority vote of the Council."

"That doesn't seem..."

"Is there someone more qualified than the head of the largest corporation on the *Universalis*?"

"No, I guess not."

"Then let us vote. All in favor?"

The two Union former-lieutenants seemed as ill at ease as the widower, but only one voted in favor. It didn't matter, though, as the two Council members also did, as did the head of the Dockworkers' Union. And like that, Tenncy Hennorr was the official leader of the civilian government of the *Universalis*.

Well, that was easy, he thought, leaning back onto the couch.

—-–

In a dark, damp, deserted hallway, Thom gasped for breath. Ralla's words shouted around his head. "You're so good at this," she had said. "I'm so happy I can count on you. You're so amazing." With every platitude, Thom's heart raced faster. With each echo, his chest burned a little more. He was shocked she didn't notice, his breathing had gotten nearly to the point of full-on gulps. She had decided — no, technically, she had asked — for him to solidify the command structure of the remaining military personnel, with him at the head, naturally. To find out who was where, what they were doing, and what they needed. And so suddenly he was in charge of men again, and just as suddenly, crippled in his response. Something about her adoring gaze, her absolute faith, had let him keep it together. He left on his "mission," stumbling directionless from corridor to corridor, trying to get away from the all the people, everywhere. He finally ducked out of sight in a disused maintenance hallway, dizzy and trembling.

He promptly threw up.

XI

THE DATA returned at a furious pace. Ralla had barely gotten back to camp when the first teams arrived. They'd had the easiest job, counting people who claimed residence mid-Basket, on or around the two crashed hulls. She had sent them back out to count one of the corners of the nearby Tent City, or so they were calling it. Two other groups were there already.

No more than an hour later, the next group arrived, and then a few more. Keeping track of where she'd sent people was hard enough, and without Dija's help, Ralla started to get overwhelmed. Stacks of census data lay scattered around the camp in once-perfect piles. She longed for even one working tablet.

Finally, she'd had enough. One of the teams returned with some markers and pens, which Ralla appropriated. She stood and approached the Basket wall. Using memory, some guesswork, and large swaths of complete inaccuracy, Ralla drew a top-down diagram of what remained of the *Uni*. Then page by page she entered the statistics of each area. Population numbers, empty and full cabins, potential supplies, all started to paint a picture of the situation, far beyond the crudeness of the drawing itself.

The drawing stretched three times wider than her outstretched arms. The Basket itself was the easiest, she noted, stepping back for a moment. It was everything she could see, with the vessel outlines and rough counts of portholes indicating cabins. Some of the interior cabins she had to draw from memory — a memory of ancient plans and blueprints. She had no idea how much had changed over the decades. She wondered if anyone did.

Ralla knew that as Dija and her team etched out their own plans, a lot of this would change, but she cast that aside for the moment. Getting a feel for the state of the ship right now was the most important factor.

More teams arrived, and she directed them toward more work thanks to empty areas on her map. It would take days at their current rate to fully complete it, but for the first time Ralla felt she was really getting a handle on their situation.

It wasn't good.

_-__--

Dija introduced herself to her team, seven men, five woman. On Ralla's suggestion, Dija went around the room and had everyone say their names and profession. It was an impressive group: two teachers of design, three structural engineers, three scientists from what they called "The Lab," and other engineers and teachers that had less practical experience with the task at hand, but still seemed really smart. They sat around a large conference table in one of the less busy wings of Medbay. Dija's voice was shaky.

"OK, well, OK, so we need to organize the Basket, and other spaces, to maximize the space and stuff there. We'll have a better idea of what materials we have when Ms. Ralla's teams get back. In the meantime, maybe we could..."

One of the structural engineers, Jos Vaee, stood and interrupted Dija without a glance.

"The important point here is to use the open space of the Basket. That means going vertical. Some of the people up there have already started. I've been working on some options using the deck plates and bulkheads of the capsized ship."

"Those bulkheads won't support any kind of weight," one of the scientists said quickly. "They acted as dividers on that ship, the structural support is from a centralized beam core and reinforced pillars."

"We're not asking them to hold much."

"Much? Any? You're talking about creating entirely new decks out of thin, non-load-bearing walls."

"What if we, what if we build out from the walls?" Dija said, her voice quiet enough to be ignored, and it was. The meeting quickly spiraled into disorder from there, with ideas shouted at each other, the days of pent-up anger and frustration bursting forth in a torrent of accusations and insults. Dija tried to interject, tried to get everyone to respond in an organized fashion, but it wasn't working. She watched helplessly as each piece in her design machine ground against the other pieces. Sitting in her chair, she brought her legs up and rocked slightly as the yelling intensified.

———

Lo was glad to take on a greater leadership role. After leading his team blindly around the ship for days, he was glad to finally have the resources and the organization to get some real work done. Each member of his original team now had their own team, which broke down further into smaller, specialized groups. He directed each squad to a certain area, confident whatever the issue was, it would be taken care of. With his own small team, he decided to survey the lower decks. Early reports said they'd collapsed when the *Uni* hit the seabed. Lo was curious, though, and figured now was as good a time as any to check.

The elevators shafts were blocked below Medbay, so Lo and his five-man team squeezed their way down an emergency stairwell. Two decks deeper the stairwell was blocked as well, crushed deck plating and debris sealing them off from going lower. It was safe to assume the bottom levels were indeed flooded, at least partially.

Each level above those, however, all the way up to Medbay, had a full lock to prevent flooding from spreading to multiple floors via a compromised stairwell. Since they were accessible, Lo figured it was worth checking them for any useful supplies or equipment, even if they were flooded.

No one had found any more drysuits, so at the bottom accessible level Lo proceeded onto the deck alone in his armor. In the flooded corridor beyond, Lo found a certain comfort in the solace of his suit. In the dark, alone with his breathing, he enjoyed the melancholy peace of it. Away from the hum of Medbay, away from the people above, Lo tried to take a moment to himself, closing his eyes and relaxing his muscles. But the faces of those he'd drowned far above were all that greeted him in the silence.

Not silence. His eyes opened to a darkness illuminated by his helmet's lights. Particles floated, catching the beams. At first his brain classified the sound as pumps, or maybe an engine. But he was too far down, too far inboard for any of the ship's engines to be that noticeable. It was too precise to be a person. Lo turned 90 degrees and tried to localize the sound, not easy in the water and through the helmet.

It was farther down the corridor, aft. He started in that direction. Every step stirred up silt, brought in with the water during the crash. He paused again, the silt hovering around him. The noise was slightly louder. There was nothing on the walls to help him with where he was and what was around him. It was a corridor like any in this section of the ship. He was a few levels below Medbay, that he knew, but that didn't narrow down the area. Offices, storage bays, he wasn't sure he'd ever been in this part of the ship before.

A few more steps, and the noise was definitely louder. Louder, but still quiet. He wasn't surprised no one had heard it before. The closest people were in Medbay, and with all that noise, it was unlikely they'd have heard gunfire down here.

Lo reached a hatch, and it seemed the noise was coming from the other side. The power was out, but the mechanical indicators had failed to open so there had to be water on the other side. Lo pushed the hatch and entered. It was an office of some sort, maybe a lab. There were emergency lights on, giving the room an eerie blue glow. A corpse floated in the center of the room, tangled in some hoses.

The corpse waved.

Lo screamed.

—ₜ--

Thom had established command, such as it was, starting with the officers at the docking bay. They'd followed normal structure, done their duty, and continued to do it. Thom emotionally thanked them, and told them to send regular reports to Ralla, and where to find her. They said a group of surviving officers had set up camp further up the Spine in a "big round room." Thom knew it, and headed towards the observation dome where he'd first seen the Fountain.

He squeezed his way past a steady stream of new arrivals, but where they broke left and right to go down into the ship, he continued up the narrow path along the Spine. The walls slowly transitioned from raw industrial latticework to partially finished bulkheads, before long old, but unworn, carpet softened his footfalls. Even knowing what it looked like, the room impressed him almost as much the second time. The walls of the round room were waist high, but from that point up was a transparent dome. Thom couldn't help but tilt his head back and marvel at the sight. They were close enough to the surface he could see sunlight filtering down through the waves. In the forward distance, a dark shadow on the surface was all the detail to be seen of the growing ice cap. He turned to look aft, and saw the dozens, maybe hundreds of small ships waiting their turn to board the *Uni*. Not that there's salvation here, Thom thought.

The room had been converted into a partial barracks. A half dozen men lay sleeping along the walls, while a half dozen more sat on foldable chairs around a foldable table in the center of the room. They eyed Thom as he entered, then one of them recognized him and bolted up into a salute. The others did the same out of reflex.

"Commander, Sir!"

Thom waved them seated, and approached the table.

"Gentlemen. Status report." He said the words almost casually. The same soldier, seemingly the highest rank in the room, spoke without hesitation.

"We're rotating through the docking bay, sir. In addition, we're shuttling pilots back and forth to park the subs no longer wanted by their occupants. We were hoping to expand our duties, but so far that's all that time has allowed. Orders, sir?"

The urge to tell them he wasn't in command was strong.

"You've done an excellent job so far. We've set up a sort of interim government, down in the Basket. Councilwoman Gattley is in charge."

"Glad to hear she's still alive, sir," one of the other soldiers said. Thom found he couldn't look them in the eyes. He could barely manage a quick look at each face. He thanked the soldier with a nod.

"If you men are maxed out with the tasks you've arranged for yourself, I'm certainly not going to argue. What can I do for you? What do you need?"

"Well, sir, to be honest we could use a bit more direction. We've just assumed there was space down below, but I'm getting reports that isn't the case."

"Correct, there isn't. Go on."

"Should we turn people away?"

"No. Not until we have somewhere else for them to go."

"Yes, sir."

"How are you communicating with the ships?"

"Ilson patched that together, sir. Ilson, center!" A form against the wall, covered by a blanket, stirred. "*Ilson!*"

The form bolted upright, seeing but not comprehending the scene. Thom recognized him as the soldier who'd first greeted him when he came aboard. A few rapid blinks seemed to clear the haze, and Ilson rose and approached the table. He had a squarish head, covered in thick, dark, curly hair.

"Yes, Lieutenant?"

"This is Commander Vargas, ensign." Ilson saluted, and seemed to waken fully.

"Ilson, the lieutenant tells me we have you to thank for the comms working?"

"Not completely, sir. I've got short range working because that was just a little antenna. For the long-wave stuff, I'd pretty much have to get access to the main systems."

"Pretty much?"

"Well..." He trailed off and looked at his lieutenant. The lieutenant motioned for him to continue. "Sir, I'm not a tech. I just fiddle with radios for fun."

"We're all a bit more than we expected right now, aren't we?"

"Yes, sir, I suppose we are. Well, if I could get access to one of the real antennas, and we could get it powered, I might be able to rig up something just using the portable equipment."

"Pardon?"

"He means he could jack into the antenna, kick it with some juice, and you could run it no different than a personal comm," the lieutenant translated.

"Well, a regular sub comm, anyway," Ilson said, suddenly bashful.

"Ilson, tell me what you need, and I'll do what I can to get it for you."

"Sir?"

"I'm promoting you to lieutenant JG, in charge of communications. We need to let our domes know we're still here, and that we need help."

"There has to be someone more qualified than me, sir."

"You're it. I'll find you help if I can, but for now figure out what you need, and don't be afraid to ask for assistance. This is your job now, and I expect you to do it."

"Yes, sir!" Ilson said with an enthusiastic salute.

"Put together a report for Councilwoman Gattley and deliver it to her within the hour. I'll be back to check on all your progress tomorrow."

He saluted, they saluted, and he left. He made it far enough down the corridor to be out of sight when the dry heaves started.

—̄--

Ralla was losing the light, and for the first time in her life, she realized how odd and artificial it was. As the picosun in the ceiling dimmed and transitioned to a more bluish hue, Ralla scrambled to add more numbers and icons to her map. Most of the teams were taking a break to find food and have some downtime before resuming their task in the morning.

The data they'd provided so far was fantastic, at least in its quality if not the reality it represented. There were far too many people, and not enough room. Already teams reported seeing fights over space and food. Thom had found some military personnel, and now she was getting reports from them. They had seen far more of what was happening, and they seemed worried, too.

Ralla looked up from the sheets of paper and out to the actual Basket, seeing it with new eyes after staring at her hand-drawn likeness. In the twilight gloom, her brain locked onto Thom's form while he was still making his way through the crowd. Her heart jumped with a burst of excitement. He looked tired, but she knew, so did she. She met him at the edge of camp, wrapping her arms around his neck and kissing him passionately on the lips. Neither made any effort to stop. Ralla dropped back down from her tiptoes, smiling.

"I made dinner!" she exclaimed. Thom looked confused.

"You did?"

"No."

"I found a transport we can sleep in tonight. It's perfect, no heat or power."

"Sounds lovely," she said, kissing him again. She looked around and, not seeing anyone close or watching, she stepped backwards toward the wall and pulled Thom's shirt to follow. He obliged. There was no more privacy at the back of the camp, but the benches blocked some line of sight, and the wall gave them something to lean against as they made out.

"Thank you, Thom," she said in his ear.

"For what?"

"For everything. For saving me on the *Pop*..."

"You didn't need me for that."

"Shush. Thank you for being here for me now. I can't tell you how much it means to me that I can count on you."

Thom heard this like she had physically pressed her finger into his chest.

"I, uh..."

"You're an amazing man, Thom Vargas. And I just wanted to say so." She kissed him again.

"That means a lot to me. Thank you. But I..."

"You don't have to say anything back. I'm not fishing for compliments. I just wanted you to know that. And that I was thinking about you when I was on the *Population*, thinking about the times we were together."

"I was thinking about that, too."

Thom leaned his head back slightly, to better look at Ralla's face. Even without her curls, her face had a quality everyone but her would have described as "cute." Now, so close to his own face, he saw in her eyes something he'd never seen before. Part of him had longed to see that look in her eyes. Longed to be here, next to her like this. But that part was being crushed by a secret. No, he realized, it wasn't a secret. More a lie.

Ralla's eyes, focused on one of his, then the other, not expecting him to say anything, just seeming to enjoy looking at his face. Then, just as suddenly, her business face snapped into place, and she stretched to see over Thom's shoulder, back into the camp.

"Did you hear that?" she asked. No part of Thom was registering anything outside of his and her bodies. "What's that guy saying to Mrs. Kelin?" Ralla struggled to get up, with only one good hand and her legs having somehow intertwined with Thom's. It took a moment for Thom's brain to shift gears, but as it did he saw a man, maybe a few years older than he, with light brown hair, thin frame, and no discernable chin, talking animatedly to the woman who'd been taking care of the camp.

Ralla was already halfway to the pair by the time Thom stood up, but he covered the distance quickly and was just arriving as Ralla spoke.

"Can I help you with something?" she said in an official tone. Mrs. Kelin was upset about something, and Ralla was now between her and this newcomer.

"I was just speaking with... wait a second, are you Ralla Gattley?"

If being recognized had fazed her at all, Thom certainly couldn't tell. In fact, Ralla took it as an opportunity to check on Mrs. Kelin, who seemed to be having trouble breathing, and was gasping for air as she looked for a place to sit down. Ralla helped her over to one of the benches, and the older woman patted Ralla's arm in thanks. Ralla took her time deciding Mrs. Kelin was indeed all right, then spun to face the interloper. The chinless man took one look at Ralla's face and involuntarily stepped back.

"Who are you, and what did you say to Mrs. Kelin?"

"No harm, no harm," he said, waving his arms in surrender. "The Council appointed me to find their missing members. A few people knew Mr. Kelin, and knew his wife was down here helping out at this camp. That's all. I was just looking for her. *Universalis* law..."

"I know the law."

"Then you know I just wanted her to come with me to meet with the Council as is her duty."

"What do you mean, 'Council'?" Ralla said, her tone still accusatory. The chinless man didn't seem to understand her question.

"The... Council. I'm not sure what you mean. They would like to meet with you, too."

"Where."

"I can take you there. They've set up a temporary chambers in my cabin," he said, pointing down the Basket and up one wall. Ralla followed his point, then looked at Thom. The hand dropped, and his gaze now followed Ralla's.

"Are you Commander Vargas?"

"He is," Ralla answered.

"Wow, this is fantastic. Can you all come with me?" he said with noticeable excitement. All three looked at the seated Ioa Kelin, who seemed to be getting over her initial shock. She motioned that she was willing to go.

After helping Ioa to her feet, the group set off down the Basket. Thom tugged at Ralla's arm, but found her expression hard to read when she looked up at him.

"Ralla, I need to talk to you."

"It will be fine."

"No, that's not what I mean."

"Thom, I'm going to need you to be there for me, no matter what this Council says, agreed?"

After a moment, Thom nodded.

—---

The meeting had devolved to shouting. Across the table, Jos Vaee sneered at a fellow engineer and ridiculed his idea. Dija, arms hugging her knees now, tried to see how she could fix this. Ralla would know. Ralla would have been able to get these people to calm down and gotten them all to do amazing work. Every time Dija opened her mouth to say something, nothing came out. Her eyes darted from one speaker to another as her grip on her legs tightened. At first, a few of the other team members had shown some concern for her behavior, but they'd gotten caught up in the argument and forgotten her as well.

Dija hadn't heard what was said, but one of the scientists got so insulted, he stormed out. Another crumpled up a piece of paper and threw it at Vaee, who just smiled a really mean smile. Dija dropped her legs to the floor and tried to speak in the momentary lull. Her voice cracked, and wasn't much louder than a whisper.

"We need to work together on this. Ralla said..."

"Look... Dija," Vaee said, taking a moment to remember her name. "You're not much use here, so if you're not going to help, either leave or keep quiet. You seem to be good at that."

The words hit as if he'd punched her. She couldn't help herself, her legs came back up and she started rocking in her seat.

—-··

Lo cycled the lock and opened the inward door. His suited companion, apparently not a corpse, collapsed on the floor. The team looked to Lo for explanation, but seeing none in his face, they looked to the breathing body on the floor. Lo clicked the button to slide back his face mask, then reached down to remove the helmet from the small man or woman on the floor. Water dripped from them both, darkening the deck plates of the stairwell. The man, it turned out, was pale, emaciated, but smiling. His odor indicated he'd been in the suit for some time.

"Sergeant Lo! Great to see you alive. Has my suit served you well?"

Lo looked at him quizzically.

"Oh, sorry. We met only briefly. Well, not met. I saw you and your companions off to rescue Ms. Gattley. My name is Koin Eliarn. I built your suit. This one, too," he said, pointing to his own.

"Have you been down here the whole time?" one of Lo's team asked.

"Since the battle? Yes. Got trapped early on. So I donned this suit. Not the initial trial I'd hoped for. Still breathing, so... success! Can someone help me up? No food for days. Not exactly mobile, right now."

—⁻--

Thom paused outside the cabin and gripped Ralla's arm gently. She looked back at him, expecting a question. He found he couldn't say what he wanted, but she took from the gesture what she wanted.

"Thank you, Thom."

They entered together, a few steps behind Chinless and Ioa. The cabin was lavish for the Basket, with lots of wood and a large open space. The view out, along the back wall, was brightly lit from the nearby, but thankfully indirect and dimming, picosun. A group of men had turned around in their seats on a central circular couch, Tenncy Hennorr stood in the middle. One looked like someone from the Fisherman's Union, of which Thom was a former member. It occurred to Thom that, among many things, not telling Ralla immediately about rescuing Hennorr was a mistake. Maybe that oversight would be covered under the larger issue here.

"Mr. Hennorr, I'm pleased to see you survived," Ralla said icily.

"Oh, did Thom not tell you? I would have figured how close you two are, and how... emotional... our first meeting was, he'd have run right down and told you."

The fact that Ralla didn't flash Thom a nasty look worried him far more than if she had.

"We've been busy."

"I'm sure you have, Ralla dear. My fellow Council members and I have been hard at work as well. Would you care to join us?"

"Us?"

"I was voted in, as prescribed by law, as Proctor Pro Tem of the Council. A pity you weren't here for the vote. Can you give us an update on your whereabouts? For instance, start with your decision to remain on the *Population* during a time of war."

Thom wasn't sure if the others in the room could tell, but Thom saw the subtle signs that Ralla would, given the opening, toss this man off the balcony. Thom took a step forward, but Ralla touched his forearm, holding him back as efficiently as if she'd blocked his path.

"I decided a role of saboteur was more important than one of politician. In addition, it was the only way to safely free the ship Commander Vargas and his people had commandeered."

"I see," Hennorr replied in a tone signifying he didn't.

"In addition," Ralla continued, some anger seeping into her voice, "Thom and I not only stopped the *Population* from damaging the Fountain, but also killed Governor Oppai."

"The freely elected leader of the *Population*?"

"What?"

"There is no need to get emotional, Ralla. You always did have such a short temper. I am merely asking the questions both the Council and I have, based on your recent actions, your lengthy tenure on an enemy ship, and dereliction of Council duties during a crisis."

"Dereliction of duties? Do you have any idea what I've been doing the past few days?"

"No, we don't, and that of course is part of the problem. You know, there were those who said you were too young to fill your father's seat on the Council. Having known you since you were a baby, plus your adorable childhood romance with my son Cern, I stood up for you."

Ralla face was flush, her eyes narrow. Through gritted teeth, she said, "I have been organizing volunteers to survey the people, find supplies, organize the Basket, and locate survivors."

"By whose authority? Don't you think that is something the Council should be doing?"

Ralla could say nothing. Her anger, and knowing she couldn't release it, had rendered her speechless.

"Well, you will hand over all the data you little team has gathered so far, and the Council will decide how to proceed with whoever you've recruited. For the time being, we'll overlook your lapse in judgment due to your condition, and the difficulties you've gone through recently. I'm sure, for example, learning about the death of your father while you were hiding out on the *Population* must not have been easy."

"Many members of the *Universalis* military survived the attack," Thom blurted out, not knowing what else to say but feeling like he needed to do something.

"Have they?" Hennorr replied, his eyes not leaving Ralla. "Well, that is good news. Perhaps that can be our next order of business." Hennorr stepped back and sat on the couch, now ignoring Ralla completely. He addressed the Council directly. "We'll need regular updates, and force strength reports, but we should also start discussing what we should be doing with our military. Options?"

Ralla was having a hard time catching up. Just minutes earlier, she was leading a group of people on their way to reclaiming the ship from the brink of disaster. Now she was a petulant, possibly traitorous child allowed in the room with the adults. The reversal had thrown her. No one even looked at her. Even Ioa, once a kind and friendly face, now seemed fully occupied with Hennorr and the Council. Even Thom seemed at a loss, looking to her for guidance. All she wanted to do was scream, or throw something at Tenncy Hennorr. All she could do, for now, was force her way into this boys' club.

"Once we reestablish contact with the domes," she said, speaking loudly, "we might need to send some troops there for assistance. I'm sure the native citizens and those Oppai left there from the *Population* aren't getting along too well."

Before Hennorr could say anything, one of the other Council members spoke. Ralla didn't recognize him, but he looked uncomfortable and out of place.

"We should check with the new arrivals and see if any of them have come from domes with conflict. Maybe we can set up a sort of 'war room' that shows where the conflicts are."

"Good idea," Hennorr said, nodding at the man. "Do you want to be in charge of that, Councilmember Appet?"

Appet seemed even more uncomfortable, and glanced at Ralla. "I guess so."

"Good, you'll liaise with the military directly. In the meantime, we'll find some space for you to set up a big map of each hemisphere.

"They're trying to rig up some long-range communications," Thom said, drawing a few glances.

"Please explain, Mr. Vargas," Hennorr said.

"A few officers have set up in the old Council chamber room at the top of the ship. One of them was good with electronics, and said he could rig up something with the long-range gear. I told him to give it a shot."

"Anything else?"

Thom shrugged and said, "Just for them to keep doing what they're doing. Didn't seem much else they could do at that moment."

"Well, we'll find something else for them to do."

"Should I talk to you?" Appet asked Thom as his gaze bounced between Thom and Hennorr.

"That's a good question, Councilman Appet," Hennorr answered. "With Captain Sarras and his direct subordinates presumed dead, we'll need a new head of the military and navy."

"I nominate Thom Vargas, as he is the ranking officer on the ship, even if he wasn't in the direct line of military succession," Ralla said quickly, seizing the opportunity. The Council members all nodded in agreement.

"Mr. Vargas. Ralla has nominated you for a promotion to rank of Captain, and leader of the marines and navy of the *Universalis*. Do you accept?"

Ralla turned to look at Thom, the triumph of this victory in her eyes. Panic surged hot from his chest, coursing through his veins and pulsing malignly from his forehead to the tips of his fingers. She looked at him expectantly, not seeing the fear in his eyes. He realized that she saw this as her way into the Council, that even if she was being marginalized, she'd at least have him there. This made it so much worse. He tried not to gasp for breath, but felt the sweat start to run down his brow. His eyes darted everywhere but towards her. He couldn't think, the world had narrowed to nothing but the fear. He could feel his mouth moving before he realized he was speaking.

"I resign my commission, effective immediately."

Thom opened his eyes, not realizing he'd closed them, and forced himself to look at Ralla. While he was sure there were many more emotions underneath, all Thom saw at that moment was shock. Looking at Hennorr, he hardly seemed able to hide how pleased he was with this turn of events.

"Well, in that case, Mr. Vargas, I hope you will be able to find a different way to help the rebuild effort. So gentlemen, what is our next order of business?"

———

Thom had made it to an elevator and had staggered out onto the darkened Basket floor before Ralla caught up to him. She was yelling for him to stop, which he eventually did. In that brief moment before she arrived, he marveled at the sight of the Basket at night. It was so quiet. Different, yet the same, as he'd seen it his entire life.

"What was that?" she barked, stepping in front of him.

"I..."

"No, what was *that?* I said I needed you. You saw what he did. Was this some kind of joke to you? Are you going to find your buddies and a bar now that you're home, is that it?"

Thom knew she meant to hurt him with that question, but instead it just made him sad. Sad about everything.

"I tried..."

"Tried what? You *betrayed me* in there."

Thom couldn't engage. She stood there before him, fuming, as angry as he he'd ever seen anyone. Angry and hurt. He could think of nothing to say that wouldn't make the situation worse.

"Ralla," Thom said, reaching out to touch her. She stepped back like he had a disease. "Ralla..." The truth was there, in his mouth, waiting to be spoken, wanting to be spoken. As much as it tore him inside to see her this way, it was better than to show her he was a coward, and a fraud. "I'm sorry," he said quietly.

Thom stepped around her and headed for elevators on the opposite side of the Basket. He didn't look back, couldn't look back, but knew she was still standing there, furious, hurt, and alone. Better she be done with him now, in anger. The elevator screeched upwards three levels and deposited him in a narrow corridor of threadbare carpet and stained walls. It was only a few paces to a hatch with hand-written letters on it he was no longer sure were true. He entered, closing the door behind him.

The cabin was as he'd left it: Every surface clean, clothes stored in bins under the bunk, bed made. A red shirt hung in front of the window, and another, pinned to cover the single light in the ceiling, both casting a warm, reddish hue. A single faded plastic flower in a cracked vase, borrowed from a neighbor, was the most obvious element of a night that wasn't to be.

Thom fell back against the hatch and slid down to the floor, unable to move any further into his cabin. Misery overwhelmed him. He *had* betrayed Ralla. She had needed him in that moment, and he had failed her. Saying "yes" to the Council would have been the right thing to do, but even in imagining himself saying it, he felt a rush of panic and bile in his throat.

Sitting there, on the floor of his cabin, he knew what incredible wrong he had done, knew how spectacularly he had failed the woman he loved, and worse, knew he couldn't do anything about it.

No, he realized, there was something even worse. Deep beneath the shame, beneath the guilt, beneath the sadness and the heartache, there was a minuscule, and unmistakable, kernel of relief.

$$\_\overset{-}{-}\texttt{--}$$

Lo found Dija at the top of the stairwell. She was crying, though it was hard to tell with her knees in front of her face and her copper-colored hair, shroud-like, covering everything. Lo dropped to one knee and removed the glove from his left hand. He hesitated, then placed it gently on Dija's exposed hands. She didn't recoil, as he expected her to. For an instant, his brain registered how soft they were.

"Ms. Yunner, are you injured?" he asked, his heavy voice echoing throughout the stairwell. Her hair shook in a way indicating 'no,' though she remained coiled and rocking slightly. Lo looked back at his men on the stairs below. Several looked concerned, likely because their leader was taking an interest in this random woman more than anything.

"Ms. Yunner, is there something we can do to help?" Her head shook more violently now, and Lo could make out mumbles from under her hair.

"He's a jerk. A jerk. ... mean... not my fault..."

Lo's tired brain tied these words together in a way that pulsed adrenaline through his system. He clinched his right hand and tried to force his voice to remain neutral.

"Did someone do something to you?" His voice shifted, "Who did this to you?"

"Just a jerk. Just a jerk. Enough fighting..."

Lo rose to his feet, towering over the huddled Dija. He looked down the stairwell at his team but addressed no one in particular. His eyes couldn't focus from the anger welling inside.

"Help her back to camp," he said, his voice now eerily quiet. He stepped out of the stairwell into the crowded hallway adjacent to Medbay. He knew this feeling before, had spent years trying to control it. With every breath, instead of calm, all he could see was the shaking Dija. He knew where she had come from. He'd heard Ralla say it. He walked into Medbay, his giant, dark presence noted by doctors, nurses, and patients alike. Those close enough to see his face stepped aside without a word. He found the room quickly enough and slammed the door open, the frame cracking with the force. The men and women around the table looked surprised and terrified at the intrusion, though whether it was from the noise or Lo's frame filling the doorway, he didn't register. His breathing was heavy, his motions abrupt.

"Dija Yunner was here. Now she's not. Whose fault is that?" he barked.

No one in the room said a word, but all eyes went to one man. Standing at the near end of the table, he had turned around when Lo burst in. Now, the papers he held fell to the floor, forgotten. He said nothing, either out of fear or obstinance.

Lo tossed him through the wall.

XII

RALLA SAT silently in the Council meeting. She had no responsibilities; her sole purpose was to vote on policy where she was regularly in the losing minority. It had been one week since she had seen Thom. Watched him slink away. He was clearly avoiding her, but she wasn't exactly looking for him either. She was so angry yet, at the same time, wanted to see him. It was driving her nuts.

For the sake of her sanity, she focused her hatred on Tenncy Hennorr. The ideas he didn't dismiss, he'd given to someone else to handle. Ralla remembered the misogyny of the old Council almost fondly. At least some of them listened.

That wasn't entirely fair. Both Appet and Ioa sympathized with her. She'd spoken to them both at length. She and Appet disagreed on most policy issues, but he enjoyed debating with her. He was a kind man, reminding her of Thom's friend, Eerre, in the endearing way he tried to like everyone.

Perhaps the best news of the week had come from the tech working on the long-range comms. He'd gotten it working, sort of, and they'd been able to contact several domes over the past few days. Things were bleak there as well, but knowing they were out there, and in return that the *Uni* lived on, gave everyone hope.

Many other domes, though, had "gone dark," as the techs liked to say. They weren't responding on their specified emergency channels, and because of the way the comms were jury-rigged, the *Uni* couldn't broadcast or receive on multiple channels at once. So those domes were either not listening, or no one was there. Worse, several domes they'd be able to contact early on had now gone dark as well, and no one was sure why.

As predicted, many domes reported fighting between the former *Uni* personnel and the *Pop* refugees now living there. Hennorr had coolly prioritized these in order of most to least important based on the resources each dome had. Big farming domes were up top, as food was the most pressing current concern. Mines and refineries were lower down the list.

Lo and his teams were another bright spot. They'd secured as much of the ship as currently possible. Other sections were either too damaged, or were open to the sea. It still didn't leave them much room: the Basket, parts of the outer ring on either side, and the one working lock on the Spine. Two more engine rooms had been cleared, but the additional power did little to help the situation. All it meant was they weren't going to run out of water or air any time soon. There was talk about assembling a team to go outside and dig out one of the locks currently blocked by debris and the seafloor, but there were more pressing matters at the moment.

There'd been one serious incident; Lo had injured some engineer on Dija's team. Since there weren't any police, military or otherwise, and Lo was too valuable to imprison, not that they had a place to do that, the issue was dropped. Ralla was also pretty sure there weren't many alive on the *Uni* right now that would say *anything* negative about Geran Lo. He'd personally saved too many of them, and indirectly helped save them all. Some leeway was certainly earned.

Dija, Ralla thought regretfully, hadn't handled the pressure of being in charge well. Her other team members had walked all over her, and she'd reverted back to her old, introverted self. She'd come around, Ralla was sure, but it would take time.

And then there was Thom. No, Ralla thought, she wasn't going to think about him. He could drink himself into space for all she cared.

There was a commotion in the room that drew Ralla out of her introspection. Ilson, the tech in charge of the long-range comms, seemed agitated. His mop of curly hair made Ralla reach for her own missing curls, finding the soft fuzz instead. He placed a box on the table in front of the Council.

"I recorded this just now. We hadn't picked it up before because, well, I'm not sure why. We can only scan a few frequencies at a time, so maybe we missed it. Or maybe they just started transmitting it. I'm not sure. If you want I can..."

"Lieutenant Ilson," Hennorr said, his tone more command than greeting.

"Sorry, sir. Please listen," Ilson pressed a button on the box, and from somewhere inside its beat-up chassis, a terrified male voice emerged.

"...*please*. Again, this is Farming Dome F183. We are under attack and need assistance."

As if to support the man's statement, sounds of gunfire were audible in the background. Ilson paused the recording.

"We would have missed it completely, but while we were communicating with another dome near F183, they picked up the distress call, so we switched over." He resumed the playback, and his voice now radiated from the box.

"F183 this is the *Universalis*. We read you," again Ilson paused the recording. "I wanted to say 'we stand by to assist,' but..." The cabin was momentarily united in a feeling of impotence. Hennorr motioned with his hand for Ilson to continue the recording. The lieutenant restarted the playback.

"The *Universalis*? Really? We thought you were gone!" The relief was audible in the man's voice. "We need help right away. Two transports docked about an hour ago, and the men inside came out shooting. They're trying to take our supplies."

"What men, F183? Are these soldiers from the *Population*?"

"The *Pop*? No, no. We have a big group here from the *Pop*. We don't know..." There was an explosion on the recording, then shouting and barrage of gunfire. The man's voice returned, this time obviously terrified, and holding the microphone close to his mouth.

"Please send help. These men are killing everyone."

"Drop that mic!" a voice shouted in the background.

"Help us! Help us! HELP..."

"I said *drop the mic*," said the other voice, noticeably closer. There were the sounds of a struggle, then a single gunshot. Then silence.

Ralla recognized the voice instantly, and suddenly felt very cold. She looked over at Tenncy Hennorr. His face was slack. He recognized it as well.

Cern.

PART 2

I

LO POPPED his head above the cover of the shipping crate long enough to survey the area, then ducked back down as the gunfire resumed. The brightly lit dome, like most older structures, was almost perfectly round, with an attached lock jutting out into the sea. Concentric circles of squat, leafy crops surrounded three beige single-story buildings. On the far side from where he and his men were, a long, gray, windowless structure hugged the interior edge of the dome for a little less than a quarter of the total perimeter. Lo's intel had said F327 was lightly defended, given its small size and marginal crop yield. "Lightly defended" seemed optimistic, as his team was pinned down just outside the main lock.

Lo looked around at his men. Seven armored soldiers, four from his team on the *Reap*, the others with decent training but marginal combat experience. Good men, all around. They'd set out from the *Uni* two days earlier.

"Thom, this is Lo. We've got some resistance down here," he said into his comm.

"Copy that. Want me knock on the door?"

"Go for knock."

Lo got the attention of his men, then made their predetermined fist-hitting-open-hand signal for the knock maneuver. He poked his head up just high enough to see the far side of the small dome and was able to witness Thom's handiwork. From the darkness outside the dome, Thom lit the transport's searchlights, creating a massively bright spot in the sea. The lights approached rapidly, at a speed clearly aimed to ram the dome. Lo knew, though his adversaries did not, that as fast as Thom seemed to be going, it was an optical illusion, using lights on extending booms to mask size and speed. The truth was, as soon as the lights went on, Thom was already slowing down. Lo held up a fist so his team knew their assault was imminent.

With a deafening *clang*, Thom rammed the transport into the dome. Lo's men were up instantly, firing and advancing across the fields against stunned and confused defenders.

It was all over in less than a minute. Lo's men disarmed the dozen holdouts. The only casualty, one of the defenders, had been hit in the leg, shattering the bone. He wouldn't be running again, but he'd probably live.

"We're clear. One of theirs will be limping, otherwise we're good."

"Copy that. Docking now... Lieutenant."

Lo rolled his eyes at Thom's jest at his recent promotion, then, for the first time, looked at the dome with nontactical eyes. Ring upon ring of green vegetables were the most numerous inhabitants. Already two members of his team were crossing the field to free the farmers held captive in the warehouse on the far side.

"So it begins," Lo sighed.

———

Dija leapt from the ledge, arms outstretched, the tiny people below oblivious to her momentary weightlessness. The cables lost their slack, and her harness snapped her back into the confines of gravity. Her momentum carried her out toward the center of the Basket, and now people started to look up. She swung to the top of her arc and began a return trajectory back toward the wall. She landed feet first against the hull of the ship formerly known as the *Ocean Voyager III*. She was one deck down from where she'd launched. Above, the site safety worker frowned down at her, but he usually did, and it meant nothing.

Her destination was the top of the "the Spire," as they were calling it, a central column of tubing and girders, welded and fastened together, reaching from the center of the overturned tanker embedded in the Basket floor all the way up to nearly the ceiling. At regular intervals, beams flayed out, waiting for floors to support. Dija had seen pictures of trees in her school years, and the Spire sort of looked like that, minus the leaves. From it, new decks would emerge, using the Spire as the central support. Far below, some already had. With such limited material available, they couldn't fashion full decks, but this at least would give some rigidity to the ever-rising ad hoc structure.

Dija landed on the top platform, currently no more than a few paces in either direction. Far below, she could see the repurposed deck plates and scavenged materials already spreading from the Spire outwards to cover the tanker like a living entity. She loved being out here, safe in the science of the safety rigging, the world open before her, away from the noise of the mob below, alone with her thoughts.

Well, almost alone. As they did the previous day, the two welders eyed her with suspicion. Their heavy fusion welder, which took up almost a quarter of their total space on the tiny platform, broke down repeatedly. The first time it had taken two days just to find out if anyone knew how it worked. Ralla had volunteered Dija to check it out, which Dija had done reluctantly. Taped to the inside of the machine's storage crate was a greasy manual. Dija read it over, took the welder apart, figured out the problem, and put it back together again. The issue was worn adjustment screws for the deflection coils. A simple fix, she mused. But every time they moved the welder, about twice a day at their current build rate, the deflection would loosen, and they'd lose the beam. It took Dija fifteen minutes to remove all the pieces to get to the part, and another ten to get it properly aligned. Like everything else on the *Uni*, the gear was old, and there was nothing anyone could do about it.

So as they had the past several days, the two welders sat and had lunch while she worked. Ralla told her they probably didn't like needing a girl to fix their equipment. Dija didn't care. Up here, working on some cool piece of gear, it was the highlight of her day. She giggled as she took the cover off and the maze of wires and circuits revealed itself.

Record time, she thought to herself. The beam fired up, and the welders gruffly said their thanks. Each level of the Spire, so far at least, started its life as the same small square platform, with two outriggers connected and fused to the outside of the ships that made up the port wall of the Basket. After attaching these, they'd start on the columns that would support the next small platform, welding them to the deck plate of the current level. Lacking a real crane, a pulley system Dija designed would fly in a new deck plate for the next level. After welding this from the bottom, they'd connect the fusion welder to the same ropes that delivered the deck plate and hoist that to the level above. Lastly, the workers would climb or be hoisted up to the next level, and the process would start again. The work far below, putting in the actual floors and rooms, was work she hadn't had time yet to see, except from a distance.

Dija wished she could stay and watch, even help weld, but there was other work to be done. Besides, these two guys did an amazing job, she saw.

"Your welds are awesome. It's really impressive," Dija stuttered as she checked her harness. The two workers thanked her, and watched in partial alarm as she stepped backwards off the platform. The safety rigging caught and bounced her slightly before she began her swing back toward the waiting gloved hands of the safety worker in the port wall.

They'd been calling it the War Room, but it was really little more than a big closet where someone had squeezed a table. The space around the table was wide enough for one person, two if they wanted to be friendly. On the table, a map showed the surface of the world on the flat, rectangular space. The computer-enabled tables the Council and military had used for decades had all been destroyed in the crash. In the place of zooming, panning, and instant unlimited data, they had a static map with a clear plastic coating they could draw on with markers. Ralla had no doubt her father would have been amused.

She was not. Pressed into her usual corner, she watched as Hennorr and his lackeys pored over the reports sent down from the radio room. The techs had been able to get a few channels at a time working on the main long-distance array, but each required their own operator with their own rig. With no way to automate the process, it was manpower-intensive, but that was one thing they had plenty of. Once Hennorr had approved payment in rations, they'd had a wave of new recruits to the newly reformed *Universalis* navy. Training had been brief, with most of the enlisted doing jobs similar to whatever they'd done before the war.

In other words, exactly what she'd been trying to do originally. Ralla put the thought out of her head. There was no point in continuing to dwell on it. A new report entered the room in the hands of a young woman, probably still of school age, had there been a school. This was the one they'd been waiting for, and from the cheers Ralla could tell it was good news. Thom and his people — no, *Lo* and his people — had successfully taken a small farming dome. It wasn't much, but with limited combat forces and escalating food needs, it was a wise first assault. Regular shuttles with supplies would commence immediately, as soon as they could find pilots.

With a small amount of trepidation, she looked over the report as it was passed around the room. No casualties on their side. As raw as her emotions were toward Thom, she still felt significant relief he, and of course the others, were all safe. Ralla forced the thought of Thom out of her mind, and did so successfully by looking at Tenncy Hennorr.

Bent over the table, looking at several reports at once, he looked every bit like a businessman running a busy company. They hadn't spoken about Cern, even though both knew the other had identified his voice on the comm weeks earlier.

Instead, and much to the annoyance of Ralla, he had started calling Cern's group "pirates." To her it was offensively overly simplistic, but it was convenient so it caught on. Now the whole Council used the term. The truth was, Cern wasn't just taking domes and goods for his own group's use. He was convincing them to join his side with promises of self-rule and lucrative trade agreements. He was essentially bribing each dome with the promise of their being their own nation. Only those he couldn't convince, he subjugated.

And all the *Uni* could do was watch. For every three domes they would contact and bring back into the fold, one would disappear to be part of Cern's pirate federation. The Council seemed far too optimistic, to Ralla's eyes at least, about the prospects of Lo's assault squad. Sure, they could secure a small dome. But they certainly couldn't *hold* that dome. After all, it had only been a month since she and Thom — *stop thinking about Thom* — had saved the Fountain, and already Cern had almost twenty domes and a fleet of ships. Well, "fleet" being a few dozen transports and fishing vessels, but it was still impressive. Nearly all the military vessels lay scattered on the seafloor, mutual destruction from the last conflict, but if someone tried to salvage them for parts or weapons, no one on the *Uni* would know about it until it was too late.

She had misjudged Cern, that was for sure. Clearly, his father had, too. With chilling ruthlessness, the elder Hennorr declared the pirates, and "whoever their leader is," criminals, ordering their capture as part of a larger mission to reestablish the *Uni*'s control over the world.

Another young messenger arrived with a new report. By the time Ralla saw it, the rest of the Council members were already discussing it. The paper said plainly: "F327 leadership back in control and requests instructions." Before Ralla had a chance to mull this over, Hennorr was already responding.

"Instruct Lieutenant Lo to secure excess supplies and proceed to the next objective. F327 is to resume normal operation."

The messenger nodded and left. Ralla wanted desperately to say something, but knew it was no use. Tenncy Hennorr was running a business and that business required materials to run, in this case food. By the time those on F327 realized the *Universalis* was powerless to protect them, it would be too late.

THE SUB faced them, lights off, unmoving. Thom and Lo stared out the viewscreen, trying to make sense of the unchanging scene.

"Hail them again," Lo instructed.

"Fishing vessel, this is *Universalis* heavy transport *Sealine Runner*, do you require assistance?"

Nothing. The smaller fishing vessel had been following them for several hours, and when they'd turned to confront their companion, the mystery sub had closed the distance and taken up position directly in front of them.

"I guess his comms could be out," Thom said aloud.

"But why just sit there, then?"

"Yeah, that's true."

"And why are their cabin lights out?"

"My old fishing sub didn't have cabin lights. Didn't have a cabin, really, and that sub looks to be about the same design."

The sonar screen in the center of the console showed a bright new dot.

"Uh oh. He's got a friend," Thom said, turning back toward the controls. Lo stepped back up into the main cabin. The *Runner* was a newer design, only a few years old. It was a hollow tube with passenger space on the top and bottom, and extensive storage on the sides. A pod on the front, connected by fins that doubled as control surfaces, held the small bridge. A similar, larger pod at the back contained the engines. It was roomy, fast, and extensively customizable. The latter aspect they'd taken advantage of already with their initial retrofit.

Lo looked down the long main top compartment, with its gently curving ceiling and sharply raked windows. His men relaxed in the cushy seating intended for far higher-class passengers than what currently occupied them.

"Trouble," he said, his tone indicating information and a command. The four veterans leapt from their seats and split in four different directions. One each descended stairs midway down the cabin that got him to the converted storage bays that held the main guns. One pulled a ladder down from the ceiling and ascended to what was once a viewport, but was now a turret. The last came right to Lo, descended the stairs to the bridge, then exited down adjacent stairs that led to the bottom compartment. Though a similar layout, the bottom was much less lavish in its design and decor. The windows here aimed downwards to offer views of the seafloor, the opposite of those on the top deck. In the back, another turret covered the back of the ship. Lo was pleased the drills had worked; it had all taken just a few seconds. The rest of his squad was already starting to don their drysuits.

"So much for no shooting," Thom muttered.

"We're not shooting yet."

"It's not us I'm worried about."

"Try to go around him; let's see what he does."

Thom moved the throttle from its stop, and the big transport crawled forward. The fishing sub matched the pace in reverse, keeping its distance.

"How long 'til the other one's on us?" Lo asked, trying to make sense of the sonar display.

"Under a minute."

"You want to find out what he wants?"

"Not really."

"Want to hail him?"

"Not really."

"Give me the mic," Lo asked. Thom handed it to him, and activated the comm. "This is the *Universalis* heavy transport *Sealine Runner*, please identify yourselves." Lo dropped the mic from his face. "Throttle up."

Thom did so, but the fishing vessel continued to keep pace. Its companion increased its speed even more.

"Unidentified vessels, if you continue to maintain comm silence we will assume hostility and take defensive measures. Please respond or discontinue your pursuit."

"If their comms are out, they can't hear you."

"Both of them?"

"I'm just saying."

"Go full throttle."

Thom pushed the throttle to its stop. Unable to compensate, the distance between the two subs decreased rapidly.

"Well, he's going to have to get out of the way now, or..."

Suddenly, the fishing sub reversed its thrusters and leapt at the transport. Narrowly missing collision, the smaller sub dove underneath while simultaneously firing out a fishing net from its aft compartment. Like a perfectly set snare, the *Runner* plowed right into it. Thom swore, as Lo turned back toward the main cabin.

"Subs are hostile, prepare to fire."

"Lo, I got this."

Thom pulled back on the controls, standing the transport nearly on end and shooting toward the surface. There was a slight tug and release as the lines of the net snapped. Reversing thrust, the loose net drifted away from the transport. Thom angled down and powered under the net and away from the pair of subs. They lacked the *Runner*'s speed, and quickly disappeared off the sonar.

"Still don't want to be in the fight?" Lo asked, half joking.

"More than ever."

—-—

Ralla did her best to avoid Thom's gaze, but she couldn't help noticing he kept looking in her direction. Lo was giving a report to the Council, and had apparently dragged Thom along against his wishes. Lo was crafty like that. Both his team's initial objectives had been successes. The first, a small farming dome, required force. The second, a remote drilling/refinery dome, had been happy the *Uni* was still around, but just needed some hand holding to sign back on. All of this had been in Lo's report, but Hennorr liked to bring people to speak before him as some sort of power statement. Begrudgingly, she appreciated the craftiness.

Ralla had already decided to tell Lo about Cern. Someone else had to know what they were getting into, and as much as she'd love to place doubt in the minds of the Council about Tenncy Hennorr, it wasn't time. But she needed someone else to know.

As the meeting started to break up, Ralla made her way over to Lo, successfully avoiding Thom's stare.

"Lo, I'm having lunch with Dija today, will you join us?"

"Oh, sure. Would you mind if Thom joins us?"

To Lo's momentary amusement, both Ralla and Thom froze.

"I, ah..." she began.

"Lo, I'm not sure if..." Thom stuttered. Lo leaned down to whisper in Thom's ear.

"I need backup," he said before standing back upright. Thom's demeanor changed instantly.

"If it's not an inconvenience to you," Thom said, speaking to Ralla though her gaze was aimed toward the balcony.

"It's fine. I'm meeting her at the camp in an hour."

—-—

Camp 1, as it had become known, was now home to Lo, his squad, Ralla, and Dija. Their original camp was still intact, with its central cooking area and benches, but it was now covered and enclosed on three sides. Inside the elevated portion, designed by Dija, held tiny rooms for each tenant. Stairs ran up along the port outside edge, going all the way to the roof, where tables and chairs made for a comfortable relaxation and meeting place. They all knew this luxury would be short lived, as the stream of refugees hadn't abated.

At the moment, four sat eating rations, three in awkward silence. Each of their gazes alternated between the food, their feet, and the view out to the ever-changing Basket. Construction projects big and small rebuilt, added, and repaired. The sparks of welders drew the eye.

Dija, however, oblivious to the tension and awkwardness, stared at the Spire and happily went over in her head possible ways to permanently fix the fusion welder. It was a problem she enjoyed thinking about. Her eyes focused back to the immediate space and onto Lo's face. Their eyes locked before the big man looked away quickly. Dija realized she had never thanked him for saving her after the crash. Then again, it's not like she'd been able to think about it much. Even now, up on the roof of Camp 1 and the gentle breeze caused by the overworked circs, the watery would-be tomb seemed impossibly far away.

"Thanks for saving me," she blurted out. It took a moment, but she realized this was the first thing anyone had said since they'd sat down. Everyone looked at her questioningly. "That first day, you know, after. Thank you." Dija didn't notice, but Thom and Ralla both saw how much Lo blushed.

"Welcome," was all he could say. For the first time, Ralla and Thom looked at each other, and smiled at mutually realizing a secret. Without a word, they understood they had a mission to undertake, and temporarily, their feud was forgotten.

"Dija," Ralla said, hardly able to hide her smile. "After lunch do you think you can show Lo the work you're doing on the Spire?"

"Well, it's not *me*. I'm not doing it."

Lo tried to burn holes in Ralla's head with his eyes. Thom elbowed Lo in the side. The burning gaze turned at Thom.

"I, uh..." Lo stammered.

"Should go," Thom finished for him. "You've been asking about it for a week."

"OK," Dija said, going back and seeming to enjoy her gruelish rations, totally unaware.

They finished the meal in silence, and Thom had to practically kick Lo down the stairs to go with Dija. His face flushed, and he was tripping over himself as he started, then stopped, then started again.

"Lo, you'll be fine," Thom said, placing a hand up on his shoulder.

"I'm not sure that's true."

Thom made a show of rolling his eyes.

"I don't know what to say," Lo said, watching Dija make her way down the stairs.

"Me neither, my friend. Me neither. Tell her what you like about her. Ask questions when she tells you something."

"You're making it sound easy."

Thom's face fell, and he looked back across the roof at Ralla.

"That it is not. Now go, before she thinks you don't want to go."

The structure shook as Lo bounded down the stairs after Dija, who had already made it to the pathway between Camp 1 and Tent City, the former park area where thousands had set up small cloth and canvas structures. She'd stopped and was waiting with her eyes on the Spire.

Thom returned to where they had been sitting, the amusement of the moment gone. It was clear the momentary respite in anger had left Ralla as well. Each waited for the other to speak. All the feelings that had driven Thom to step down still burned in his chest.

"Ralla, I'd like to explain."

"Explain how you betrayed me when I needed you?"

"It's not like that."

"Really? I remember it being exactly like that."

"No, I mean..." Thom wanted to say it, but he just couldn't get it out. It welled in his throat like a stone. Ralla's gaze held no mercy.

"I saw things in you I guess weren't really there."

"No, Ralla..."

"You know what? I don't want to talk about this. You've upset me enough, and I'm done. I need to tell you something that's important to the security of the ship, and I expect you to tell Lo when he's done with his date. Think you can do that?"

Thom's brain hung on "done," but he could see he was getting no farther right now. He nodded for her to go on.

"I'm reasonably certain the leader of this group we've been fighting is Cern Hennorr."

Thom's brain flashed back to when he and Ralla returned from the *Population* after their first escape. Ralla holding the hand of this tall, handsome, athletic man, and the crowd cheering as they kissed. Then, many weeks later, the same man losing his mind at the idea of Ralla donning an armored suit and staying behind with the intent to save everyone on board their stolen cruiser. Thom was oddly not surprised that this impulsive, entitled playboy would have taken charge of something so negative.

"How can you be sure?"

"I heard his voice on the comms from a farming dome."

"Does his father know?"

"I think so."

"You *think* so?" Thom shot back, suddenly angry. "Ralla, you're telling me the Proctor of the Council's *son* is the leader of the pirates, and he *knows*?"

"Well, yes, but..."

"But? He's sending Lo, he's sending me and the squad and Lo, into *combat* with these people. How do you know they're not working together?"

"I'm sure they're not."

"You're sure."

"Yes, well, as sure as I can be. They're not communicating through any means I can discover. If they are, it's some private method no one else knows about. For that matter, the first thing Tenncy did after we all heard the recording was to declare them all criminals and order their capture. You should have seen it, it was cold."

"Well, that I believe."

"That's why I'm telling you. Look, I need help. Tenncy is dangerous, even if he isn't working with Cern."

"Because he disagrees with you?"

"What? No," she replied, shocked.

"I'll tell Lo all this if you want me to, but what he does with this information is up to him."

"Then maybe I should talk to him."

"Maybe you should." The balance of the conversation had shifted, and Thom stood angrily. "Ralla, this is reckless. Reckless of you to hold something like this secret."

Thom left the roof, leaving Ralla alone and them both wanting to return to an earlier moment.

———-—

Thom had once joked that his cabin was "cozy." With Lo inside, taking up nearly the entire end wall with his muscled bulk, it devolved to something more like "cramped." Geran shifted uncomfortably, brushing against two walls as he did so. Thom handed him a newly poured drink. Lo took a sip and grimaced.

"My friends and I made it with a still and restaurant leftovers," Thom said, pouring himself one.

"What did it taste like before it went bad?"

"About the same."

Lo painfully gulped the rest of the brown alcohol down and handed the empty cup to Thom.

"Another?"

Lo nodded. Thom removed the stopper from the jug and poured another serving into the clear jars they were using as cups.

"So... Ralla," Thom said.

"Yep," Lo replied, taking a big gulp of his drink. He had come to Thom directly after talking with Ralla.

"What do you think?"

"She thinks you were being an ass."

"What do I have to do with this?"

"No idea, but she seemed pretty upset about it."

"Yeah, well..." Thom had known Lo for a while now, but this was the first time they'd really spent any time together outside of "work." He felt mildly uncomfortable jumping into such a personal topic. Lo seemed to sense his unease.

"Would you rather I talk about something else?"

"Very much. How'd your date go?"

"It was not a date," Lo replied.

"How did your not-a-date go?"

"Maybe we should keep talking about Ralla."

"Sorry. Look, how about this? You talk to me about Dija, I'll talk to you about Ralla, and we can try to be normal guys for a few hours."

Lo bobbed his head slowly and took another drink. "I get uncomfortable talking about this stuff," he said quietly.

"Same here. It's too bad my friend Yullsin isn't around. He was this little guy, but had this amazing ability to chat up *anyone*. He'd turn on this charm and there wasn't a woman on this ship that wouldn't be captivated."

"What happened to him?"

"I don't know," Thom replied regretfully. "I didn't see much of him, or my other friends, when the war started. I've gone by their cabins, but..."

"Me too. With my friends, I mean."

The silence hung heavily. Thom raised his jar in a toast, and Lo did the same.

"We've lost so many people," Thom said. "No one's had time to mourn."

Lo nodded. They drank in silence for a few minutes.

"So... Dija?" Thom asked.

"You're going to say she's too smart for me."

"Why would I say that?"

"I don't know. Sorry."

"Lo, let me make something really clear. I don't find any humor in making fun of others. For that matter I am — was — something, with Ralla, and she is *way* smarter than me. So if you think this girl likes you, or would like you, or whatever, I'm in. I'm for it. I'll help in any way I can."

"Thank you for that," Lo replied.

"Hey, if we're going to be friends, we might as well speed up the process. Who knows what's going to happen tomorrow."

"Good point," Lo agreed.

"So Dija."

"There's something about her. Not sure I have the words to explain it. I don't suppose you get that."

"I don't *not* get it. Does that makes any sense?" Thom asked.

"No."

"I dig her hair, how about that. And I think if she relaxed a bit, she'd be fun to spend some time with." Thom said.

"She is a little... manic, isn't she?"

"A bit, but it's charming."

"Adorable," Lo said.

"Sure..."

"I rescued her and some other people on that long day after the crash," Lo began. "She just curled up in this ball and didn't move after that. I remember thinking, with all that was going on, here was someone I helped. Here was someone I could protect."

"Whoa..."

"Not the best reason to start a relationship, I know."

"It's a little creepy, yes."

"That was just the start of it, though. That was just a harmless crush. It helped me get through some... not great stuff that happened after."

"I am familiar with 'not great stuff,'" Thom replied honestly, taking another sip of his drink. Lo noticed, as if he had forgotten his drink, and took a swig of his.

"I know she doesn't need my help. But I can't shake the crush, you know? I guess I just wanted to see what she was like. The actual Dija."

"And?" Thom asked.

"She's weird, but in a really interesting way. She sees things I'd never notice. She's... different. I like that."

"And the hair."

"And the hair," Lo agreed.

"Well my friend, my advice is to leave the 'protection' bit in your cabin. Some women like that kind of thing, but if she's anything like Ralla, she'll throw it right back at you."

"Seems like good advice."

"Maybe. What do I know? I can't even tell Ralla I'm having panic attacks." Thom froze. They both did. He hadn't intended to admit that. He hadn't even ever called them that before. It had just slipped out. He looked at Lo, who held his glass just in front of his face, seeming to realize this was a new level of the conversation. He lowered the glass slowly.

"Is this something you want to talk about?" Lo asked. Thom thought for a moment, not finding the courage to say what he had so easily blurted out. "Right," Lo said, as if Thom had answered.

They drank in silence.

—-—

Ralla knocked on the door to Dija's room. It was merely a piece of plastic from a shipping container, which she moved aside when Dija said she could enter. The corner room was almost perfectly square, half taken up by a cot pressed against one wall. The windows were as large as the structural integrity would allow, or so Dija had said. The light outside was fading, offering a stunning twilight view down the length of the Basket. Welders, working into the night, created pinpricks of vibrant light and showers of orange sparks from their efforts. Below, across Tent City and into the lower levels of the Spire, lights turned on as families huddled together in the tiny spaces they called their own. For a moment, Ralla couldn't help but marvel at it all, at the resilience, at the strength and ingenuity. She couldn't help but find it humbling. Allowing herself see the hope in it put her in a better mood.

Dija lay with her back on the floor and legs on her cot, reading through a detailed and illustrated manual with a worn cover and water-stained pages.

"How'd your date go with Geran?"

"My what?" Dija said, without looking away from her reading.

"Your, uh... how's Geran? He seems nice."

"Real nice. He was fun to talk to."

"Think you'll see him again?"

"I would guess so. Doesn't he work with you?"

"I mean, outside of that."

"Oh. That would be nice. He is handsome."

Ralla smiled to herself, figuring that was as far as she'd be able to get. They could all use a distraction like what these two could be starting.

"Would you like to get a late dinner?"

"Sure," Dija said, turning a page. "Let me know when you go."

III

RALLA HAD NEVER had a problem sleeping before. Now, she tossed and turned, waking up frequently. With her mind going full speed, she saw little reason to try to fall back asleep. She put on pants and a thick red tunic, wrapped her blanket around her, and went up to the top of Camp 1, like she normally did. In the early morning, the Basket was peaceful and quiet.

On the roof sat a fidgety man with slick black hair; he sat with papers spread around him in a half circle, lit by a yellowish portable lamp. He tapped at a wrist computer with incredible dexterity. He turned as she approached, and squinted at her in the semi-darkness.

"Ah," he said, getting to his feet. "Ralla Gattley. Hello. My name is Koin." Ralla was surprised at his small size, only slightly taller than her. His clothes, though well worn, seemed to fit his frame oddly well. He moved with an abrupt manner.

"You made the suits."

"I did! Thank you. Lots of work. Wish I could build more."

"Surely we can find you an office or something to work in. Geran Lo and his team found you in your flooded lab, correct?"

"Yes. Such a pity. So much equipment. No. This is fine."

"Do you want quarters? I'm sure we can find something for you here, if you don't mind sharing."

"Thank you. I don't sleep much. Too much to do."

"Me neither, these days," Ralla said before looking over at the papers by his feet. "What are you working on?"

Koin frowned.

"Many things. Several things. A few things. Trying to see if we can empty the Garden. Trying to see what we can shore up and save. What's destroyed and lost. Mostly... something else."

"What's that?"

"I am a fan of Thom Vargas."

"Uh..." Ralla said, unsure where this veer in the conversation was going.

"He is a fan of you, correct?"

"I guess, sure."

"I trust him, he trusts you, so I trust you. Correct?"

"Yes, you can trust me, Koin. What is this about?"

"I need to go to the surface. Can you help with that?"

"I suppose. What's on the surface?"

"The Fountain."

_-__--

Dija stared down the hole like it was about to eat her. The jagged edges were teeth; the murky, brackish, churning water far below, the gullet. She had taken three ladders and a long walk down a poorly lit corridor to get to this spot. Now that she was here, all she wanted to do was flee. An explosion during the final battle had ripped open the hole. The space below was a bay with repair and docking facilities the *Uni* desperately needed. Some piece of equipment the workers were using had failed, and the call had gone out.

Now, actually standing here, she couldn't even remember what the equipment was, what it did, what it looked like, nothing. Her brain was being consumed by the hole. Two workers dressed in orange manned the hoist that would lower her down, and they looked at her expectantly.

"The water's not that deep," one said as he handed her the harness. She reached for it instinctively, forgetting she was clutching her tool kit. "Here, let me hold those while you get buckled in." He pried the kit out of her hands, and she watched him place them on the deck. The harness was a struggle, as she was unable to look at it, her gaze now fixed back on the hole. "Now easy... It's not that far down."

Dija grabbed the rope with both hands as the worker swung her out over the maw. Her breath came rapid and shallow. He spun her slightly, and placed her tool kit in a pouch on the back of the harness. The worker running the hoist started the motor, and she began to descend. Her breathing sped up as she passed the lip, the serrated metal nearly touching her face. Then the dark. Partially submerged work lights cast shimmering shadows on the walls. Ghostly, derelict submersibles littered the deck. A crew of six stared up at her, their faces in partial darkness.

The rigid weave of the harness prevented her from drawing her knees to her chest, but that didn't stop her from trying. The fabric cut into her thighs, the pain a distant sensation.

"Stop wiggling," shouted a voice from above. Dija couldn't stop, her leg muscles fatiguing from the effort. Her tools. Her tools were there. Dija tried to reach for them, but the pouch was in the middle of her back. She reached violently in one direction, then the other, then back again, doing little but spinning around. The hoist stopped. She could hear them, she registered what they were saying, but it seemed too far away.

"What is she doing?"

"Freaking out or something."

"She keeps moving around like that, she'll snap a line. Hey! Stop jerking around like that."

"What a spaz. Keep going, maybe she'll calm down when she gets her feet on the deck."

The hoist resumed. Her pants were soaked through where the harness had cut her legs. Her brain focused now on the water. It was the deepest point on the planet. Its depth was infinite, and she was wearing clothes that would drag her down. And this *harness*, it was weight. It was going to drown her. Dija tried to rip at the buckles that trapped her. Somehow, she successfully yanked one loose, and she spilled partially out the side.

"Someone catch her!"

Upside down, Dija flailed. Her kit fell open and she watched, as if in slow motion, her shiny tools as they fell past her and into the black water below. Everything was lost. She tried to look up. Beyond her feet she could see The Mouth. She'd been swallowed whole. Desperately, she struggled against her shackles. The flickering walls contracted toward her. She swung wildly now, still swiping at the other buckles. Shapes below reached out for her, trying to capture her. Drag her down. She pulled upright, the harness now digging into the back of her thighs. Finally, with a solid tug, Dija freed her right leg. The imbalance caused her to fall backwards, now dangling from her left leg. She heard a loud pop, and pain shot up her left side.

Suddenly, weightlessness.

Dija hit the cold water hard, and thrashed against its assault. Rope twisted around her, binding her, snaring her, limiting her movement despite her increasing fight. There was no breath, only water. There was no escape.

Then hands, air, a grip. She was out of the water, held fast by an unyielding grasp. She opened her eyes, not remembering she closed them. A dirty, unshaven face in front of her own revealed no emotion. The hands distantly attached to the face pressed her arms to her sides, and kept her feet above the water. Other hands pulled ropes off her.

"Is she hurt?" a voice from above asked. The face spoke,

"I don't know. She looks pretty out of it. I think she's gonna pass out."

Darkness.

—---

Ralla reached the top of the ladder and was helped to her feet by a woman, about her own age, about to head down it. Ralla thanked her, then the woman was gone. The floor beyond was structurally complete, and was the fourth that used the Spire for support. However, there were no walls yet: just a floor and ceiling separated by air. The levels above this one were mere skeletons; the levels below had already started filling out with tiny rooms partitioned by scavenged materials. Each floor stretched out nearly to the ends of the capsized tanker. There were already discussions of extending them outwards, well, technically toward starboard, to meet with the construction taking place on the cruise ship lying on the opposite side of the Basket.

The first levels were already inhabited, and some of the residents had been referring to their new home as Tanker Town, or more often, T-town. Apparently "the Spire" lost all meaning once the walls and floors were in place. Ralla had wandered around the first few levels briefly, and had nearly gotten lost in a maze of dimly lit passageways and random dead ends. Once a few paces from a ladder or stairway, the only successful method of navigation was to follow the hastily strung wires and leaky pipes back towards the Spire where they all seemed to link up and go vertical.

On the fourth level, of what everyone assumed would be over two dozen, the openness was refreshing. She walked to the edge for an unobstructed view. Ralla was nearly eye level with the top of the toppled cruise ship across the way. Construction there was progressing slowly. Most of the available resources were being allocated for T-town, but those who had staked a claim opposite didn't feel like waiting. Ralla had half-jokingly suggested they call it Cruise City, but this was rejected soundly. So far most people were calling it the Terraces. It was easy to see why. All over the upwards-facing starboard side, builders were constructing level platforms jutting out from the former hull and linking back with the starboard wall. Lacking the support of something like the Spire, they took a more traditional, cautious approach with their found building materials. Each level was a little smaller, and therefore lighter, than the one below. They angled backwards like giant steps of decking and composite plating.

Ralla stepped back from the edge and started to wander around the mostly empty fourth floor of T-town. The Spire created enough central rigidity to cantilever each level outwards, enough so that small supports at each corner were all that was needed, or so said the engineers. This allowed maximum deck space on each level. The back wall, still inhabited by those with cabins originally overlooking the Basket, were soon to lose their view entirely. Somewhere above, where the tanker had sat for so many decades, Ralla knew additional construction was reinforcing the bulkheads and building out new cabins.

A middle-aged, and slightly plump, woman knelt near the aft end of the deck. As Ralla approached, she noticed the woman drawing on the floor, marking her desired territory.

"Your turn in the lottery?" Ralla said, the answer obvious. The woman looked up with a kindly smile.

"I'm getting us a room with a view!" she said, rising to her feet and brushing her hands on her skirt. She was tall, with her light auburn hair tied back in a braid.

"I'm Ralla Gattley."

"Ralla Gattley! You serve with my husband on the Council!" Her big cheeks and large eyes seemed incapable of anything but a smile.

"I do?"

"Sorry, I'm Vellya Farre. My husband is Pell Farre."

"Oh, of the Dockworkers' union."

"Once, yes. Not many docks around here anymore."

"We'll change that soon."

"I hope you're right!"

"What are you doing up here?"

"I told Pell we were *not* to get any special treatment. It's bad enough he got roped into that Council thing." Vellya brushed some imaginary dust off her hands again. Ralla said nothing. "I was a docker's wife for many years. I don't need some luxury cabin."

"I'm sure you don't."

"Well, thank you. That's nice of you to say. But we were in the lottery fair and square, and I'm sure going to slice us off this nice little corner. It won't be much, but maybe I can have a little garden."

"You grow?"

"Oh, nothing much. A few herbs, something root-y once in a while. We had a cabin tucked up in the corner of the Garden, great light in there, so I used what space we had the best I could. Sold what we couldn't eat down at the market."

"That's wonderful."

"Pell promised we'd settle down in some farming dome somewhere, get our hands dirty in our old age. Then all this happened."

"That it did."

"But I'm determined to make the best of it."

"With your own little farm," Ralla said with a smile.

"Big in heart, though!"

"I'm sure." Ralla found it hard not to like this woman, despite her husband's fealty to Hennorr. "Well Mrs. Farre, it was a pleasure to meet you."

"And you, little one."

"I can't wait to see your new home."

"When it's ready, I'm going to invite you up for dinner."

"Mrs. Farre, I'm looking forward to it."

IV

LO STOOD in the camp, fidgeting.

"Geran? Are you all right?" Ralla asked as she approached.

"I just got back. I heard something happened to Dija. I wanted to check if she was all right."

"She's probably upstairs. She has been since they brought her back."

"I know."

"So why don't you go talk to her?"

"I don't want to disturb her if she's busy, or something."

"Busy?"

"I don't know," he said, scraping at a rust spot on the deck plate.

"Geran, go up there. If she wants to talk to you, she'll talk to you."

"Can you..."

"No. Go."

Lo made his way up the stairs, nearly tripping twice. Once inside, he knocked gently on Dija's door panel.

"She hasn't spoken to anyone yet," Ralla said from the hallway behind him, having apparently followed him up. "Here," she said, sliding the panel open.

Lo hesitated, then entered. He expected Ralla to be behind him, but she had disappeared. He left door open anyway.

Dija lay coiled on her cot. Her legs were bare except for bandages around both thighs. A T-shirt that would have been big on Lo draped her like a dress. It had the emblem of one of the *Uni*'s old sports teams. Lo remembered hating the team. From his pocket, he fumbled out a small box and tried to hand it to her. She didn't move, but her eyes had followed him since he'd entered. He placed it on the cot in front of her, but she kept watching him instead. He stepped back nervously.

"It's some candy. We found a crate of supplies on a recent mission. I thought you might like them. If you don't, that's fine too."

Dija's eyes flicked downward to the candy, then back at Lo.

"I heard something happened. I, uh, I was worried," he said. Thom's advice rang like a bell in his head. "Not that you need my help or anything like that. I just..." He realized he had no idea where to go with that statement. Her eyes didn't waver off him. Suddenly, he felt like he was intruding. He shouldn't have come, shouldn't have given her the candy, shouldn't have set foot in this tiny room. "I'm gonna go. I didn't mean to bother you. The candy you can keep, if you want, or you can..." Lo stepped backwards toward the door.

"Stay," Dija said, her voice barely a whisper. Lo froze, unsure if he had heard her at all. She hadn't moved. Her eyes were still locked on him. He looked around the room again, as if another look would reveal anything new. There were no chairs, or room for chairs. Other than the cot, he was the largest thing in the room. Unsure what else to do, Lo carefully sat on the floor.

Dija slid one hand slowly across the bed, grasped the box, and pulled it back toward her. A moment later, a smile appeared on her face. It told him many things.

Geran Lo decided that, all things considered, this floor was not at all a bad place to be.

—ᵀ--

Dija eventually wanted to walk. Lo was happy to oblige, his joints stiff from sitting on the floor. He waited downstairs while she changed clothes. Soon they were walking through Tent City at a leisurely pace. Lo wanted to put his arm around Dija, just some kind of basic physical connection, but she gave no indication this was desired. Instead, she kept looking up, carefully following the lines of the ever-growing Spire, the filling out of the levels of T-town, each and every ship in the walls of the Basket, the staggered lines of the Terraces. Everything but him.

So they walked. They walked along the darkened corridor where T-town bridged the gap to the Basket wall. They walked through the crowds by the elevators. They walked up into the construction of the Terraces and down into the low-rise structures growing from the sides of the fallen hull. They ceased having a direction, just walking with the sole purpose of walking. They walked for hours. Lo eventually allowed himself to relax. There was comfort in just being with her. Occasionally, she'd reach out and touch his arm, to point out some new structure or feature. There was a little electric shock each time she did it. He gave up trying to think of things to say. Words so often failed him, but she didn't seem to need him to say anything. If her legs were bothering her, if anything was bothering her, she said nothing.

They climbed the ladder in the Spire, emerging on an open level. Heights were never one of Lo's favorites, but as a seemingly fearless Dija bounded to the edge and looked down, he swallowed his nerves and approached.

"I could stay up here for hours," she said, sitting on the edge, feet dangling over the side. Lo hesitated, then joined her. It looked to be four or five stores to the top of the tanker, and another few to the actual deck of the Basket. Killed instantly, he figured, if they fell. He wanted this to offer some comfort, but it didn't. He leaned back as nonchalantly as he could. Doing so gave him a perfect angle to marvel at Dija, feet swinging back and forth, a big smile on her face.

"Ralla and Thom were on the surface. Did you know that?"

"He told me, yeah."

"Can you imagine? I want to go."

"I really can't," Lo said, images of open skies and horizons making him even more uneasy.

"Thank you for before. I get these... moments."

"It's not a big deal."

"I wish it wasn't."

"No, I mean... a friend of mine gets them. So I understand a bit, I think."

"I'd like to talk to your friend. Most people just think I'm crazy or weird."

"I don't think you're crazy or weird."

"Thank you," Dija said, pushing her hair behind her ears and giving Lo a long look.

"I think everyone is going through something. How could they not with all that's happened?"

"Are you going through something?"

Lo tensed, his mind going back to the thieves he beat up, and the engineer he put through a wall.

"Nothing new."

Dija waited for more, then looked out at the Basket.

"You can kiss me now."

It took less than a second for Lo's brain to shift back to the present.

"What?"

"If you don't want to, that's fine. I just thought it would be nice."

So he did.

—-\--

Ralla wasn't sure, the distance was too great, but from the sizes of the participants she was pretty sure Dija and Lo were making out on the edge of one of the unfinished floors of T-town. The balcony where she stood now was far above and across the Basket, but it offered an unobstructed view. The sight made her happy, happier than she'd been in weeks. As it so often did, her mind went to Thom. It was too raw still, she was mad, but couldn't deny that the reason she felt so betrayed was how much he meant to her. To stop herself from being distracted by that, she let herself be distracted by the bright hair next to the massive man so far in the distance. With everything else going on, this made her day. She hoped it would make getting through the next few hours slightly more bearable.

Turning back to the cabin that'd become the Council chambers, she looked over the gathering. Hennorr had yet to arrive, as usual. Appet and Ioa, the two she felt were at least somewhat her compatriots, were leaning back on the sofa talking. They were similar in age, and as her mind was still fresh with thoughts of Di and Lo, she decided these two Council members would make an excellent couple. Not that she had any interest in trying to make it happen, but she enjoyed the idea.

Next she focused on Pell Farre. He was a large man, typical of a former dockworker: broad shoulders, thick forearms, muscular legs. Even at his age, he seemed strong enough to go back on the job and embarrass many of the younger workers. Though they hadn't spoken often, Ralla got the feeling she'd misjudged him. Her negative opinion couldn't be entirely correct; his wife was too nice a person for that. Maybe there was more to his loyalty to Hennorr than first appeared. She had assumed they knew each other before the war, friend backing up friend. Maybe that was the case. Maybe not. Pell Farre didn't know it, but he was about to become Ralla's new hobby.

Tenncy Hennor finally arrived, two assistants in tow. He always seemed rushed; they always seemed flustered. Ralla wondered if it was all an act. He sat down without a greeting.

"Let's cut right to this. I don't have a lot of time," he said, taking a notepad handed to him by an aide. Don't have time, Ralla thought. What else do you have to do? The two aides, a man and a woman, both young, could be sources for finding that out.

"At the current rate, we'll be out of food in less than a month."

The Council seemed shocked, with the exception of Ioa, Appet, and Farre. Ralla was more surprised at the surprise, though it made clear these other Council members spent little time down on the deck.

"And that's if we don't see an increase in refugees. If we start turning away people now, we might be able to get a few more weeks from our supplies, but that's a stopgap, not a solution."

"Have the engineering reports come back on the Garden?" Ralla asked, knowing, thanks to a heads up from Koin, that they hadn't.

"We can't wait for one scientist to determine our course. We need to act now."

"What do you propose?" Farre asked. He had a raspy voice, like he'd damaged his throat at some point.

"There are hundreds of subs resting on the seabed outside. I propose we establish a merchant fleet, to reestablish trade routes with the hundreds of farming and other domes we have yet to contact."

"And do what? Are you expecting them to just hand over what they're producing?" asked Farre.

"Pell, don't start. You know that I, of all people, want to get the economy started. The fact is right now we have high demand, no supply, and nothing to trade. These domes, and those formerly owned by the *Population*, need to support us in our time of need."

"And if they don't?"

"Let us see if we can ask first, before we jump right to threats. All in favor of establishing a merchant marine?" All were in favor. "Councilman Bannis, I'd like you to organize and lead this new fleet."

Ralla couldn't help but see Hennorr's plan behind the plan. Bannis was loyal to Hennorr, but not sycophantically so like some of the other Council members. If Ralla or Ioa had a good idea, Bannis was just as likely to support them. Not the case with some of the others. Only Wess, the Engineers' Union lieutenant, was a similar swing vote, only even less so. Standoffish with everyone, Wess usually voted in line with the majority, and that was always Hennorr and his lackeys. Now, with Bannis gone to run the merchant marine fleet, Hennorr's vote would break any tie, even if his vote was what caused the tie in the first place.

So, in one brilliant move, Hennorr had nominated someone inherently qualified for the position, while at the same time reduced the Council by one in such a way as to ensure no further opposition.

Ralla desperately wanted to fight it, but knew she'd have no support. Bannis was a good man, a capable organizer, and the perfect choice to run the new department. Hennorr said what was on her mind.

"Of course, this would mean you'd need to step down from your current duties, as active fleet personnel aren't allowed to serve on the Council."

"Surely we can make an exception this time," Ralla offered. She was gratified that her idea was at least considered before being shot down.

"No, I wouldn't feel right about it," Bannis answered. "Besides, I'm going to have way too much work getting this all up and running. Thank you for the opportunity, Proctor Hennorr."

The two rose to shake hands. Hennorr had just given himself a fleet of ships, uncontested, with the explicit approval of the entire Council. This wasn't any different than any previous Proctor of the Council, but Ralla couldn't help but feel concerned.

Still, she thought, the *Uni* did need food. There was no denying that. And they didn't have anything to trade. They were going to have to beg for supplies from domes that were likely already overburdened.

Ralla had a difficult time seeing what Hennorr's end game was here. He was already the leader of the *Uni*. With Lo's squad he already had a small military force he could send wherever he wanted. Now a fleet of merchant ships under his control — well, the Council's control... Ralla began to feel she was jumping at shadows. If he was making a play here, she couldn't see it.

Hennorr was unpleasant, rude, and arrogant, but it seemed like he was making a decision that was unquestionably *for* the citizens of the *Universalis*, with an added byproduct of limiting her oppositional voice in the Council. While she'd found no reason to trust his motives so far, and had no intention of starting now, she knew there wasn't anything she could do about it.

What it did solidify in her mind was the need to start expanding her own sphere of influence. No more tentative thinking, no more considering options. It was time to start acting. She was sure her father would approve, after voicing his annoyance it had taken her so long.

_–_

"So then I kissed her."

"After she told you to," Thom replied with a jovial smirk.

"I think you're missing the big picture," Lo returned.

"No, no. I'm not. Consider me proud, and a little jealous."

"That's more like it."

"What's your next move?"

Lo leaned back in the copilot's chair of the *Sealine Runner* and put his feet up on the console. They were on their way to convince a farming dome to rejoin the *Universalis* family. Hennorr had thought a friendly request, delivered in person by an armed force, was the right method to convince this particular dome. He'd apparently worked with the governor before.

"I want to make a joke here, about my time-tested and always successful techniques, but we both know that's not true. I have no idea what I'm doing. How did you make it work with Ralla?"

"Not sure I did. There were... extraneous circumstances."

"Eh, you give up too easy."

"That, my friend, is the truth," Thom said. He sat up, adjusted the trim control, then sat back. The quiet hum of the engines, the water rushing over the hull, and the distant banter of Lo's squad, Thom found all very relaxing.

"She wants to talk to you."

"Ralla?"

"No, Dija. Well, I'm sure Ralla wants to talk to you too."

"*You're* sure, maybe."

"Di told me about these... she calls them 'moments.' I told her a friend of mine had them too," Lo said, continuing. Thom frowned, but said nothing. "She wanted to talk to someone about it. As in, not me. I'm not trying to push anything, but maybe you can help each other out."

"I don't even know what's going on."

"Then maybe she can help you. I don't know."

Thom looked annoyed. "I don't know when I'll have time. After this run I'm taking a group of scientists up to the *Pop* to poke around."

"Perfect, she wants to go to the surface."

"That wasn't an invitation."

"I'll have her meet you at the dock. What time are you leaving?"

Thom scowled at Lo, then he turned back to the console.

"Just after lunch the day after we get back."

Lo said nothing about his victory. The *Runner*'s noises once again took over the cabin.

"Why are you pushing this?" Thom asked, more curious than annoyed.

Lo frowned. Thom waited.

"Before you made it back to the *Uni*, I beat up two guys trying to steal some soup from Dija."

"Why would that…"

"I nearly killed that engineer that was part of that group she was running."

"Wow…"

"Everything that's happened, is happening… right before you got back I let a whole bunch of people…"

Thom flipped on the autopilot and swiveled in his chair, giving his friend his undivided attention.

"I have… anger issues," Lo said finally.

"Who doesn't?"

"No, I mean 'this tribunal determines you have anger issues.'"

"Oh."

"I thought I had put that all behind me. But now… it seems to be getting worse."

"What happens?"

"Do you want to talk about your panic attacks?"

"No."

"Then here we are," Lo answered, crossing his arms and putting his feet up on the console. With a bit of a stretch, he could touch the toes of his boots to the viewscreen. Thom rubbed his temples with both hands.

"It's like I lose grip on reality," Thom said, finally looking up. "And this other reality slides over it. I can only fixate on one thing. One bad thing. When I try to push that one thing aside, or when some part of me realizes that the one thing isn't real... something else bad slides in, and I focus on that instead."

Lo nodded, then looked out the viewscreen to the dark sea.

"For me," Lo said, "everything disappears. The anger is all there is. Whatever set me off, I believe I can fix by hitting it. I finally got to a point where I could feel the slide and be able to stop it, take a breath, focus on something else. After a while, stuff just didn't bother me like it used to. But something happened in those days after war..." In Lo's mind, he saw the woman's face as she drowned in front of him. He tried to shake it away.

"Seems like we both got pretty messed up."

"I've been like this a long time. A long time. This is new for you?"

"I think so. At least like this. I don't know. It's not like I've ever had responsibility before. I avoided it. I was really, really good at avoiding it. I spent a lot of years on the happy end of a bottle, too. Maybe if I hadn't, I'd have noticed. Maybe my dad was the same way," Thom said, the words coming out before his brain fully registered them. He sat back, realizing much about his life, and his father's.

The quiet cabin whir once again became the loudest noise as the two men sat with their thoughts.

"You should tell Ralla this," Lo said.

"I tried. I couldn't."

"Why not?"

"She thinks I'm all tough, that I'm this thing I'm not."

"Well, it seems she thinks you're a lot of things right now, and I doubt any of them are 'not.'"

Thom started to roll his eyes at Lo, then nodded dispiritedly.

"So are you afraid you're going to hit someone? Dija?"

"No. Never. I'm afraid Dija is going to see me hit someone else. That she'll see this side of me and run."

"Well, I'm afraid Ralla's going to see that I'm a failure."

"Well, if it makes you feel better, I don't think you're a failure."

"It doesn't, but thank you. If it makes you feel better, I'm not scared of you."

Lo laughed. "You should be."

—¯--

Ralla caught up to Appet in the corridor after the Council meeting broke up.

"Were you as surprised as I was that the rest of the Council didn't realize there was a food problem?"

Appet gave her a wry smile. His face changed when he did, looking far more the kindly old man she'd heard he was. Ioa certainly talked about him that way.

"I didn't imagine I was the only one to have picked up on that."

"I know we often disagree about policy matters, but…"

"Skip ahead."

"Excuse me?" she asked, puzzled. Appet stopped.

"You want to ask me something. We don't need to mess around with the pleasantries. I respect you, and on top of that, you remind me of my daughter. So you're already on solid ground. Let's not waste time. Ask your question."

For a moment, Ralla couldn't decide if he was kidding, but the smile hadn't wavered, so she tried to laugh, awkwardly.

"Well, it's not a question specifically. Can we keep walking?" she asked. Appet motioned with an outstretched hand. Ahead was an intersection, and she turned them left toward an overlook of the Basket. "I feel like I can trust you. Ioa says I can, is that true?"

"If it wasn't, how would you know if you could trust my answer?"

"A fair question."

"I have no love for Tenncy Hennorr, if that helps."

"It does."

"I think we're in a real mess, more so than I think the rest of the Council, save you and Ioa, realize."

"I agree."

"I also think something that might surprise you."

"What's that?" she asked. They had reached the overlook. They were midway down the Basket, roughly halfway up the starboard wall. Below, the Terraces swarmed with activity.

"I think you should be leading us, Ralla Gattley."

"Sorry, what?"

"You don't need to be coy. I've heard what you did for the refugees on the *Population* I've spoken to many of them. I know what you risked to get them to safety. Ioa told me all about how you, barely out of Medbay, organized rescue teams, damage parties, and more. You are a remarkable young woman, Ralla. A natural leader. I am sure your parents would be proud. I'll support you, whatever your next move is."

Ralla didn't expect the lump in her throat, and somehow resisted the urge to hug him.

"That means more to me than you can imagine."

V

"KOIN." Thom yelled, spotting the scientist lugging a ratty net barely containing his bulky gear through the waiting area. The small man trudged toward the lock, not noticing how many he jostled in the crowd as he progressed.

"Greetings, Thom. I was told you were our pilot."

"I wasn't even told you were *alive*. Glad to see you made it."

"I am as well. Almost didn't. Your friend Lo found me. Gave him a bit of a fright."

Thom stepped off the sub and hoisted Koin's gear easily over his shoulder.

"Somehow I find that hard to believe."

"Believe or not. It's the truth."

Thom stacked the multiple boxes of Koin's gear on a bench in the modified transport sub. Since there was no ship in existence built for egress onto the surface, the small transport had been modified with a second hatch on top. On the exterior a long ramp had been attached that they'd be able to pivot and use as a gangplank.

"Anyone else coming?" Thom asked, firing up the sub's engines. This time of day they were lucky the deck officer had spared them as much time as she had. Thom didn't want to waste any more of it than he had to.

"Just me, I'm afraid. Other scientists are busy on other projects."

"Well, we'll have one more, a friend of mine. There she is," Thom said, looking over his shoulder and seeing Dija's hair bounce through the crowd in the waiting area. "Koin, Dija. Dija, Koin."

"You designed the suits," she said, extending her hand.

"I did. Are you the Dija that keeps the fusion welder running on the Spire?"

"That's me!" Dija said, so excited she bounced.

"Your work is invaluable."

"Thank you! I'm just fixing it, though. I wish I knew more so I could just keep it working."

"I'd love see how you're fixing it. I tried and was rather baffled."

"Well, it's all in the focus."

"Ah… How did you overcome the field harmonics?"

Thom lost interest in the conversation immediately, and continued readying the sub for departure. Hatch sealed, he signaled the deck officer, and thrusted away from the *Uni*. Koin and Dija had increased the pace of their discussion to a blur of sounds with an occasional recognizable word.

It didn't take long before the broken *Population* appeared. A shadow, surrounded by bluish light sneaking past snow and ice. He figured this was as good a time as any to interrupt.

"You guys want to see this?"

The conversation stopped immediately, and Thom felt the presence of a head above each shoulder.

"Impressive. The hull is still intact. Mostly. The construction methods must have been excellent," Koin said as the *Pop* revealed itself further.

"See how the ice has surrounded it, that's all since Ralla and I crashed there."

"Impressive," Koin replied. Dija was silent, looking instead at the sunlight filtering past the waves.

They surfaced a short distance from the ice, and Thom maneuvered so they were scraping against the edge. The noise was distressing, having been something all had been trained from birth to mean imminent danger. Koin assured them that the modern transport hulls were significantly stronger than any piece of ice. Thom stepped back into the cabin and spun the wheel on the top hatch. With a hand on the latch, he smiled.

"Congratulations, you are the third and fourth person to breathe fresh air, and set foot on the surface in modern history."

It was clear neither had thought of it this way. Koin smiled, Dija teared up, but still looked giddy. With a tug, the hatch dropped inwards and they were hit by a blast of cold, dry air. Koin stepped toward his gear and pulled out three heavy, dark ponchos. Handing them to Thom and Dija, he held the last up in front of him.

"Lined with fiberweave. Several layers. Should keep us quite warm," Koin said before throwing the black cloth over his head. Thom and Dija did the same, flipping up the hoods and cinching the cloth at the waist. Koin bowed, arm extended toward the rope ladder hanging from the hatch. Thom stepped back, allowing an exuberant Dija to scramble up the ladder and disappear.

Standing on the top of the sub, they could see the hulk of the *Pop* over the snowdrifts, and, in the distance, the Fountain spewing white powder into the clear blue sky.

"The air seems different," Dija said, nose high in the air.

"We breathe a different mixture," Koin said. "Better for us down there. Easier to manufacture. Other benefits."

"It's always sunny up here, I don't know why," Thom said, still awed by the scene.

"Near the pole. The sun is above the horizon. Always, this time of year," Koin replied, dissecting the *Pop* with his eyes.

"You would know that."

Dija bounced excitedly. Thom swung the gangplank toward the ice, and it just barely touched. Dija was across before Thom could secure it in place. She scurried up the ice and jumped off the top into the snow beyond.

"Can you help me with my instruments?" Koin asked. The gear Koin had brought consisted of eight containers of various sizes. The smallest was not much bigger than a helmet, the biggest somewhat smaller than a table. Their weight, Thom noticed, seemed opposite to their size. They were extra careful crossing the narrow gangplank, and it took them several trips. By the time they reached Dija, she was covered in snow and eating handfuls while jumping into the drifts.

"I was terrified when I was here last, and she's jumping around like a kid on a playground."

Koin looked at Dija, as if noticing her behavior for the first time, but said nothing before going back to his gear.

"I'll need a few hours. Also, I need to set out sensors. Will we have time to explore the *Population*?"

"You work on your stuff. Di and I will try to make a path."

"Ideal. Thank you."

Koin had fashioned small rectangular sections of textured carbon-composite for them to slip over their boots. Thom caught up to Dija and handed her a pair before sitting in the snow to attach his. Thom thought the footwear looked ridiculous, but a after a few steps in the snow, and not sinking to his waist, he realized Koin's genius.

"Let's head towards the *Pop*, make a bit of a path."

Dija nodded, and together they stomped their way across the snow field. As before, snow fell lightly, despite the bright sun. Thom had to squint from the light bouncing off the snow. Dija walked awkwardly at first, bouncing from leg to leg, but she soon settled into a smoother cadence. She kept tripping herself up every few steps, mostly because she couldn't stop looking at the sky, the Fountain, the horizon, everything but her feet. Thom watched his feet.

"How long were you here?" she asked.

"Not long, a day or two, I think. We beached the ship, called for help for a few days, then Ralla got sick."

"She's really mad at you."

"I know."

"What did you do?"

The crunching of their feet filled the silence that followed.

"She wanted... she needed me to do something, and at exactly the wrong moment I couldn't do it."

Dija said nothing. They continued walking, making a reasonable path for Koin and their own return. Thom knew the path would be gone in a few days, if not a few hours, but it helped for the moment. Finally, Dija actually tripped and fell face first into the snow. Thom could hear her muffled laughter. She rolled over and spread her arms and legs, then moved them up and down like she was swimming.

"What are you..."

"Do this! It's amazing!"

Dija's smile was infectious. While she watched, he leapt in the air, spun halfway around, and landed on his back beside her. The snow conformed perfectly to his body, and found its way in through every slight opening in the poncho and his clothes. Staring up at the sky, real sky, he couldn't help but forget all other concerns. He moved his arms and legs like Dija was doing. She giggled beside him. It was the most relaxed he'd been in recent memory. Since, well, those first few hours *last* time he was here, he realized. This thought made him think of Ralla.

"Can I ask you something?" Thom asked. He could hear her stop moving.

"OK."

It was still hard for him to say out loud, but he could hear Lo's voice in his head, and this convinced him Dija would understand.

"I have these... I'm not sure what to call them. I guess panic attacks?"

"Oh... I get those sometimes," she said, sadly. Thom felt a pang of guilt for bringing her down.

Her silence begged him to continue. "A lot of people... died." He could feel a lump in his throat. "Actions I took, commands I gave... I killed a lot of people, Dija."

She sat up, popping into his view of the sky. The snow caught in her hair had melted, then refrozen, wadding strands together in icy clumps.

"Did you want to hurt these people?"

Thom sighed. "I wish it were that easy."

A change came over Dija's face. The playfulness was gone.

"I'm not saying anything's easy. I'm just saying that I think you're OK. I don't know what everyone else thinks."

"Well... thank you, Dija."

She stood up, wobbled a bit, then offered a hand to help Thom up. It was little help; he outweighed her by double. Once on their feet, she hugged him. They stood there for a long moment, in silence in the snow. He hadn't realized he needed something as simple as a hug, but he did.

"Ha!" she exclaimed suddenly. "They look like person-sized fish."

Thom followed her gaze and saw their imprints looking just as she described. She let Thom go, then jumped, her wide, flat shoes scattering the snow from her fish-shape, then continued toward the *Population*. Thom followed, staring up at the hole in the hull where the escape sub had launched. As if reading where his thoughts went after that, Dija slowed so he could catch up.

"You should talk to Ralla. Tell her what you told me."

"I tried."

"Tried? She knows I get 'attacks,' and it doesn't seem to matter to her."

"Yeah, but it's not the same thing."

"Why not?" Dija said honestly. She looked up at Thom with genuine confusion. Thom wasn't sure how to answer.

—---

They searched along the base of the *Pop* for several hours, covering roughly half the visible length. Despite numerous hull breaches, there didn't seem to be an easy way in. Most decks had collapsed. Thom assumed they could have gotten inside where the hull had split, as ice had formed all around it, covering the submerged remainder of the hull. That had been too far to walk on this expedition, so they started back. The path they'd made meant return progress was easier. As they got closer to their own sub, they noticed several metallic sensors, and holes in the snow where others had presumably been thrown.

Koin, as they had expected, was crouched over his instruments, furiously taking notes on the readings.

"Everything all right, Koin? You looked spooked," Thom said, sitting down to remove the planks from his feet. Koin looked up, seeming to just notice their arrival.

"Too soon to say. I need to go over the data. How was your walk?"

Thom detailed what they'd found. Koin didn't seem to pay attention, instead continued inputting data from one piece of equipment to another. When Thom finished, Koin nodded.

"You are right. Most logical entry point is the main breach. We'll have to return with a salvage team." Koin stood up, stretched, and ran his fingers through his dark hair. "If you would help, please, with the gear, we can return."

With Dija's help, they got the equipment back on the sub in two trips, then, after sealing the hatch they began the return voyage. Thom could hear Dija trying to talk to Koin, but one-word answers drove her forward to Thom. She seemed melancholy, so he figured it wouldn't matter if he resumed their conversation from earlier.

"What happens when you have an attack? What do you do to get over it?"

"Over it?" she said with a morose laugh. "I'll let you know."

"Sorry, that's not what I meant. I just was asking if there were any tricks you've used to help make it pass."

"I wish I did. The panic just takes over me. I just want to shrink away from everything."

"What triggers it?"

"Well now, it's been being trapped. When Geran found me, me and some others were trapped in this flooded room, I sort of shut down. That's what happens now, I can't help it. I shut down and just want to disappear. I can't breathe, my body goes numb, and I just kinda feel like I'm separate from myself. All I can do to hold on, is to hold on, physically, to myself."

"When did you first start having them? Has it just been since the war?"

"No, they started when I was young, when my... No. It's been a long time. When I feel safe, or out in the open, it's not a problem."

"Thank you for talking to me about this. I sort of thought I was the only one."

"You're definitely not the only one. I am glad we talked, too. Helps me sort out stuff in my brain too."

"Please don't tell Ralla."

"You're not that lucky. That's all you."

The *Universalis* came into view, resting on the seabed like a decaying carcass. Dija frowned. She stepped back into the main cabin and sat on a bench, her knees rising to her chest.

"*Universalis* Control," Thom said into the comm. "This is transport sub S992, requesting clearance to dock."

There was a delay, but finally the comm crackled to life. Behind the speaker's voice, he could hear shouting.

"Cleared for immediate dock, S992," came back an alarmed voice. "Secure the door!" the voice screamed at someone in the background. The comm clicked off. Thom turned around to see if his passengers had heard that. Dija had, her eyes wide from behind her knees.

"Koin, there may be trouble. Get your gear together."

The scientist looked up from his work, seemed to replay in his mind what Thom had just said, and nodded.

As he navigated the approach, Thom saw the dock was clear of any ships, waiting or otherwise. He touched down, and heard the umbilical seal to the rear hatch. Thom motioned for Dija and Koin to remain on the sub, while he found out what was happening. The lock cycled, revealing chaos.

VI

IT WAS THE SCREAM that did it. Ralla finally looked up from her paperwork and realized she had been hearing a commotion for some time. Sitting on her cot, leaning against the wall, she surveyed the papers before her as if seeing them for the first time. All the while, she strained her ears for more clues. A single scream, though not good, certainly wasn't unprecedented. There were a *lot* of people crammed into the Basket, and it was inevitable some squabble, some surprise, some shock, would cause someone to scream.

Sure enough, she could make out the sounds of raised voices through her pane-less window. She pushed the papers from her lap onto the pile on her cot, and stood shakily. Her knees popped, telling her how long she'd been sitting cross-legged on the bed. It was all busywork, reports someone on the Council had to read: Details of food shipments, reports on maintenance completed and desired, estimated population totals, but nothing pressing and little actually interesting. The hallway outside her room was clear, so she made her way to the other end and knocked on Dija's door. Ralla slid it open immediately, remembering

Dija had gone to the surface with Thom some countless hours of paperwork earlier.

From Dija's window Ralla saw the makings of a full-scale riot. A mob of people, pressing and surging together, piled up against a former storefront the Council had been using to dispense rations. The storefront sat between where Ralla stood and the forward end of the Terraces. Multiple hodgepodge levels had been grafted on top, connecting where possible to other, similarly grown structures, and eventually to the wall or the fallen cruise ship itself.

They weren't out of food, Ralla knew, so what was the problem? No one was happy with the small portions, but everyone got the same. The total crowd looked to be in the hundreds, though the real excitement was right in front of the store, where dozens pushed and shoved. The small building shook when someone got knocked into it, sending tremors through the many connected structures above. Even at this distance, Ralla could make out anger on many faces.

It clicked in her head, and she dashed back to her bedroom. Tossing papers left and right, she finally found the one she was looking for. An expected food shipment from a nearby friendly dome hadn't arrived, and attempts to raise them had gone unanswered. Normally this wouldn't have been an issue, but the potential shipment had allowed the maintenance crew to finally start repairing a dangerously leaky passage that led to the main ration stores. They weren't expecting to be done until later that night. It was all presented very matter-of-factly in the report, something that likely didn't matter to the hungry and angry people outside.

Ralla slipped on her worn — and getting a whiff, brutally odorous — brown boots, and headed out. At the bottom of the stairs she caught sight of Lo, relaxing but alert on one of the benches. He watched the crowd, then let his gaze drift over to Ralla.

"It's worse than it looks," she said. Lo stood, but she waved him back down. "Let me see if I can get them to calm down."

Lo looked conflicted. He didn't follow her, but he didn't sit back down either. Ralla reached the outer edges of the crowd quickly and tried to push her way toward the center. The dense swarm swallowed her, and knocked her around indiscriminately. She worked her way to the front of the store, dodging elbows and stomping feet. The storefront counter was empty, and the male and female clerks huddled in the back looked terrified.

"I'm Ralla Gattley," she shouted at them, while being pressed from behind into the counter. "You need to tell them there's food on the way."

"Is there?" a young male clerk asked her.

"There should be, soon."

The clerks approached the counter and tried to shout at their former customers, but to no avail. Seeing this, Ralla jumped up on the counter and started waving her arms. With full lungs, she let out a scream.

The fighting continued.

"Well, that worked before," she said aloud, though no one could hear her. She ducked back down into the storefront. "Do you guys have any ration packets? Any at all?"

"We have one box, but it expired three years ago," the same clerk informed.

"That's fine, give me a couple."

The clerk dug out a greasy box and handed Ralla two foil ration packets. She jumped back on the counter and started waving them over her head. It got the crowd's attention, but not in the way she'd hoped. They surged forward, crushing those in front. The fighting escalated. A stray elbow knocked Ralla's foot from under her, and she doubled forward and crashed into the crowd. Suddenly all she could see was feet and legs. A foot stepped on her good hand, and she snatched it away, smarting and holding it to her chest. As she struggled to get to her knees, another foot stepped on her injured hand.

Ralla screamed like she never had before in her life. The intensity of the pain shot up her arm, then took her breath, causing bright white and red to tunnel her vision. With both hands now clutched to her chest, she leapt to her feet, crashing into a barrel-chested man with graying hair. She opened her mouth to apologize, and comprehended the fury in his face moments before his fist hit her jaw. She staggered back, bumping into someone else, who shoved her back toward the man who hit her. In that moment, Ralla saw how far she'd come. There was a time that being punched in the face would have shocked her system, dropping her to a quivering mess on the floor. That time had passed.

With her good hand, she slugged him right back, hitting him square in the nose. She thought she could hear it crack, but even if she didn't, the results were obvious. Blood gushed from his nostrils like she'd broken a faucet. She felt proud and slightly ashamed at the same time. He looked more shocked than anything, as if she had hit him out of the blue, for no reason. Now it was his turn to stagger backwards, away from her. Guiltily, she noticed the fighting had escalated from shoves and shouts to blows and kicks.

The massive bulk of Geran Lo burst through the crowd in front of her like he was walking through water. He took one look at her cradling her hands, noticing the blood on both at the same time she did, and in one motion picked her up and swung his free arm around, knocking over four people. With little apparent effort, he charged back through the crowd like they were paper cutouts. Before they reached the safety of the camp, Ralla was already squirming.

"Put me down," she demanded. He did, gently. "Don't *ever* pick someone up without asking." The rage in her voice caused him to step back.

"Sorry, I..."

"Do you realize how demeaning that is?"

"No."

"No, I suppose you wouldn't."

"I'm sorry. I had to help."

"Well, did you at least see me punch that guy?"

"No, sorry."

"No! Aw, it was *awesome*."

Ralla paced as the energy and adrenaline worked its way out of her system. Her face soon twisted into a frown as she slowed down. The pain in her hand demanded attention. She looked at the bandage, the top now soaked with blood.

"I could have handled that better," she said, shaking her head. "I should have."

"Maybe not," Lo answered. "Look," he said gesturing toward Tent City. The melee had spread, or spawned similar fights across the Basket. The emotions of thousands of hungry, desperate people, were finally erupting.

"We need to get to the Council chambers, try to organize. This could get out of hand."

"If it hasn't already."

Ralla removed her belt and cinched it around her wrist, slightly above her bandaged hand. Thinking about the best direction, she headed toward the nearest exit to the Basket, a starboard-side corridor that led through the interiors of the myriad ships that made up the wall of the Basket.

"You coming?" she yelled back at Lo, who was watching her go, unsure if he should follow. He did immediately.

Thom pushed his way through an angry mob toward the ad hoc military barracks and HQ at the top of the ship. The corridor was packed with people; some trying to push forward, some trying to retreat. Angrier and angrier, Thom began shoving people against the bulkheads if they didn't yield to his shouts. Dija and Koin followed in his wake. Thom had no weapon but his voice, which he used to command several men in the process of assaulting the door to the HQ to stand down. The rioting civilians paused long enough to see who was talking to them. One recognized Thom and immediately instructed his companions to stop their pounding on the door.

"Are you taking charge here?" he asked.

"If you people don't clear this hallway immediately, I'm going to instruct the men inside to arrest and subdue the lot of you, with whatever force they deem necessary. Is that clear?"

Three of the men took this as a challenge, but the one who recognized Thom whispered something to them, and they allowed Thom, Dija, and Koin to pass. The same man reached out to Thom and gently touched his arm.

"I know who you are, and what you did, but we have nothing. We don't even get rations anymore. We're *starving*. Please do something. That's all we're asking."

Thom suddenly viewed the men with different eyes. Their anger had abated somewhat, and Thom saw them instead as husbands and fathers, pushed to desperation.

"I didn't know. I'm sorry. I'll see what I can do."

"Thank you."

Thom pounded on the door.

"This is... Commander... Vargas. It's clear out here. Open the hatch."

Thom could hear some arguing from the other side of the door, but it eventually slid open. Thom entered and motioned for Dija and Koin to follow. The men in the hall watched the door close in their face. There had been some organizing since Thom's last visit. The room was lined with cots, and thick cables led off to what he assumed were the main comms several decks below. It was a sort of central hub for military activity, though a far cry from the war rooms flooded and destroyed in the bow.

"Report, Lieutenant," Thom said, affecting his military voice. The lieutenant saluted Thom, which Thom returned. No use telling this soldier he was no longer in the military now, he thought. The man's nametag said "Merella," and he finished his salute as crisply as he had begun it. His short-cropped black hair and rigid demeanor said "military."

"We have reports of riots throughout the ship. It started when we didn't get a vital food shipment."

"What about the ration stores?" Koin asked, stepping up to the central table. A plastic-coated diagram of the ship lay on top, acting as an incident map. Red X's marked where fights had broken out. There were a lot of X's.

"We closed off the passage to the food stores for maintenance. The crews reported serious leaks and minor flooding. It was unsafe."

"When will they be done?" Thom asked.

"In a few hours, but that's not the problem. This isn't an organized revolt. There isn't some group that is demanding more food or better housing. This is just angry people, feeding off the anger of others."

"Inevitable, I suppose. Too many people," Koin said, staring at the map.

"What have you done so far?" Thom asked.

"I've got a few teams stationed in key areas like the engine bays, but as you can see, we can't even control the passages up here. There are apparently fights breaking out all over, but we don't have a clear picture of what's going on or where and so I... I don't know what to do, Commander. What are your orders?"

And like that, Thom froze. His hands gripped the table, as if breaking off a piece would somehow release his panic. His eyes darted from the lieutenant to the other soldiers who had gathered around. All looked to him, waiting. Each added to his intense and crippling anxiety. Even Koin looked at him, tilting his head questioningly. He could feel the sweat dripping from his brow, back, everywhere.

Suddenly, a hand. Thom's eyes darted down to it, as if seeing it intertwined with his somehow made it real. He followed it up to its shoulder, neck, and then head. Dija's head. She looked nearly as panicked as he did.

"Thom," she said, her voice shaky. "Can I borrow you for a moment?" He nodded, oblivious to the looks he received. She led him away from the table and over to the deserted cots along the curved wall. Her eyes didn't waver from his.

"Are you having an attack right now?" she asked quietly. Thom nodded. "OK, I nearly had one in the hall." Thom looked over to the door, as if he could see out into the hall packed with rioting people. "I'm barely holding on. Look up."

He did. The clear dome above them showed teal-blue water, and sunlight twinkling far above. For a moment, they were no longer in the room, but standing atop the *Universalis*, the open ocean spreading in all directions. He looked back down. Dija's copper hair, matted and still wet from the melted snow, framed her pale face. *Now* he understood what Lo was talking about.

The panic had subsided, but as he thought about returning to the table, it returned. She gripped his hand tighter, and he realized she hadn't let go.

"What part is freaking you out?"

"I don't know," he answered.

"Focus."

"The orders," he blurted out.

"What do you think we need to do?"

"Find Ralla."

"Good idea. Start with that."

"Lieutenant Merella," Thom said, turning around and returning to the table. "Are you able to locate Councilwoman Gattley."

"No, sorry, Commander."

"How about Lieutenant Lo?"

"Lo returned to his quarters a few hours ago. I think they're on the bow-end of the Basket."

"They are. How many—" Thom felt the panic swell inside him, and it took all his concentration to push it back just below the surface. "How many men can you spare?"

"Just a few, sir."

"We need to find Ralla Gattley and Geran Lo."

"Should I make that a priority?"

Thom forced himself to take a slow breath.

"Yes, Lieutenant. Send word to your men to find either of them, and do whatever they instruct."

"Yes sir, Commander." The lieutenant saluted and turned to give orders to his men nearby, including those monitoring the comms. Thom turned to Dija, who gave him a smile, which quickly returned to a look of distress.

"Now what?" Koin asked. Thom almost laughed as another burst of adrenaline pulsed through him.

"What do you think we should do?" Dija asked Koin.

"I can't help with food," he said. "I will stay here and compile my data." He held up a tablet, the only piece of gear he'd carried with him, as proof.

"I'm sure the lieutenant can spare you some space, Koin," Dija replied, but Koin had already turned to speak with the lieutenant.

"And us?" Thom asked Dija. "I don't suppose you can go down into the mess below?"

"No…" she said, shrinking away from the very idea.

They stood for moment, unsure what to do. Out of place and in the way.

"Wait," Dija said. "Data. We can help with data."

"Help Koin?"

"No, help Lieutenant Merella. We can get him data. If we go down to one of the cabins overlooking the Basket, we can get an overview of what's going on and help him organize his people."

Thom nodded, relived to be doing something, ashamed it seemed so little. "Lieutenant, would it help if we got some eyes on the situation for you?"

—--

Ralla increased her speed to a jog and, noticing Lo keeping up, sped up to a sprint. Every footfall caused a throb of pain from her hand. She couldn't help but be angry. It had been healing so well. Who knew how many weeks this would set her back. Not that she relished the idea of her mangled hand out where everyone could see it, but the bandages were annoying, even if she didn't have to change them as often as she used to.

She nearly ran into an old man leaving his cabin, so she refocused on the mission at hand. She'd decided trying to get down the length of the Basket would be folly, so her chosen path was to go up into the ships. It would take longer, with lots of zigzags and many flights of stairs, instead of one straight walk and a quick elevator ride. There were fewer people this way, though, and less chance of getting caught in another riot.

The first portion had started easy, long corridors through tankers or along the backs of stores. Then she spotted a crowd, so up she went, Lo in tow. The next levels up were all personal cabins where the corridors varied in width and cabin density. Often progress was impeded by groups of neighbors gathering in the halls to discuss what was happening below.

Another floor, another set of stairs, she and Lo were getting closer and closer to the right cabin. There was no guarantee the Council could do anything, but they were good people at their core, and she was certain they'd at least try. That was where she needed to be. Once a plan was decided, then she could go help more directly. There was no way she was going to let Hennorr decide some brutal action without her vocal objections.

With just a few levels to go, Ralla was out of breath, and her legs ached. She looked back at Lo, and was disheartened to see him barely winded and hardly sweating.

"Don't make me carry you," she shouted back at him. She didn't bother to see his response. Just saying it made her feel better. They exited on the level of the Council chambers, but it was still far in the distance. They could see something was wrong immediately. Ahead was the bank of elevators that dropped to the floor of the Basket. Outside of them, blocking their view further down the curve of the corridor, was a densely packed and visibly riled mob. She skidded to a stop, not wanting to enter the crowd without a plan.

"Maybe we can cross over and come around from the other side?" Lo offered. They knew it would mean crossing over the Basket via the Spine, then going aft, making their way through the personal yachts and cabins along the stern face, and coming back forward. Already exhausted, Ralla didn't love the idea. Also, she couldn't be sure the crowd was any less dense on the other side of the Council doors further down the corridor. Or, she realized, in front of the elevators on the port side. It might be more running just to put them no closer to the Council than they were now. At least the passage that led to the Spine was between her and the mob, making that an option, at least.

The men at the back of the mob noticed Lo and Ralla's arrival.

"We should go," Lo's bass voice rumbled quietly, trying to stare down the rioters. More turned to face them. Some looked as if they were bracing against an imminent attack. Others eyed Lo and Ralla as fresh prey. One proved he was the most dangerous.

"That's Ralla Gattley! She's on the Council!" he yelled. This got the attention of dozens more. They broke off from the main pack and started advancing down the corridor toward Lo and Ralla. The makeshift weapons in their hands, no more than slabs of deck plating and construction tools, seemed far more dangerous in the hands of the furious.

"Please stop, I'm here to help!" Ralla yelled, trying to sound assertive. The group continued forward. Ralla took an involuntary step back.

Lo did not. He clenched his fists.

"Lo, don't."

He didn't hear her. Instead, he stepped forward between Ralla and the advancing mob. Lo didn't wait for one of them to strike first. He swung his right fist into the face of the closest rioter, breaking bone and crushing cartilage. As that first man's hands went to protect his already destroyed visage, Lo snatched the club-like piece of deck plating from his hands and swung it like a bat, connecting with the stomach of an adjacent attacker. The mob tried to swarm him, but they weren't used to fighting as a group. Lo was well used to fighting alone. The club swung and jabbed, connecting with more body parts beyond his noticing. Jab after jab he blocked, taking on as many as could fit near enough to hit him, the narrow confines of the corridor acting in his favor.

There was no choreographed elegance. No rules to the engagement. Whatever hand, elbow, forearm, knee, or foot was closest to hit or block, Lo used it. Knives and prybars sliced at his arms, hammers swung at his head. He flowed on pure instinct, only staying ahead because they hadn't been able to get around and attack from all sides. As it was, he was still fighting four or five at time, and they were pressed together, limiting their options. As one would fall back, another would take his place. Whatever reason had brought these men here was irrelevant. Now they saw this man, this giant, violent man, as the target for their hatred. Through the shouts and screams, the wet thud of solid impacting flesh, and the crunch of broken bones, was the sound of Ralla screaming for them to stop.

Gunfire echoed down the hall, stopping all. From the passageway to the Spine, two soldiers leveled their rifles from the ceiling to the crowd. One by one, the rioters dropped their weapons, and retreated toward the elevators, as directed by the muzzles of the guns. Layer upon layer peeled away from the army assaulting Lo. The lucky ones walked, the wounded limped.

Finally, all that remained was Geran Lo, surrounded by carnage. Bodies lay at his feet. Blood coated his arms and spattered his clothes. He dropped his club, the clang echoing in the sudden silence.

Behind the soldiers stood Thom. But at Thom's feet Lo saw Dija, shrunk to a ball on the floor, rocking back and forth.

$$—\overset{-}{--}$$

"You, soldier. What's your name?" Ralla said, taking command of the emptying hallway. A few cautious protesters helped their injured compatriots to their feet and toward the elevator. Others were carrying the unconscious away from the scene with care.

"Ensign Bylin, ma'am."

"Ensign, take Lieutenant Lo to Medbay. Make sure he gets cleaned up, then both of you report back here."

"I don't need an escort," Lo said without conviction. He hadn't moved, his eyes fixated on the trembling Dija.

"Ensign, do what I said," Ralla said to Bylin. "Go." The ensign slung his rifle over his shoulder, and gently guided Lo by the arm. Whether from exhaustion or shock, Lo followed.

"You, what's your name?"

"Ensign, ensign, ensign..." the young, skinny soldier had fixated on the blood. Ralla slapped him upside the head.

"*Hey*," she barked. "Go to your commander and tell him what happened. Tell him we need a security detail posted outside the Council chambers. Go."

The young ensign seemed to acknowledge what she had said, and turned to head back up the ramp toward the Spine.

"Wait," she said, pausing him in midstride. Ralla removed the ensign's sidearm, then motioned for him to continue.

"It won't matter, the lieutenant doesn't have any men to spare," Thom said from his position against the wall.

"Then here," Ralla said with a sneer. "Make yourself useful." She jammed the pistol flat into his stomach and walked down the corridor to the Council chambers.

Within a few minutes, the hallway was clear. The injured had been helped or carried to Medbay. The soldiers had yet to arrive. The blood on the floor, small pools and splatters, remained a grisly reminder of what had happened. Thom half helped, half lifted Dija to her feet, then half walked, half carried her down the corridor toward the Council chambers. Outside, he sat them both against the wall. The gun lay on one side of him, Dija on the other. He put his arm around her and sighed.

VII

"**DO YOU UNDERSTAND** what just happened out there?" Ralla shouted at the Council. All looked unnerved by the siege, but none wanted to admit it. Ioa and Appet stood on the balcony, looking down at the riots still unfolding on the floor of the Basket.

"This is all for nothing, they'll have their food in a few hours," Hennorr said from his seat on the couch, seemingly distracted by a report gripped in his hands.

"This isn't about the food," she snapped back.

"Of course it is. Don't be naive."

"Naive? What does... Do you honestly think one late meal caused riots? *That's* naive."

"Ralla, calm down," he said, reluctantly looking up from the report.

"Don't tell me to calm down. I just watched my friend put a dozen people in Medbay protecting me from an irate mob. Go look outside right now. The riots are still going on."

"I don't need you to..."

"Well, you need *somebody* to."

Hennorr slammed down the report and leapt off the couch, freezing everyone in the room. He towered over Ralla and jabbed his finger in her face.

"I don't need a lecture from you. I am perfectly aware of what's happening here. *You* are the one who has no idea. No idea about what's happening. No idea about the ship. No idea the pressure I'm under keeping this all running. *No idea.*"

Ralla was pretty sure everyone else in the room expected Hennorr to slap her. He was in the position to, had the intensity to, and after that explosion of anger, no one was sure what to expect. She couldn't help but consider it a victory, but saw something in his eyes that made her feel guilty. The strain was getting to him. He looked like a man on the brink. Ralla spoke slowly and quietly.

"I never said I did, Proctor Pro Tem Hennorr. I am merely informing the Council of an incident I experienced firsthand. Perhaps it is not I that needs to calm down. Would the Council agree?"

Hennorr leaned away from her and looked around the room. All eyes were on him, and all saw him in a new light. Ralla almost felt sorry for him. Almost.

"We need to figure out some way to defuse this, without hurting anyone else," Ralla said, asserting herself as Hennorr walked back to the couch in a daze.

"We need to get everyone's attention," Ioa said, stepping in from the balcony. "We can't let this keep going on its own. Who knows when it will snuff itself out."

"I agree," Appet said, following her in. He rubbed Ioa's back gently, who looked like she had been crying.

"There's an old public address system built into the spaces between the ships," Pell Farre said. "We considered using it during a strike when I was still a local rep. No idea how to access it, but all the equipment is there. Or at least it was."

"Ralla, why don't you go ask your tech friends if they can take a look," Hennorr said, seeming to get his wits back. "Perhaps you should hurry?"

Ralla hated doing his bidding, but could barely contain her shock at such an obvious lapse. Sure, she'd be happy to go talk to the entire ship.

—---

Ralla nearly tripped over Thom and Dija in the hallway. His arm was around her, and she had her legs pulled up to her chin. It was rather intimate, and she couldn't help but feel a twinge of jealousy.

"Ralla..." he said.

"Not now. Any idea where the PA system access is?"

"PA system?"

"Never mind. When Lo and Ensign Bylin get back here, have them lock out the elevators and defend the Council chambers until I get back or the riot is over."

"Do you want me to come with you?"

"I can take care of myself."

—---

When Lo returned, he looked exhausted. When he saw Dija tucked under Thom's arm, he looked dejected. Thom had watched him since he stepped off the elevators. Lo hadn't looked to the left at all, at the remains of his handiwork that was now likely a permanent coloration to the hallway. As he approached, Dija wiggled out from under Thom's arm, and headed the opposite way down the corridor. She reached the end without looking back, and disappeared around the corner. Lo looked down solemnly at Thom.

"Not sure what to tell you," Thom said, looking down the hallway where Dija had fled. Lo continued staring at Thom. "What?"

—-⁻--

It wasn't hard for the Council to find Thom and Lo; they hadn't left the corridor outside the chambers. It was obvious to everyone in the room that the two of them wanted to be anywhere else. It was obvious to Thom that Lo was completely out of it.

"Lieutenant Lo," Hennorr began. "The Council has decided it needs you to go on the offensive. The shipment we were expecting, the one whose absence prompted these riots, was withheld deliberately. It seems the pirates convinced the dome to redirect the shipment their way. Worse, they've convinced them to not send us any shipments in the future, either. This is not the first dome to go dark on us, and we suspect it won't be the last. We need you to show that we won't sit by and let them starve us."

"Yes, sir."

"We need you to get that shipment and secure the dome for us."

"Yes, sir."

"Do you understand my meaning?"

"Yes, sir."

"Good. Are you all right? The bandages on your arms look fresh."

"I was... part of the altercation outside. I'll be fine."

"I see. Thom Vargas, can the Council count on your support?"

"I'll drive Lo wherever he needs, if that's what you mean," Thom replied.

"Good," Hennorr said, getting up suddenly. Thom couldn't help but notice a few people in the room flinch. What had happened when Ralla was in here, Thom wondered. Hennorr approached with an outstretched hand.

"I know we've had our differences in the past, but we... I could really use your support right now."

Lo and Thom each shook Hennorr's hand, neither putting much thought into it.

"Gentlemen, we have been passive too long. It's clear a strong hand is what's required right now. I am pleased you two understand that."

Thom wasn't sure he understood the difference between Hennorr's new strategy and Hennorr's son's current strategy. He looked to see if Lo had any interest in bringing this up, but the big man seemed lost in his own thoughts.

"When can you set out?"

"As soon as we can get the team together," Lo replied after a pause.

"Excellent. Thank you, gentlemen."

—-—

Ralla didn't bother asking for permission from the Council, she made the announcement herself. The techs, once learning the system existed, were able to find it and patch in with their equipment easily. Ralla couldn't see it from her cramped seat next to the comm equipment, but she was told the biggest effect her broadcast had was actually just making a broadcast. Her speech was so loud, people covered their ears. It paused the violence long enough for people to hear what she was saying.

"People of the *Universalis*, this is Councilwoman Ralla Gattley. I am in charge of distributing the rations and anyone caught rioting or fighting from this point on will receive half rations for three weeks." There was a certain "mom" tone her mother had never used, but her friend's mothers had. She was channeling that. "The current food shortage is temporary, and we will have the issue solved in a few hours. I ask you all to return to where you're staying." She softened her tone, and hoped the people below were as focused on her words as the techs around her. "I know it's hard. We have all lost so much. I lost both my parents." The words unexpectedly caught in her throat. She could feel the weeks of repressing her feelings swelling to the surface. It suddenly became clear to her how much of her anger at Hennorr, at Thom, hadn't been really anger at all. She let it loose.

"I lost my parents and I couldn't be there for them. I lost friends I've known my whole life," she said through the tears. "I know you have, too. We have all lost so much. Everyone around you has lost so much. Everyone. So much is gone." Her emotions were real, but her mind was already moving ahead. The sniff to clear her nose, the rustle on the mic as she brushed against it to wipe her eyes on her sleeve. She hadn't really needed to do this things. She was now consciously doing it for effect.

"But not everything," she said, her tone hardening. "This ship may not be what it was, but it is still our home. We will make it thrive again. The people around you, together we will all rebuild. Look around. Look how far we've come in such a short time. Imagine where we'll be in a few months! There are going to be hiccups along the way, but we'll get through them. But we'll need work together. I need your help. In some way, I don't know what yet, but maybe you'll need mine.

"For now, let's all head back to wherever we're staying. Introduce yourself to your neighbors if you haven't already. Tell them your story. Listen to theirs. Tell them of people you've lost. Console them as they tell you theirs. My name is Ralla Gattley. I lost my mother, Awbee, and," she choked up a bit again, for real, "my father, Mrakas. We will get through this. I will help you however I can. I hope you'll do the same for me."

She clicked off the mic and let out a long slow breath. The techs around her had mix of red-eyed emotion and admiration. She gave them all an appreciative nod and wiped her eyes, for real this time.

—--

Though a few fights resumed, the tension had broken. The vast majority of people dispersed after Ralla's speech. Some did as she asked, talking with their neighbors. Others didn't, but that didn't seem to bother anyone. A few hours later, shortly after the picosuns dimmed, food got distributed, and people settled back into their evening routines. The Medbay was slammed throughout the night, but most were minor injuries.

By the time Ralla got back to her Camp 1, the Basket was quiet, like nothing had happened. Ralla wanted to feel proud, but instead all she could feel was relief. She knew all she'd accomplished today was preventing things, temporarily at that, from getting worse. Those future issues, of food shortages and supply issues, lay in the future. She allowed herself the moment of respite.

She noticed Thom moments before he noticed her, as he walked down the stairs from the cabins above Camp 1.

"I was just checking in on Dija," he said.

"I was about to do the same."

The silence pressed between them. Her speech and the day's events had put Ralla in an introspective mood. She realized, standing there in front of him, how much their fight had become about the fight, and not what caused it. Too much had happened, between them, in the world, everything, to let something small come between them. She opened her mouth to start that peace offering, then he ruined it.

"Hennorr asked Lo and I to attack and capture a farming dome. We're leaving in the morning."

She turned away and climbed the stairs to her cabin.

———

Ralla knocked on Dija's door and slid it ajar. In the corner, on her cot, Dija sat crunched into a ball. Ralla sighed, entered, and sat on the floor, leaning back against the bed.

"Geran scares me, Ralla."

"I know," she replied sadly. He was protecting me, she wanted to say, but knew it didn't matter.

———

Ralla awoke, everything from her neck to her legs sore from being on the floor so long. She looked over her shoulder and saw Dija, still in the same position, but at least asleep. Making her way to her own cabin, she realized with dismay her brain was already going far too much to fall back asleep again. She turned left, out to the stairs, and climbed up to the roof.

She figured it was early morning. The picosuns hadn't started their color shift to daylight, but something felt like morning.

A portable lantern cast a yellowish glow across the roof. Bench and chair legs cast long shadows that became increasingly wide the farther they fled from the light. Koin sat next to the lantern, dozens of papers spread before him. His small frame cast its own huge shadow. He looked up as she approached.

"Good morning, Ms. Gattley."

"Morning, Koin."

"Lab still leaks, unfortunately," he said. Ralla recognized this as his humor, and gave him a laugh.

"That's fine. What are you working on?"

"Too soon to discuss. Need more help first."

"What kind of help? People, things? I'm on the Council, you know. I can probably get you what you need."

"Hennorr is on the Council. Is Council, probably. No help there."

"Maybe there's something I can get you that he can't."

"Hmmm, yes. Not things. People. Not many left. Do you know Cirin Wess?"

"Councilman Wess? Yes, of course."

"Need his expertise."

"Have you asked him?"

"Not yet."

"You should ask him. I'm sure he'll help."

"Yes. Good. Thank you. Much appreciated, Ms. Gattley."

"What do you need his help for?"

"Smart. Good with… things."

"Things…"

Koin looked up, then slowly around the Basket as if seeing it for the first time. "This is not our problem."

"What is that supposed to mean?"

"Too soon. Cirin Wess first."

"All right, Koin. Well, you go talk to him if you need to, and let me know what you're thinking as soon as you can."

"Yes. Will do."

Ralla started back for her cabin, amused that each time she spoke to Koin she learned few answers and gained new questions, usually unrelated. What she couldn't remember, past that Cirin Wess had been the number two guy in the Engineers' Union, was Wess's area of "expertise."

—˙--

"Farming Dome F109, this is the *Sealine Runner*, please respond." Thom keyed off the mic and looked across the cockpit at Lo. The big man was brooding, and not paying attention. "You, ah, want to give me some advice here? They're still not answering."

Lo sat still, lost in his thoughts, but finally turned to look at Thom.

"Unwilling or unable?"

"Does it matter?"

"I suppose not," Lo answered, twisting in his seat toward the main cabin. "Gear up!" he shouted. He was already in his armor, helmet resting on the floor beside him.

"What's your plan?"

"Is there an easy way in?"

Thom peered out the viewscreen. Farming Dome F109 was a long, semicylindrical structure, with a central square tower housing dormitories, processing, and main locks. Set near the top of a rise, the facility was visible from quite a distance away.

"Nope," Thom answered.

"I'm sure the central tower is going to be heavily defended, if anything is. Think the ends have emergency or loading locks?"

Thom keyed up a schematic on the console.

"Yep, one on each end, designed to get heavy farming machinery in and out for maintenance."

"Flip me live," Lo said, nodding at the comm. Thom did as asked. "Dome F109, this is Lieutenant Lo of the *Universalis*. We have come to negotiate a trade agreement. Please respond." They waited in silence. "Dome F109, we are assuming you are having comm problems. We will return in six hours with a maintenance crew. Please have your main lock ready for our arrival."

Thom turned off the comm.

"Go now," Lo instructed.

"Yep."

Thom nudged the throttle away from its stop, and the *Runner* began moving. Pulling back on the controls and powering up, they sped away from the dome for several minutes, eventually rising above the thermal layer. The Dome disappeared off their sensors, but its glow remained visible through the viewscreen. Thom spun the ship back around and held position far above the Dome. Cutting the power and the lights, he took on just enough ballast for them to sink slowly back through the layer.

His positioning was perfect. Unless someone was at the end of the facility and somehow able to see out — it was extremely bright inside, and dark outside — the *Runner* was just a shadow in the darkness. Thom trimmed out the ballast as they approached the seafloor, gently coming to a rest beside the end of the dome.

"Nice work," Lo said.

"Used to do it all the time when I was fishing. Didn't want to scare the fish."

"I guess that's my job."

Lo stepped off the bridge, helmet in hand. The smell of his armor was comforting, going a long way to calm his nerves. But he still couldn't focus, as much as he wanted and needed to. All he could see was Dija's horrified stare.

His team had connected the umbilical, and on his command, opened their end. The still-wet outer hatch of F109 glistened just a few paces away.

"We're assuming they're hostile," Lo said, the six men from the squad stopping their prep and listening. "But don't shoot unless I do. Clear?"

Each man in the squad said their affirmatives.

"Standard deployment once we get inside. We'll advance on the tower in groups of two. Clear?"

"Clear!" they responded. Lo fastened his helmet and snapped it shut with a press of the side. The umbilical sagged as he stepped off the *Runner*.

—-—

Ralla awoke to quiet voices, unsure how long she'd been hearing them. It didn't take much to wake her these days. At first the voices had woven with a dream. Now that slowly faded as she focused on their reality. She realized she was hearing Ioa and Appet. Ioa's cabin was below Ralla's on the ground floor of Camp 1. The voices were drifting out, then in, the glassless windows. She tried to ignore them, tried to go back to sleep, when she heard her name.

"And Ralla. She just tries so hard, the poor thing," Ioa said.

"She's a natural, like her father."

"Still, I see how much it's eating her up…"

"I don't think there's anyone who could do better."

"That's not what I mean."

"I know what you mean," Appet said. "But a lot of people are going to have to do a whole lot more before Ralla Gattley can do much less."

"It's not fair."

"No, it isn't."

In the silence, Ralla heard the unmistakable sound of bottle touching glass, and smiled at the idea of the two getting drunk together.

They were such kind, sweet people. Supportive and caring when they had no reason to be.

"My daughter would be about her age now," Appet said.

"Did she die in the attacks?"

"No, it..."

"If you don't want to talk about it, I understand," Ioa interrupted. There was another moment of silence.

"It was a little over four years ago. The anniversary, if you want to call it that, was the day before Ralla and Thom arrived back on the *Uni* that first time. Seeing Ralla safe softened the pain that week for my wife and I."

Ralla heard another clink of bottle on glass. She wanted to fall asleep, but was too fascinated to know more about this kind man and his history. She also felt bad for eavesdropping, but it wasn't as if she had tried to hear what they were saying.

"Turri was on a school exchange program with a farming dome. It was her first time away from home. She was supposed to be there for half a year, but after a few months, she wanted to come home."

"Homesick?"

"No. Well, I don't think so. She wasn't like that. She was smart, strong, independent... That's why I say Ralla reminds me of her. No, I think she just didn't like it, and didn't want to waste any more time there. Something happened on the shuttle ride home..."

"Oh no."

"It took them two weeks to find the sub. They'd gone off course. The investigators said something went wrong with the scrubbers, so they probably all just fell asleep, but I just can't help but think..." Appet's voice cracked.

"I know."

"And she was there alone..."

"I know."

Ralla's heart broke, hearing the pain in his voice. She was so glad he and Ioa had found each other. That they all had found each other. Them, Dija and Lo, Thom... Then it all hit her all over again. Her father was gone, and she'd never see him again. Her mother was gone, and she'd never see her again. Gone. She let the sadness take her and for a moment, let herself forget about all the rest of the world. In the now quiet dark of the *Universalis* night, Ralla cried herself to sleep.

In the morning, Ralla joined Appet and Ioa for breakfast on the roof of Camp 1. She was sure her eyes were as red and puffy as his. Neither said anything, but they exchanged a nod of acknowledgement. The simple gesture made her feel a little better, a little more connected to him, as if they were sharing a secret. After they ate their rations, they all made their way to the improvised Council chambers in comfortable silence.

The Council meeting started the same, with mindless greetings and insincere platitudes. It seemed the new Council members were picking up the habits of the professionals. All, Ralla noticed, except for Wess. His mind was clearly elsewhere, staring out to the balcony and the Basket beyond. Something was bothering him, but clearly it had nothing to do with this room or the people in it.

Hennorr called the meeting to order and laid out their agenda for the afternoon. It was standard concerns; dealing with resources, shift changes in the engine room, an administrator was needed for a farming dome F268, where to allocate repair and construction crews, and so on. The boring day-to-day stuff that needed attending. Wess ignored two votes in a row, his eyes still focused far past the opposite walls of the Basket.

"Mr. Wess, would you care to participate?" Hennorr asked. Wess turned at the sound of his name.

"What?"

"I know this is boring, but it's our duty as members of the Council to govern."

"Oh, sorry." Wess stood up, and without looking at anyone in particular, said, "I resign from the Council, effective immediately."

He reached the door before looking back at the calls for an explanation. What Ralla saw on his face gave her chills. He looked at them with total detached apathy, as if they were no different than the sofa on which they sat. Ralla expected him to say some parting sentiment about them, or why he had quit, or something. Instead, he stared at them blankly as if he hadn't heard anything they had said, then turned and left.

Everyone spoke at once, either upset, affronted, or trying to understand what had just happened. Ralla silently leaned back in her seat. Koin.

—---

Thom sat on the stairs to the bridge with a clear view down the cabin, through the umbilical, and to the open hatch at its end. It was the perfect place to guard the only access to the ship and still monitor the comms. He wasn't sure how long the squad had been gone, it seemed only a few minutes, before a terror-stricken voice screeched over the comm.

"Lo's been hit! The lieutenant's been hit!"

VIII

THOM LEAPT halfway across the cabin, was down the umbilical with another leap, and dove through the open lock with one more. The dome was searingly bright. Even squinting, it was hard to see. The end where they'd entered looked like a storage area, with crates and boxes piled haphazardly. Thom tried to peek through the gaps but was unable to place where the squad had gone. He checked his sidearm, his only weapon, and clicked off the safety. Gunfire erupted from farther down the dome. He reached the edge of the stacked crates and peeked around.

The yellow grains at this end of the dome appeared to be in mid-harvest. A giant blue and green combine sat parked in the center. Mounds of dirt lay at regular intervals, while deep trenches stretched out behind dozens of huge mechanized plows.

The squad was spread out behind all of these, two behind a dirt mound to the left of the combine, three similarly ensconced on the right, and a single soldier behind the combine itself. They raised their rifles above cover and shot blindly toward foes Thom couldn't see. What he could see was the armored body of Geran Lo, lying motionless in the middle of the field. Even from a distance, Thom could see the crushed and scored armor plating.

Somehow, for the moment, Thom was able to push from his mind thoughts of his friend being dead. First, he had to get to him. It was a straight shot across the field to the back of the nearest plow. From what he could tell, the defenders were holed up all the way down in the central tower.

Thom sprinted from cover and dove behind a plow. The dirt reminded him of the smell of the Garden. Another leap and he was behind the next plow, and slightly closer to the squad. He realized now he probably should have told them he was coming. Another leap to another plow, then to a mound of dirt just behind the staggered line the squad held. The soldier behind the combine noticed Thom and waved him over. The boxy machine towered over him and seemed a safe place to be. Rolling out, he got his first taste of incoming fire. Bullets hit the ground around him with thumps that were immediately drowned out by the returning fire of the squad. He made it to the combine. Lo's motionless body lay just forward and to the right side of the combine. Out of reach of them all.

The soldier who had motioned Thom over, Private Lenn, cupped his mouth to Thom's ear. It was so loud, he still needed to shout. The terror in his voice came through clearly.

"We started taking fire right after we started our advance. We took cover while Lo kept going. His suit worked great, then something happened. The front of it just exploded. We took cover but we can't get to him."

"Is he dead?" Thom shouted back.

"I don't know."

"What's the plan?"

"Plan?"

"Who's in charge?"

Private Lenn, turned to look at Lo's body, then down the scattered line of soldiers, then back at Thom.

"You are," Lenn shouted.

Thom wasn't sure why he was surprised by the answer, but a new level of panic gripped him the same. He realized the absurdity of it, trapped behind a combine under fire from an elevated position, and it was the fear of *command* that had paralyzed him.

"What are your orders?"

Thom felt like he was going to throw up. He tried to wave off the private, but Lenn was too terrified himself to register what Thom was going through. Bullets ricocheted off the combine chassis.

"If you're not going to give us orders, then we need to get out of here. NOW."

Thom knew he was right. These men weren't a trained military squad. They had seen a bit of action, trained for a few weeks together, but they were far from a cohesive unit. He could see them all, some panicking in their own way, all hiding behind cover, not even trying to aim as they held their rifles over their heads and pulled the trigger. Bullets sprayed out, hitting nothing of importance. Lenn grabbed Thom and shook him.

"We need to get out of here!" he screamed in Thom's face.

Thom couldn't do it, the words catching in his throat. He couldn't even bring himself to tell them to retreat. The panic had burned from his chest outwards, consuming him entirely.

Private Lenn pushed Thom away in disgust and started waving at the other soldiers to get their attention. He gestured back the way they had come, toward the hatch, toward the sub, toward safety. Thom dropped to his knees, the barrage of gunfire, shouting, and bullet impacts wrapping him in a cocoon of noise.

From his new vantage point, Thom could see under the back of the combine, between the enormous tires, and out across the field. Lying there, face up, was the partially charred body of Geran Lo. There was no way they were taking this dome, that much Thom knew, but they were *not* leaving Lo here.

Thom gripped Lenn's leg, and getting his attention, stood up.

"We can't leave him here," Thom shouted.

"What do you want to do? We can't get him," Lenn answered angrily.

Like pushing against a current, Thom struggled to get the words to his mouth. They finally spilled out.

"Drag him back here. We need to coordinate covering fire... then drag him back here."

"Are you crazy? He weighs more than all of us combined."

"We are not leaving him."

Most of the soldiers were already looking in their direction, waiting for a retreat order that hadn't come. Thom went over who was where. The three from Lo's team on the *Reap*, the ones he considered the combat veterans of the squad, were flanking the combine, split two on the right, one on the left. They had the same armored suits Lo wore, the last of their kind, and relics of the last war. Relics, Thom realized, despite being only a few months old. The other men, one on each side, and Private Lenn, were new recruits. They wore carbonweave vests and leggings, the best anyone could find on the *Uni*. These were "bullet-resistant" according to the labels, with a dark, reflective coating that should deflect or absorb some energy weapon fire, but not a lot. These were not for use on any sort of front line troop, and yet here they were. The hand signals he'd learned months earlier all came back.

Thom gestured to the two on the left of the combine, and they signaled they understood the plan. He turned to the three on the right. He signaled he wanted the rookie to help Thom and Lenn in supplying covering fire, backed up by the two on the other side of the combine. Meanwhile, the two armored vets would get Lo and drag him behind cover. All signaled they understood.

Thom waved to the left, both rose to a kneeling position, and sighting over their dirt-mound cover, aimed fire at wherever they saw muzzle flashes on the tower. Thom signaled to the right. He and Lenn ducked out from behind the combine and started firing. For the first time, Thom had a solid view of the central tower. It was greenish-black glass, with shaded, covered balconies draped with vines: excellent cover, with a perfect view of the battlefield. Out of the corner of his eye, Thom saw the two armored vets leap over their dirt mound and sprint toward Lo.

Muzzle flashes lit up the tower as the enemy realized what they were trying to do. To their credit, none of the *Uni* soldiers stopped firing or ducked back behind cover. The armored suits held; Thom could see the force of the bullet impacts cause the two soldiers to jolt in response as they kept running.

The two men had reached Lo and were halfway to the combine with the body when the lone rookie took a round in the chest, knocking him backwards and out of cover. Lenn flinched as if to go after him when a flurry of bullets traced up the rookie's side, exploding his face in a spray of red.

Thom screamed, but no one could hear it. The solider dragging Lo's right arm made it behind cover. Thom grabbed the charred front of Lo's armor and helped drag the body behind the combine. The other soldier, still in the open, turned as if to go after the fallen rookie. Then Thom heard a new noise.

It sounded like a rapid turbine spool-up, followed by a tremendous metallic *clang*. The soldier's right arm vaporized, the impact spinning him around till he fell face first into the dirt. The projectile seemed to impact several yards behind them at the same time, exploding and showering them with soil. Ears ringing, Thom could see into the soldier's ruptured suit, the arm and half the torso missing.

This time Lenn screamed and bolted from behind the combine back toward the sub. No sooner was he out in the open before his back was riddled with bullets, tracing a path up and exploding his head.

Thom's brain had passed the point of registering shock. He looked to the surviving soldier next to him, who looked up from checking on Lo. The big man had taken the impact in the center of the chest, with the blast scoring radiating outwards across his torso. It was dented inwards severely, and was likely pressing on Lo's internal organs. The faceplate was smashed, and the face behind it coated with blood.

"Is he breathing?" Thom shouted. The soldier shrugged, ashen.

With the remaining squad members all behind cover, they were safe for the moment. Then they heard the sound again. This time a projectile, from what Thom assumed was a mass driver repurposed from an old attack sub, hit the front side of the dirt mound hiding the rest of the team. It showered them with dirt, but did no damage. This struck Thom as odd. They knew there were people behind the combine, but... *They didn't want to destroy the combine*, he realized. The two soldiers behind cover looked over at Thom. He reached up and tapped the back of the combine without breaking eye contact with the team. The farthest soldier nodded, pointed forward, then made an open-door gesture with his hands. Thom ducked around the side and peered forward. The massive and knobbed front tire was easily as wide as Thom, and much taller. Above it the cockpit door hung open, left that way, Thom assumed, by a fleeing farmer.

"When this thing starts moving, just go with it," Thom yelled to the soldier near him. Turning to the rest of the team, he caught the eye of the same soldier and motioned for them to get behind the combine as soon as they could.

There was enough space under the vehicle for Thom to crawl. His view forward was blocked by the wide cutter bar in front, which suited Thom just fine, as it hid his progress. As soon as he reached the back of the front wheel, he rolled out from under the combine, scrambled up the knobbed wheel, and was in the cockpit before anyone knew he was there. The controls were mechanical, unlabeled, and well worn. He figured Dija would have grasped what they all did just by looking at them. He wasn't so intuitive. The view out of the all-glass cockpit was almost serene, with the tower in the distance, the curve of the dome above, and uncut grain swaying in the recirc breeze before him.

He heard *the sound*, and braced himself for the impact. Eyes closed, he heard the explosion and something hitting the wide viewscreen. After a moment, when his brain registered he was still alive, he opened his eyes. A wide oval, a few paces in front of the combine, was bare of grain. Clumps of dirt and stalks littered the small shelf in front of the viewscreen. *I was right*, he thought, *they weren't going to risk destroying their equipment*.

Thom pressed the most used-looking button on the console, and the engine rattled to life somewhere behind him. There were three groupings of levers, but on the far side of the ragged-looking steering wheel was a lone, long black one. On a hunch, he slammed it back toward the seat.

The combine lurched forward, knocking Thom off balance and onto the floor. It was just as well, as rifle fire began impacting the viewscreen, cracking the old-fashioned glass into webs. He reached up, pushed the lever back where it had been, and with a grinding noise, the combine lurched to a stop. This time he pushed the lever forward, and the massive machine reversed course, lumbering along slower than a walking pace.

Suddenly, the viewscreen shattered, covering him with glass. Thom rolled out of the cockpit backwards, hit the ground hard, and dove underneath the moving combine. Ahead of him, toward the back of the machine, he could see Lo's feet. The soldier dragged him by the arms, trying keep pace. Thom crawled as fast as he could, barely moving faster than the machine above him.

Thom emerged from under the combine just as it was about to overtake the soldier dragging Lo. Between them and the sub lay four plows, the crates, and way too much open field. In textbook form, the remaining soldiers covered each other as they retreated back behind a nearby plow. Gunfire from the tower was keeping them all suppressed, but they were making progress; slow, but steady, progress.

The back of the combine passed the plow where the two soldiers held cover, one veteran, one rookie. The vet stood, firing toward the tower, and the rookie dove toward Thom. After checking his squadmate had made it, the remaining soldier turned to follow. He was already in motion when they all heard the sound. The projectile from the mass driver canon hit him mid-leap, tossing him like child's toy through the air. He landed, crumpled unnaturally in a pile against the crates at the end of the dome.

The death, like the others, registered in some part of Thom's brain, but was subdued by the overriding terror of the moment.

"Take him!" the soldier carrying Lo shouted, and the rookie sprung to his aid. He struggled to drag the body the necessary pace.

Unslinging his rifle, the soldier pressed against the rear of the combine, and started firing forward down its right side. "They're advancing in the open!" he shouted back at them. Thom had spotted a different problem: a plow lay in the path of the reversing combine. For the moment all they could do was wait for that upcoming narrow window of time when they could reach the plow under the cover of the combine, but before the vehicle hit it. When that happened, Thom wasn't sure what the result would be, but it was a variable they didn't have margin for.

The gunfire continued, an almost constant stream of noise. Then they were finally up to the plow. The rookie, deflected by its front angle, came perilously close to the edge of the safe zone behind the combine. He squeezed past the plow, still dragging Lo. Thom, instead, vaulted straight over it and tried to start the tiny motor. It fired up with a bang, but there was only one gear: forward. Thom leaned on the right handle, deflecting the plow to its left, but there wasn't enough room. The blade dug in under the combine's left rear, the power of the two machines acting to wedge them together, and together, into the ground.

The now-stationary plow acted like a pivot point. With the combine's left corner stopped, but the right side continuing, it began to rotate in a circle. The front swung right, opening up a direct line of sight between the tower and the rookie, now standing in the open. He hadn't noticed, looking behind him as he walked backwards pulling Lo. Thom shouted at him, but it was too late. The turbine sound, the *clang*, and the top half of the rookie's body vaporizing in a mist of red. Lo's body limply fell to the ground.

Thom could see the hatch, at the lower left of the end face of the dome. At a run, he could be there in a moment. Through that hatch was the *Sealine Runner*, and through that, home. The combine continued its swing, nearing perpendicular to the length of the dome. He figured half the distance he'd need to travel now would be covered by the shadow of the combine. Thom holstered his sidearm. It wasn't a hard decision. He leapt.

With one vicious tug, Thom yanked Lo's body back behind the combine before anyone was able to shoot at him in the open. The sole remaining soldier had moved farther down the length of the combine. Now blocked by the cutter bar, he had gone prone and was shooting underneath the combine at the advancing enemy.

"Grab his feet!" Thom yelled. The soldier jumped up and did as instructed. Thom grabbed Lo's arms at the shoulder, and they set off at a laden, awkward run. Bullet impacts peppered the containers ahead of them, and the soldier twisted to put his armored body between the guns and Thom. They were almost there. They maneuvered around the containers, which offered some protection from the gunfire. Some had fallen over, leaving an open space between them and the hatch. If they miss here with that mass driver, Thom thought, the projectile would go right through the superstructure. The dome would flood in minutes. Some safety, then.

Step, then step, Thom concentrated on moving his feet and not tripping while running backwards. He heard the sound.

Spool up. *Clang.* Before Thom's eyes, the front of the soldier's armor bulged outwards, and he lurched forward onto Lo, putting them all on the ground and trapping Thom's legs under them both. The impact crater on the back of the soldier's armor was already filling with blood. Thom, in a horrified frenzy, flailed to free himself as more gunfire showered on his position. Shrapnel from splintered, bullet-riddled crates sliced his face and arms. All he could see was the boxes before him, the still spinning combine beyond that, and the roof of the tower in the distance. All he could hear was the gunfire, the combine's engine, the shouting, and a scream. His scream.

With a final jerk, he got one leg from under Lo's body and used it to push himself free. He rose to a half crouch and took a round in the right arm, causing him to spin and fall. In desperation, he looked how far he had to go. Close! He was almost to the hatch. Something hit him hard in the face, nearly causing him to black out. When he tried to open his eyes, only one would open. Something was wrong with his jaw. His mouth tasted like copper. With his left arm, he pulled on Lo's. No matter how hard he pulled, he couldn't free him from under the other soldier's added weight. A head popped over the top of the combine. Thom couldn't lift his right arm, but the hand and wrist still worked. He was able to unholster his sidearm, and take a few shots from hip level at the exposed head. All missed, but the head ducked back down.

Gripping Lo's wrist, Thom dug his feet in and pulled as hard as he could. Lo slid free, causing Thom to fall backwards. His head rested next to the hatch. He repeated the process. He fell into the umbilical. More heads. He fired again, two rounds hitting the crates, three glancing off Lo's armor. Feet. Pull. Fall. Feet. Pull. Fall. Why weren't they at the *Runner* yet? Feet. Pull. Fall. As his eyes adjusted to the darkness of the umbilical, the hatch's opening bloomed with brightness.

A silhouette of a head. Thom fired till his sidearm clicked empty. Feet. Pull. Fall. This time, his back hit something hard. Turning, he saw he was at the *Runner*'s exterior hatch. Tossing the sidearm into the cabin, he gave one more pull to get Lo inside, and sealed the door with a slap of a bloody hand.

Thom tried to stand, and found he couldn't. He tried again, wobbled, and fell to the deck. His strength had gone. Or maybe there was something wrong with his legs. He couldn't tell. He was covered in blood. He couldn't remember if he had left the engines idling. Half-crawling, half pulling himself a across the deck, leaving a trail of blood on the carpet, he made it to the stairs to the bridge. Pulling himself up one step at a time, he made it onto the bridge and slumped into his chair. With the one part of his body still working, he jammed the throttle to its stop, snapping the umbilical and launching the *Sealine Runner* into the dark.

IX

RALLA GATTLEY RAN. People and walls and bulkheads blurred past. She felt like a passenger inside herself, watching it all flash by. Her hair had grown enough that she could feel it bounce on its own. Her feet hit the deck hard. Her hand throbbed with each footfall, a familiar and comforting, if malevolent, friend. She didn't bother waiting for the elevator, instead bounding down the nearby stairs and bursting out into the crowded hallway. She followed the blood.

At the entrance to Medbay she slid to a stop, nearly falling into the very red fluids that caused her skid. On one table, a doctor straddled a body that could only be Geran Lo. With a hand-held saw, he attempted to cut off armor designed to stop bullets. The front was crushed and scorched.

On the other side of the emergency room, another group of doctors swarmed a Thom Vargas covered in blood. A doctor moved, and Ralla caught sight of Thom's face. Reflexively, her hand covered her mouth and she turned away. It didn't matter. She couldn't un-see it, bone, blood, and gore.

A nurse approached, and distantly Ralla recognized her.

"Kera, are they going to be all right?" Ralla asked, the words sounding childish in her ears. Nurse Kera looked upset, pushing Ralla nearly over the edge.

"Ralla, you shouldn't be in here," Kera said softly, gently reaching her hand out to touch Ralla's shoulder. Ralla sniffed, feeling pressure behind her eyes. Thom and Lo, Lo and Thom.

"Are they going to be all right?" she asked again, this time feeling the lump in her throat. Her eyes settled on the glimpses of Thom through the cloud of doctors. "Is he...?" For the moment, her anger at him turned to guilt, her disappointment, yearning. A doctor tore apart Thom's shirt and jumped onto the table. With both hands together, he began pushing on Thom's chest. Ralla stepped forward, and Kera placed her hand gently on Ralla's chest.

"There's nothing you can do."

"Is he going to be all right...?" Ralla whispered. She tried to move forward again, and Kera's hand became an immoveable object.

"Ralla, there is nothing you can do," Kera said, the words becoming a command. The sounds of her voice filtered through to Ralla's brain as the tears began. An eerie calm spread from her temples, drawing her eyelids to slits, pushing her mouth to a frown, clenching her jaw, then her arms, then her fists. Through water-blurred eyes, Ralla watched as they pushed Thom's bed from the emergency room, the doctor still on top of him, pushing hard.

"There is," she said, stepping backwards, turning, and leaving the Medbay with anger, but not at them.

—---

"Get *out*," Ralla growled, fists clenched, tone leaving no room for discussion. The Council, seated on the couches, looked at her like they'd never seen her before. "Get. Out. *Now*." Her gaze burned holes into only one, but the rest knew she was talking to them. Ioa nudged Appet, and both stood to leave. As they passed, Ioa touched Ralla's arm, but said nothing. The others, on a wave of the hand by Hennorr, left as well. Ralla heard the door latch behind her, but Hennorr began before she could.

"I'm sorry your friends got hurt."

"You need to talk to your son."

"What?" Hennorr said, obviously feigning ignorance.

"We both know he's behind all this, and you need to contact him and tell him to stop."

"I think you're mistaken."

"I heard his voice, and so did you."

"It's not that simple."

"*Don't* tell me what is simple. Don't you dare condescend to me."

"Well, Ralla, it *isn't* that simple," he snapped back, finally agitated.

"He is attacking our people. This is no better than the war. You need to contact him and tell him to stop."

"Or what? I'll take his allowance away? What magical powers do you think I have?"

"He's killing our people!"

"And why shouldn't he?" Hennorr's words echoed off the walls of the cabin.

"What?"

"Why shouldn't he? What do you think is going on here? Do you really think things are back to normal? Did you really think we could all just go back to being one big happy community like before? Our world worked because we had military power, and we had economic power. The Council ruled because they had control of those powers. Now we have *nothing*, Ralla. We can't force people to trade with us because we have nothing to trade. We can't bully people to give us supplies because we have no arms. This," Hennorr said, tossing the papers on the table in front of him to the floor, "is a *joke*. We rely on charitable donations from domes nostalgic for the way it was. The *Universalis* was never self-sufficient. And in a time when we were a hub of trade and in charge of a navy, we had all the bargaining power. Domes would send us what they could, because we would give them something in return. That's gone.

That's all gone now. These domes, they don't have to send us anything. Some do because they can, some do out of loyalty. But others can't, because they're starving. Other's won't, because it's in their best interests not to. All Cern has done is what we should have done in the first place, if we'd been able. He set up a trading system, and then took whatever he needed if he couldn't get it."

"You're... you're *proud* of him."

"Why shouldn't I be? He's doing what he can for his people."

"There are *thousands* of people *here*, on this ship. *Tens* of thousands."

"Ralla, you naive little girl," he said, shaking his head. "This ship, maybe this world, can no longer sustain the current population."

"What?"

"There is not enough food. People are going to die."

"No. No, that can't be true. That's unacceptable."

"Unacceptable or not, that's the way it is. Without the Garden, and whatever analog they had on the *Population*, there just isn't enough food."

"What if we—"

"We what? If you have ideas, I'd love to hear them. What if we fish more? Great, where do we process it? How do we get the fishermen to their subs? Even more important, how do we get the fish off those subs? We have one working dock. It barely handles people. What if we turn refugees away? Fantastic, where do they go? What if we send people to live in the domes? Brilliant, which ones? Which will take them?"

Ralla tried to find words, hearing several of her initial ideas shot down before she'd been able to say them.

"The domes weren't meant to support large numbers of people. We'll be able to save some people by sending them to the larger domes, but those numbers fall far short of what we have here now, and more are arriving every day. And where are they arriving from? Domes that kicked them out because Oppai dumped them there."

"You're giving up, is that it?"

"Giving? No, Ralla, gave. *Gave.* Gave up. I've been looking at these numbers for weeks. That food riot? That's just be the beginning. I'd hoped that Lieutenant Lo and his team could have secured that dome for us. It was supposed to be lightly defended. Had they succeeded, I don't know, maybe we could have started to push Cern back, but now... are they all dead?"

"I don't know."

"It doesn't matter. They'll be prepared for us now, and it's not like we have soldiers and weapons to spare."

"You are giving up," Ralla said, quietly, almost to herself.

"We still have a few domes loyal to us. Current estimates show we'll run out of food in about eight to ten weeks, on the outside. Even if we started now, with the bottleneck at the dock, it's not likely we'd be able to get everyone off the ship in time. And that's if we even had a place to send them."

"We have to try."

"Those people down there, that you love so much, nearly tore this ship apart when they were *hungry.* Can you imagine what they'll do when they find out most of them will *die* in two months?"

Ralla stepped back, stumbled against a chair, and fell into it. Her anger and energy from just minutes earlier, gone. Her body and mind, numb. Hennorr sat back as the weight of what he'd said pressed on him as well. There was no celebration in his lashing, just ruthless fatalism.

"Does the rest of the Council know?" Ralla asked morosely.

"No. I haven't told them yet. My assistants know; I had to tell them. They were starting to figure it out anyway. I've been trying to keep everything sequestered. That's why we had the mix-up with the rations that caused that riot. None of the people who keep track of supplies have the big picture. They know their area, and that's it. I know you dislike me, Ralla, but if you were in my position, you wouldn't have done anything different."

She barely registered his words. In her mind, Ralla saw the Basket. She saw the construction of the Spire, the expansion of the Terraces, and the thousands in Tent City. She didn't want to understand it, didn't want to let Hennorr be right, but if they told these people right now what was happening, the panic would be uncontrollable.

She looked at Hennorr. Her anger had blocked her from really looking at him in weeks. He seemed to have aged a decade since he'd been rescued. He'd already given up. He was beaten. It might have been greed and desire that had put him in this position, but to his credit, he had tried. This was the situation, and he had followed it through as he saw fit. He could have left at any time, but didn't. No, instead he had tried to work something out, that was clear now to Ralla, and it had beaten him. His concession would result in the deaths of thousands, perhaps tens of thousands.

It took her a moment, but it hit her that this could be the final fatal blow for their entire species. Too few in number to survive. All that effort to save the Fountain, and they were going to lose everything anyway. In a way, Ralla realized, Oppai had won.

Ralla stood and went to the balcony. It all seemed so futile now, trying to hobble together places for people to stay, to live. She leaned out and looked down, the floor of the Basket teeming with people so many levels below. She had lost her father, and her mother, countless friends and colleagues, all in just a few weeks. She saw their faces. She longed to hear her father's voice, to feel one of his massive hugs. To hear Thom's voice, his embrace. But her father was gone. Right now, Thom could be gone, too. So much time wasted being angry over what? Ralla realized she was crying again, and resting her arms on the balcony railing, she let her sobbing face fall into them.

She tensed as an arm draped over her shoulder, then felt Hennorr beside her. He stroked her back gently, and then all the other feelings dropped away, replaced by one. Ralla shrugged him off, and stepped away. Hennorr wasn't looking at her, but out into the Basket with a resigned look of defeat.

Ralla realized, in that moment, she didn't need her father there. She didn't need Thom there. She, Ralla Gattley, was all the strength she needed. And that strength told her one thing:

Fight.

X

RALLA WASN'T SURE how long she was walking. It had started with anger and vigor leaving the Council chambers, her mind leaping from problem to problem, convinced there was a solution to The Problem facing them all. After a while, her pace slowed, and her mind calmed.

It was night in the Basket, quiet, dim. Ralla walked, still wrapped in her thoughts. Sounds echoed in the darkness: A pot falling, a laugh, a baby's cry. Ralla walked. Up some stairs to cross the Terraces. Construction had halted for the night. A rickety bridge made of metal trusses and carbon-composite plating stretched tenuously over the Canyon, connecting the Terraces to the lower reaches of T-town. Ralla paused in the middle, near the exact center of the Basket. Above her to one side towered the Spire, on the other, the stepped-back upper levels of the Terraces. Fore and aft, the long stretch of the Canyon, and in the distance, Camp 1. More and more, she thought of the little camp as home, despite its sloppy construction and tiny accommodations. It was where her friends were; Dija and, with a lump in her throat, Geran. As fired up as she'd been earlier, the darkness and solitude had snuck in a heavy melancholy.

Voices drifted up to her, either from the small camps in the Canyon below, or from the open walls of T-town and the Terraces, she couldn't tell. They were the quiet conversations of the weary, the respectful, the doomed. She couldn't let these people die, of that she was certain. Hennorr had resolved to let some die so others could live. Maybe that was the pragmatic option, but it wasn't an acceptable option.

Ralla's whole life had been one infused with optimism. As much as Oppai had tried to beat it out of her, deep in the nightmare bowels of the *Population*, he hadn't succeeded. But here, now, the future weighed on her. It was going to get worse, much worse, and there was no guarantee it would ever get better. She'd once heard a Councilman friend of her father's refer to something as "the new normal." Was this the new normal? Rations, scarcity, overcrowding, and death?

For the first time, she realized how tired she was. Beyond tired — drained. In her mind, she traced the steps it would take to get back to Medbay. Many. She traced the steps home. Many. Instead, she realized where to go. She continued across the bridge to T-town and found a passage that wove through the makeshift structure and into the wall of the Basket. From there, it was a short walk.

Thom's cabin was unlocked, as she knew it would be. Entering, she felt like an intruder, like he would step out of the tiny bathroom and confront her. He didn't, of course. How many times over the previous months had she thought to come here? It was cleaner than she figured it would be. The bed was unmade, and a towel hung from the porthole. She fell onto the bunk. The pillow smelled of him. She held it tight, and cried herself to sleep.

—-̄--

Morning cast its harsh light, and Ralla wished she hadn't looked at herself in the mirror. Puffy eyes, hair matted on one side — not that she could do much with it at this stage. She looked tired, but inside, she was not. Sometimes, she thought, you've just got to cry it out. With a laugh, she imagined saying that to her father.

Maybe Thom was dead. Maybe Geran was dead. There was nothing she could do about that now. There was something she had to do first. Her walk to the Council chambers was brisk and invigorating. She knew what she had to do, and was prepared to do it. She was the first to arrive and greeted each member as they entered. Ralla was able to talk with Ioa and Appet privately for just a few moments before Hennorr arrived. They all sat as one of his aides went through the agenda. As they all anticipated, it was about food, logistics, and what to do about the still administrator-less Farming Dome F268. It had turned out none of the surviving resident farmers knew the first thing about actually running the place. The last item on the agenda, a presentation by Koin, Ralla hadn't expected.

Ralla followed along with the pretense of the meeting. Hennorr kept stealing glances at her, like she was going to erupt and spill about their conversation the day before. That her calm was unnerving him amused her greatly. Finally, it was time. Ralla's heart jumped from the excitement. Hennorr said the words she'd be waiting for.

"Next on the agenda, the situation on F268. It seems they're still having management issues. Thoughts?"

Ralla took a breath, and tried to speak as casually as she could.

"I nominate Councilman Pell Farre for the administrator position," she said, looking at Ioa.

"I second the nomination," Ioa said, perfectly deadpan.

Farre looked surprised, but Hennorr did not. In Ralla's mind she screamed at him not to figure it out yet. Appet then played his hand,

"I think that's a great idea. It's vital we have someone we trust in charge over there. It's one of our biggest food providers, right?"

"Well, uh... yes. But..." Farre, caught off guard, was obviously trying to go over every pro or con. Ralla could see when it clicked; she saw in his face the exact moment when his mind was made up. "If the Council so wishes it, I would be proud to serve."

"Vote?" Hennorr asked. Not wanting to insult their friend, all voted for Farre. He wore a broad, genuine smile. Ralla bit her tongue, intensely hoping someone else would say the next step so she wouldn't have to. One of Hennorr's lackey Councilmembers finally did.

"So does this mean we only have five Councilmembers now? I mean, he can't serve on the Council from F268 can he?"

Hennorr shot Ralla a glance, which she saw out of the corner of her eye. He'd figured it out too late.

"The law says we need five for a quorum. So we'll still be able to function for now." Ralla's answer seemed to satisfy those it needed to, as everyone stood to congratulate Pell Farre.

"If you don't mind, I'd like to go tell my wife, she's going to be thrilled," he said with a smile. Yes, she is, Ralla thought.

There were more handshakes, then he was gone. As he opened the door to leave, Ralla saw Koin fidgeting nervously in the hallway. Ralla could feel Hennorr's eyes on her, so she turned to stare him down as she spoke.

"I propose the immediate dismissal of Tenncy Hennorr as Proctor Pro Tempore of the *Universalis* Council of Concord for gross negligence and subversion."

"Seconded," Ioa said immediately. If Hennorr was surprised, Ralla couldn't tell.

"Vote?" Ralla asked.

Ioa, Appet, and her hands went up. The two remaining former Union lieutenants did not. It didn't matter, it was three to two.

"I nominate Ralla Gattley as Proctor," Ioa said with a wry smile. Now here, Ralla knew, they weren't entirely inside the law. Technically, Ralla couldn't vote on her own nomination, but there was nothing in the bylaws that said what to do in the case of three Councilmembers nominating their only other member as Proctor. Ralla doubted anyone would know the Council laws as she did. The three raised their hands anyway, and they moved forward as if it had passed. Hennorr stood to leave, but Ralla wasn't finished.

"In accordance with the laws of the *Universalis*, I hereby dissolve this Council of Concord until such a time as a full and legal election can be held to determine new members."

The cabin was silent. Ralla knew, if it came down to it, there was no reason for any of them to go along with what she had said. Sure enough, one of the lieutenants started to balk.

"Now wait a second, what? You can't do that."

"Mr. Hennorr has been concealing the fact that the leader of the pirates that steal our food and kill our people is his son."

"What?"

Hennorr walked toward the door, and looked back at Ralla with his hand on the latch.

"Take it," he said. There was no malice in his voice. If anything, Ralla thought, there was relief. He let the door swing wide as he left, a confused Koin watched him leave from across the hallway.

Ralla's heart surged with bittersweet triumph. It was a huge, important step. Hennorr would have led them to certain destruction. There had to be a better way, and Ralla was determined to find it. Her view was so different from the night before. Hennorr hadn't *wanted* it. He ran the Council like an ill-fated company, destined for extinction.

Ralla was terrified, but it was a good feeling. A feeling of hope. Across from her, Ioa and Appet seemed to share in her optimism. Tomorrow, maybe the day after, they'd hold elections. The people needed a voice, and *then* they could find out about what was happening. Give the people a say in their future, and maybe, maybe they'd see this not as an ending, but as just another surmountable obstacle. The people of the *Uni* were resilient, and those she'd met on the *Pop*, many living here now, were as well. They'd get through this, somehow, and then... and then... the promise of a future on the surface. She wished her father was here to see this. He'd have been so proud, she knew.

Koin wandered in, still fidgeting, still nervous. Ralla waved him over as the other, now former, Councilmembers left, leaving just Ralla, Ioa, and Appet.

"What can we do for you, Koin? We've had a bit of a shake-up, as you can see."

Koin looked at the Ralla, Ioa, and Appet in turn, but didn't seem to register any of them as a real object.

"We must discuss my findings."

"That's fine. You don't have to be nervous. It's just the three of us."

Koin focused on Ralla, and the hair on the back of her neck stood on end. His eyes were dark and hollow, as if he hadn't slept in days.

"You are not the cause of my anxiety, Ms. Gattley."

"Well, spit it out then," said a frustrated Appet. Koin nodded.

"The Fountain is not working. We have failed."

PART 3

"RALLA WON. I don't know if you heard. Well, I mean she won Proctor. She ran unopposed in her Rep election. We haven't really talked yet, but the nurses said she came by several times when I was out. That seems like a good sign."

Thom adjusted his sling, and winced as his arm moved.

"The doctors say I'll have limited function in my arm for a few weeks, at best. Seems like the bullet tore up the muscle pretty good. That's nothing compared to my leg. I tore a tendon, so I'm going to be limping for a while, and that's *with* a cane. And then there's my eye..."

Thom reached up with his left hand, and touched the bandaged right side of his face.

"Eye. Face. Whatever. If you were wondering why my voice sounds weird, it's because I can't open my jaw. I'm gorgeous." He laughed then winced in quick succession. "Dija's on the surface with Koin. They won't tell me what's up, but I can guess. I'm sure you can, too. I've never seen him so freaked out. Ralla looks older now. Seems older, maybe that's the right way to say it. I wonder if I look older. I feel older. I guess I don't look like much right now, that's for sure. Sorry, I'm rambling."

Thom leaned back in his wheelchair and closed his eyes. The drugs kept the pain suppressed, but it was still there, in the background. Looming, waiting, ready to strike.

"I tried to talk to Dija. She's easy to talk to, in her way. Very honest. Too honest. I'm not sure if I helped anything. She just needed to be on the surface, to get out of here. I get that. I bet most people can get that, now. Not that I liked the surface. Too open. But not being here anymore... She's a dear friend, but more than that... Maybe this is what having a sister feels like? Not that any of us would know. What I'm trying to say is, I know what you were thinking in the hallway after the riot, and I know you didn't want to ask me about it, and I'm just telling you that there's nothing between us. She's a friend, and I know she feels the same about me. I should have told you that before, but it was weird and then it was... well, you know the rest. I'll look after her, for you."

A lump welled in Thom's throat, making it hard to swallow. He instinctively brought his hand to his face, wiping the tears from one eye, and clumsily brushing the bandage in front of the other. He winced again. A nurse hovered nearby, and he motioned her over. She pushed Thom's chair away from the bed and bandages and tubes and machines and the body that trapped the mind of Geran Lo.

_-__

Dija soared through the air, for what felt like an eternity, even though it was just a fraction of a second. Face first, she landed. Even with three layers, a heavy jacket, and the poncho Koin gave her, Dija was still cold. She loved it. Jumping into the snow was a type of fun she felt wrongly denied her in her youth. So she figured she'd make up for it now. Koin was absorbed in his instruments, so she figured he wasn't bothered by it. She rolled onto her back. The sky was clear, filled with tiny glistening snowflakes. Though designed to spread its frozen water bounty evenly, a ring roughly the same distance from the Fountain as it was tall, showed heavier precipitation, creating a ringed hill circling the Fountain that gave them a spectacular view following a strenuous hike.

Dija sat up and looked down the hill where they'd come. White powder had nearly swallowed the *Pop*. A few glimpses of the hull, revealed by the wind, were all the only signs that there was a man-made thing down there. Otherwise, it was just an enormous mound surrounded by snowdrifts on the edge of the sea. The rest of the science team were inside, she knew, digging around for supplies and salvageable materials.

This, this was where she wanted to be, Dija decided. She didn't know how, but she wanted to live here. Maybe she could find a cabin in the *Pop*. Maybe she could fashion some sort of hut and live in the snow. It was impractical, and unlikely, she knew, but this place felt like home. Not even "home," all the way back in the farming dome where she was born, had felt like this. It had always seemed so artificial. At least, that's how she remembered it now. At the time she just wanted to get away, or at the very least, be left alone in the fields with the tractors and other machinery.

It helped she was here with Koin. Smart, completely accepting, nonjudgmental, and just as weird as she was. He wasn't exactly *fun*, but that was understandable given the circumstances. The circumstances, but not the location. Dija packed some snow into a ball shape, and lobbed it at Koin, missing him completely. He looked back at her, studying her.

"Fair play, but don't hit the equipment," he said, before turning back to the big red box they'd dragged up the hill. Somehow, his acceptance of the snowball attack had taken the fun out of it.

"Anything I can do to help?"

Koin studied her again, as if his brain was running as slow in the cold as the gear he'd brought. He shook his head and went back to work. The sun was lower in the sky than the last time they'd been here. Koin had told her that in a few more weeks it'd be gone completely. The other scientists had heard this with some trepidation, but then, they didn't seem thrilled to be on the surface anyway. No one did, really. Ralla had said every time the idea of a surface settlement came up, the Council members unanimously and emphatically said no, claiming none of their constituents would want to live on the surface. Some apparently implied mutiny if the idea was even put to a vote. Ralla had tried to explain it, explain how some people couldn't shake the fear they'd been trained since birth to have about the surface. Dija didn't get it, but that didn't bother her. She'd spent her whole life thinking differently from everyone around her. She scooped up some snow in her mittened hand and ate it. It was so quiet here, just the sound of the wind, and so peaceful.

The sight of a bloodied Geran, looming over the bodies in the hallway, pierced her mind. She frowned. Ralla had told her later he'd been protecting her. Thom said the same thing. But a person that could *do* that. And now he lay in the Medbay, the doctors saying that if he woke up, he may not be the same person. He had taken too much damage. Dija recognized a sliver of guilt in her emotions, but couldn't deny that more than guilt, she felt sadness. At least she should have spoken to him. Now...

"Ready to head back," Koin said behind her.

"Good or bad?"

Koin shook his head.

—-‑--

Ralla convened the Council. They sat on the roof of Camp 1, on uncomfortable folding chairs, using crates as tables. They were eight, in total. One representative for each wall of the Basket, one for the Terraces, and two for T-town and three for the ever-growing Tent City. Ioa and Appet had both won, as had the remaining former Union member. The latter turned out to be a solid guy, Ralla realized, once he was out from under the thumb of Tenncy Hennorr. She didn't trust him yet, but he didn't seem to have any agenda as far as she could tell. As for Hennorr, no one had seen him. Or at least, no one admitted to having seen him. A concern for another day. This meeting was about relocation.

The new members of the Council still didn't know about their collective tenuous position, something all four of the original members had agreed on. The group would be kept in the dark for at least another few days, so they could approach the problem perhaps more objectively than those who knew.

Ralla, Ioa, and Appet had already decided the most fair way was to hold a lottery, with the winners given the choice, as much as could be offered, where to locate. If they didn't want to leave, even after gentle prodding, their names would go back in the queue. In the meantime, they'd been contacting friendly domes. So far, of the dozen domes they'd contacted, most said they'd be able to take a few refugees; some as little as ten, others a few hundred. It was a start, and it presumed Cern wouldn't get there first. In a few cases, the dome administrators admitted they'd been approached by Cern or one of his people. Ralla had to assume the others had been as well, but they were cooperating for now and for now, that was enough.

And what to do about Cern? As she had become very adept at doing, Ralla filed that in a compartment to deal with at another time.

"Ladies and gentlemen, shall we begin?"

II

RALLA STARED at the drink in Thom's hand and the bottle on the floor. They were the most important objects in the room, both knew. He was a mess, though she'd been prepared for that. All the time spent in Medbay, and the days since his release, hadn't been enough to fully mend his broken body or, apparently, his mind.

Little remained in the bottle. How much there'd been to start, she didn't know. Thom sat on the bed, leaning against the wall, his good leg firmly planted on the floor. He'd told her to enter. He must have recognized her voice, Ralla thought. His eyes were glossy, but his stare was steady. His eyes slowly dropped to look at the bottle, then back up at Ralla. He seemed to be fatalistically bracing himself for an expected onslaught.

She'd known him like this. Known him to drink until there was no more booze to be found. But he'd claimed that was behind him. She'd expected that was why he'd ditched his responsibilities and betrayed her. It seemed a long time ago. Here seemed proof.

Thom, for his part, expected a barrage of negativity. Here was all the proof Ralla needed to explain his behavior since the war. The painkillers, mixed with the booze, mixed with recent events, had blended into a numbness of him not caring. If she wanted to yell, she could yell, and he'd tell her to get out and never come back. This was none of her business.

The silent tension tugged at them both. Ralla opened her mouth to speak. Thom opened his to scream at her to stuff it.

"Do you have another glass?" she asked timidly. Thom's jaw snapped shut, his prepared, mentally rehearsed response now no longer fitting. He was unsure what to do. He reached out to hand her the glass he held.

"This is the clean one. I'll find another."

Ralla shook her head.

"No, it's fine. Tell me where. I'll find it," she said, already scanning the room to find another cup. Thom pointed to a cabinet above the bunk where she found a spotted and chipped, brown glass tumbler. She wiped it out with the bottom of her blouse, unsure which was cleaning which, and poured herself a drink. After chugging it back, wincing as the harsh liquid burned her throat, she poured herself another. "May I sit?"

Thom motioned toward the other end of the bed, the only other area worthy of sitting, other than the floor. Ralla sat, but wasn't sure where to start. She didn't want to bring up his injuries, or the battle that had caused them. She knew he knew about her election and new position. He must have been told she'd come to visit him when he was unconscious in the Medbay, but also knew she hadn't come when he was awake. Nothing had passed between them other than terse "hellos." Not until now. She had come here for a reason. Best to get right out with it.

"This is pretty terrible," was all she could think to say.

"I agree."

"I don't suppose you want to start," she said lightly, hearing it fall flat as she said it.

"No."

"Me neither."

Thom raised his glass to her and took a drink. She did the same to him.

"I didn't mean to hurt you like that," he said to his glass.

"You tried to tell me something. I should have listened. What did you want to say?"

Thom took another sip of his drink and studied the worn paint on the wall.

"You thought I was this big hero."

"You are."

"No, I mean you saw me as this thing. I was a fisherman, and you turned me into this leader. That's not me." Ralla bit her tongue, knowing if she said he really was, he'd ignore it. "I know how you see me. I can see it in your face right now. But I'm not that." He finished his drink, so Ralla poured him another. She realized silence was working for her, and stuck with it. "I see their names, Ralla. I see all names and names and faces. So many of their faces. Not enough of their faces. And somehow, I'm sitting here, Lo's in Medbay, and they're all dead. Because of me. I'm a *fisherman*, Ralla. That's what I was supposed to be. Not this."

He fell silent, looking ashamed and embarrassed. Ralla knew he had been right about one thing, she did see him differently. She knew that he'd made the best decisions he could, and they had broken him. She understood now why he'd acted the way he had. Guilt welled inside her, but that seemed a waste now. Now that there was so little time left. Being mad, it seemed such a waste, too.

Thom finally looked at her, trying to judge what she was thinking. She knew he expected to be chastised. She finished her drink and placed the tumbler on the floor.

Ralla reached out, wrapping her fingers around the glass Thom held in his hand. She loosened it from his grasp, sliding her fingers between his. This glass, too, she placed on the floor, bringing Thom's stray leg onto the bunk as she returned. She lay down beside him, kissing him gently on his unbandaged cheek. He looked surprised at her actions. She ran her bandaged hand down Thom's bandaged arm.

"Some of my parts aren't working so well," he said.

"Which parts?"

"Not those parts."

She leaned in to kiss his cheek again, but he turned his face and met her lips with his. She helped him to lie on the bed.

"I missed you," she whispered in his ear.

"I missed you, too."

—-—

Ralla awoke the next morning, cramped from spending the night on a bed designed for one, but happy to have spent it with two. Thom lay on his back snoring quietly. Early morning light snuck its way past the towel he used as a curtain. There hadn't been much sleeping, yet she felt rested and relaxed. She dressed quietly in the dark.

"Can I see you later?" Thom asked as she opened the hatch. He seemed such a sorry mess there on the bed. She saw him differently again in that moment, more the shiftless pilot she'd met nearly a year before. In that instant, she saw two futures. One, where he healed, got over his physical and mental trauma, and became the man she knew he was. In the other, he didn't. He was permanently hobbled by one or more of his injuries, mentally or physically limping along. She knew which she'd prefer, but had to admit that, regardless, he was in her future.

Well, whatever future any of them had.

"Have dinner with me tonight?" she asked.

"I know the best restaurant."

Ralla smiled and left, the weight of the day beginning to press down on her with every step away from the cabin. It couldn't squash the kernel of happiness buried deep inside. There was just something about him, she thought with a smile.

—-—

Dija was there when he woke up. The nurses later told their colleagues he woke up *because* she was there. The doctors scoffed at this, but couldn't deny the coincidence. However, they pointed out, they'd expected him to wake up for several days. Lo blinked; the light from the intensive care room left no shadows. He smiled at Dija. She was the first thing he saw, her copper-colored hair pinned back from her face with paperclips. She smiled politely in return.

"What happened?" she asked.

"I have no idea," he answered, his voice raspy.

"The doctors said you got hit with something."

"If they say so."

"What do you remember?"

Lo tried to remember, but it was just flashes of events. He knew he had gone somewhere with Thom, but where and what happened, there was nothing.

"I don't know, I..." He stopped in midsentence, remembering vividly the fight in the hallway, and Dija's state afterwards. He frowned. "I upset you."

"You did, yes."

"I'm sorry."

"Is that what you're like?"

His heart sank. Whatever drugs they were feeding him clouded his mind, but he could tell by her tone this was a battle he'd already lost. Why was she here, then?

"I'm here because Thom and Ralla asked me to come."

Had he said that out loud, Lo thought.

"Yes," she replied.

"Can we do this when I'm better?" Lo asked, trying to look down at his body, but unable to lift his head far enough. Worried, he tried to move his fingers and toes. Everything seemed intact, but distant.

"I would like to do this now, so I know if I need to come back."

Lo thought it a weird response, then instantly worried if he'd said that.

"You did," Dija replied. She lifted a tablet and read from it.

"It says here you spent a month in the brig for assault."

Lo didn't think he could feel any worse, but now he did. She'd found his record. She was reading it, here, *to* him. There was no hiding anything now.

"When I was a kid, yes."

"And two months under cabin arrest."

"Later, yes."

"It says you were arrested, but not sentenced, for nearly beating a man to death."

Lo said nothing; he didn't need to.

"Is there more?"

"Yes."

Dija dropped the tablet away from her face.

"You hurt people."

"Yes."

He knew it was pointless to get upset. Part of him expected something like this to happen. He'd just hoped it would happen when he'd be able to defend himself.

"Well?" she asked.

"I did those things. I've accepted the consequences. You think I'm some monster. I can't prove that I'm not. I don't know that I'm not."

"So you won't even try to explain?"

"Explain what?"

"What happened."

"You've read what happened."

"No, I've read the results."

"I don't... Dija, I'm really tired, and there's nothing I can say that will make you think any better of me."

Dija placed the tablet on the bed.

"Try, please."

—---

Dija held Lo captive, sitting, unmoving and silent, next to his bed. Monitors beeped while the groans of other patients filled the space between them. He finally broke the silence.

"I was a heavy kid. I've always been big, but I didn't get tall until I was nearly out of school. Kids are mean, and that upset me. It didn't matter how many times the teachers or my mom told me to forget about it, or not to let it bother me. It did bother me. And sometimes when it would bother me, I'd lash out. Some kid would say something, and I'd hit him. Always, he'd run to the teacher, and because I was bigger, *I* would get in trouble. Of course, all of his friends would say I started it. Kids are crafty like that."

Lo focused back on Dija, the drugs making his recollections especially vivid. She listened intently.

"Then my dad left. He went to live in some dome. I got in more fights, so they put me in therapy. Three times a week, plus a weekly group session. It doesn't matter, except to explain what happened next. A few years go by, and my mom starts dating this guy. He didn't treat her well, but then, neither did my dad. The guy shoved her around a lot, but he never really hit her. I used to yell at him to stop, and he'd threaten me in every way you can imagine. But he never hit me. Smart guy. One night, he hit her. I was a little older then. Still not tall, but big. I just sort of snapped. I threw myself at him. I whaled on him. Broke his jaw. It wasn't hard for him to convince the judge, with my record, that I was dangerous. My mom didn't have a scratch on her, and didn't say a word in my defense. That was the brig."

A nurse came by to check on him, and slid some ice chips into his mouth. He mumbled a thank you.

"I didn't go home after the brig. I made a place for myself between two ships on the outer ring. It was a little camp. I made myself a bed out of discarded clothing, fixed up a heating plate, and scavenged whatever else I needed. It was terrifying, but great. I still went to school. Not sure why, I guess that's just what I felt like I needed to do. When I smelled too bad, I'd shower in the school's gym. It was this weird freedom. What the kids said at school didn't bother me as much. Or maybe they didn't tease me as much, I don't know. The teachers didn't think anything was wrong, as they never saw my mom anyway. I'll tell you, Dija, I wouldn't do it again, but living on my own like that was the best decision I ever made. Eight months later, and I remember because it was right before midyear break, I decided I wanted a few of my old things so I'd have something do while school was out. I got it in my head about these things. Toys and stuff I didn't need, hadn't needed, but I just wanted them. So I snuck back into my mom's cabin, and tried to get them."

Lo paused again and motioned toward the cup of ice chips on the table beside the bed. Dija got them and slid a couple into his mouth. He mumbled a thank you. She took one herself, examined it, then began to chew on it.

"I thought the place would be empty. I'd scouted it for days. I knew when they were working, so I figured I could get in and get out. But he was there. I think he thought I'd come back to kill him. I just wanted my toys, and to get away from him. But he was too fast. He pinned me down and kept punching me in the stomach. I found out later that word had gotten around that he'd been beaten up by a kid, and everyone had made fun of him for it. My mom was there too, and eventually she tried to stop it. When she went to pull him off, he backhanded her. I exploded on him. Rolled him over, and used my weight to keep him down. While my mom called for help, I choked him. I didn't kill him. I didn't want to kill him. I just wanted to scare him like he scared my mom. She testified this time, and he was sent to some mining dome, but I was sentenced to cabin arrest. Technically it was attempted murder, but the prosecutor knew no jury would convict me, so they just locked me inside a cabin for two months."

"So that's the beating a man to death thing?"

Lo shook his head, on the verge of tears.

"No," he said, his voice cracking. He knew if he kept going he'd lose whatever hope he had to be with her. He couldn't stop himself. "That was years later. After I'd finished school. I left a bar late one night and stumbled across some guy forcing himself on some girl. They were drunk, but she was trying to push him away. I don't remember what happened, but at the trial they said he spent two months in the hospital."

"Oh..."

"They knew my past. They knew what I'd done before, and even though I was defending that woman, I'd kept beating that guy after I'd knocked him unconscious. My choice was exile to a mining dome, or join the military. Obviously, I did the latter."

"Oh..."

"I got better. I swear I did, Dija. Or, I thought I had. But that first night you were in the camp? When you were curled up and wouldn't eat? Two guys tried to steal your soup, and I knocked them around."

"Why did you do that?" she asked, furrowing her brow.

"I was exhausted. I'd been working, trying to save people, not being able to, practically nonstop for days. There was just something about those two, trying to steal from you. You were helpless; my anger just got the better of me. It was the first time that had happened in years. It's not an excuse, but you remember what those days were like."

"Tell me about Jos Vaee."

She knew, he realized. But then, of course she did. Did she know it all? When did she find out he'd put Vaee through a wall? Why hadn't she ever mentioned it? Had he just said that out loud, too? He looked at her face, but she was hard to read even when he wasn't doped up.

"He hurt you. I hurt him. I won't apologize for that. I shouldn't have been so violent, but no... I know this isn't want you want to hear, but if anyone hurts you, I'll hurt them. That's how I am. But telling you all this, lying here, I've never been so sure that I don't want to fight anymore. Fight anyone. Ever again. I don't want to be a soldier anymore. But even if you walk out of here right now and never want to see me again, I'll will bring such violent fury down on anyone who causes you harm that it will be unlike anything seen before on this planet."

The words hung in the air, surrounded by the beeps, the breathing, and the bawling. Lo couldn't understand, her face revealed no emotion, yet she didn't move. Finally, slowly, at the edge of her mouth, a twitch of a smirk revealed itself.

"'Unlike anything seen before on this planet?'" she mocked lightly.

"Well, yeah. What?"

"I like you, Geran Lo. You're weird. Like me. Well, not like me. You still scare me a bit. Is that OK?"

"I would never hurt you."

"I think I get that now. You should have told me all of this sooner."

"It's not exactly a story I like to tell."

"Makes sense."

As they so often did, they lapsed into a comfortable silence.

"Mind if I sit here a read for a bit? I have some work for Ralla I have to finish."

"Only if you don't mind if I lay here for a bit."

She squinted at him.

III

IT WASN'T GOING WELL. Ralla had tried three times to quiet the Council, and the arguments and shouting continued. Oddly, most weren't directed at her. She had informed them of the dire food situation. It affected them all, so they all needed to decide what to do. Taking a cue from her fondly remembered school teachers, Ralla rose her hand. It worked better than she expected. After a few moments, everyone settled down and looked her way.

"For the moment, I need all of you to promise this doesn't leave the Council. I need your word. I think you understand that we can't afford another riot," Ralla said. The Council nodded, in some cases reluctantly, but all seemed to understand the reality. "Proctor Hennorr established a merchant marine program. While it never really got off the ground, I think it's worth it for us to push that program. I'm sure there are many pilots sitting around out there, and it would be great to give them something to do."

"Can we pay them?" one of the new members asked.

"If you can think of something we have to give them, sure. I can't. The best I can think of is an extra entry into the lottery, or maybe a promise they can keep their sub if everything goes well, or if it goes sour. Of course, neither of those things we can promise at the moment. Not before we decide to tell everyone what's happening."

"Who's to say these pilots won't just steal the subs, or sell their supplies on the black market?" the same Council member asked. Ralla had already considered this.

"It could happen. We have to assume it will. Right now, we don't have much of a choice. If we send out twenty ships, and eighteen come back with food, maybe that buys us another week or two. That's how we have to look at this. I'm open to more permanent solutions, but we can't let ourselves govern for the long term when we likely don't have a short term." Ralla took their grumbling as agreement.

"There's one other thing," she continued. "The leader of the so-called pirates is Cern Hennorr, as most of you know. His father was unwilling to open communications with him. Despite my history with him, our desperation supersedes any personal feelings. Well, at least on my part. Hopefully, he will feel the same. I will offer to meet with him in person, to plead our case."

"Someone else should go with you," Ioa said, her motherly tone a welcome change from the harshness of the others. "To plead our case if he does still have personal feelings." Ralla knew Ioa was familiar with the whole story. In the circles of the Council and the Yard, Ralla and Cern's long relationship was common knowledge. From the looks on some of the other Council members' faces, this was the first they'd heard of any of it.

"What kind of 'personal feelings'?" one of the younger Council members asked.

"We've known each other since we were children… and we dated for many years," Ralla answered, figuring there was no point hiding the truth. As she expected, several eyed her with suspicion, others whispered to those next to them. Ralla held up her hand again before the meeting got away from her.

"You have every right to be suspicious. You should know that I broke it off with him shortly after we were first attacked by the *Population*. I didn't know he survived the war until I heard his voice on a transmission we received from a farming dome he was capturing. I am happy to take someone else with me, more than one if you want, but you have to realize, without Cern and his people on our side, or at least not against us, we have little chance of surviving. One of you mentioned earlier about the black market. Understand they *are* the market. We need him to help us, not capture him or bring him into our economy. We're not the most important anything anymore, at least not to him. Don't fool yourselves. Proctor Hennorr was right when he said we have nothing to offer, nothing to sell, nothing to trade."

"So what are you going to do?" another Council member asked.

"Beg."

—⁻--

Ralla was exhausted by the time she got back to Thom's cabin. It was cramped and dark, and she loved it.

Thom kissed her as she entered, and she could tell by his breath that he was at least one drink ahead of her. She took the glass he offered, and attempted to catch up. He had other ideas, as she suspected he would.

Later, as they lay there, Ralla's mind raced. Her head on his chest, she played with his hair distractedly. She wanted him with her when they went to meet Cern. Sure, he was a good pilot, but of course it was more than that. She wanted *him* there. Confronting Cern was going to be hard enough, and a little backup wouldn't hurt. Cern would have no way of knowing Thom was her new... whatever this was.

But then there was Thom's leg. He was getting around with a cane, barely, and it was clear he enjoyed sitting a lot more. Well, and lying down, she thought with a smile. Thom started snoring quietly. They'd have to go down to Camp 1 to get their dinner rations. Maybe she could talk to him there.

As she imagined him painfully going down the stairs, one by one, wincing if he turned his foot wrong, she realized her desire was entirely selfish. Worse, Ralla was sure he'd *want* to go with her. No matter how much he'd claim his leg and arm were fine and his face didn't hurt, none of it was true. He'd made it clear he wasn't leading anyone, ever again. He didn't want to be near any sort of combat. But she knew as soon as she told him what she was doing, he'd insist on going.

She couldn't let him. He was broken, in more ways than one. Going with her on this mission of mercy would do him more harm than good. He needed to heal, because if her mission didn't go well, all their lives would get a lot tougher.

Thom's snoring stopped.

"Don't stop," he whispered in a half-awake voice. She hadn't noticed she'd stopped playing with his hair, so she resumed. It was better for him not to go. She knew it, but why did it feel so wrong?

— - --

The transport detached from the *Uni* and powered south. The Council had chosen Appet to go with her; it was simultaneously a wise choice, and a welcome one. He had a calming presence in Council meetings, and she figured that couldn't hurt on this mission.

In the end, she'd told Thom a few hours before she left. As she expected, he wanted to go. As she expected, he was angry at how little notice she'd given him. But maybe because she wanted to see it there, or maybe because it actually was there, she could have sworn he looked relieved when she'd insisted he stay.

They'd signaled the dome where Cern had set up his headquarters, or at least, the one they'd been told he was using by *Uni*-friendly domes he'd contacted. Even though they'd accepted a meeting under the flags of trade and truce, Ralla couldn't help but be nervous. Worst case, she figured, they'd say no, and the *Uni* would be no worse than where they were now. Hopefully, Cern and his people wouldn't see that where they were now was desperate indeed.

—‾--

Thom limped his way down to Medbay for his almost-daily visit to Lo — the days when one of them wasn't unconscious, getting prodded by doctors, or otherwise incapacitated, anyway. Lo'd been moved to a recovery area, in what seemed to Thom as the farthest point from the main entrance as possible. Lo still had wires connected to his cast and bandaged body, sensors that kept track of his vitals. He was eating on his own, a notable improvement according to the doctors.

"Took a dump today," Lo informed as a sort of greeting.

"Congrats?" Thom replied, borrowing a wheelchair from the unconscious inhabitant of a nearby bed.

"I guess it's an even bigger deal than the eating. It means my insides aren't permanently messed up."

"It's the little things, apparently."

"After you've been in bed for this long, it tends to be all little things."

"Ralla went to meet with Cern today."

"Really?"

"She asked me to stay here."

"Really..."

"I was pretty upset, but she had a good point."

"That you can barely walk?"

"Pretty much, yeah."

"I didn't fight her as hard as I could have. I should have insisted. I'm feeling pretty guilty about that."

"So you'd be there to protect her?"

"Lo, we both know that if anyone is able to take care of themselves, it's Ralla Gattley."

"Yes, but..."

"Yes, I feel guilty because I want to be there to protect her."

"Ahhhh, you talk a big game, but there it is."

"Like you're any better."

"I'm not, but at least I'm honest about it. Look at it this way," Lo said, adjusting slightly in the bed and wincing. "If you were there, and something happened, she'd have to rescue the both of you. How annoying would that be? For her."

"You're not wrong."

They both watched a nurse approach. She smiled professionally at them both, checked Lo's chart, then the myriad instruments connected to him. Thom spun the wheelchair slowly in circles.

"I spoke to Dija," Lo said, after the nurse moved on other patients.

"Oh yeah? How'd that go?"

"Well, we spoke. That's more than I was expecting. She said she was scared of me."

"You look like a lumpy roll of wet toilet paper. Terrifying."

"A lumpy roll of toilet paper that's more than twice her size and chronically violent."

"I don't know about chronically."

"Thom."

"Sorry. What do you want me to say? I know you're a good person. A good person who occasionally messes up bad persons. Have you ever hurt someone who didn't deserve it?"

"Not in the way you mean, no."

"That's good enough for me. Maybe it's good enough for her."

"What if I do?"

"What if you do what? Lo, are you telling me you have so little control that you'll randomly pummel someone? That nurse didn't say hello, how about her? I annoy the crap out of you? How about me?"

"It's not like that."

"Tell me what it's like."

"I lose control. I can't explain it. I just get so angry sometimes."

"Everybody does."

"But not everybody puts people in Medbay when they do," Lo said. Thom looked at him quizzically. Lo told Thom about the soup thieves, and his trouble when he was younger. Thom listened intently, absentmindedly scratching at his bandaged face.

"I didn't know," Thom said finally.

"Now do you understand? Of course she's afraid of me. *I'm* afraid of me."

"What I understand is it's been a rough few months. I understand that you nearly died upstairs. And I understand that Dija means a lot to you. After you told her this, did she run?"

"No."

"Well, that's something."

"And she came back this morning."

"That's something better."

"I'm not sure what she's thinking. She keeps her distance."

"Lo, she probably doesn't want to break you."

"Maybe."

"Give her some time. She's making an effort, right? If she didn't want to see you, there's plenty of places she could go instead of here."

"I know. And I know what you meant before. I'm just so done with it all. I don't want to be a soldier anymore. I don't want to fight."

"Then let's hope Ralla doesn't provoke us into another war."

Lo shook his head the small amount he could.

"I can't, Thom."

"Me neither."

"No, I mean I really can't. The idea of getting back into it. I can't do it. Even if I was physically able. No more. This isn't even about Dija. I'm not going to let it kill me."

Thom looked away and sat silently for a few moments.

"Me too," he said quietly. He turned back and looked Lo in the eyes. "I haven't wanted to say anything, but, yeah, me too. The panic thing, about being in charge? That's part of it, but I just can't, I mentally just can't, be in a place where I'm responsible for someone else's death."

Lo nodded, the best he could, understanding completely.

"Aren't we a sorry bunch?" Thom said a few moments later, trying to clear the mood.

"A little more me than you, my mobile friend. Plus, I did die upstairs. They brought me back."

"Me too!"

"Then we are definitely a sorry bunch. Lucky, but sorry."

—_---

Ralla tired of the monotonous drone of the engines. Appet sat a few seats behind her, going over reports he'd brought with him. She took a seat closer.

"Would it be inappropriate to say I love watching you and Ioa together?"

"Pardon?"

"You and Ioa. You two are so adorable together."

"Adorable, eh? There was a time in my life when I would have considered such a critique... rather pejorative."

"I didn't mean to—"

"No, no," Appet said, finally cracking a smile. His voice sounded like he was always on the verge of coughing. "I take it as a compliment."

Ralla sighed with relief.

"You make it look so easy."

"Easy? Yes, I suppose. When you get to be our age, you realize what's important, and what's not."

"So what's that?" she asked.

"And ruin the surprise?"

"That's not a surprise I'd care to keep."

"I gather not," Appet said, his smile broadening. "Ioa tells me things. Things about your private life a man my age should not be privy."

"It's fine. I've spent most of my life without much of a private, private life."

"Indeed. My wife knew your father well. She dragged me to enough social functions that even I heard about you... and the boy Cern."

"Not a boy now."

"Perhaps not."

"Forgive me, but what did you do before the war?" Ralla asked, trying to pivot away from her love life. The topic change seemed to please Appet as well.

"I taught master classes in business, actually."

"No wonder you're so good at Council stuff," she said, motioning to the reports now scattered on the seat beside him.

"I suppose. Not much other use for me, I'm afraid."

"What? Don't say that."

"A man my age doesn't have a lot to contribute to our new society."

"That's not true."

"Ralla, please."

"We need teachers. We're going to need teachers."

"Maybe so, but right now, we need fighters, and engineers, and the strength and stamina of youth. Otherwise, none of us will survive."

Ralla couldn't think of anything to say.

"Ralla, there are many things I admire about you. My wife, had she gotten to know you as I have, would have adored you. Of that I'm sure. But I do want to caution you against too much faith in your idealism. You're going to have some tough decisions coming up, even if Hennorr the Younger agrees to set aside our differences and become our benevolent benefactor."

"I know."

"I hope you do. I wouldn't want to be in your shoes. We're on the brink of something here, Ralla. We all thought the war would be either the end or the beginning. Turns out it was neither."

"What do you think we should do?"

"Well, I'm here."

"So you think making a deal with Cern is the best option."

"I fear it's our only option."

"That's sort of best, then," Ralla replied, trying to smile.

"I suppose. Have you thought about what you're going to do if he says no?"

"I have."

"As have I. I gather you haven't figured out any better options?"

Ralla shook her head. "I had hoped," she began, "if we hung on long enough, the Fountain would work just enough for some of us to live on the surface."

"That was going to be a tough sell, even in ideal conditions."

"I know. Most people I've spoken to seem terrified of the idea."

"Me too. The ones I've spoken to, that is," he said.

"Can't say I blame them. Everyone alive was taught from their earliest days that the surface meant death. How do you convince people otherwise?"

"I don't know you can."

"Would you live on the surface?"

"I'll tell you, Ralla, even knowing the science, and being told by smart people it's safe, I don't know if I'd go willingly."

"Oh."

"I'm not sure I'd even want to *visit*, and I understand what's happened. There will be countless people who won't understand the science and will just reject it out of hand. Out of fear. Fear is powerful, probably the most powerful emotion. It pushes aside all logic and reason, and just becomes the truth of the moment."

"The Fountain's not working correctly, so I'm not sure it matters," Ralla said, reaching up to run her hands through her hair. She'd had time for a quick shower at Thom's place before heading out. It had been refreshing, but the dank transport made her feel grimy all over again.

"I have Koin's latest report here somewhere. You've read it?" he asked.

"No, but I talked to him after he got back. My best friend is working with him on it."

"And?"

"They're still trying to take more readings, but it seems right now that the Fountain is drastically underperforming from how it was designed."

"Weren't there supposed to be more, smaller Fountains to supplement the main one?"

"Yes, but even separate from that."

"Oh."

"I asked him not to put this in the report, but from what he's estimating now, it could be decades before we see any appreciable drop in water level."

"So it is working."

"But too slow for any of us to ever see actual land."

"If we had to, could we live up on the ice now?"

"Koin says that once the sun sets, the temperatures will plummet. He doesn't think they'll even be able to walk around up there, it will be so cold."

"Certainly people lived in cold climates before."

"I wondered the same thing. But they had specialized clothing, extensive heating, and insulated habitats. If we had time, or manufacturing facilities, or time, or time, or time."

"We don't seem to have any of those things."

"That's the worst thing about the damage to the *Uni*. The domes provided the materials, we provided the goods. Now all that is gone. Maybe eventually we can dig out some of that manufacturing equipment, but..."

"Time," Appet said quietly.

"I'm sure you have it there in your report, but we're down to three weeks of rations. When we get back, I'm cutting everyone but children and Medbay down to half rations."

"That's not going to go over well."

"Remember what you said about hard decisions?"

"Remember what I said about your shoes?"

IV

RALLA HAD NEVER seen one of the *Population*'s domes before. She'd seen their locations on maps, seen layouts and surveillance photos, but to see one in person was a different experience. The *Uni*'s engineers, using the latest innovations and components, designed elegant shapes, maximizing space and minimizing raw materials. They were, in Ralla's mind, clean. The *Pop*'s engineers, lacking the advancements of their counterparts on the *Uni*, took the tact of brutish overkill. Even at a distance, the massive girders that made up the superstructure gave a ghoulish appearance, like there was an enormous, multi-armed creature tightly embracing the dome from above. Only the slivers of light that snuck past the trusses revealed the overall "X" shape to the structure.

Ralla pointed the pilot toward the docking bay they'd been instructed to use. There had been no indication by Cern's people that they'd be greeted well or poorly, only that they were open to a meeting. It was on their turf, which Ralla agreed to as a show of good faith. Looking at the ominous dome before her, she began to second guess that decision. Appet joined her in the transport's cockpit.

"I hope they're friendlier on the inside," he said.

"I never appreciated how beautiful our domes were, until now."

"Perhaps you should start getting used to not calling them 'our,'" Appet said, his tone attempting levity, but not succeeding.

The transport docked with a thud at the far end of the facility's n-pole-facing arm. The sounds of flushing water and latches thrown echoed through the small cabin. The pilot, on Ralla's command, unlocked the rear hatch remotely.

Despite her hopes, but living up to her expectations, the hatch cycled to reveal a dozen armed men, guns drawn.

_-_--

The walk across the field was unceremonious, but allowed Ralla to marvel at the dome. Though similar in function, the appearance was unlike any she'd ever seen. The clear, open aesthetic typical of the *Uni*'s domes was developed to minimize the claustrophobic feelings many early settlers experienced. People born in the domes, and on the *Uni*, didn't mind the closed-in feeling, as they knew nothing else. Within a generation, the need to see out into the sea was merely a design choice, not a necessity. She'd written a paper on the phenomenon in school, but it wasn't until now, walking through this dome, that she understood there was a lot more to it.

While the exterior's metal supports gave an almost insectoid appearance, the extensive interior latticework inside reminded Ralla of a wire mesh, except the wires were the diameter of her torso. What made it all the more creepy was the light from inside reflected off the support beams outside, constantly catching the eye. As if something menacing lurked in the water.

The leafy vegetables grown in this section of the facility didn't look familiar to Ralla, but her eyes stopped focusing on the plants after a few paces. The saucer-like central building appeared to hover over the center of the station's four-branched X shape. Supports arched across the open areas, appearing as legs stretching out from its ovoid shape. Like the rest of the facility, it was glass, with thick metal muntin bars separating the individual panes. The overhead lights that ran the length of each long branch of the dome reflected brightly off the top of the saucer, but otherwise the view in was clear. As they approached it, she could see dozens of rooms, all swarming with people busy at work.

At the center of the station, before her group ascended the stairs in one of the legs of the saucer building, Ralla had a view down the other three arms of the facility. She was surprised to see they were mostly storage. Shipping containers of all sizes were stacked nearly to the ceiling.

The leg itself was dark and cramped, with bare lightbulbs unevenly spread up the incline. Lo wouldn't have fit here at all, Ralla realized. It smelled of mold and rust.

Appet was heavily winded by the time they reached the top of the stairs, entering an orange and brown waiting room somewhere inside the saucer. Lightly cushioned couches sat wilting under hand-drawn murals depicting farmers at work. The blue "sky" above the farmers' painted heads had been augmented with cartoonish fish, seemingly drawn by children. Everything looked faded and worn.

The guards pushed them on, through a maze of glossy white plastic corridors. An occasional open door revealed windows where Ralla could see out into the X. Glimpses of freedom, except, not. The outside curved shape of the saucer was something of an illusion, she realized, as all the panes of glass were flat, just angled slightly to one another. A central circular stairway led them to the top level. Glancing down the stairwell, she estimated eight floors total for the saucer. At the top of these stairs, Appet flashed her a look of exhaustion, which surprised her since the climb hadn't been that strenuous. A short, dark, and bare hallway led them to what Ralla assumed was the edge of the saucer, judging by the incline of the wall. Another stairway curved up along the wall, bringing them up to the well-lit top floor.

The top level was quite small, but the arc of the saucer allowed a high ceiling for the circular room. The muntins cast crisscrossing shadows of latitude and longitude from the intense lights not too far above. The glass must have been tinted pretty heavily, she realized, as the room itself wasn't overly bright. Near the stairs, two yellow sofas surrounded a low brown table. Sitting on the edge of a long desk on the other side of the room, gnawing on a bright red fruit, was Cern Hennorr. He smiled.

"Thank you, gentlemen," Cern said to the guards. They returned back down the stairway without a word. "Sorry for the stiff greeting," he said through the smile. "Most of my people aren't big fans of yours. Not since you shot up a few of our domes."

"Your domes?"

"Please, sit down. Would you like anything to eat or drink?"

Despite her thirst, Ralla shook her head. Appet requested a glass of water, his brow glistening with sweat. A small wetbar stood adjacent to the stairs they'd ascended. Cern poured three glasses of water from a chrome fixture and carried them carefully to the low table. Appet introduced himself, and they shook hands.

"Sorry for the décor," Cern said, waving his hand over the paper-strewn desk then toward the worn path in the vibrant green pile carpet that now separated them. "The previous occupants were a bit... of the soil, shall we say?" Behind him the view out was superb, Ralla noted, down the curve of the saucer, and out all the way to the end of each arm of the X in the distance.

Ralla hesitated, but drank the water anyway. She wanted to slap the smug smile off Cern's face, but knew that wouldn't be a good way to start their meeting.

"So," he said, leaning back on the couch. "What can I do for you?"

Appet looked at Ralla, and suddenly she was nervous. His glance, in her mind, represented the tens out thousands of people about to starve to death on the *Universalis*. She'd known Cern her whole life. This was going to be fine. He was a good man, always had been.

"We, well... um, well, first let me say thank you for seeing us."

Cern tipped his drink slightly in her direction.

"We, the Council of the *Universalis*, would like to open trade negotiations with you and your," criminal, she thought, "organization."

He stared at her intensely as she spoke, and slowly took a sip of water before answering.

"Now that is interesting. Not quite what I was expecting you to say."

"We feel a mutually beneficial trade agreement–"

"Ha! No."

"What?"

"No. Why would I do that?"

"Pardon?"Appet said, looking every bit as alarmed as Ralla felt.

"What do you have to trade?"

"Well, we have–" Ralla started, before Cern cut her off.

"No you don't. Look, you came here under false pretenses. I know you have nothing to trade and nothing to offer."

"Thousands of lives are at stake," Ralla said, trying to keep her voice neutral.

"I agree, they are. My people. I'm surprised at you, Ralla, I thought you were smarter than this. Charity only works as long as those giving have something to give."

"Are you seriously trying to tell us that among all the domes you run, there isn't *anything* left over?" Appet said, annoyed.

"Mr. Appet, I'm saying that as far as you're concerned, yes. We have a delicate equilibrium, and I'm not about to throw that out a lock by inviting thousands of new mouths to the table."

"But we'll *die!*" Ralla said, finally allowing some emotion into her voice.

"I'm sure you're right," Cern answered casually. "Huh," he said, as if something just occurred to him. "You all probably will die." He became lost in thought.

"Are you seriously going to do nothing? You're going to let all of those people die when you could have done something? Anything? How can you do that?" Ralla asked, incredulous.

Cern took a moment to bring his mind back to the conversation.

"I didn't cause the events that destroyed our former home. I didn't start that war. And I certainly didn't provoke the *Population* into some insane suicide mission."

"Provoke? What's that supposed to mean?" Ralla snapped back. "Is this... is this about *us*?"

Cern laughed, the remaining water in his glass sloshing over the side and soaking into the couch fabric.

"Us? Wow, you are some kind of narcissist, aren't you? I'd hoped this would go different, but I guess not. Look, you are welcome to stay the night. I've had two rooms made up for you. You are welcome to dine with my people; there's a cafeteria on level 4. Judging by the looks on your faces, though, I'm guessing you probably won't. We can talk again in the morning, if you think of anything else you want to discuss. Now, if you'll excuse me," he said, standing up. "I have some work to finish up before dinner."

Neither Appet or Ralla were willing to shake his proffered hand. Cern shrugged and walked over to his desk. He pushed some papers aside and activated an intercom.

"Please escort my guests to their rooms."

A soldier, unarmed this time, rose from the stairs. Cern was already absorbed in some papers on his desk as Ralla and Appet followed the soldier out of the room.

"Well, what do you think?" Appet asked when they were in the hallway below Cern's office.

"Let's try again in the morning. He was always more amiable in the morning."

"Do you really think he'll just cast us out like that?"

"The Cern I knew wouldn't do that. But he seems different, now. The old Cern had never really worked a day in his life. This Cern, he's seems all business."

"Maybe you could... talk... to him later?"

"Are you joking?"

"I suppose."

The adjoining rooms were small and narrow, but comfortably appointed. The low bed stuck out perpendicular to the center of the wall, taking up nearly half the total floor space. The mattress was thin, but the white sheets looked clean. Through the single pane of glass that made up the one "exterior" wall, Ralla could see all the way down the farming arm they'd crossed from their transport sub. A few soldiers seemed to be running up and down the length, probably for exercise, she thought.

The desperation of the moment finally hit her. This had been their one shot, and as of right now, she'd failed. She was glad they were staying the night. She'd at least be able to sleep on the problem, and face it fresh the next morning. Her stomach growled. Maybe the cafeteria was a good idea. She tried the door.

Locked.

_-_--

Pounding and shouting at the door did nothing, as Ralla expected. She tried pounding on the wall separating her room from Appet's. His muffled response told her nothing other than he was there and had heard her. The window was thick glass; actual glass too, it seemed. It rose above her, the top angled into the room compared to the bottom. No matter where she tried to stand, Ralla realized that if she were able to smash it, there was a high likelihood of glass falling on her. Last resort, she decided.

A few deep breaths calmed her down. She'd been trapped before, and in far worse places than this, she thought. She took stock of her situation. There was no immediate danger. Had Cern wanted them killed, there'd be no reason to lock them up. Why he'd captured them at all was the mystery. He knew the *Uni* had nothing to trade for ransom, he'd made that very clear.

Ralla skipped forward a few steps in her mind. *Why* he'd taken them prisoner wasn't important right now. Getting out was. She pressed her face against the window to see what she could see. Her cabin was roughly straight-on with the arm they'd walked down. The soldiers had stopped their exercises and were walking back toward the saucer.

The pilot, Ralla thought. She'd left him to take care of the sub. If Cern had taken her and Appet, it was likely he'd tried to take the sub pilot as well. Part of her hoped the pilot surrendered unharmed. Another part of her hoped he got away to notify the *Uni*. Her escape plans, regardless, would have to assume the sub was no longer there. Pressing her face even harder against the glass, she could just make out a sliver of the next closest arm. This one, too, faced roughly toward the n-pole. Mostly cargo containers, but in the distance... *Yes*, she realized, the arm was noticeably shorter than the farming arm. There was a good chance they'd retrofitted a lock or shipyard down there. The size was right, but it could also just be a loading dock. At the moment, that was her likeliest target, but hopefully she'd find something better.

Cern had said they were all about to have dinner. Maybe they cycled down the lights at night like they did on the *Uni*. Every little bit helped. She began checking the room for something she could fashion as a weapon.

—-¯--

He came to her a few hours after the lights dimmed. Cern shut the door behind him, and Ralla heard the lock click from outside. She knelt on the bed; not as threatening as standing, not as helpless as sitting. One false move, and she'd be on her feet and at his throat.

"I'm sorry I had to lock you in here."

Ralla said nothing.

"I needed to buy a little time."

"Time for what?"

Cern casually moved away from the door. Ralla tensed.

"You said something before that got me thinking. You said that without my help, you'd all die. You're probably right, but as I said, I can't help you. Not without endangering people who've come to trust me. It's a fragile balance right now, Ralla, as I'm sure you can imagine. Or maybe you can't; you did come here for help."

"Get on with it."

"So I thought to myself, once I denied your request, what would you do next? You would go back to the *Uni*, and either then, or shortly thereafter, initiate a mass exodus. Tens of thousands of people, spreading forth seeking asylum wherever they could. You see, as much as it pains me to say it, the *Universalis* is a disease. Right now, it festers, secluded at the n-pole. But once you got back, it would burst, spreading that infection worldwide. You would send your people to find shelter wherever they could, at any dome they could find. The domes just barely hanging on would fail, causing more people to flee, causing to more domes to fail. Don't you see? Cascading failures, pop, pop, pop. The crisis would grow exponentially. Right now, it's contained, quarantined, if you will. But once you got back, you'd start something that would kill us all."

"I will not accept the deaths of my people, *our* people, because you're too unimaginative and selfish to help find a solution."

"Selfish? Ralla, come on. I'm being anything but selfish. If anything, I'm being pragmatic. I'd hoped you'd be the same. I'd hoped you'd come to the same realization."

"You can call it what you want, but what you're doing will mean tens of thousands of people will die, including my friends."

"There is… another option," Cern said. The way he said it made the hairs on the back of Ralla's neck stand on end. She scowled.

"You could… I mean I'd like it if," he stammered as his whole demeanor changed. "I'd like it if you stayed, you could stay here. With your friends too, if you wanted. You'd be safe. Here."

She laughed derisively, and hard, for longer than was really necessary. Cern stepped back as if slapped, then seemed genuinely hurt. He grasped behind him for the handle, seeming to forget it was locked. He'd started to recover by the time he knocked, and when the door opened, he was back to his confident self. Confident-*seeming* self, Ralla realized.

"You didn't have to do that," he said as he stepped out. "Not that it matters. You won't be allowed to leave. The chain reaction you'd cause if you got back to the *Uni* would be the end of everything. In a few weeks this will all sort itself out, and then, well, then I don't care what you do or where you go. Goodbye, Ralla."

The door shut forcefully and locked.

Ralla rose to her feet.

V

"THEY'RE OVERDUE to check in," Dija told Thom. He swung his legs over the side of his bunk, using his good arm for assistance. She eyed his cabin suspiciously.

"By how long?"

"Six hours. They sent a signal they'd arrived, and were supposed to check in after they met with Cern."

"Could the meeting have gone long?"

"Too long to check in?"

"Yeah..."

"I know you're not... I just thought you'd want to know," Dija said.

"Was there a backup plan? Did she at least give some idea how we were supposed to get her *out* if something happened?"

"Honestly, I don't think she thought anything would happen. They used to date, you know."

"Trust me, I know."

"If there's a discussion about going to get her, do you want to be a part of it?"

Thom sat up, and rubbed his hands through his greasy hair. The comment had brought no panic, as he'd expected it would. But it seemed the deep black of intense apathy he'd felt recently had been cracked by this news.

"Are you all right? You know, with the thing?"

"Yes," Thom replied.

"OK, good."

"Also, yes."

Dija smiled.

"Don't get all smiley yet. As proof of how much use I'll be, I need you to help find my cane."

———

Ralla didn't want to wait, but she knew there was no way she'd be able to break open the door. Some heavy prodding of the window suggested it would require serious effort to break as well. Her plan, annoyingly meager, consisted of waiting for someone to return, or waiting for an hour or so, and complain about needing the bathroom. Waiting, or waiting; Ralla liked neither option but knew, for the latter option at least, it was difficult to deny someone's use of a toilet. That was a pretty universal need. There had to be a guard outside the door, and if he or she opened it, for whatever reason, she'd be on them.

Ralla also figured there was little reason to keep her alive now, so any return had to be considered a mortal threat. Kneeling on the floor, just outside of the swing radius of the door, Ralla tried tapping on the wall shared with Appet's room. Quietly at first, then a little bit louder with each series of taps. Finally, she got a response: a series of taps matching her own. He was still alive, at least. It hadn't gotten any darker in the dome since the initial dimming a few hours earlier. It was a lot brighter than night on the *Uni*, however.

Something told her it was time. Whether she was tired of waiting, or tired of going through endless sequences of ill-fated future events, she wasn't sure. Either way, the waiting was over. She knocked the door as gently as she could.

"Excuse me, I need to use the bathroom." No response. She tried again. "I need to use the bathroom, please."

The door clicked. The classics never die, she thought. The rifle barrel stuck into the room first, sweeping with the door until it found her. The soldier looked about her age, with a day's worth of stubble and a week's worth of dirty hair. His eyes didn't waver. A pro, she thought. He stepped back into the hallway, the gun still pointed at her. He removed one hand from the rifle and motioned for her to spin around. She did, with arms raised.

The hallway was empty and made of the same shiny white plastic she'd seen everywhere else. He indicated for her to head down the hallway, in a direction she hadn't gone before. It curved to the left, limiting her view. They passed white plastic doors, nearly invisible, their only indication a thin black seam. By her count, they had passed four doors after Appet's, probably other small cabins like her own.

"Left," the soldier said abruptly.

The bathroom was disappointingly lacking any reasonable escape route: Tiny vents, no other doors. Just the single toilet and a showerhead that turned the whole room into a shower. The shiny metal fixtures reflected the harsh light like bathrooms everywhere. Ralla realized, ironically, that she actually had to go to the bathroom.

So relieved, but no less free, they started back toward her room. Knowing there was no way she was getting locked back in her room, Ralla tried a different tact. She faltered for a half-step, bringing the guard closer. Pretending to trip, Ralla dropped to all fours. The soldier, though watching her, was midstep and wavered as he tried his best not to trip on her. Instantly, Ralla spun to her back and kicked upwards with all her strength. Her shin didn't connect where she'd wanted it to, but the guard was caught off balance, which was almost as good. Like a trained professional, he didn't drop the gun. Sliding sideways down the corridor wall, he landed hard on his gun arm. Ralla had already rolled to her feet and jumped on the rifle, crushing the soldier's hand underneath.

Not wanting to risk any further trouble, she kicked him in the chin before removing his sidearm from its perfectly exposed holster. Point, safety click, grin...

"I'm going to step off your hand. Raise your rifle and I'll kill you. This is not the first time I've held a gun. Nod if you understand."

The solider nodded. Ralla stepped off the rifle. The soldier made a show of removing his finger from the trigger, before slowly sliding his hand out. She motioned for him to get up and to continue back toward her room. She reached down and slung the rifle over her shoulder after he passed.

_—_-_-_

The look on Appet's face was not what she expected. There was something almost debilitating seeing a man of his age gripped with such fear. He trembled slightly.

"What have you done? How did you get those?"

"A guard. He's in my room."

"Is he..."

"Dreadfully embarrassed, yes. Now, we need to get out of here. Any ideas?"

"Out of here? I don't... how could we possibly?"

"We can't stay here."

Appet looked around the room like there was something he hadn't seen that could help him.

"Maybe if we reason with him. Apologize, and see if he'll let us be on our way."

"It's not like that. He told me he has no intention of letting us go back to the *Universalis*. Ever." Ralla explained what had happened in her room earlier. Appet nodded slowly as he absorbed the information.

"I guess I'm with you. Do you think we can we make it back to our sub?" he asked.

"We have to assume our sub is gone or captured," she said, peeking into the hall. It was still clear. "Once you and I missed our check-in with the pilot, he was supposed to signal the *Uni*. Somehow I doubt this place would be as quiet as it is if he'd been able to do that." She turned back to see Appet still nodding slowly in agreement, seemingly going over options in his mind. Ralla checked the charge on the pistol, then the rifle. "I also think it would be risky to check. We'd be exposed running through those fields."

"They must have other transportation. Or maybe we call the *Uni* for help. Or at least warn them."

"Not a lot of people on the *Uni* in much shape to help us at the moment. We're on our own," Ralla said.

"What's your plan?"

"The top of the saucer legs are, what do you think, two levels below us?"

"I suppose."

"That's our first step. Then we can decide which leg to try, and then which arm of the station. No need getting ahead of ourselves." Ralla stuck her head out into the hallway, and immediately pulled it back in. "Too late."

"Throw your weapons into the hallway, and you will not be hurt," a voice shouted.

"How did they find out so soon?" Appet asked.

"It doesn't matter. Here," she said, pushing the pistol into his hands. "I don't doubt they're going to try to kill us. If you have any doubts, say so now."

Ralla watched a change come over Appet's face. He had always given off a fatherly vibe, kind, if occasionally stern. A deep frown emerged, his bushy brow furrowed.

"No, no doubts."

"Ever fired one of those before?"

"Yes."

"At someone?"

"No."

"Well, just point it in their direction and they'll either duck or they won't."

Ralla stuck her head out of the doorway to look down the hallway toward the stairs. As she expected, two helmets peeked out, one high, one low, both paired with rifle barrels. No sooner had she pulled her head back in then they began to fire.

The noise was deafening. Shards of plastic from the door and frame splintered into the small room. Ralla staggered backwards, firing blindly into the hallway. The rifle had a slow rate of fire, but from the sound and recoil, fired sizeable ammunition. Dinner-plate-sized craters in the wall opposite the room were impressive in size, if not importance.

"Now what?" Appet yelled over the din.

"Cover the door!" she yelled back. They switched positions, Ralla stepping up on the bed, Appet moving cautiously toward the wall. One round from her rifle was all it took to shatter the floor-to-ceiling window. Glass rained down, but no sizeable pieces hit either of them.

The glass crunched under her feet. She could tell by feel but not sound. Standing in the frame, Ralla quickly took in the curve and slope of the saucer, the arches of the dome. It was going to be a long run to the dockyard, if that's what it was. With a clear view down that arm, beyond a curved sea of glass reflections, Ralla saw cargo containers packed in tight from just beyond the edge of the saucer all the way to the far wall. Long and boxy, the containers, some stacked four or five high, created narrow passageways. Perfect for an ambush. This wasn't going to happen, she realized. They'd have minutes, at best, before the whole facility was alerted to their escape, if they weren't already. Ralla turned back around, determined at least to get Appet out of this room. He crouched awkwardly by the bed, firing off shot after shot, closing his eyes and flinching with every trigger pull.

"Come on!" she yelled. "COME ON!"

He looked quickly in her direction, saw her motion for him to get moving, then stood, firing a few more rounds at the door, hitting the frame, wall, and ceiling.

"We're going to have to run, are you up for it?"

He peeked around her to the outside of the saucer, then down the length of the arm. The resolve disappeared, replaced with sadness.

"No," he said, shaking his head.

Ralla's brain jumped rapidly from idea to idea. Maybe they could barricade the door, give them time to think. Maybe they could fight their way past these guards and get to another level. Maybe they should...

"Go," he said. She barely heard him and started to shake her head. He looked so sad, all she wanted to do was hug him. It was her fault he was here. This had been her terrible idea, another of many. She was not going to let him die. Not here.

"No! I have to get you back to my mother!"

Appet cocked his head to the side, unsure of what he heard.

"Ralla, I'm not going to make that."

"You're going to try," she shouted back, pulling him toward the remains of the window.

—⁻--

Ralla leapt out the window and slid perilously down the side of the saucer before catching her footing. Appet wobbled as he slid, flailing. She caught his right arm with hers, wincing as he hit her partially bandaged hand. Somehow she kept her balance without losing the rifle slung over her other shoulder. They set off at a jog across the slippery angled surface. Slightly ahead and down slope lay the nearest leg support. Something buzzed past her ear. Dropping to one knee, she spun and fired the rifle. The bullets shattered the glass where they hit, shards and dust exploding outwards, while the rest of the panes fell inwards. In a diagonal between her and Appet's room, a line of gaping holes in the saucer now appeared.

She didn't bother to see if she hit anyone. Running on the glass surface was awkward; every few steps one of their feet would slip out, and they'd grab on to each other or drop to a knee and grab one of the nearest muntins for stability. The leg arched out from the saucer like a shoulder, then down to meet the junction of the two arms of the X. The leg blocked their path, so she diverted them up slope so she could see around it. She could see all the way down the station, and in the wall at the end, past all the stacks of containers, was a lock big enough for cargo. Next to it was a smaller, person-sized lock. There had to be some sort of dockyard on the other side, she thought, trying to convince herself. Anything was better than here. There was no clear way down, so they climbed up the top of the leg.

Layers of dust and dirt artificially darkened its aging white paint. More gunshots. Ralla looked quickly back the way they'd come, and saw four solders scrambling across the saucer's surface, while two more fired at her from one of her newly made openings.

Half sliding, half running, Ralla and Appet made their way down the leg, jumping to the top of a rusting shipping container. Her view now close to ground level, she saw the difficulty of the situation. If they jumped down to the floor, they'd be trapped in a labyrinthine maze of narrow corridors that may, or may not, lead to the lock at the far end of the arm. But if they stayed on the shipping containers, they'd be easy targets for the soldiers. The containers, stacked at different levels, created a peaking and random ridgeline all the way to the back wall. In her head, she pictured it from her viewpoint on the saucer a moment before. Plenty of places hidden from direct line of sight. She looked at Appet; he was sweating profusely, his skin taking on an eerie pallor. She heard shouts above her as the soldiers reached the top of the leg. *Move.*

Jumping over from their shipping container, Ralla landed solidly on the next. She motioned for Appet to follow, which he did, landing shakily next to her. The distance wasn't far between the containers, little more than a big step, so they did the same with the next and the next. Tall, narrow containers were their next obstacle, but were stacked far enough apart to squeeze between them.

Ralla allowed herself a look back, and as she'd imagined, she couldn't see the saucer. Appet leaned against the container, and she let him catch what breath he could as she looked around. The containers created a multicolored, corrugated façade above and around them, limiting her view of the rest of the dome, but fortunately also the dome's view of them. She mapped out a path for what she could see, and turned back to check on Appet. He made no indication he wanted to give up, but didn't seem interested in continuing. She squeezed his arm, then jumped across to the next container, motioning for him to follow. He did, and they jogged across the tops of more containers. She could hear the gunfire, so she zigzagged, but if the shots were getting close, she hadn't noticed. Ralla could hear shouts from ahead now. Word had gotten out, or they'd heard the gunshots; either way, they were surrounded. At the moment, though, none of the soldiers ahead had left ground level. Ralla looked over the edge; they were two containers above ground. A fall wouldn't kill them, but they'd almost certainly break something.

More long containers, this time stacked vertically and close. Ralla indicated for Appet to head toward the space between the containers and the metalwork superstructure of the dome. As they entered this narrow corridor, she felt the glass radiating the cold from outside. The gap and stacks shadowed them from the dome's main lighting. The heavy girders supporting the dome structure crowded them in like menacing arms of steel. Gripping a beam to get around it, she realized that not only were they massive, but also I-shaped. She looked up the curve of one, arching upward to the top of the dome, then at Appet.

"Ralla..." he said, wheezing. At first she thought he was about to try to get her to go on without him, but when she saw his face, she realized that wasn't it. "I... I don't want to die here." Once again, seeing him so fearful gripped a deep part of her psyche. The situation seemed more terrifying because he was afraid.

"Our path ahead is blocked by soldiers, the path back is blocked by soldiers. We can't stay here. We need to go up into the superstructure. The beam here has ridges on the inside, like steps, and at the top is a maintenance crawlspace. Look. That buys us some time, and there should be a way into the dock from above." Ralla hoped the last part didn't sound like too much of an assumption, but she couldn't leave him here.

Appet looked up the arc of the beam and shook his head, defeat in his eyes. Ralla grabbed his tunic and pushed him toward the girder. "Climb."

Their climb was slow, but steady. More importantly, unseen. Ralla struggled with keeping the rifle, slung across her back, from clanging into the metal. The curve of the girder was steep where they'd started, but had leveled off as they ascended. By the time they reached the long spine superstructure that ran the length of the arm, it was nearly flat. All the lights hung from this long spinal support, their glare hiding Ralla and Appet from view completely.

They had a perfect view of the search below. They watched as the two groups of soldiers fanned out to cover all the alleys between the containers. The height made Ralla dizzy, so she stopped looking down. Appet didn't seem to be enjoying the view either.

The spine girder proved much larger than it had seemed from below, with a small, integrated walkway/crawlspace. Ralla insisted on going first, and even though they both had to crouch, they could still walk. The sides were frightfully open and lacking any safety railings, but it offered her and Appet passage down the rest of the arm toward the end wall.

Ralla stared forcefully at end of the walkway, not wanting to look down during their careful walk along the spine. The end wall had clearly been built after the rest of the dome. Where it bisected the spine girder some sloppy-looking welds inspired no confidence. There was a small hatch at the end of the walkway, sporting the same patchwork welds. She knelt before it and gave the handle a tug. It slid open to reveal the smallest lock she'd ever seen. The hatch on the opposite side was half transparent, revealing an even narrower crawlspace beyond. She turned back to Appet, who had gone even paler than she thought was possible.

"I can't do small places like that."

"It's not much worse than a small sub."

"I don't do those either, and this is far worse. Ralla, I'm not even sure I can fit in there."

Ralla took a second look at the lock, not having considered this. Most of the time her world involved her not being able to reach something, or a sub's controls being too far from the seat. She'd never given much thought to *not* being able to fit somewhere. She peered over the edge of the walkway. The soldiers below had converged on where she and Appet had started their climb. It was only a matter of time now.

"You're going to have to try."

"You don't even know if that goes anywhere."

"It has to go somewhere," she said, starting to crawl through the opening. "We can't stay here. If this doesn't work, we'll try something else." She tried to sound confident, but she wasn't sure she was convincing herself either. She was keenly aware that if the crawlspace dead-ended, they wouldn't have anywhere else to go. Appet reluctantly joined her, their shoulders rubbing against each other and against the sides of the lock. With her foot, she managed to close the hatch. The lock cycled, and their ears popped with a noticeable increase in air pressure. The hatch before them opened. Just outside the lock, hooks along the walls held well-used tools, lengths of wire, and rubberized tape in thin but tall spools. Ahead, the crawlspace narrowed and angled up toward the top of the dome. Ralla motioned for Appet to go first; they'd have to go single file. After he had cleared the small area outside the lock, she took the largest spanner she could see and braced it inside the frame of the hatch, preventing it from closing. With any luck, she thought, the lock's safeties would prevent the inner door from opening, at least temporarily slowing down their pursuers.

Ralla pushed the rifle in front of her and followed after Appet. Small lights in the floor pointed the way, and as they rose, the passage ceiling became the dome itself. The glow from the surface trickled through the ocean, lighting the crawlspace with shimmering, diffused sunlight. Ralla started to shiver, the dome surface absorbing all the heat they had and freeing it into the water beyond. Ralla became very aware of the weight of the sea above her. They passed small openings, staggered along the crawlspace. An arm's length away, lights hung from support girders. The cutouts, as that's what they seemed to be, seemed just large enough to allow maintenance access to the lighting grid, but small enough that the crew wouldn't fall to the dock floor below.

Ralla stuck her head out one of the openings. The wall opposite the one they'd just crawled through was glass, with panels of similar size to the central saucer, giving a clear view of the sea beyond. Below her, two long moon pools took up most of the space in the dock area, each with a handful of dockworkers loading cargo onto floating sleds. Attached to the sleds, though, were tug subs, all looking ready for launch. If they could get to them...

Appet called her name, his voice higher in pitch, and wavering. She pulled her head back in to see his feet moving backward towards her. He pressed himself against the left wall and pressed his head against the other side so he could see her in the space between his body and the wall.

"The hatch. The hatch...it won't open."

"Is it sealed?"

"No, there's something wedged against it on the other side."

"Well, that's funny."

"Why is that funny? That's not funny."

"No, I mean... forget it. Hold on a second." Ralla's mind raced. They could go back the way they came, but there was nothing that way. "Could you see in?"

"Yes. It was a full-sized lock, with two hatches on the side walls and another on in the ceiling."

She leaned through the cutout again. As she suspected, metal access stairs ran along the top of the glass on the end wall to a lock at the end of their crawlspace. It wasn't flashy, partially blending in with the rest of the structure, like all good maintenance gangways did. She brought her head back in and once again was disturbed by the look of fear on Appet's face. He was sweating profusely.

"I think I can fit out."

"What?"

"I think I can squeeze out, climb down, and let you out from the other side."

Appet looked back up the passage, as if he could verify what she was saying.

"I don't think we should split up," he said nervously.

"It's fine, I can do this."

"It's not you I'm worried about."

Ralla looked at the cutout. It would be a tight fit, but it seemed possible. From there all she had to do was climb down the girder and up the stairs. Basically, the reverse of what they'd done to get up here. That was all easy, of course. Doing it unseen, on the other hand...

"I'm not going to leave you," she said.

"Right. I don't want to split up."

"But for both of us to get out of here, we have to get out of this passage."

"I knew we shouldn't have gotten in here."

"There are subs waiting below. From the bottom of the stairs to the closest sub is nothing. You could practically jump from one to the other." A slight exaggeration, they both knew. Appet looked back and forth between the far hatch, Ralla, and the way they'd come.

"I never should have come. I should have stayed with Ioa. I should have stayed home."

"We're almost out of this."

"Don't leave me here."

"I'm not leaving you."

"I don't want to die in here."

"It will be all right," Ralla said again, touching his ankle gently. She looked through the cutout again. They were about even with the girder closest to the far outside wall. This was the best chance they had. She knew it. "Here's what I want you to do. I'm going to climb out. Once I'm there, I want you to move where I am, and hand me my rifle."

"I don't..."

"Appet, this is what I need you to do. Can you do it?"

"Yes, I think so."

Ralla twisted the best she could and stuck her arm through the opening. The I-beam girder was just to the side, so she gripped the lower flat portion and slowly pulled her torso out. One glance down to the floor below was enough. Even if she was above one of the pools, it was still high enough the fall would probably kill her. She felt the heat from the half-domed lights, even though they hung from the I-beam itself. The cutout scraped along her sides, but she fit. Bracing herself on her hands and left knee, she brought her right leg out onto the beam. And like that, she was out. Appet stared at her from the passage, trapped and terrified. He shakily handed the rifle out to her, which she slung over her back.

Ralla gave him a nod she hoped would be reassuring, then started down the beam, watching the dockworkers below. They loaded cargo into the sleds, unaware of her presence. As she neared the floor, she spun carefully around so she was feet first, then slid down the steep part to the floor. There was a gap, maybe twenty or thirty paces, between where she was and the stairs. Ten dockworkers unloaded the sled farthest from her. Ralla waited until they all seemed preoccupied, and made a dash for the stairs.

Wobbling under her feet, the metal stairs seemed far less safe than she expected, but then she was bounding up them two at a time. As she neared the top, she realized she was in the safety of shadow, with the harsh dock lights hanging below where she was now. The hatch opened easily, and she shut it behind her. She looked out the window of the lock and saw no one following her. So far, so good.

The lock itself was octagonal, with another door opposite her, presumably connecting to stairs just like those she'd come up. Above her, a hatch with a dropdown ladder implied access to the roof of the dome for exterior maintenance. The small hatch to her left continued the add-on look of the walkway and crawlspace, with even more sloppy welds and here, mismatched paint. A broken mop handle leaned against it. She tossed it aside easily and gave the hatch's handle a solid tug.

Nothing.

She pulled at it again. In the darkness of the porthole, she could see Appet crawling toward her. Ralla looked around frantically for some sort of override. Along the frame of the hatch, there were a series of error lights. One was lit, she leaned closer to read it: "Opposite hatch ajar." Her heart sank from her chest. She'd blocked the other hatch open, and now this one wouldn't release. This was her fault. She pounded at the handle with the butt of her rifle. The sound reverberated around the little chamber, causing her ears to ring. This didn't make any *sense*. There was *no reason* for this not to open. It was all the same *pressure*. She recovered as Appet pressed his face against the porthole.

"You have to go back and close the other hatch!"

"What?"

"The hatch. The hatch we came through. It's open. You have to close it."

"What?"

Appet turned around suddenly to look back down the passage. For a moment Ralla had hope he'd figured out what she'd said. One look at his face when he turned back revealed how wrong she was.

"Ralla, you have to get me out. I can hear people coming."

"I can't!" she cried.

"Ralla, open the hatch. Please open the hatch."

As Appet turned away again, Ralla swung at the handle with the rifle. The sound echoed viciously. She looked back into the porthole. Appet looked back at her, his face pleading, not understanding why she hadn't opened the hatch.

His body shook as the bullets riddled his body.

Ralla screamed, in horror and in anger. She placed the rifle against her shoulder, aimed at the porthole, and fired into the passage above Appet's lifeless corpse. The porthole shattered, and she could feel herself screaming, but couldn't hear either over the gunfire. She dropped to her knees as the soldiers at the far end of the passage returned fire, showering her with metal and composite shrapnel from the lock behind her.

"Get up. Get up. Get UP!" Ralla shouted at herself. She rolled sideways and onto her feet, the emotional part of her brain sealing itself off. The rifle led the way out the hatch and down the stairs. The dockworkers had heard the commotion, but weren't sure where it had come from. Ralla fired at them from the stairs, spooking them back toward the station proper.

As they tried to leave through the locks in the far wall, soldiers entered. Hiding behind a stack of containers, Ralla checked her clip: only a few rounds left. She could see the soldiers advancing, using stacked palettes as cover. All she had was open floor between her and the nearest sub, rocking gently in the pool.

She didn't bother thinking about her plan any further. She aimed above the heads of the advancing soldiers and fired a single round into the dome's ceiling.

The round passed through the glass easily, puncturing it and spreading cracks outwards. The alarm was deafening, even louder than the gunfire in the lock. Ralla stumbled, falling to her knees and grabbing her ears. She could feel the air currents change, as atmosphere vented into the sea above. She twisted around to see the soldiers fleeing toward the locks. Suddenly, freezing water soaked her clothes, the pool having surged over the edge. Ralla splashed her way to the tug, now bobbing vigorously as the water rushed into the dome, impeded less and less by pressure.

Ralla sealed the tug's hatch behind her, the alarm still audible through the hull. It was a tiny vehicle: a one-person cockpit in the front and a long bench in back that likely doubled as a bed for long hauls. She strapped into the chair and surveyed the console. It had been nearly a decade since she'd gone through the mandatory sub operation course in school. She was pretty confident that even what she'd forgotten wouldn't have helped her here. The buttons, through years of use, all lacked labeling. The main display was cracked, but still working. It showed full engine power was available. Through the viewscreen, she saw the sub was starting to bump against the sides of what had been the moon pool.

Pushing the yoke down, and the throttle up, the little craft dove downwards into the water, and out into the sea.

VI

"WE HAVE TO GO get them!" Dija pleaded before the Council. Thom, having limped up the stairs to the roof of Camp 1, sat off to the side, rubbing his injured leg.

"I agree," Ioa said, the stress audible in her voice. "We have an obligation to get them. They would have checked in by now. If we hear from them while the rescue party is en route, all they have to do is turn back. But we *have* to do something. Thom, how long will it take to get there?"

"If we take the *Runner*? Half a day. But that's not the problem."

"What's the problem?" a Council member whom Thom didn't know asked.

"Who's going to go inside?" he asked, tapping his cane on the deck. The question stopped all of them for a moment. Even Ioa opened and closed her mouth a few times in response.

"We can get some people together," Ioa said finally. "There have to be weapons somewhere. What about the Navy guys running the dock upstairs?"

"Weapons or not, throwing untrained men, or men not trained for combat like those upstairs, is irresponsible. They'll be killed. Trust me, I know."

"You want to do nothing?"

"Oh, I *want* to do something. I'm just not *able* to do something. I think we should definitely go, offer what assistance we can, but when it comes down to it, she's going to have to get them out of whatever trouble they're in. Fortunately, in my experience, Ralla Gattley doesn't need much rescuing.

Ralla was in trouble. Water pooled at her feet and the controls were sluggish. After finding the button to release the sleds, she'd made fast progress away from the facility. A patrol had jumped her, and no matter how much speed she tried to put on, they kept with her. A torpedo detonating near the hull had knocked out two of the six engine pods, and torqued the hull just enough to split a seam in the side, and killed the integrity of the hatch seal. The little tug might have been sturdy, but it hadn't been built for combat.

Alarms growled and screamed. Ralla was certain every light on the console was either lit, or flashing. Maybe Thom could have made sense of this, she realized morosely. Another explosion knocked her around, straining the seat's harness. It occurred to her they must be using improvised equipment, just as the *Uni* had done with Thom's *Sealine Runner*. That was the only explanation she could imagine as to why she wasn't an imploded chunk of debris sinking toward the seafloor.

Except, she *was* sinking toward the seafloor. The water lapping around her knees, and the missing air it represented, saw to that. She had the remaining engines at maximum throttle, and more than half their power went to just maintaining depth. That was only going to get worse. The more buoyancy she lost, the harder it would be to stay at level. The sub would get less and less buoyant, she'd have to go slower and slower as she diverted power upwards instead of forwards. Then she'd just hover.

Hover until the circling subs finished her off, or the cabin filled with water.

Sensors indicated a layer just above her. Thom had used the layers to evade subs dozens of times. With little else left to try, as her ailing sub strained against its increasing inability to float, Ralla pulled back on the yoke, tipping the bow lazily upwards. The water in the cabin rushed backwards, dropping the level in the cockpit to her ankles, but submerging half of the aft cabin. Two more explosions shook the craft, this time, from below her. The layer was invisible to her eyes, but its effects became apparent on sensors as she passed through it. For a moment, the enemy subs disappeared. As she expected, but feared nonetheless, the two attacking subs followed her through the layer. Their menacing blips on the cracked sensor screen trailed a short distance behind her.

"It was worth a shot," she said aloud in the cabin. The sub continued its upward trajectory, getting slower with every tick of the depth gauge. Ralla looked back at the sensor screen. The subs still pursued her, but had fallen back. In fact, as she watched, they let their distance increase even as her own pace decreased.

They think I'm dead, or trying to figure out what I'm doing, she realized. With a momentary respite from the attack, she tried to envision what a trained sub pilot would assume about her actions. She'd weaved around a bit at the start, then after the big explosion, she'd done nothing but travel in a slower and slower straight line. Then this bizarre slow ascent towards the surface. If she'd been knocked unconscious, or killed, this is pretty much how the sub would react without a pilot. Ralla released her grip from the controls carefully. Whether that was what they were thinking or not, there was no need to change her actions. Not that she *could* change anything.

The enemy subs stopped abruptly. Through the viewscreen Ralla could see the shimmer of the surface and smiled.

"I know something you don't know," she said bitterly at the sensor screen. Her pace had slowed so much, it was hard to determine if she was still moving at all. She risked diverting more power upwards. The depth gauge clicked slightly shallower. The water crept around the edges of the seat, still pouring in from the cracked hatch seal. Ralla released the safety harness, and leaned forward, away from the water. *Come on*, she said in her head at the depth gauge. She tried to push the throttle and trim further, but found both at their max. The alarms and rushing water put her back to a different place, trapped in an engine room. She pushed off the seat and pounded on the viewscreen.

"COME ON!" she screamed. The surface was so close, she could see the underside of the waves, feel their force rock the little sub in a tantalizing rhythm. The gauge hadn't moved in minutes, but it hadn't fallen yet either. Each swell turned the sub slightly, sloshing the water around. She knew what to do.

Ralla waited, hand on the yoke and throttle, until she decided she had it right. The subs below, if they were still there, wouldn't miss this one. At the right moment, she pushed the yoke forward. All the water in the cabin rushed forward in a deluge, knocking Ralla into the viewscreen. The stern rose up, and got caught by a swell, pushing it forward. With a mouth and nose full of brackish, oily water, Ralla pulled back on the yoke and pushed the trim on the throttle to full forward thrust.

The wave held the little sub in a brief, loving embrace, before releasing it into the trough behind. Water beaded off the viewscreen revealing a black sky the likes of which Ralla had never seen.

The next wave washed over the hull, but she had done it. The tug was on the surface. Water had stopped rushing in from the hatch, and she hoped enough of the hull was in the air that some water would start to drain out.

In the air. Ralla sloshed through the waist-high water and popped the hatch. The sky was dark, yet lit by countless tiny specks of light. She remembered reading something about this in a science class in school, but had retained none of it. Another wave surged past the sub, but only a splash made it inside. Ralla pulled herself onto the roof of the submarine, and braced herself on the undulating hull.

Countless emotions fought for attention: jubilation at being alive; awe at the near infinite distances of rolling dark waves around her;

awe mixed with terror at the actual infinite bowl of lights above her; triumph at her success at escaping her captors; fierce sadness at Appet's death. She lifted her head up and screamed at the sky in furious victory.

The sub rode a little higher with each passing wave, as tiny waterfalls cascaded out of unseen cracks in the hull. The air was surprisingly warm. Quite a change from the air around the n-pole, she remembered, so far away in time and distance. So Ralla stayed on the roof of the sub instead of trying to find a dry space in a flooded cabin. After locking the hatch open and dangling one leg inside for safety, she lay back. The adrenaline dissolved in her body, leaving behind introspection, solitude, and depression. Her brain devised patterns in the beauty of the lights above. The water lapped against the tug's hull. A hazy mixture of white and blue, too far away and bright to be clouds, stretched nearly from horizon to horizon.

It was the most beautiful thing Ralla had ever seen, and became hard to see through the tears.

—-—

"The surface science team just radioed this down," the comm officer said from the door of Dija's room.

"The science what? What?" Dija said, struggling to wake.

"They said they've received a signal from Ralla Gattley. She's requesting assistance."

Her brain still not fully around the idea, Dija nonetheless was awake instantly.

—-—

Thom awoke with the first knock, the pulse of panic soaking through him, a familiar friend. No good news came in the middle of the night.

"Yeah," he said to a cabin barely lit by darkened picosuns dimmed further by the dirty towel hung over the porthole. The door opened, revealing the petite frame of Dija, silhouetted by the slightly brighter hallway lights. "What happened?" he asked, dreading the answer. Dija entered and slapped blindly against the wall, searching for the light switch.

"No, don't turn on the—"

The overhead light blazed on, causing Thom and Dija to squint in response.

"She's alive. She's on the surface. The science team picked up her transmission. Her transport is damaged; she needs someone to pick her up."

Thom felt a deep relief, though he wasn't sure if it was from Ralla being all right, or that all he'd have to do is pick her up. Thom tried to make sense of the information Dija had just given him.

"So she's floating on the surface… and can't submerge to send a signal to us directly?"

"I think so."

"The *Runner* has a hatch on the top deck, that should work."

"Can I come?"

"Di, I *need* you to. I can barely walk," Thom said, swinging his legs around the side of the bed.

"Cane?"

"Pants."

———

The slow rocking of the tug had caused her to throw up twice since she got the comm working. Out in the fresh air, with a brightening sky to look at, her nausea abated.

Her pain did not. She couldn't stop seeing Appet, trapped and afraid, begging her to let him out of the crawlspace. He had died thinking she had trapped him there. That she had let him down. And she had. The thought made her want to cry out in agony. So she did. She *had* trapped him there. She had killed this kind old man who had been her friend.

Ioa. She'd have to tell Ioa. She'd have to relive it all again. Ralla lay down on the roof of the sub, and wanted to sink through it, down into the sea.

Instead, she slowly rolled with the sub, which rolled slowly with the waves. By chance, she was looking in the direction of the light and saw the sun the moment it appeared on the horizon. She just stared at the light. It was unlike "sunrise" on the *Uni*. The picosuns ramped up their intensity with precision and without drama. This, what she figured was the first real sunrise anyone, or any *thing*, had seen in decades, appeared as a slow-motion explosion. Colors she didn't think possible shifted, blended, brightened and disappeared, all in the briefest of moments. The sun hurt her eyes as it rose higher, yet she couldn't look away. Soon, she felt its power on her skin, a welcoming warmth.

By the time it reached overhead, she'd had enough of it and its heat. Sweat dripped from everywhere, and she knew without fresh water to drink, that was a bad thing. The tug lacked any useful supplies, so she lay down in the cabin, the water having almost completely drained during the night. The wet bench and watery floor cooled her off as the air became hot and humid.

She knew they were coming; that's what made it bearable, but how had people done this? It was too hot during the day here, too cold up by the pole. From what she'd heard, it was going to get even colder up there in a few weeks. Impossibly cold. There was logic, an order to submarine living; a controlled, perfectly temperate environment. She didn't fear being on the surface, though staring out at the terrifyingly distant horizon, she could understand why others did. After less than a day, she didn't want to live here either. Most, maybe all, of the people below had been taught since birth to fear the surface. A deep-rooted fear told them that to approach the surface meant a certain, and painful, death. At some point in the near future, the Council would have to suggest that some people move to the surface. The mere suggestion would lead to more riots, of that Ralla was sure.

Even if she, the Council, even Koin told them the surface was safe, there would be many who still wouldn't believe them. Wouldn't take

274 | GEOFFREY MORRISON

the chance that some unseen toxin or radiation would kill them and their family.

Even those who did believe, what of them? Only a small minority could fit on the few shuttles, transports, and emergency pods they had left. Even in shifts, how would they get off the ship? Where would they live if they did? Cern had been right, she just hadn't wanted to admit it to herself. Koin seemed confident they could create some sort of habitat on the surface, but what kind of life would that be? Some would choose death below to death above, on a freezing, horrifying, dark surface.

She couldn't blame them.

—˙--

The sun was setting when she heard a new noise outside the sub. The hot afternoon had left her parched and tired, despite falling asleep several times. Poking her head out the hatch, she saw the long arched back of a ship that could only be the *Sealine Runner*, and with it she felt a palpable sense of relief. A hatch on the upper deck, well above the waterline, opened, revealing the unmistakable form of Dija. They waved excitedly at each other.

She knew without looking Thom was in the cockpit. Of course he'd come for her, injured or not. Ralla couldn't deny a feeling of love underneath that feeling of certainty. The *Runner* maneuvered closer to her tug, and as their hulls scraped, Ralla jumped. Her shoes found no purchase on the wet, curved surface. She fell flat, and slid down into the water between the slowly separating submarines. The sea was warm, warmer than she'd ever felt seawater before. Bobbing there, looking up at a concerned Dija, Ralla realized the tug was probably drifting back toward her. She twisted around in the water to see it looming there, the setting sun giving it a bright halo. The waves were pulling it farther away. She looked back up as Dija secured a rope to a cleat inside the door. She tossed it out, the knotted brown braid landing in the water nearby.

Checking once again to make sure the tug wasn't an issue, Ralla waved for Dija to join her in the water. It didn't take much convincing.

She shouted something back into the cabin Ralla couldn't hear, then leapt from the door, splashing spectacularly, nearly on top of Ralla.

"It's so warm!" Dija said after resurfacing. Her wet hair matted against her face.

"Isn't it?"

"I've always wanted to swim on the surface. That's one thing I *really* couldn't do when we were at the pole."

"I bet not!" Ralla said with a smile. Dija's eyes went up toward the door, and Ralla's followed. She was glad to see Thom there, with his amused smile. She and Dija shouted for him to join them, and for a moment, it looked like he would. His eyes caught on the rope, and he shook his head.

"His leg hurts really bad," Dija said, as an explanation.

"I know. Another time," she replied. The words were said with levity, but the weight of them increased as she realized the scope of what was to come. Suddenly, being in the water felt ridiculous.

"What?" Dija asked.

"We should get going."

"OK."

Dija scrambled up the side and disappeared into the hatch. Ralla, realizing how much the day had taken out of her, found the climb strenuous. Thom offered a hand as she reached the hatch, but she didn't take it, preferring not to put any strain on his broken body. Instead, as she rose to her feet in the lavish cabin, she hugged him, transferring seawater from her clothes to his. Something about how he didn't pull away or even flinch made her want to hug him more.

"Are you..." he whispered in her ear. With her head planted against his chest, she could feel his voice.

"Are you?"

"Walking hurts. Also, sitting, lying down, standing," he answered. She hugged him tighter. "And hugging. Definitely hugging." Neither let go. "Appet?"

Ralla felt the joy of the moment drain out of her, seeing Appet's pleading face so clearly. Her arms went slack, but Thom didn't let go. He didn't seem to need a further explanation.

"Wow," they heard Dija say quietly. Thom and Ralla looked over at Dija, who looked past them out the hatch. The sun was nearly at the horizon, casting even more beautiful colors than it had that morning.

"That's incredible," Thom muttered reverently. Ralla wrapped her arms back around Thom. After a moment, Ralla motioned with her head for Dija to join them. Ralla wrapped an arm around Dija, who did the same to her. There, in the open hatch, all three stared out and watched the sun descend in silence.

Slowly at first, then seeming to pick up speed, the deep orange disc dropped below the horizon, leaving an ever-darkening multicolored sky.

VI

"WE HAVE TO EVACUATE the ship," Ralla said flatly, the other conversations among the Council members ceasing immediately. She, Dija, and Thom had been back for less than an hour. Just long enough to get cleaned up, nibble on some rations, and get the Council assembled on the rooftop of Camp 1. Ralla had tried to talk to Ioa first, but when it was clear Appet wasn't with them, she didn't want to speak of it. Sitting with the Council, stoic and composed, Ioa's appearance belied the pain Ralla knew must be underneath.

"I thought we had weeks left on our ration supply," one of the Council members said, looking though his notes for confirmation. Word had already spread that Cern had tried to hold Ralla captive, which was as definitive a "no" as anyone could imagine.

"I believe Cern intends to quarantine the *Universalis*."

"Quarantine? As in, trap us here?" another Council member said.

"Yes."

"That's insane."

"Sadly, no, it's probably not. He thinks what he's doing is right. He thinks we'll flood the remaining domes with people, causing more of them to fail like we saw happen when the *Pop* tried the same thing during the war. Then, as each dome fails, it sends those people to other domes, which will fail, and so on. He's trying to contain the situation. The fact that everyone remaining on the *Uni* will die is a consequence, but not his motivation. If this makes him more or less dangerous... honestly, I don't know. I don't really care either. Look, we're getting off topic. This is happening, and we need to act. We can't just announce what's happening or we'll never get the ensuing riots under control. So we need an evacuation plan. A quick, and *quiet* evacuation plan," Ralla said. Everyone started talking at once, and all at different levels of understanding the situation.

"We don't have enough ships," said a member.

"Where will we go?" asked another.

"You don't expect us to live on the surface, do you?" asked another. Ralla quickly lost track of who said what.

"Who decides who stays and who goes?

"Please, everyone, we need to focus," Ralla said, holding her hand up. "We need to tally what ships we have available, including the emergency escape subs, and get as many people off the *Uni* as possible. It's as simple a start as that."

"Surely we can reason with him. This is ludicrous. We need to try to reason with him. Did you try? What happened?"

"He won't let all of these people die. He's bluffing!"

"Everyone *STOP*," Ralla shouted. In return, she received a moment of silence. "I have known this man my whole life. I have no reason to believe he was lying. And we can't take the chance I'm wrong. If he intends to use his fleet to blockade the *Uni*, we can't stop him. If he does, we all die. We need to get as many people away from here *now* as we can."

Ralla saw she was losing them, panic setting in. Panic, mixed with disbelief in some, and self-preservation in others. Thom and Dija sat off to the side, trying to look supportive. They were in this with her, no matter what she decided. They'd had the entire ride back to the *Uni* to figure out a plan, and it had always been some variation of running: Evacuate some people to the surface and hope the subs provided enough shelter in the cold; evacuate others to the transports and shuttles that lay scattered in the seabed around the ship, sending them to whatever safe harbor they could find; evacuate a few more via the remaining emergency escape subs. Evacuate. Run. No one knew how many they'd be able to get off in time. A few hundred people, probably. A few thousand? Maybe. Once the evacuations started, and people felt they might get left behind, they'd tear the ship apart. Who could blame them? What then?

The cold logic of Cern's decision couldn't be denied, but that didn't mean they had to go along with it. However, even if they used every sub and every spare moment, there would be people left behind. Left behind to die.

As guilty as it made her feel, she'd always assumed she'd be on a sub to somewhere. It wasn't until just then, standing in front of the Council, she realized she'd been making this assumption. Had been.

"I'm staying," she said, once again silencing the conversations around her. Out of the corner of her eye, she saw Thom and Dija look at each other.

"You said everyone who stayed would die. What are you going to do?" someone asked.

"I'm going to fight."

—‾--

"And then she said 'I'm gonna fight.' You should have seen it, it was *amazing*," Dija said, trying not to struggle with Lo's left arm draped over her shoulder. They walked, slowly, down the Medbay corridor. Her enthusiasm was infectious, causing Lo to smile through the ache in his torso.

"I always did like her."

"Right?"

"Did she say what exactly we'd fight *with*?"

"We're working on that."

"No doubt. Can we sit down a second?" Lo asked, eyeing a bench they were passing.

"No. The nurse said you needed to do a full lap."

"If I start sitting down, there's not much you can do to stop me."

"Try it. What I lack in size I make up for in leverage and cunning."

"I'd like to see your cunning move three times your weight," he said, trying to smile. Dija reached up with her left hand and gently intertwined her fingers with Lo's. "Well played, Di. Well played. But seriously, I've barely gotten out of bed in over a week, my legs feel weird. I don't want to fall on you. I promise I'll finish the lap."

She squinted at him with suspicion, but allowed them to sidestep to the bench. Lo sat down, relieved.

"I want to stay with Ralla as long as possible," Dija said, sitting down beside him.

"I figured you would."

"You don't have to."

"I'm staying with you."

"You can barely walk."

"And last week, I was barely dead. Look at my improvement."

"Geran..."

"I'll help however I can, but I'm not running away."

"I figured you'd say that."

She hadn't let go of his hand. It wasn't lost on Lo that this was the most they'd touched since the incident. With his insides still a mess, and everywhere outside a mess, he took a moment to enjoy holding Dija's hand, sitting on a plastic bench in a Medbay corridor like it was in the middle the Garden, back before it all.

—-⁻--

Half a ship away, Thom winced as he tried to lie down on Ralla's bed.

"Is it bad?" Ralla asked, worried.

"I'm fine, I'm fine. Grab my foot... Gently! Gently, Ralla. Thank you."

Thom, propped up slightly against the wall, saw Ralla fretting as she looked at his condition.

"You always look at me like that, and it's fine. It only hurts when I move it. And sometimes when I don't move it, but it's fine."

"You keep saying 'it's fine' like it means the opposite."

"Ralla, I'm... Just come here, will you."

She lay down beside him on the narrow bunk, half on the lumpy mattress, half across his torso.

"You should take Lo and evacuate to the surface."

"Why, is that where you're going to be?" he asked sarcastically. She ignored him.

"Di isn't going to leave me, and he's not going to leave her, unless you tell him to."

"What makes you think *I* want to leave?"

"It's just your... you know,"

Thom wanted to crack a joke, change the subject, but realized he couldn't. She had a reasonable point. He wanted to be able to say he could rise up and lead thousands to defend their home, but even that quick thought stirred some panic in him. He could feel his heart rate increase, and assumed Ralla could feel it, her head on his chest.

In her, in *their* time of greatest need, he knew he'd collapse in a heap. They couldn't risk it. By fearing he'd put someone's life in danger, he'd put everyone's life in danger. Mentally, he felt like fleeing the room and running... somewhere. That is, until he looked down and saw Ralla looking back up at him. There was no judgment in her eyes.

"I'll fight for you," Thom said.

—-̈--

Ralla awoke early, the meager light from the dimmed picosuns barely lighting her small cabin. Nestled in the crook of Thom's arm, she didn't want to move, yet knew she had to. It was going to be a long day and days. The few hours of sleep she'd had would be the last for a while.

The bunk was small for one, cramped for two. She stared a moment at Thom's face. Still asleep, it was contorted in a tight grimace that told Ralla he'd awake to some agony. They'd never had a real bed, she realized sadly, and never would.

As gently as she could, Ralla removed herself from the bunk and positioned Thom's legs in what looked like a more comfortable position. The tension in his face dissipated. She poured him a glass of water from her battered red carafe and positioned the last of his pain pills beside it on the scratched brown bedside table. Ralla had been using a knit blanket Ioa had found as a shawl. Draping it over her shoulders, she left the cabin.

In the quiet gloom as she walked down the steps she saw Ioa just as Ioa saw her. The older woman approached, arms wide, motioning with her fingers for Ralla to come near. At first it seemed to Ralla that Ioa wanted to comfort her. Ioa's face looked to be filled more with concern than sorrow. Ralla welcomed the hug, for how it felt, and what it meant. There was no blame here, just the sadness of circumstance. The older woman, slightly taller, pressed her face into Ralla's shoulder. Ioa held Ralla tightly, protectively. Then something changed or maybe, Ralla realized, just her understanding of it. Ioa's embrace loosened, and instead her grip on the shawl tightened. Ralla could feel Ioa's body start to shake as the sobs came. Ralla hugged her tighter. They stood there, Ioa's tears wetting Ralla's shoulder, the sounds of sadness loud in Ralla's ears, loud as they boomed from the walls, loud as they echoed throughout the ship.

Then Ioa pulled away, wiped her wet eyes, smiled a sad smile, and Ralla realized the sound had just been here, between them. Ioa squeezed Ralla's arm, then walked back into Camp 1. The ship was again quiet, but different.

Ralla walked to Tent City, only the few stirrings of early morning risers audible: a tired mother walking her young son to the communal bathroom, a man stretching as he emerged from his tent, a couple arguing in hushed tones as they resecured the tarp acting as their home. All around, Ralla heard the snores and rustles of the sleeping.

Passing through Tent City, she entered one of the lower entrances to T-Town, the narrow maze of corridors dark and silent. She moved up the flights of stairs, past the mismatched walls and across the multicolored scavenged deck plating. The view out from one of the remaining open floors was its usual beauty. She noticed a few lights in the cabins in the wall across the way. Below, the Canyon between the two fallen ships showed the glowing embers of cooking fires. This was frowned upon, but who was going to enforce the rules now? She was impressed by their ability to scrounge enough combustible materials for a fire.

Back down the imperfect stairs, Ralla started to cross one of the connecting bridges to the Terraces. In the middle, she paused, taking in the early-morning beauty of the Basket. It barely looked anything like what it was, yet all the thousands of new people gave it a character it hadn't had before. There was a home here, despite the adversity and terrible conditions. Ralla didn't fool herself into thinking everyone here wouldn't happily move somewhere better in an instant, but they'd made the best of what they had. In the face of impossible odds, they all had tried, and in so many ways succeeded. As much as she was sure so many hated it, she was just as sure they'd fight for it. They'd fight for their lives, their families, their friends, and this overcrowded, dilapidated mess, because it was *their* mess. Their home.

Later today, she knew the preparations would begin for the fight and flight of the current, and possibly last, population of the *Universalis*. Already they'd turned away subs looking for refuge and had begun quietly putting people on subs and sending them away. Large families, or groups of friends, anyone who could fill a sub without letting the word "evacuation" slip. Ralla had no doubt these were friends of Council members, but for now secrecy outweighed fairness. Every person they got off the ship now was a victory. Today they'd work on the next step, and the step after that, and whatever came after that.

When she'd started this walk, she hadn't had a destination. Now, though, she realized the walk was the destination in itself. In a few hours, she was going to ask tremendous things from these people, impossible things. She had to be ready herself to do anything she asked of them. And without question, she knew she was. She had let Appet down, but that would not happen again. He had believed in their cause, and had died for it. She wouldn't let his death be in vain. Wouldn't let Ioa's pain be for nothing. In the face of chaos, it was her job to unite. That was her mission. All these people came from different backgrounds. Some came from the very ship the *Uni* had fought for decades, yet they had been living here together in peace. This is where Cern and the *Pop*'s late Governor Oppai had it so wrong, she realized. We were, we *are*, all one people. A great people.

Walking through the random angles of the Terraces, she made her way back to her room. She needed to prepare.

—˙--

Standing on the roof of Camp 1, a microphone connected to the ship's PA waiting, Ralla looked out at a sea of faces. Many crowded in front of Camp 1, but many more looked on from Tent City, and thousands leaned out windows of T-Town and the Terraces, with even more peering out from portholes and cabins the length of the walls of the Basket.

This was all on her. If she failed here, if she couldn't bring these people together now, how many more would die? In the panic and the riots, what then? What then, of the future of the species? The weight of the moment pressed down on Ralla. Her father had never had this kind of responsibility. No former Proctor had been so directly responsible for so many lives. Oppai, with his cold, severe malevolence, had been driven nearly mad, or at least myopic, from his burden of leadership. Ralla felt the stress, felt the weight, but reveled in it. Without knowing it, she had trained for this her whole life. Her whole life had built to this moment, so she could be standing here, able to address this amazing group of people. It was terrifying. It was exhilarating.

Ralla stepped up to the microphone.

VII

"**MY NAME** is Ralla Gattley, Proctor of the Council of Concord. I stand before you not as a leader, but as a citizen of the *Universalis*, a resident of the Basket, and member of a family of survivors that have made this mighty ship our home. Over the past weeks and months, we have done amazing things. We have taken a ship nearly destroyed by war and made it livable. We have built new buildings, the first in generations. We have triumphed in the face of great adversity. We have embraced refugees we once called enemies, and rightly treated them as our own brothers and sisters. We have made life from certain death." Ralla paused, her words echoing loudly through the Basket. As they died down, the silence hit her like a wall.

"Now, we face a new challenge, and I need your help. People we once considered friends have turned against us. The Council and I have tried to reason with them, but to no avail. They have diminished our access to food and supplies and hindered our ability to forge new alliances. I refuse to sit idly by and let these *pirates* dictate how we live our lives." Ralla paused again. She still didn't like the word, but knew it was the most efficient way of getting everyone to understand their adversary. She saw before her rapt attention, a good sign.

"As you know, we have no Navy. Our military force is almost nonexistent. This makes us appear weak. But we are not weak. The weak would have surrendered to the sea long ago. We have a strength in each other far beyond what's measured in ships and guns. I know it. You know it. So I ask you to join me. We can fight back. Our strength against their force. I won't lie to you, the situation is dire. If we don't succeed, everything we've accomplished is in jeopardy. More than that, everything our parents accomplished, everything their parents accomplished, is in jeopardy. This submarine may lie deep in the silt, but it is not a tomb. We will not let it be a tomb. Those who can fight, I ask you to fight. Fight with me. Fight for me. Fight for us. Thank you."

Ralla stood at the microphone, and raised her fist over her head. She'd expected an immediate response. Probably not rioting, having left out the really terrifying details, but she'd hoped for at least some clapping or cheers. Even boos were preferable to silence. She'd been taught in school not to focus on her audience, but instead focus her eyes on the back wall. It made public speaking easier. Now, the movement in front of Camp 1 drew her eye, and was the most chilling sight she had ever seen.

All eyes were on her, and one by one, single fists rose in support. She could see hands in the air all over the Basket, in greater and greater numbers. She knew it hadn't been the speech, it hadn't been nearly as good as those she'd read — and cribbed from. These people, these incredible people, she was right about them. They knew they were looking down the edge of the void, and they weren't going to be pushed over by anyone.

Ralla heard noise behind her and turned to see the Council, plus Dija, helping to support Thom and Lo as they all stood, fists held high.

She had never felt so proud, so part of something. Cern and his people were on their way, and they had no idea what they were getting into.

—˙––

Ralla sat down reluctantly, surrounded by her friends, a bowl of soup in her hands. Ioa smiled her motherly smile, trying to hide the sadness, and went back to tending her bubbling cauldron of savory liquid beneath the overhang of Camp 1. The smell had attracted a small group, who eagerly awaited their helping. Thom, Dija, and Geran sipped cautiously at their own steaming bowls, gathered together on the benches. It had been a busy day, the busiest she could remember. After her speech, the Council had dispersed among their constituents, inundated by pledges to fight, and requests to flee. Many wanted to help, even if they weren't in any physical condition to take up arms. Many questions were asked, most went unanswered, but for now that had to be.

It had been a day of quick decisions, the ramifications of which she'd only know in the coming hours and days. She signed off on defensive plans with a quick glance, approved sub passenger lists based on the reputation of the person handing it to her. She agreed to plans that seemed too outrageous to work, but too promising not to try. Plans within plans, within plans.

It had been a day of trust. There was too much to do, and too little time to do it, for any one person to make every decision. Ralla delegated to those she trusted: Dija, Ioa, the ranking military officers. She trusted Koin when he told her the science of an outrageous project. She told him to get started, to take whatever he needed to make it work, and trusted that he would.

It had been a day of forgiveness. Councilman Bannis had never been a friend, and had been loyal to Tenncy Hennorr. There hadn't been enough time to form much of a merchant marine fleet. He came to her midday and pledged the support of every ship and pilot he had ready.

It had been a day of understanding. Thom had been by her side from the moment she'd stepped away from the microphone. He'd helped keep track of meetings, people, important issues. She'd wanted to ask him for more, even gently pushed in that direction, but understood he could not. He would give all he could. Late in the day Pell Farre had sent word from F268 that he had rejected an offer from Cern Hennorr and was ready to assist however he could. In the short exchange that followed, he agreed to take several dozen subs of refugees, but that was as many as he could feasibly take on.

It had been a day of pride, of hope, and of intense stress. It had been a day of guilt. She had told these people the truth, but not the entire truth. That weighed on her, but she saw only the negatives of unleashing such facts about their potential starvation and destruction. There was still a chance, somewhere in all this mess, that they could survive. But Ralla had to admit to herself, she wasn't sure how.

"Ioa is going to think you don't like her soup," Dija said between slurps. Ralla looked down at the cooling bowl in her hands. How Ioa still found enough ingredients with such limited rations, Ralla couldn't figure out. How she kept going with the death of Appet so fresh, she wasn't sure she'd ever be able to understand. The woman had a strength Ralla wasn't sure she had. Ralla took a long sip, the broth warming her mouth, throat, and stomach.

"I think this is my first food since yesterday," she said before taking another gulp.

"This is my first food since, um..." Lo replied, his own bowl still close to full. He took a tentative sip. "Not sure what it's going to do to me."

"Look at you, eating like a big boy," Thom said over the top of his own bowl. "Pretty soon we'll let you sit at the grown-up table and everything."

Lo narrowed his eyes, "Suppose I don't want to sit at the grown-up table."

"You have to," Ralla answered. "At some point, everyone has to."

Thom answered with a loud slurp.

"I'm sorry," Thom said, his mouth full. "Were you saying something?"

"Di, maybe we can make our own table for us adults," Ralla, said making a show of turning away from Lo and Thom. Dija looked up at her, eyes wide, eyebrows slowly rising. Her lips turned to a frown, and soup leaked out from the edges and dribbled down her chin.

"I just want you to know," Ralla said, "I don't like any of you."

"We know," Dija replied.

"But you don't like me less than these other two, right?" Thom asked, mock sadness on his face.

"Much less."

"Good," Thom said, smiling. Ralla couldn't contain her own smile any longer, and tried to cover it by having more soup.

"I love you guys," Lo said, his deep voice suddenly filled with emotion. He looked intently at his bowl. The levity of the previous moment disappeared. Thom reached over and put his hand on Lo's arm.

"I love you, too," he said, but locking his eyes with Ralla for a moment, before they both looked away.

Dija walked over to hug Lo, bringing her bowl of soup with her. Seated on the bench, he was almost taller than she was while standing. After a long hug, she sat down beside him to finish her soup. Their legs touched. Ralla and Thom eyed each other before each making a show that the space next to them was available. They laughed.

"I'll sit on your bench if we sleep in my cabin tonight," Ralla said.

"I don't care what bench or what cabin, as long as I'm with you."

Both realized this was the first time either of them had said anything like this out loud.

"Oh, Thom, you're just—"

"Please don't make a joke."

Ralla stopped herself, as that was exactly what she was about to do. She felt uncomfortable, but didn't know why. It was obvious to them all their lightheartedness had been a defensive cover. No one was in a joking mood, but the forced humor made the tension of the day almost bearable. Lo had cracked the ice, Thom had just shattered it, and now all three of her friends looked on, intrigued, like they were watching a vid. Thom stood and walked to her. He took her hand in his.

"I've spent too much time apart from you. I don't share your optimism about the next few days. I wanted you to know how I feel."

Ralla stood and looked Thom in the eyes.

"I feel the same way," she said, standing on her tiptoes to kiss him.

Dinners finished, the couples retired to the roof of Camp 1, finding it empty. They moved chairs around so they could put their feet up on the ledge and look out across the Basket.

The sparks and glow of welders in T-town and the Terraces pierced the growing darkness as the picosuns dimmed. Newly erected barricades rose knifelike out of the deck plating near the elevators and down the Canyon. The people of Tent City, contributing what they could, built a wall around their district. Its mosaic of colors and textures segregated yet united them. The multistory structures spilling off the end of the Terraces and onto the floor of the Basket showed the signs of hours of reinforcement, diagonal beams bracing walls, paneling covering open windows. Workers carried materials up into the forward stairwells, rushing to finish a project Lo had recommended for adding another lock. A steady stream of people, mostly children and mothers with babies, filed calmly through the Canyon toward the elevators, hoping to board one of the last shuttles out.

Guilt gripped Ralla again, wondering how many more would have chosen to flee if she'd told them all the truth. As it had so many times that day, the logic of the averted riots outweighed the lie. No, she realized, the hidden truth. Maybe Cern wouldn't come, she thought and hoped, not for the first time. Maybe all of this had been for nothing. They'd send more and more people away, each group cast out letting the *Uni*'s reserves last a little bit longer. That much more time to figure out what to do. It always came down to time. She reached down and wove her fingers with Thom's.

"That doesn't look good," Lo said, his deep voice breaking the silence. They all followed his gaze and saw a lone figure running from the elevators, struggling past the long line of future refugees. As he exited the Canyon, even in the low light they could see his uniform. Without moving, they watched him come, not wanting the urgent news to disturb their peace. They felt vibrations through their chairs as the uniformed man bounded up the stairs on the side of Camp 1. They turned to watch him approach. He held a thin, torn slip of paper, their supplies of clean paper having run out days earlier.

"Proctor Gattley, I was told to bring you this."

"Thank you, Ensign," she said, holding out her hand. She read it, and squeezed Thom's hand. The rest waited for her to speak.

"It says sensors have picked up a fleet of ships, headed our way."

"From what direction?" Thom asked.

"Every direction."

VIII

THE LINE to board a shuttle wound from the elevators, up to the Spine, and down to the one working lock. Ralla gave up trying to be polite and started shouting for people to make way as she tried to get to the de facto command room at the top of the ship. They had finally just started calling it Command for the lack of a location better suited for the name.

"Report!" she shouted, barely in the door. The troops looked on edge in their armored vests and helmets. Their outfits were a far cry from the heavy battle armor that saved Lo's life, but it was all they could scavenge. Lieutenant Merella looked up from a large whiteboard that lay on the only table in the room. It was a swift reminder how far they'd all fallen since the high-tech tables and tablets from a few months earlier. Ralla stepped closer to the table. It showed a top-down schematic of the *Uni*, with corridors, cabins, plus their new makeshift battlements. On the outer edges of the board, an ensign drew small submarine shapes.

"We've detected twenty-five ships," Merella said, "pretty evenly spaced out around us. There may be other ships behind them, but it's getting pretty noisy out there, so we can't tell."

"Have they taken any of our subs yet?" Ralla asked.

"The last one launched right before we detected the enemy. They had comm silence instructions unless they were attacked. So either they made it through or were destroyed outright."

"How soon before your next launch?"

"Five minutes, maybe more."

"Five? How long are you taking per sub?"

"Twenty minutes?"

"Twenty *minutes?* What is taking so long? We had said ten minutes, maximum."

"That turned out to be unrealistic. We're lucky to be making twenty, ma'am. It's not just the loading, it's getting the sub, transferring a crew, getting it back here, picking up another crew, and so on. Please believe me, 20 minutes is impressive."

Ralla did the numbers in her head. Three subs an hour, fifteen to thirty people per sub, so around seventy people per hour. That was so low. Too low. Stupid, she thought, I should have been up here overseeing the evacuation instead of wasting time at dinner. She looked out the door and down the hall. She could see the line as it made its final turn toward the waiting room in the distance. She saw Thom come around the corner, limping his way toward Command.

The comm in the lieutenant's ear momentarily diverted his attention.

"We've launched the next sub," he said as he reached for and pulled out a worn black metal box from under the table. Its front was a worn fabric grille, its top several faded buttons. He pressed the largest of these. "There was no point in keeping comm silence now, so we're having the pilot relay what he sees." The box crackled to life as it connected to unseen computers and eventually out to the escaping sub.

"There's a circle of ships, looks like it goes around the *Uni*." The pilot's voice sounded thin through the box on the table. "They're above us, too. I'm sure they saw us detach. There are two... they look like cargo haulers, right above the stern. They haven't moved to follow us yet."

Ralla didn't get her hopes up.

"We've passed them. I can see more subs in the distance. They've got their running lights on. They're not hiding at all. It looks like there's another ring of ships out here. Smaller subs though, more like small transports and tugs. I'm going to try to run for it."

"So what do you think, Lieutenant," Ralla asked. "Fifty subs?"

"If there's a second ring? Sure, at least."

"They're definitely coming for us now," spoke the panicked voice of the sub pilot. "Two of them, they're behind me now, but I think they're tugs or something." The room went silent, as all present listened to the comm. "They haven't shot anything at us yet, but the sensors say they're still closing. I wonder if—" A loud clang cut off the pilot, then silence. A moment later, it cut back in, this time the pilot's voice sounded terrified. "They're ramming us! They're trying to take out the thrusters. I'm going to—" Another clang. "They're driving us into the seabed. HELP! HELP US!" A slow scraping noise overwhelmed the sound of his voice, which stopped suddenly, replaced by silence.

"That was probably just the comm antennas," the lieutenant offered.

"Not just that," Thom replied, staring at the black box.

"Ma'am, if you want us to go after them..." the lieutenant said cautiously. Ralla held up her hand.

"If they're alive, and we are in a few hours, we can go get them."

"Yes, ma'am."

Ralla looked around the room. She had just condemned those people to die, and no one called her on it. Later, she knew that would haunt her just as much as the actual decision would. If there was a later, she thought morosely. Lieutenant Merella awaited her orders.

"Phase 2, Lieutenant."

"Yes, ma'am."

He activated his comm and sent out the order. Military personnel all over the ship switched gears. Down the corridor from Command, they saw the first rumblings of the new directive. Shouts of confusion and alarm spread down the line of awaiting escapees. Three officers, waving flashlights, led a procession of people back down the line and down away from the Spine. The line curved and went with them, everyone following the person in front of them, turning around and heading back down into the ship proper. After a few minutes, the organized retreat had cleared the corridor along the Spine, offering a clear view all the way to the lock.

"The retrieval team is docking now. After they secure the ship, we'll start reinforcing the lock."

"Seal it off, Lieutenant."

"Ma'am?"

"After they're through, seal it off. Nothing good will pass through that door any time soon. Seal it off."

"Yes, ma'am."

The lieutenant issued the command into comm, then repeated it to an apparently incredulous subordinate on the other end.

"Is there something I can do to help?" Thom asked. The lieutenant looked him up and down, pausing on his cane.

"Is there?" he asked, his tone without malice.

"I can help with the barricades."

"Can you weld?"

"A bit."

"Have at it."

Thom winked at Ralla, out of sight of the lieutenant, and hobbled down the corridor. The lieutenant listened to his comm again.

"Ma'am, we've got a signal coming in. It's Cern Hennorr."

"Can I hear it on this?" she said, pointing to the black box. The lieutenant pressed another button on the top, and they heard a hiss. The lieutenant motioned for Ralla to speak.

"This is Proctor Gattley of the *Universalis*. To whom am I speaking?"

"Well *Proctor* Gattley, this is... *Commodore*... Cern Hennorr. See, now we both have impressive titles."

"Mr. Hennorr, if you would like to discuss terms of trade, please remove your fleet to a respectable distance. Your current formation is aggressive, and seemingly hostile."

"Well *Ms.* Gattley, I'm sorry to tell you, but it is indeed hostile. You see, in order to get all these ships to agree to help with a quarantine, I had to promise them something. Being entrepreneurial men, they all wanted the same thing. You. Well, your ship. There are a lot of valuable raw materials and equipment buried in there."

It was clear some of the men around her were shocked by Cern's comments and had already imagined them out to the logical conclusion. Ralla, however, wasn't shocked in the slightest. What did these soldiers think was going to happen?

"You're to have us believe that you found enough people who had no qualms killing tens of thousands of people, for their own profit?"

"No, Ralla, you're still not understanding. As far as we're concerned, you're already dead. We won't let you inundate domes that are barely self-sufficient. These men are protecting their homes, preemptive as that protection may be. They come from domes all over the hemisphere. Domes that barely survived the *Pop* dumping thousands of their people on them, and they won't let you do the same. I've merely incentivized them with the promise of resources, supplies, machines, and lots of other vital… well, let's call it what it is: bounty."

"It's interesting you assume we won't fight back. This is a powerful ship." Ralla had prepared the line in her mind, for this very situation. She hoped it came across as genuine. There was silence on the comm. Merella pressed and held a button on the top of the box.

"Sounds like you spooked him, ma'am," he said with a smile. Ralla didn't share his jubilance and made a circle motion with her finger. The lieutenant's smile faded, and he released the button. The comm clicked to life a moment later. Cern's voice lacked the sarcastic tone it had a moment earlier.

"My father is sure you're bluffing, and he was certainly right about you before," Cern said. Ralla scowled. Of *course* Tenncy Hennorr had run straight to join his son, Ralla thought. Cern started talking again. "Surrender now and I promise we'll evacuate you and your friends."

Ralla almost laughed out loud, stifling it into a snort at the last moment. When she recovered, her voice had turned icy.

"My friends are many. We are strong. You are warned."

Ralla pressed the power button on the box and noticed the pride and resolve on Lieutenant Merella's face. He gave her a nod of respect.

"Send the Alpha teams," she instructed.

—˙--

Lo heard the order on his comm, and signaled to his men. They were hard to see in the dark. The bay's lights, along with its primary exterior lock, had been partially destroyed by the impact of the *Uni* with the seabed. Sand, silt, and water covered the floor of the bay, but the air pressure had prevented total flooding. Lo knew his men were tired; they'd been digging for six hours straight. Now, though, their real work began.

One by one, they turned off their suit lights and walked/swam through the partially open lock. As Lo's eyes adjusted to the darkness, he saw the faint glow through the lock, and the hole they'd dug out to the sea beyond. He wished he could go with them, odd as that seemed. But however tempting that was, and how doubtful they'd find a suit in his size, he knew he'd just hold them back. It hurt to move, never mind swim. His chest still ached from neck to navel, far more than he'd let on. So instead, he watched them disappear into the open sea. It was a weird mix of feelings: his desire not to fight, combined with his need to be with his men.

His team of six emerged from their tunnel. The jagged, crushed exterior of the *Uni* belied the life within. They followed Lo's instructions to the letter. In the low light, their black suits blended with the hull as they slowly rose past it. Gaping, serrated holes and protruding beams made the ascent perilous. The hull curved away from them toward the Spine. Now they swam, assisted by two ancient and underpowered thrusters. With the drag of three bodies, the thrusters propelled them slowly toward their chosen target: a stationary transport sub holding position above the *Uni*. Within moments, the team was in the open, the citysub stretching away from them like a craggy, sleeping monster, half embedded in the silt. The seafloor beyond stretched even further, as far as they could see. The shadow of the slowly growing icepack ominously darkened the distance.

They approached the transport from underneath, then spread to either side, taking on some ballast in waist-mounted bladders, giving them neutral buoyancy. They swung around to the top of the sub and carefully, quietly, they attached a magnetic explosive charge to the top of the hull. Job done, and so far seemingly undetected, the moved to the next phase of the plan. Splitting into two groups, they proceeded to the next closest submarines, just barely visible in the murky coldness.

Lo, anxious as he returned to the Basket, knew no word was good word. Only if they were discovered would they send a signal. Grunting as he trudged up the stairs, he keyed his comm to check if the other team had launched on schedule.

———

Dija struggled to get the welder back together. In her rushing, she fumbled with pieces and dropped others. The men around her looked on with impatience, arms crossed, as if it was her fault they couldn't fix their tools. Finally, she got the coils aligned and slammed the rest of the pieces back in place. No sooner did she have the access panel reattached then the welders fired it up and went back to work. The corridor filled with the smell of burning paint as metal fused with metal, igniting layers and layers of ancient colored enamels. Dija had been running from job site to job site, with only the brief, and wonderful, break for dinner. As the stress welled inside her, she just pictured being back with her friends, with Lo. It wasn't much, but it helped.

Her skills repairing things had become too valuable. She was needed in many places at once. All across the ship, defensive fortifications, mixed with targeted repair work, meant there was too much to do for those who could do it, and infinitely too much work for those needed to keep the machines running. It seemed to Dija that as smart as the engineers on the *Uni* were, none had much experience with the day-to-day devices used by the average worker. She knew they'd be able to tear down one of the big generators that powered the ship faster than she could — though she'd figure it out *eventually* — but they seemed hopeless when it came to basic tool repair. The fusion welder being the most obvious example.

In her mind, she checked the welder off her to-do list and planned the fastest route to where she was needed next: a portable air compressor on the portside upper deck. Three stairways, the first right up ahead, then along a corridor, and to the right. She started to jog.

———

Ralla watched Thom struggle as he dragged a slab of carbonweave paneling down the Spine's corridor. She wanted to help him but knew her place was in Command. Around her the military, her military, barked orders to subordinates, gave updates to their superiors, and spoke rapidly into comms. The ink-colored hands of those crowded around the whiteboard showed how rapidly they drew, then erased, new information.

Standing there, with the excitement and energy around her, she wondered if this was how Proctor Jills had felt, or Captain Sarras, in those moments before the war. She wondered how her father had felt on the eve of his war. She found it hard to imagine him scared of anything, but looking at the faces of the soldiers around her, not much younger than he was at the time, she had to concede it was likely. He wouldn't have shown it, of course, just as Ralla tried not to show her own current emotions.

As at other times of great stress in her life, Ralla felt herself grow calmer as the hour approached. There was a stark realization that they'd done what they could in the time they had. Whatever came next, came next. She was still mildly terrified, but that feeling hadn't gotten any worse.

Time to make it worse.

"Are we ready?"

"Yes, ma'am."

"Then get me Cern Hennorr, please."

The lieutenant keyed his comm and waved the others away from the table. The ugly black box waited. He nodded to her and pressed the power button.

"I hope you've decided to reconsider already. We're certainly in no rush." The smugness in Cern's voice had returned.

"This is your last warning. Leave now," Ralla said, her voice stern and calm.

"Stop playing around. You're bluffing. I know it, you know—"

The sound cut out as Ralla spun her finger in the air, and Lieutenant Merella pressed the power button on cue. She realized in that moment that she'd picked up the hand gesture from Thom.

The lieutenant barked an order into his comm. In tiny crawlspaces just inside the outer skin of the *Univeralis*, thirty-six volunteers manually activated torso-sized rockets, held securely in their own launch tubes along the upper hull. All each heard was an ear-piercing hiss of air as the rocket launched, then the heart-wrenching splash as water filled the tube to replace it. Two people were killed instantly, their tubes bursting, flooding their tiny compartments.

All along the back of the ship, thirty-four flares emerged from their tubes in two longitudinal rows, and shot upwards, creating a piercing white light and temporarily scrambling the sensors of every ship in the vicinity. Trails of smoke and bubbles followed the flares towards the surface. The flares reached the top of their ascent, well shallow of the surface. Curving over, the tiny suns of fire and noise began a slow glowing descent back to the bottom.

Everyone in Command knew to close their eyes, but even so the light was blinding. Through the transparent dome above their heads, they had a clear view of what happened next.

Ralla couldn't see the initial flash of the next explosion, not with the afterimages of the flares still seared on her retinas, but she could see the enormous bubble released as a result. Six subs, trailing bubbles themselves, sank quickly to the seabed. The sounds of their implosions reverberated through the hull of the *Universalis* like an enormous hammer rapidly striking the hull.

"Commodore Hennorr is signaling."

"Don't call him that. Put him through." Ralla paused as the connection was made, then spoke quickly. "Are you surrendering?"

"What did you do?" Cern's tone indicated less of a question and more of an accusation.

"Surrender, now."

"It is not your place to dictate—"

The lieutenant cut off the comm again on Ralla's indication.

"You enjoy doing that, don't you?" he asked. Ralla ignored him.

"Make sure your men are ready. Patch me through to the PA," Ralla ordered. The lieutenant complied. "People of the *Univeralis*, this is Proctor Gattley. The sounds you just heard were six enemy submarines. They have rejected my order to surrender. We expect them next to assault the ship. Follow your defense plans. Listen to your group leaders. We will get through this." Ralla deactivated the mic just as they all heard a loud clang. Ralla looked questioningly at the lieutenant.

"That would be a ship landing on the hull," he replied stoically.

—-—

"Lieutenant Lo, there are subs landing on the hull."

"How many?" Lo asked.

"Seven… no, eight." It took Lo a moment to recognize the voice of the leader of Team 1, Denn Breka.

"Have any of them headed towards the bow, or the Garden?"

"Not that we can see from here. We're pretty far aft, along the Spine," Breka replied.

"Can you give me rough coordinates of the ones you can see?"

"Yes, I think so."

"Do that and move to your next objective."

Lo reached the next landing in the stairwell and dropped to one knee, winded. His chest radiated sharp pains outward with each breath. His team started sending estimates on where the subs had landed along the hull. From their viewpoint, still outside but far aft, they had a tough time judging distances. Lo scratched the locations into the stairwell wall with his knife.

"That's all we can see for now."

"Keep me informed, Lo out." He rose shakily to his feet and keyed a different frequency into his comm. "This is Lo," he said. "I've got sub locations."

—˙--

"Go," Merella instructed from Command. As Lo relayed the estimated locations, the lieutenant drew on the whiteboard. Ralla watched as the invasion took shape. Four subs had latched onto the sides of the *Uni*, presumably for easy access to some of the manufacturing equipment in the flooded outer areas. They weren't a threat at the moment, and easily ignored. Two had parked themselves on the stern, near the engineering compartments. Even as Merella took the locations down, he waved at his subordinates to get teams there. The final two subs seemed more threatening, landing above the Basket, in line with the top rows of ships. With little difficulty, they could cut through the hull and have easy access to the entire ship. Or worse.

"Should we evacuate and seal off those corridors now?" Ralla asked. They had discussed the very real possibility of Cern trying to flood the Basket by burning through the ceiling. It would take time to cut through the armored and multilayered hull. Time enough, they hoped, to deal with such an attack directly.

"I don't want to give them a chance to get that far. I'm sending teams now."

—˙--

Dija watched the two soldiers freeze as orders came over their comms. She focused on her repair work while they started shouting to others around her. Having helped Ralla in the planning, Dija didn't need to look up to understand what was happening. The two soldiers were in charge of ten volunteers each. The residential corridor, moments earlier a busy workplace, became a staging area. Even the welders dropped their torches and picked up crowbars. To watch it all happen, she was less sure of its potential success. As a group, they filed down the corridor, stopping a short distance away. At first, Dija thought something was wrong, unsure why they had stopped. Then it occurred to her: They were cutting through *here*. As if to confirm her fears, the men and women of the volunteer squad looked above their heads nervously. She was on the highest level of the port wall of the Basket, and it had been identified as one of the likeliest targets for infiltration.

Low metal barricades, secured to the floor, provided some cover. The threadbare purple carpet was now torn and scorched, as if the barricades had burned their way up from the floor below. The nearby elevators acted as the final fallback point. The point most important to defend. The idea had been to add barricades all the way down the corridor, but they hadn't had the time. Dija heard the latch click on the firedoor in the corridor beyond the elevators, another step in the operating procedure. Next, Dija knew, they'd be locking out the elevators. The only escape now from this area was the stairs, on the other side of the mass of angry workers-turned-soldiers. She was trapped. Her pulse quickened.

The mob milled about nervously, occasionally pointing at different areas thinking they saw something. Cern's people must be cutting their way in, she realized. Dija knew if their plan was to flood the ship, starting here, the hammers, knives, and screwdrivers held by the mob would do nothing. Fatalistically, she realized that thanks to the precautions she'd help set up, if they did try to flood the ship from this point, all they'd flood would be this section of corridor. It would kill her and everyone else here, but the rest of the ship would be fine.

The mob had spread into two groups, leaving space between them, above where they all had suddenly focused their attention. Earlier that day, Dija had estimated five to ten minutes to cut through the outer hull, with good equipment. That would flood one of the cells between the outer and inner hulls. Figure another five or so minutes on the inner hull. A lot of that water would vaporize while they cut. That meant pressure. They were too close.

"Move back! Move farther away!" she shouted as she stood up, arms waving. A few at the back of the mob heard her, and looked at her vacantly. A glow appeared on the ceiling, shouting ensued.

The first lance of flame shot down out of the ceiling, but it was almost immediately replaced by a stream of boiling water, which vaporized as soon as it hit the *Uni*'s dry air. She could hear the screams of those closest who'd been scalded. The cloud of steam rolled along the ceiling as water continued to drain out, now in a steady narrow column. As it slowed to a trickle, the torch beam began moving in a circle. The paint on the ceiling started burning, adding its own yellowish smoke to the haze.

Dija crouched behind a finished barricade. The barricade in front of hers rested against plastic crates, waiting for workers who had been waiting on Dija to finish with the welder. The crowd parted to let the wounded retreat. Two men, their faces deep red and swollen, looked to be in significant pain.

Now, with a better idea where the enemy was entering, the crowd had fallen back some. The plan had been to stay far enough back to let the enemy enter, then swarm them, but emotions were running high.

The torch ceased, not having completed the circle. Something heavy stomped on the ceiling, pounding the partially cut disc away. Dija didn't see the person drop through the opening, but saw the result. The mob surged forward, hammers and crowbars swung in huge arcs over their heads, then gunfire. She wasn't sure who was firing, but saw someone else fall from the ceiling, lifeless. More gunfire, this time Dija could see muzzle flashes as rifles appeared over the heads of the crowds, firing into the submarine above. Shouts and screams filled Dija's ears, audible over an intense ringing.

The body of one of the invaders, his face beaten nearly unrecognizable, got dragged through the crowd and dropped unceremoniously in the corridor between the mob and Dija. She wanted to look away, but couldn't. Beyond, one of the *Uni*'s soldiers, hoisted by his team, pulled himself up through the opening into the hole. He reached down and helped up another, a plainly dressed worker.

Dija knew what would come next. She turned back around, hands shaking, and continued her repair on the welder. Now it was even more important.

— ¯--

"We've taken one of the subs," Lieutenant Merella exclaimed. The news was met by relief more than excitement. "They're reporting now," he said, tilting his head down as he listened. "No serious casualties. They want us to warn the other teams about steam buildup at the cutting locations. The sub itself is in good shape, they're going to proceed to the next... Say again?" The lieutenant looked up at Ralla. "They say there's no ordnance on the sub."

"Should there be?"

"They say it's got the racks and guidance for offensive weaponry, but no actual munitions."

"A good thing, Lieutenant."

"I know, I'm just surprised. How does he expect to fight without weapons?"

"With guns, men, and water. He doesn't need anything else."

"You're right, of course."

"He also assumed, rather correctly, that we didn't have any either."

"The *Universalis* must have stockpiles somewhere," the lieutenant asked rhetorically. They'd gone over this earlier, to no satisfactory conclusion.

"If we did, that information died with Captain Sarras and his officers. Instruct your men to move as quickly as possible. Right now our only weapon is surprise, and for that weapon, we don't have much ammo."

"Nor for the other weapons," the lieutenant said bleakly.

—˙--

"We're approaching the first sub," Breka told Lo over the comm.

"You're good to go," he whispered back. Poking his head around the corner, he got a better look at what he'd glimpsed a moment earlier. The *Uni's* soldiers and civilian militia hadn't followed protocol. They'd cowered behind low barricades near the elevators while the enemy dropped heavy cases from the hole they'd cut in the ceiling. Now, as Lo watched from the stairwell, one of them jumped down behind the cases, impervious to the *Uni* soldiers' fire. Lo had a perfect shot, from his place at the head of the stairwell, at their unshielded backs.

Had he a weapon of any sort.

IX

"SHOULD WE KNOCK?" Breka asked his team.

The two other men looked scornfully at him through their helmets as they floated nearby. He shrugged and reached toward the lever on the top of the transport's hull. Modern subs had safety mechanisms to prevent exactly what Breka was about to do. This was not a modern sub. The lever released easily. Wedging a crowbar between the hatch the top of the hull, he only needed to push and pull slightly before water and air found their equilibrium. In a split second, the transport sub flooded, killing all eighteen men inside instantly.

"Lo, we've taken the first sub," Breka said over the comm as the sub sank away from him to the seabed below.

"Fine, keep going," Lo whispered. I'm busy, he thought but didn't say. He pressed himself against the wall of the stairwell, knowing how futile the effort was for someone his size. The gunfire was moving closer, indicating that at least some of the enemy troops had left their initial position and were moving in his direction. He didn't want to fight. For that matter, he wasn't sure he could. Climbing stairs winded him. A few days ago, he couldn't even get out of bed. But he was the only thing between these intruders and the rest of the ship. He was happy his men had captured one of the subs attacking engineering, but that was a small battle in what was becoming a much larger war.

There was a fraction of a moment as Lo's brain registered he was looking at a man's face, and that face was connected to other body parts that eventually grasped a gun. From the look of surprise on the face, it was clear this man wasn't expecting to see Lo either. The transition from surprise to menace was all that another part of Lo's brain needed. As the gun pivoted toward him, Lo's hands reached out, grabbing the man's black combat vest. In one fluid motion, Lo yanked him off his feet and tossed him toward the next landing, one flight below. What bones caused the cracking sound on impact, Lo didn't know, and didn't bother to check.

Another face appeared around the corner and was so shocked at the sight of his companion so far away, and in an unnatural pile, he didn't notice Lo's fist headed toward his head. The blow staggered him backwards, and he collapsed in his own pile on the far side of the corridor. Blood gushed. Lo moved on autopilot, stepping into the hallway and found the third and last of the squad. He was covering the hallway down which they'd come, firing over the heads of two cohorts holding fort underneath their sub. Lo used the man's vest as a handle and beat him against one wall of the corridor, then the other. The man dropped to the floor like a doll the moment Lo released him.

Kneeling down, realizing his crewmembers' bullets wouldn't know him from enemy, Lo took the rifle from his fallen victim. Winded and unable to aim the rifle well, reality started to crack into the scene. The realization of what he'd done started to seep into his consciousness. He fought it back just long enough to fire four rounds each into the two remaining soldiers, then he dropped the rifle and sat down hard on the floor.

Five men, all in the matter of seconds, he realized. After Dija had seen the carnage he'd been able to unleash, and after nearly dying on the dome in the middle of nowhere, he'd felt no desire to fight. He didn't want even the slightest form of conflict. Even as this battle loomed, he'd requested a backup role, organizing troops, nothing aggressive. His days of violence behind him.

Apparently not. From around the enemy's makeshift box barricade, faces of his crewmembers peered. His shape was known to them all, and they rushed over to see if he was hurt. Lo heard their voices but didn't hear their words. On some level, he knew what he'd done was right: protecting the ship. There were people below who couldn't defend themselves. On that level, it was his duty to help. He'd pledged his adult life to their protection. That cost, it seemed, was this. More than guilt, Lo felt disappointment and despair. It wasn't that he had hurt these men; they would have done the same to thousands of others. It's that he hadn't, on any level, *thought* about hurting these men. It had been a base instinct, uncontrollable, that had taken over. Bypassing all logic or good intentions, he slipped into machine mode. A machine Dija would never be able to fix, and that, once unleashed, killed. As he stared at the threadbare carpet and the rusty deck plating that peered through it, the sadness quickly overwhelmed him.

_-_--

Dija supervised the welding of the inner hull above the corridor's ceiling. She wasn't remotely qualified, but she was the closest thing to an engineer the area had at the moment. The soldier and his assistant, an amateur sub pilot apparently, had sealed themselves inside the sub. They would wait until the welding was finished before flooding the seal and going on the offensive.

The fusion welder made short work of the repair. The outer hull, with its ablative armor and carbon-composite base layer, was unrepairable with the equipment they had available. Maybe Koin had some gear in his lab, Dija thought, but that was dozens of decks below. The metal interior hull, however, was designed to handle pressure, and the fusion welder had its way with it. Within a few minutes, it was better than new. She heard the water rush in as the soldier released the seal, and a slight scrape as the sub lifted off.

— ¯ --

Within moments of each other, two subs rose away from the *Universalis*, their mission explicit: havoc. The sub captured near engineering, its occupants still in drysuits thanks to the flooded interior, acted as a mobile dive platform. Rising quickly behind another of the blockading subs, it disgorged its occupants and attempted to repeat their success from earlier. One, the pilot, stayed on the sub. The other two swam toward their target. It didn't work. Before they'd made it halfway, the other sub throttled up and shot away.

The other captured sub, after lifting off from the newly sealed hole, made no such attempt at subterfuge. With full throttle and expert aim, the *Universalis*'s burgeoning Defense Fleet scored its first victory. Impacting precisely at the right spot, the captured sub hit the enemy tug's port thruster nacelle, ripping it from its mounts. The crippled sub rolled starboard, the tears causing rapid flooding. The tug never righted from its list, and started to plummet toward the seabed.

— ¯ --

"Team 2 just took out a sub," Merella relayed to Ralla. "But Team 1's target scooted. It's a safe bet they know we're out there." Ralla nodded, looking down at the whiteboard. "The squad on the port side are welding the hull as we speak, and expect to launch momentarily."

Ralla allowed herself a moment of cautious optimism. So far, they were surviving. They'd repelled the boarders, capturing three subs and destroying another in the process.

"The aft team is radioing for assistance on a casualty. They say he's too big to carry. He doesn't seem injured, but they can't move him."

"Geran. That must be Geran Lo. How badly is he hurt?"

"They don't know, ma'am. They say he doesn't look injured, but he's comatose or something. 'Comatose' being their word."

Even though she knew she couldn't go, she struggled. Lo was a good man, and her best friend cared for him a great deal. So did Thom. For that matter, so did she. The Proctor part of her brain told her not to say what she was about to say.

"I need you to find Dija Yunner. Find her and tell her to get up there. She'll know what to do."

Ralla knew she probably *wouldn't* know what to do, but the two of them had a bond just like she and Thom did. Actually, Ralla realized, *nothing* like she and Thom had, but it worked for them. The lieutenant searched his board and checked with his nearby subordinates. They looked to be tracking her down.

"Wait, that was three subs," Ralla said. "I thought you said there were four?"

———

Breka's team had struck out again. The hatch on the target sub below theirs had been fully electronic, with no way to bypass from the outside. It was attached to the *Uni*'s hull with a skirt of carbonweave, uncuttable by their knives. The lip, vacuum pressurized, suctioned to the hull tightly. There was no way to dislodge or sabotage it.

"Lo," Breka sent over the comm, "we can't get in. Should we destroy the sub?"

They waited, receiving no response. Up along the slope of the *Uni*, they saw a new problem. Breka changed channels on his comm, and keyed the mic.

———

"The team on the stern says a big transport sub is landing at the main lock," Lieutenant Merella said, looking at the board and making a notation. Ralla looked down the hallway, the series of barricades blocking her view to the lock at the far end. Armed soldiers at each gave her some hope they'd be ready. They all heard the scraping.

"That would be them dragging our shuttle off the landing pad," the lieutenant informed Ralla, though she already knew. "Our other two subs are proving rather ineffective. They're annoying our visitors, but they're not able to inflict any actual damage. They definitely know what we're trying." Ralla looked up through the clear ceiling, unable to make out anything distinct.

"Should we fill the last captured sub with refugees then?" she asked.

The lieutenant thought for a moment. "I don't think so. I think we need as much going on out there as we can."

"Agreed."

They heard some shouting from down the corridor. Thom limped into Command and gripped the table to steady himself.

"Barricades are nearly done. They're definitely trying to get in, though. Where do you want me?"

The lieutenant looked up from Thom's hand.

"Arm yourself. We'll need it," Merella answered, not waiting for Ralla. Thom looked to her for her answer, and she agreed.

Dija knelt beside Geran Lo and placed her hand on his shoulder.

"Are you hurt?" she asked quietly. The others in the hallway had moved away to give them space. She spotted the bloodstains on the carpet. "Is that your blood?"

Geran looked up at her slowly, his face a mixture of pain and longing for forgiveness. She reflexively grimaced, and caught herself before she pulled her hand away.

"OK, maybe we can go somewhere else? What do you think?"

He clearly didn't believe her.

"Where would we go? Everywhere is here. You should go," he said quietly.

Dija looked up and down the corridor. A welding team had nearly completed repairs to the inner hull on this level. Soon they'd be moving to another level for more defensive construction.

"Yunner!" a soldier yelled from down the corridor. "Command says they need you up there. Their welder just went down."

"Lo, come with me to Command. Thom and Ralla are there."

Lo couldn't imagine facing Thom. Dija tugged at his arm.

"Come on. I want you to come with me. Please?" She stuck her face right in front of his. "Geran, please?

Her hair slid down in front of her face, framing it in copper. Her eyes showed she was worried, and Lo knew that for the moment, that worry was for him. Later, it wouldn't be. He saw what would happen next. She would be in trouble, and he's need to do something terrible to save her. And in that doing, he'd lose her forever.

Well, he thought, if that was the case, so be it. I'd rather live in a world with her alive and hating me than the both of us dead.

Lo shakily rose to his feet.

—-‒--

"Your attack failed. It's time to talk about this," Ralla said at the dented black box. In her mind she could see Cern, his face twisted in contempt. When she heard his voice, she knew she was right.

"Failed? Those subs? That was a single overeager gang of morons. I told them not to, but they tried to go it alone. Serves them right. And your men zooming around up here. What do they hope to accomplish? They're an annoyance. They're keeping our pilots awake, that's all."

"Cern, we can end this now. We can figure out a solution. It doesn't have to be like this."

"You know it does, Ralla, and if your father was alive, he would tell you the same thing."

"I'm glad to see you didn't know my father any better than you knew me."

She regretted it as soon as the words left her mouth, but Lieutenant Merella smiled proudly at her, presumably that she'd stood up for herself. Ralla noticed Dija and Lo in the room for the first time, and briefly wondered when they'd showed up. Dija gave her a thumbs-up. Ralla smiled in return, but the silent black box heightened her fears. It crackled.

"You're right, Ralla. It doesn't have to be like this. Here, listen in," Cern's voice moved away from the mic, but they all could still hear it as he spoke into what they assumed was another microphone. "Gentlemen, this is Hennorr. They're refusing to yield. Given their surprising aggression and our regrettable casualties, I feel it is no longer in our best interest to blockade and quarantine. You now have full and complete access to the *Universalis*, any and all salvage you acquire is yours to keep. I needn't remind you they will resist. Use your best judgment on how to proceed. Hennorr, out."

"Cern, no!" Ralla pleaded. "This is pointless. We're just throwing rocks at each other."

"I have more rocks. Goodbye, Ralla."

X

"THE WET TEAMS are reporting multiple ships closing on the *Uni*, all directions," one of Merella's subordinates relayed.

"Keep them away from the Garden," Ralla ordered.

"Sir, they're cutting through the lock!" another shouted. They all turned to look down the corridor, even though they knew they couldn't see that far.

"Miss Yunner, we could use your assistance on the welder," Merella said.

"Right," she answered, and tugged on Lo to follow. Silently, he did. The sounds of objects hitting the hull reverberated up to Command.

"Can you get the wet teams into position as spotters? Put them up here even," Ralla said, pointing at the dome above their heads. The lieutenant nodded. She turned to Thom.

"I'm going to need your help soon. Are you up for it?" she asked. Thom nodded, sure in his response, unsure in his ability.

The sounds of gunfire echoed down the corridor.

"They've made it through," the lieutenant said redundantly. He motioned with quick jabs of his hands for his subordinates to get their weapons. Ralla noticed she was the only one unarmed.

"Lieutenant?" she said, holding out her hand.

"Sorry, ma'am, of course," he handed her his own sidearm, and took another from a nervous ensign struggling with a rifle nearby. Down the corridor, gunfire mixed with screams.

—⁻--

When her hands shook, it made the complex and exacting work impossible. When the bullets cracked off pieces of the barricade, she lost her concentration as well. As each piece failed to fit, she became more flustered.

"Geran... I..." she said, dropping another piece. Looking at it, she wasn't even sure what it was. Lo, having been keeping an eye out the best he could, turned back to Dija. He read her face instantly, and it was all he needed. Pulling her away from the machine, they ducked behind the next barricade, stepped to the connecting hallway, and headed down into the ship.

—⁻--

Outside, salvage tugs, haulers, and transports of all sizes, all outfitted with softlocks, descended en masse toward the *Universalis*. Inside them, crews with cutting tools, or teams with drysuits and handheld thrusters, readied themselves for the imminent scavenging.

One by one the subs attached, some along the flooded edges of the citysub, others along the roofline, all ready to bore their way in.

—⁻--

"Slow down, slow down. All right, say again," Lieutenant Merella shouted into his comm. As quickly as he could, he noted on the board where the spotters said the subs had latched on. His remaining three subordinates helped mark the map and relay orders. Merella directed these men, they directed their respective crews. As much as it worked, it was working. The gunfire behind them got louder. He kept looking up, and strained to see down the hallway.

"Lieutenant, you should see to your men," Ralla said. "We can't lose that corridor. Give me your comm. I'll take over here."

The lieutenant hesitated, then pulled out the earpiece and handed it to Ralla. She wiped it cursorily before slamming it in her ear. He pointed to the three remaining subordinates.

"They'll know what to do and where everyone is," he said. "I'll be back in a moment." He checked the clip on his pistol, and headed toward the corridor. As he passed Thom, they exchanged a salute.

The comm came to life in Ralla's ear, the spotters reporting more and more landings. She stepped around to the other side of the board and started marking down locations. She hadn't been counting the subs the lieutenant had added, and not being able to hear the spotters, she hadn't known. But now, really looking at the board, and putting more spots down herself, the magnitude of their problem seemed overwhelming. There were at least thirty ships already on the hull, and that was just the ones they knew about.

Ralla caught Thom's eye as he looked back and forth between her and the hallway. They shared a glance, her feelings obvious to him. He nodded despairingly.

Suddenly, Ralla had an idea. She looked at the three remaining officers.

"How many teams do we have, with comms, near these landings? The priority landings, I don't care about the outer ring."

"Fifteen, I think," one said. Ralla figured the soldier was school-age, had there still been school. "Fifteen near some of them, at least..."

"I want you to have them report which of these landings has visible signs they're breaking through. I'm talking about actual cuts in the inner hull. If their spot *doesn't* have signs they're cutting in, relay that landing to our 'fleet' outside. Understand? I want them to gets these bugs off our back while we still can."

The officers started talking immediately into their comms.

"Thom, find out how the lieutenant is doing."

"You got it."

Thom limped down the corridor, moving carefully from cover to cover. The gunfire from the open hatch at the far end was sporadic, but sporadic bullets killed just as easily. He finally found the lieutenant, two-thirds the distance to the hatch.

"We've pinned them, they've pinned us, is that what you came up here to find out?" Merella said between looks over the top of the low barricade.

"More or less. What are the odds you'll be able to take their sub?"

"Not good. We can't get close, and we don't have any grenades or smoke to clear them out."

"What's your advice, then?"

"We're pretty well set in here. They're the ones that want to come in. I say we wait, let them come to us. We can pick them off one by one."

"Understood," Thom replied before crouch-walking back toward Command.

_-__

Lo placed Dija against the wall around the corner from the Spine's access tunnel. He couldn't tell if she was ramping up to a panic attack, or coming down from one. Her breathing was shallow and rapid, but she still seemed lucid.

"Tell me what you need."

"I need to fix that welder," she replied.

"No, you don't."

"I need to fix that welder."

"Dija, look at me. Di, look," he said, resting his big hand gently on her shoulder. She finally locked eyes with him. His face was close to hers, his breathing slow and steady. "I'm freaking out right now," he calmly. "Can you help me?"

She looked him up and down. He looked almost placid.

"Well, you look terrified," she replied.

"I'm stronger than I look," Lo answered.

"I suppose you'd have to be."

"What should I do?" he asked.

"You could kiss me, if you think it would help," she said. Lo did, an awkward kiss while trying to lean over her with shooting pains in his chest. He finally leaned back and rubbed his sternum with his hand. "Well, that made me feel better, though you still look like a wreck," she said, the corners of her lips showing the barest hint of a smile.

"We can't stay here, Di."

The gunfire started again, in earnest this time, from the Spine. Dija jumped at the noise. Shouts and screams echoed down their own corridor. Lo assumed that Cern's people had found another way in and were spreading through the interior. He wondered clinically how many, and how quickly.

"Geran, I don't want to die here."

"We can get down to the Basket; we shouldn't stay up here anyway."

"No, I mean I don't want to die on this ship. Does that make me a bad person?"

"What? No." Lo looked nervously both ways down the corridor. This was a bad place to be having a conversation.

"Because I think Ralla does. I think she means to. You have to tell Thom."

"What's Thom going to do? Look, we need to get down to the Basket. Thom and Ralla can take care of themselves."

Lo stood up, the sharp pains in his chest now joined by soreness in his legs. Even with the excuse of being bed-bound for a few weeks, Lo was annoyed at himself for being so out of shape. He offered Dija his hand and she pulled herself up. Lo keyed his comm.

"Command, this is Lo. Dija and I are falling back to the next checkpoint."

"Roger that, Lieutenant Lo," returned a voice he didn't recognize.

"The hallway out here may be compromised. I can't see anyone, but I can hear something."

"Thank you, Command out."

Lo shook his head. There was no time to worry about what was happening in Command.

—-—

Ralla wanted to scream over the comm in aggravation. Reports were coming in from all over the ship now, some real, some imagined, of intruders. The limited nature of the crippled comm system meant she could only talk to certain people. Often, she'd issue an order just to find out she was talking to the wrong person. Even the military officers were having trouble keeping track.

The gunfire, almost constant now, only added to the confusion. If they could hold the invaders where they were, Ralla figured, and they had done their planning well, they might be able to prevent them from having the run of the ship. It didn't matter that they weren't explicitly trying to take over the citysub; their looting would cause far more damage. She thought she heard one of the officers say Lo's name. She asked for confirmation.

"He's falling back with a 'Dija' to the next checkpoint."

That meant downstairs, in the Basket. That was probably a good idea. Mixed with the gunfire, Ralla was sure she heard a rhythmic pounding, like someone hitting the... she looked up. One of the spotters, Ralla had no way of knowing for how long, had been slamming his fist against the dome. Once he saw he had gotten her attention, he pointed at his helmet.

"What channel are the spotters on?" she asked. The officers looked at each other. She snapped her fingers. "Come on, come on."

"Twelve, I think."

Ralla dialed in the correct channel, and the spotter's panicked voice overloaded the tiny speaker in the earpiece.

"They're landing another sub," the spotter shouted. Ralla could see him point toward the landing pad.

"How? They've still got a sub there," Ralla said, peering down the corridor out of habit to double check. The gunfire meant they were still fighting someone.

"No, they're landing a sub *on* the other sub."

"Understood," she answered.

That meant reinforcements, potentially unlimited. Had the enemy needed to move their current sub, at least that would have allowed the *Uni* soldiers a brief respite to reload and reinforce. Now, a steady stream of fresh troops.

"Thom," she yelled, waving him over from his station at the door. "They're landing another sub *on* the sub that's there."

"Time to go?"

"Tell the lieutenant to fall back to the next checkpoint."

Thom nodded and limped off. They had prepared for this, but Ralla took another look around the room: stained mattresses, empty food containers, loose bedding. There was nothing here anyone would miss. She started erasing the board with her hand, and after a moment the other officers assisted. It was going to be a dangerous run through the barricades to the access tunnel, but then it was a clear shot to the elevators and down into the Basket. She picked up a small green box from the table and headed for the door.

$$—\,^{-}\!--$$

"Try Lo again," one of Breka's team shouted into the comm. They stood on top of an enemy sub, watching murky shadows swarm the *Uni*'s carcass.

"Lieutenant Lo, we are requesting orders. The enemy sub has penetrated the hull. How should we proceed?

Surprising them all, he responded.

"This is Lo. Stand by," he said. Lo stepped out onto the deck of the Basket, with Dija close behind. He hadn't seen the fortifications from this angle, and they looked intimidating. It was like the wall of a fortress he remembered from an old book. Except it was all metal, connecting the aft wall and the stern of the fallen cruise ship. There were even guard towers and a gate. He waved at the guards on the ramparts and the gate opened, one benefit of being recognizable at a distance. The door scraped open, revealing the open staging area beyond.

To get the necessary material for the new walls, crews had torn up the floor, leaving dangerous-looking gullies between thick pipes and narrow crawlspaces. White carbon-composite paneling, laid end-to-end, connected the small islands of remaining floor in a sea of industrial-looking demolished openness.

Lieutenant Merella's second in command, Lieutenant Ilson, was in charge down here. While the bulwark, and its twin on the far side of the Basket, blocked enemy movement from the elevators, it was all still a perfect shooting gallery, with tens of thousands of windows and portholes looking down onto the floor of the Basket. Men and women, gathering in a sort of militia, took cover wherever they could, each visibly scanning a different part of the walls above.

"Lieutenant Ilson," Lo said, partly as a greeting, partly to get the man's attention. He got it. Ilson was using a pile of crates as a base of operations, stacked near the center of the open space between the barricades. His trademark dark curly hair was matted to his square head with sweat. "Are you in charge of the engineering defense team?"

"I was, yes."

"Was? You've lost contact?"

"No, not contact. We've lost it."

"Lost engineering? So they're in there now? Doing what?"

"Nothing good."

"Get Command, we need to get in there. They could take out the power for half the ship."

"Command isn't answering."

"Di," Lo said, waving her over. "What would happen if we flood starboard engineering?"

Lo saw a change come over her face, from eyes darting and general anxiety, to intense focus.

"Most of the heavies are protected, they'll cut out as soon as there's water. The breakers, though..." she trailed off, and looked up at the picosuns. "I'm not sure. It could cut half the lights on the ship, or just double the load on the other generator. I don't know."

"Would that be worse or better compared to what some of Cern's people could do in there?"

"Umm... Well, if they just want the parts, they could rip out pretty much everything and it wouldn't affect the other gennie. They're connected in parallel, but the relays are fail-safes. They snap open at the first sign of trouble. We had the same setup in my dome growing up. They copied the *Uni* design."

"And if they don't just want the parts?"

"They could spike the generators and they'd both go down."

"Down, as in..." Lo asked.

"Dark. We'd be in the dark."

"Command, this is Lo, the enemy has taken starboard engineering. Requesting orders. Repeat, we have lost starboard engineering. If you don't respond, I am ordering the wet team to flood it."

They waited, silence. Dija looked worried, and Lo knew why. Ralla wasn't answering. There wasn't time to worry about that. He switched his comm to his team.

"This is Lo. Flood it."

"Say again?" Breka responded. "Did you say *flood* it? Flood engineering?"

"Flood it. The water will do less damage than they can."

"What about our people in there?"

"Sergeant, if the enemy is in there, our people are dead. Flood it, this is an order." He looked at Ilson, whose face showed grim determination. Lo turned to Dija. "Di, I hope you're right."

There wasn't time for her to respond before a deafening *crack* plunged them into absolute and total darkness.

XI

THE BLACK was palpable, weighing on them, separating them. It was as if their eyes had stopped working. Through the ringing in their ears, screams sounded and echoed all up and down the Basket. It seemed everyone was making some sort of noise, in reaction or fear to the darkness. Everyone, Lo realized, except Dija. She was close enough that he could hear her muttering.

"Tick, tick, tick, *pop*, now," and as if on her cue, the lights snapped back on, partially. The picosuns far above shone at half brightness, casting the dim light of dusk, but with the warm color of midday. Around them they could hear continued popping sounds as bulbs burst with the strain of inferior power.

"The gennie will spool up," Dija said, paler than normal.

Lo didn't want to ask if she'd known that was going to happen.

"So we'll get full light again?" Ilson asked.

"I don't know. I doubt it. There's a lot of ship to run on one generator," Dija answered. "I hope Ralla is OK."

Crouched behind a barricade, Ralla didn't see the shot that killed Lieutenant Merella. The few moments of darkness had been less traumatic for the men and women defending the Spine than the rest of the ship. Though this hadn't stopped Ralla from lashing out with her arm to find Thom in the dark, only to hit him in the jaw, which he now rubbed silently. The light from the enemy sub let them see enough, and even helped, silhouetting their targets on the bright background. As the main lights sputtered back on, the lieutenant turned to order his men to retreat. Either a ricochet or shrapnel had buried itself into the back of his head. With no exit wound, everyone thought he'd fainted. Realizing he was dead, Ralla assumed direct command immediately.

"Covering fire! Get back to the elevators." It was an orderly retreat, the pair closest to the enemy sub emptied their clips into the hatch while those behind them fled. Then the rearmost team did the same, firing over the heads of their retreating squadmates. Ralla didn't want to, but she had no choice but to leave the lieutenant's body. After they were all clear, they sealed the hatch to the access tunnel.

Ralla removed the green box from her pocket. Four switches and a button, it was that simple. She flipped the top two switches, and they all could hear and feel the massive watertight doors slam shut just around the bends of the corridor. The elevators arrived, and the twenty soldiers and officers, plus Ralla and Thom, entered. She flipped the next two switches, sending all three starboard-side elevators to the floor of the Basket and locking them there. As they descended, Ralla pressed and held the button.

A small charge, attached with packing tape to the dome, blew out a fist-sized hole. The force of the sea rushing in, and the air rushing out, fractured the rest of the clear panel. Water rushed down the Spine, flooding the enemy sub parked at the end.

Ralla arrived at the makeshift fort with Thom and a handful of soldiers.

"What happened?" she asked the group, skipping any greetings. Dija looked happy to see her, but when all eyes turned to her to explain, she got nervous.

"I, I thought... since they had gotten in engineering they could have shut down the ship. So we flooded it. There was less chance of damage."

"Because there were safeties against water," Ralla stated, just realizing it herself.

"Right," Dija said, happy her friend got it so quickly.

"Will we get full power back?"

"Doubtful," Ilson answered.

"Fine, we'll do the best with what we can. What else?"

"I've got reports of intruders all over the ship," he replied.

Ralla looked up and surveyed the Basket. Many windows on the walls above were covered by hastily attached panels, but not all. T-town and the Terraces showed the results of the recent fortification work, but even those barricades looked marginal compared to the vast open spaces and infinite angles available for gunmen. All it would take would be a few snipers to set off a panic.

"Ilson, we need..." Ralla's voice trailed off. She was going to ask him to station more men down the Canyon and around Tent City, but to what end? To show those people they had them protected? They didn't, and everyone knew it. Sure, in terms of raw numbers, the survivors on the *Uni* outnumbered their attackers. But from a soldier-to-soldier standpoint, they were clearly at a disadvantage.

"Ilson, Lieutenant Merella is dead. You're ranking officer." Ilson looked shocked for a moment, then nodded. "Right now I want you to order your men to fall back if the fighting gets too hot."

"Ma'am?"

"My father taught me that on some level, all wars are wars of attrition. Either of men or resources, one side has more, keeps more, finds more, whatever. We set up our defense with the idea that we could hold them where they land, and worst case, fall back. We were wrong. There is no way we can hold them, so we have to yield."

"You want to surrender?" he asked incredulous.

"No, we need to *flow*. Let them hit, we fall back. Let them come. They may have more soldiers, but there are more of us."

"You expect the civilians to fight? We've already signed up everyone who was willing."

"Then the nonwilling will have to fight, too. Once they see their homes destroyed, they'll fight."

"The casualties will be staggering."

"Lieutenant Ilson, I hate to be so blunt, but this is a question of some dead versus all dead. Cern saw to that when he started all this. I don't want anyone to die, but if these people don't stand up for themselves, none of us have any hope." She looked around to the soldiers gathered to hear her. "We can win this. I know it looks bleak, but we just need to work together."

It looked to Ralla that some of the soldiers believed her, and thankfully, those who didn't, didn't say anything. Thom offered a comforting smile. Dija, as Ralla expected, looked energized. Lo looked at Dija, clearly not having bought a word Ralla had said.

—⁻--

The initial fusillade of gunfire didn't hurt anyone, but it successfully panicked the troops. Ralla and Ilson had barely started working on a new plan for defense. Lo scooped Dija up in one swipe and dove into a nearby trough. Thom and Ralla ducked behind the crates they'd been using as tables and quickly realized Ilson was on the other side of the same crates.

"From where?" Ralla yelled. Thom shrugged, and stuck his head up over the crates while Ralla scanned the wall in front of them.

"I don't see anything."

After the initial shock, some of the *Uni* troops started firing blindly into the walls. Ilson shouted at them to stop. Ralla looked over at Dija extricating herself from Lo's mass. Ralla elbowed Thom in the side. "We planned for this," she said before spreading the crates apart so she could see Ilson. "We planned for this," she yelled again. "Let those in cover stay here. The rest of us need to fall back to the Canyon." Ilson nodded. The gunfire started up again. This time they could see the bullets impact the deck. Shrapnel from the deck plating showered everyone in the open. Ralla screamed as a piece sliced open her arm. Thom leapt to her, clamping his hand on the wound.

"It's fine, it's fine, I'm fine. We need to go," she yelled over the noise, pushing Thom's hand out of the way and replacing it with her own. It was a lot of blood, she noted analytically. On her signal, she, Ilson, and Thom sprinted toward the cover of the Canyon, Thom barely using his bad leg, wielding his cane deftly. Another barricade had been set up, looking more like the entrance to another fort than an exit for the one they were in. As they ran, they could hear more bullets impacting around them. Thom could feel the safety of the huge fallen ships looming over them, their heavy shadows a surprisingly comforting darkness.

Lo half lifted, half tossed Dija out of the trough. Across the deck, in the safety of the shadowed gloom, Thom and Ralla watched anxiously as Dija ran toward them. Halfway, she stopped, and looked back at Lo, who was struggling to get onto the deck. She ran back to help him.

"Crap," Thom said, dropping his cane and limp-running out to assist. In slow motion he watched bullets hit the deck plating in an advancing line. The one that struck Lo's outstretched arm caused an eruption of blood.

Dija screamed and fell back. Lo's face twisted into a harsh grimace. Thom reached Dija and the two of them tried to pull Lo the rest of the way out of the trench toward the relative safety of the Canyon. Ralla started to run out to join them, then stepped back, still holding her bleeding arm. She pointed awkwardly with her joined arms toward the area high up on the wall where she'd seen the muzzle flashes.

"Covering fire!" she yelled to the troops around her. They aimed where she was pointing and opened fire. A long white yacht that made that section of the wall disappeared under the impact of hundreds of bullets. With Dija pulling Lo's good arm, and Thom lifting his legs, they half-carried, half-dragged Lo to the shadow of the Canyon.

_-__

The second wave of attackers had begun their breach. Dumping into the upper corridors, dozens of armed men spread out like flowing water. Finding little of value, and the path to the elevators locked out, they made their way to the stairs. Here they found heavy resistance. At every landing, shots exchanged resulted in casualties. Each floor, barricaded and defended, funneled the pirates lower and lower in search of easier prey and plunder.

_-__

"They're on multiple levels," Ilson shouted to Ralla. Having wrapped a few lengths of gauze around her own arm, she was attempting to do the same for Lo. No sooner did the thin white cloth go taught than it soaked red with blood. Thom scanned through the narrow space above them for signs of the enemy. Dija gripped Lo's big hand in both of hers.

"So far we have them contained in the stairwells," he announced.

"They're going to hit the bottom and start bouncing back up," Ralla said, tying off Lo's bloodied tourniquet.

"We'll be ready for them," Ilson said quickly.

"We haven't been so far," Ralla muttered to herself.

_-__

Eventually, they found it: a half-welded hatch gave way, offering access to T-Town. The initial rush swarmed the first cabins, knocking over people and furniture alike. The dark corridors came alive with bodies, falling into walls, kicking open doors, trying to make room for the relentless surge behind them. The thin, makeshift walls of T-town started to give way. First, it was accidental; a wrong step, an overly heavy push, and someone would fall through a wall.

The screams of those cowering inside were nearly matched by the triumphant invaders, destroying everything in their wake.

— ¯--

Everyone below knew what the screams meant.

"Lieutenant Ilson, have your men on the Terraces take positions to defend the bridges," Ralla ordered. Ilson looked up at the two swaying rope-and-paneling bridges that offered easy, if alarming, passage between the two areas. A single covered bridge offered better protection, but in its own way was easy to defend. Ilson conveyed orders over his comm.

"We need to get Lo better cover," Ralla said, looking down at her injured friend. His face was pale and moist with sweat.

"I can walk," he replied hoarsely.

"I hope so," Ralla answered. "But right now, just help Thom and Dija move you under that overhang."

The sounds of gunfire and screams pressed down as Ralla watched an injured Thom help an injured Lo closer to one of the few areas of cover they actually had.

Shouts from above and from the other side of the gate told Ralla that Cern's people had broken through to more areas.

"Just a bit longer. Just a little bit longer," she said aloud, though no one could hear her.

— ¯--

Firing from a covered balcony high up on the Terraces, Corporal Ebel, last of his unit, knew his was going to die. He could hear the sounds of the enemy breaking down the door behind him. Ahead, he could see the destructive signs of the enemy trashing entire levels of T-town. The structure visibly shook with their efforts. His girlfriend and her parents had just moved to level six, a lucky win in a lottery of only losers. Their floor was gone now, just debris and bodies. She hadn't been there, but her parents had. For a quick moment, he felt guilt for being glad he wouldn't have to tell her that her parents were dead. Someone else would, and would tell her the same of him.

Ebel brought his rifle to his shoulder, sighted down the long barrel. A relic of another time, he had cast and stuffed the cartridges himself. The noise it made was from another world. The massive boom echoed off the walls of the Basket for what seemed like an eternity. Ebel saw the bullet impact its target, knocking the man backwards and spraying blood behind him. Ebel chambered another round. *Boom.* The sound was terrifying, but he didn't notice. Another target down. This one lost a leg from the thigh down.

Boom.

Passing through one target, Ebel's shot caught a second in the chest. They went down together. Below, he could hear his shipmates firing as they spotted enemy soldiers trying to find a way across the open space between the ships, and the narrow bridges that connected them.

Boom.

Ebel missed his target thanks to a last second dodge. Steadying the barrel on the balcony's railing, his next shot found its mark. He cycled another round, then noticed his hand fall from the stock. He looked down as it hung limply at his side. Slowly, he felt himself fall to his knees. There was no pain, only an intense desire to fire his rifle one more time, many more times. The stock fell in front of him as he collapsed forward, face pressing against the balcony wall. He wished he could pick it up. He wished he could kiss his girlfriend goodbye.

He felt the pressure of the kick more than anything, knocking him onto his back. Corporal Ebel looked up and smiled, the second to last thing he would do, or his enemy would see.

—-—

The explosion shook the whole ship. Fiery debris rained down on the Canyon. After the initial shock, Thom stepped in the middle of the Canyon and tried to see where it had come from.

"It looks like it was up in the Terraces," he said as the gunfire restarted above.

"Ilson, did you plant demolitions?" Ralla asked, brushing off some ash.

"Of course not."

"Find out what happened," she ordered. It would make sense for Cern's people to have brought explosives, she thought, but if they were going to use them, why hadn't they used them on the doors and barricades already?

"The explosion was near one of our guys," Ilson reported. "There are fires. People are panicking. I have to get up there."

Ralla thought about it for a moment, then agreed.

"Go. Take charge. Report back when you can."

Ilson nodded and took off at a run. Ralla tuned her comm to the general channel, and tried to make sense of the layers of intense chatter. Two things were clear: More subs were landing, and the invaders onboard were spreading.

___-__

Lin Ott missed her son. Cowering in her tent, she tried to block out the sounds around her the best she could. Born on the *Population*, she'd been raised to hate the people of the *Universalis*. Forced to live among them, she'd been shocked at how gracious and friendly they all were. Her son, Lume, not always the easiest to reach, so typical of his age, had come around more slowly. But even he had started to make friends with the other children in the place everyone called Tent City.

Lin knew her son would always need his mother, but when she saw all the people trying to evacuate, she had made the hardest decision of her life. Lume was a good boy, independent and smart. He was young enough to make the cut for the first round of evacuations. Lin gave her seat willingly. There were too many other boys and girls far younger than Lume needing their mothers. She felt bittersweet about Lume's tears as he'd been ushered away. So sweet that he cared so much about her, despite not giving any indication for months, and so bitter that they'd be torn apart, especially after they'd survived the horrors of Oppai's reign on the *Population*. Now he was gone, hopefully safe.

Tent City had become increasingly chaotic. As more and more people ran past her tent, Lin bravely peered out to see what they were running from. She could look down one of the main paths, down the small hill, toward the bow of some great fallen ship. Ever intrepid, the *Uni* engineers had built some massive tower out of materials they'd scavenged. She'd watched in awe as the floors went up, and filled out with walls and windows, balconies and stairways. Now, armed men poured out of it like a leaking seal. Unable to cross to the Terraces, another marvel, they were climbing down the bow and into Tent City.

Lin had known men like this before. She'd watched Oppai's rise to power and the greed he awoke in like-minded men. Selfish men. Men like Lume's father. They wouldn't stop at Tent City. They'd swarm through it, raping and stealing, just as their kind had done for all history. And then what? Then they'd spread out, finding more helpless individuals to enslave or imprison.

Well, not me, Lin thought. Not again. And not my son.

Stepping out of her tent, Lin Ott felt a resolve she'd never known before. Dirty, tattered clothes trailing behind her, she started at a jog down the small slope toward the pirates. She passed tent after tent, the wide eyes of forgotten women and cowardly men staring at this blur of a frail form running toward danger. Fleeing residents stumbled to get out of her way. Legs pumping fiercely, Lin Ott let loose a wailing scream heard though all the tents and hovels across Tent City.

She ran, headlong into a gathering mass of pirates that had no idea what was happening.

"Apparently," Ralla said, relaying the chatter on the comm to her friends, "some tiny lady just attacked a bunch of invaders over in Tent City."

"That's awesome," Dija said, suddenly smiling.

"It's going to take a lot more than that. At least ten more subs have landed. More are landing on the backs of other subs like what we saw upstairs. And they're working their way down."

It took them a moment to notice, but the gunfire from the "fort" between the elevators had taken on a new level of intensity. One of the men on the gate yelled over to Ralla.

"They've found a way in. They're inside!"

"Get our people in here. Have them fall back. Wait, what am I saying?" Ralla tapped her comm. "This is Ralla Gattley, all troops near the elevators, fall back to the Canyon. We will regroup here."

At the top of the gate, Ralla saw the soldiers waving for their colleagues to hurry. In the yard beyond, soldiers with cover fired out at an advancing group of invaders. Unable to cross to the Terraces from T-town, they had begun climbing down the stern of the overturned tanker and into the makeshift fort. The more that poured out from the stairwells into T-town, the more that had to make room by getting to the ground of the Basket. There seemed to Ralla very little organization among their enemy. Small groups, probably known to each other beforehand, stuck together, but apparently the only cohesive plan was a sort of instinctual swarm. With limited places to go, Ralla felt it safe to assume they'd eventually start communicating, organizing.

The pirates still on the open levels of T-town shot down at the soldiers inside the fort, supplying suppressing fire for their comrades climbing down onto the Basket floor. Once in the fort, Cern's people easily made it into the trenches and started clearing them of resistance. For every one *Uni* soldier that had escaped to the Canyon, two others had been cut down in the attempt.

Finally, the gate was closed. The Canyon, with its partial cover supplied by the hull foundations of T-Town and the Terraces, became the new shelter for twenty armed but frazzled soldiers, some wounded casualties, and many more terrified noncombatants. Those who had claimed the Canyon as home tried to make room in or around their tarps and tents for their defenders.

"Ralla, something's happening in Tent City," Ilson said over the comm.

_-__

There had been too many to contain, and now they spread viciously through Tent City. Lin Ott's assault had inspired many others, so instead of an easy advance through a destitute and hungry populace, the invaders now found themselves with a fight on their hands. More and more civilians joined the defense as they tried to push the enemy back. With nowhere to go, their backs against the tanker and outer walls, the invaders escalated their violence. Up until that moment, they'd been fighting off their unarmed assailants with the butts and stocks of their weapons, sometimes with a slash of a knife. But all it took was one.

The machine gun sounded like a saw shredding itself to destruction. In a vast sweeping arc radiating outward from the thin, frightened pirate, scores of people fell, bloodied or dead. Against such force, the largely unarmed civilian residents of Tent City began to flee. The flight became a stampede, crushing tents and people alike as the mob ran outward. Like frantic ripples in a pond, the ever-growing circles of people caused further terror, and soon the thousands of remaining civilians in Tent City began running, or trying to run, from the now easily advancing pirates.

People soon reached the walls, erected to protect, but now pinning them in. The panic spread like a wave.

_-__

"Ralla, they're losing it over there. One of the pirates just slaughtered a bunch of people and they're all panicking," Ilson shouted over his comm. "I'm going to try to get over there. If that mob breaks free, it will be like a lock bursting. There's no way we'll be able to contain it."

"Understood. Take some of your men and see if you can flank them, or at least sneak into Tent City along the forward edge of the Canyon. I'll take some of the soldiers here and, I don't know what. I'll try to get our people's attention or something."

The troops around her that weren't tending their wounds knew she was about to ask them for something, and had already started to assemble before her. They all turned as the ramming began on the gate.

Cern's men pounded with their weapons and tried to shoulder their way through the gate. It wasn't substantial, a piecemeal of repurposed metal decking, just like the rest of the flimsy new wall. Ralla knew it wouldn't last long. Within a few moments, they would break through and her people would have nowhere to fall back to. The gate at the far end of the Canyon wouldn't hold either. And from the Canyon, the invaders could easily take the Terraces, and worse, surround Tent City. Ralla could hear the pounding against the gate, and in the distance behind her, the pounding of thousands against the walls of Tent City. The guards at the top of the gate had stopped firing on their attackers and now held on for dear life. Ralla watched as one lost his grip, and fell off into the enemy beyond. It wasn't going to be moments, she realized, it was imminent.

Ralla looked at Thom and could see in his eyes he knew. He knew what she was about to ask. Standing guard over the wounded Lo and lost-looking Dija, Thom lowered his gaze as Ralla approached.

"Why are they still coming after us?" Dija asked. Ralla could hear the nerves in her voice. She didn't like tight spaces, and this one was getting tighter and tighter. "Why won't they just go loot and leave us alone?"

"Because we're shooting at them," Thom said dryly.

"Are you saying it'd be better if we surrendered?" Ralla asked angrily.

"No, I'm saying we're shooting at them, so they're trying to get us to stop. But because they won't stop, we're shooting at them."

"What are you saying?"

"Just sayin'."

Ralla could see he was already breathing more quickly. His response came from a place of anxiety. Well, she thought, there wasn't anything she could do about that.

"Thom, I need you to take charge here. I have to go help Tent City."

She saw him swallow. As he looked up his body sagged.

"Ralla, I..." Thom said.

"Thom," she answered. In her look was more than an order, it was a plea. "It is time for you to fight."

Thom knew what she meant. He had been in combat all day. Now it was time for him to fight something else. She didn't wait for him to respond. Ralla turned, gathered half the remaining troops, and headed off toward the far gate and Tent City beyond.

Thom watched her go, hearing in the back of his mind the pounding on the gate. The remaining troops looked to him. "Troops" was generous. Few had been military, fewer still seemed to know how to hold a gun. Many were injured. All were terrified. He looked at Dija, watching Ralla go, hand covered in Lo's blood as she gripped his arm tight. Lo looked up at him, pale and drawn, looking eerily like Mrakas Gattley, Ralla's father, had on his deathbed.

And that was what did it. His mind connected events rapidly. From the elder Gattley and his bed, to the commission Thom received, to the ship he'd commanded, to the people he'd killed and the people he'd gotten killed. Faces lost to the sea. Bodies crushed forever in metal cocoons. In a rush, the terror overwhelmed him. His eyes could only focus on the faces of those around him, all waiting for his orders, waiting for him to get them killed. A cold sweat soaked his skin, his breathing short and shallow. The pounding of the blood in his ears syncopated with the pounding at the gate. Any moment, they'd break through and have the run of the ship. Thousands would die. Ralla had counted on him in this moment, and he'd let her down. He half fell, half sat on the deck. Because of him, these people here would die. Because of him, everyone on the ship would die. Because of his failure, he was a failure, just as his father said he'd be. He failed, and now Lo would die. Dija would die. Everyone would die, even...

A white-hot sphere of loathing and panic and fear consumed Thom, blocking out all the screams and sounds around him. Some of the terrified young guards and soldiers now started to flee while others rushed toward the gate in an attempt to hold it up. Welds gave way, gaps appeared. And the white-hot sphere in Thom's chest flared in a last celebration of his utter failure, and imminent death.

...Ralla.

Thom grabbed the sphere. He could see it now, like a physical object. Thom stood up. With the world collapsing around him, the wails of the dying and the cries of the fearful, he held fast his sphere of panic. He was terrified, more than he'd ever been in his life, but he held the sphere. Held it.

It didn't hold him.

"You, start firing into those gaps," Thom shouted powerfully. "You two, find something to wedge against the hulls and the gate. You guys, start throwing anything heavy you can find over the top. NOW!" Thom picked up a discarded rifle and limped toward the gate. A face appeared in a gap. Thom fired, the rifle kicking powerfully in his hands. Another face. Thom fired. He shouted more orders to the soldiers cowering on the floor. In his mind the sphere fought to consume him. In his mind, he gripped it tighter, and kept firing.

XII

THEY WERE ABOUT to lose it. With the few men he had available, Thom knew there was no way he'd be able to hold the gate. Even as more and more of Cern's men left to search out other ways around, more showed up to take their place.

Ralla, the Council, everyone knew it would be difficult to defend the ship. There were too many places to get in, too many passages throughout, and too many people to protect. Ralla had sold them all on it, and Thom wondered now, as then, if she'd believed a word of it.

The so-called pirates were working together now, running at the gate. It swayed a little more with each hit. It was time to go.

"Di, I need you to help Lo fall back to the next checkpoint."

"No. Leave me here," Lo mumbled.

"Where's that?" Dija asked Thom.

"Um, Camp 1, I think. Just get going. Anything on the other side of the next gate is better than here."

"Thom, I can barely walk," Lo said.

Thom looked at Lo for the first time in many minutes. He looked emaciated from the blood still oozing from his wound. Thom locked eyes with Dija.

"Go," he said to her.

The panic in his brain was trying to sear its way to the surface, but for the moment he could still focus. Thom surveyed the wounded. Those who could walk, he sent down the Canyon. Those who couldn't, he checked their weapons. Every one who could still shoot was willing to serve. Those who weren't able to shoot, he knew were too far gone. He morosely took their rifles and clips, redistributing them to those who could use them.

"Ralla," he said into his comm. "We're about to lose the aft gate."

"How bad?"

"Bad. Di and Lo are headed your way, along with some injured."

"How far behind are you?"

He checked on Dija and Lo's progress. Somehow her tiny body was supporting what looked like most of Lo's weight. They shuffled down the Canyon.

"Hold the gate open, if that's what you're asking."

"Thom," she said. He could hear the fatigue in her voice. "It's not good here either."

"Just a little bit longer, right?" he said, trying to be supportive. He cringed that it almost sounded like he was mocking her.

"I hope."

Thom shouted at his men to prepare to fall back. If they were lucky, they'd have a few seconds head start before the gate came down. With no one supporting it, it wouldn't last long.

"Get ready!" he shouted.

—*--

Ralla ran along the outside edge of Tent City. The barricade still held, but thousands were pressing against it, trying to escape. Part of her wanted to pull it down and let the people inside flee. But that anarchy was bound to cause more harm than good. What she needed was a way to stop their panicking, or get them to turn on their attackers.

"Ilson, status?"

"We're dropping in behind you."

Ralla turned and saw a group of dark-clothed men scaling down the multistory shacks that hung off the bow side of the Terraces. Rooftop to balcony to rooftop, each time one of them landed, the entire structure shook. How people had built so many levels and rooms in such a short amount of time, she had no idea.

"Ilson, I still see smoke, did you get the fires out?"

"Negative. They're too far gone."

"They're *what*?"

"They're burning too hot. There are no hose hookups in there. Everyone daisy-chained pipes off of pipes. By the time it reaches the outer cabins, it's barely a trickle. We had to give up."

"Fire is worse than the invasion."

"I know that, ma'am, but we have to take on the enemy we can fight. I lost three men to the fire already."

Ralla felt herself losing grip on what little remained of her calm. Things were rapidly spiraling out of control. There seemed an endless supply of invaders, and now a fire was eating its way through the Terraces. If that didn't kill them, the smoke would. She needed more time and more people.

—"--

The fire had driven them from their homes. The homes they'd made out of the remains of the homes of others before them. Ziran Rinner, proud patriarch, led his family up into the *Uni*. His great-granddaughter, held tight by her mother's arms, was amazingly quiet as they snuck through the darkened halls. All told, there were sixteen of them, including husbands and wives of the extended Rinner clan.

The stairwell had been sealed off at every floor, but that didn't matter. He knew where they needed to go. There was a lock at the top of the ship, and if there was a way off this soon-to-be inferno, that was it.

He was pretty sure they'd reached the right floor, or at least it was the top of the stairs. He'd gotten turned around, with so many flights. He always liked the word "spry" and liked to think that even in his advancing years, he still was. But he couldn't deny he got confused sometimes. He picked a door, and called for the husband of his granddaughter. The young man climbed the last few steps to join Ziran on the top landing.

"This one's not welded shut," Rinner said. "See if you can unlock it."

"Z," the young man said. Ziran insisted everyone call him that. "It's locked for a reason."

"To keep us out, just like they always do. There's a shuttle on the other side of this door, son, and we're going to be on it."

As if to punctuate his point, they could smell faint traces of burning composite in the air. The fire was following them. The young man began playing with the panel adjacent to the big door. Ziran never had any interest in electronics, even as a boy. He'd always been a farmer, but the war had stripped him of that, too.

"Well, that should do it. Hmm, it seems to be stuck."

"Let me try."

—-−--

Ralla felt the air shift, like a fan had turned on. Her first impulse was to look at the fire, and sure enough, the black smoke bent at an angle. Then she heard something that sounded like a distant roar.

"Thom, I think we have a problem," she said over the comm.

"*A problem?*" he replied. Ralla could tell he was out of breath.

"I think we have a hull breach."

"Understood."

Ralla stopped running. She was in the small open area near the bow end of Tent City, the front portside corner of the Basket. The dozen men following her stopped as well, curious at first, but then heard what she heard. She didn't need to tell them to keep following her as she doubled back, headed toward Camp 1. Reaching it quickly, she bounded up the stairs two by two. From the roof, she could see the crowd pushing against the walls of Tent City, and the advancing invaders. She knew she'd only have a moment before someone saw her and made her a target.

The crowd against the Tent City walls was at least twenty people deep and spread around nearly half the wall. Most pressed forward, some pressed back, trying to make room for themselves. Some stood still, no doubt hearing the roar. It would only be a matter of time before they all did. Right before she turned to run back down the stairs, she caught sight of Lo, and Dija carrying him, with Thom limping close behind. The gate to the Canyon slammed shut behind them and swayed as something on the other side hit it hard.

"Ilson," she said into her comm.

"There's a hull breach, I know. Busy."

—˙--

Ilson knew there was a gap between the crowd of people trying to escape Tent City and the small number of pirates trying to seize it. Ilson knew he had no time for a plan, so it would have to be a simple smash and shoot.

He kept up the momentum of his men and hit the Tent City barricade at full speed. The overlapping patchwork had given the wall surprising strength, but where it met the hull of the tanker, it was just a simple weld. One of Ilson's men immediately went at it with a fusor set on split. The intense heat liquefied the metal of the hull and allowed them to pull the corner of the wall away. They snuck in at the bottom of a small rise, unseen. He pushed his men on, adrenaline surging. As they reached the top of the crest, he saw in dismay the handful of pirates he'd seen earlier had been reinforced to at least thirty. It was too late now. As they crested the rise, Ilson started firing blindly at the group of pirates, as did all his men. He was proud of them in that moment, the last feeling he'd experience.

"I can't reach Ilson," Ralla said, meeting up with Thom's group. Behind them, the guards at the forward gate fired into the shadowy Canyon with rapidity. Ralla covertly squeezed Thom's hand before surveying their group. The dozen soldiers who followed Ralla were healthy and ready to fight. Even as they stood there, they had their rifles ready and were watching the mounds of Tent City and the eviscerated T-town for signs of hostiles. Acrid black smoke continued to plume out of the Terraces and looked menacing enough that even Cern's men had given up trying to take it. She could see them climbing down into the Canyon and Tent City, and she presumed into the base at the other end of the Basket. There seemed to be no end to them, but she knew that even just a few thousand armed invaders would seem like a much greater force, given the circumstances.

Thom's group, however, were clearly not ready for combat. Lo could barely walk, and the other soldiers showed visible wounds. Three of the ten were so heavily bandaged, Ralla was amazed they could hold a rifle. Thom looked from the Terraces to her.

"Do you think the hull breach is behind the Terraces?" he asked.

"That would explain the way the smoke is moving."

"Di?" Thom asked. Dija and Lo moved as a unit, but it was clear Dija was driving. She turned Lo so she could see the Terraces, and froze, seeing them for the first time. Thom knew instantly what she felt. "Di. Di, look at me," he said, gently touching her arm. She turned reluctantly. "Di, I need you to do your thing. If there's a breach up there, how long do we have?"

She didn't seem able to focus, almost like she didn't know where she was.

"I... If the... Maybe, not good," she stammered. Thom saw in her eyes what he was sure everyone else had seen in his only minutes before.

As he watched, her eyes went wide. He turned to follow her gaze as the screams began.

_ _ ˉ _ _

Water burst out horizontally from a cabin mid-way up the Terraces. As it found fire, it vaporized, the steam mixing with the smoke in huge plumes. The stream itself wasn't huge, no wider than a hatch, but the pressure and flow looked intense. Those who could see it yelled in terror; those who hadn't, quickly turned to see.

For those trapped in Tent City, it was too much. With renewed intensity, they surged forward. The weakest point in the wall gave, creating a tiny seam. This became the new focus as people pushed, grabbed, and shoved to get to it. Finally, the weight too much, a panel gave way, barely wide enough to fit a single person. Four, five, six people at a time attempted to push their way through, slicing their clothes and skin on the serrated panels. The screams intensified.

From their view in front of Camp 1, Ralla knew people were being trampled and crushed. There was nothing they could do. The flow of women and men increased as adjacent panels broke free. It was only a matter of time before there would be a full-fledged riot. The pounding on the Canyon's last gate had gotten louder and faster. Cern's people, seeing the water cascade down into the Canyon behind them, realized they needed to get out even more than they had wanted to get in.

Thom looked at the shaking gate, the plumes of smoke from the Terraces, the seemingly endless stream of pirates leaving the ruins of T-town, the shouts and screams from Tent City, the terrified people running in every direction, his wounded men, his dying best friend, feeling the throbbing in his leg, and finally, he saw the panic in Dija's face. He knew that same feeling was inside him, ready to burst to the surface. In his mind the white sphere had engulfed his hands, swelling to take the ship. He looked back at Ralla.

"Ralla..."

"If we can get some of the Tent City people to help with the fires, maybe we can..."

"Ralla."

"No, we just need to get their attention. They'll want to help, I know it. We just need to get a few of them together."

"Ralla."

She finally realized he was saying her name. She looked at him and could tell what he was thinking. She saw it there, the quiet resolve of defeat.

"No. I'm not giving up. We can still do this. We are *not* going to lose this ship." Ralla felt like stomping her foot. Thom just looked at her. He was too calm. She couldn't understand how he could be so calm. He reached out and took her hand.

"Ralla, it's time."

She finally let herself see what he was seeing; the fire, the water, the invasion, the imminent swarm of people. They had failed. She had failed. There was nothing left. Thom was right, it was time. She let go of his hand, and keyed her comm.

"This is Ralla Gattley," she spoke, her grief audible. "We have lost the *Universalis*. Best of luck to you all."

_–_

Charges fired along the back of the *Universalis*, sending puffs of bubbles toward the surface, and releasing dozens of small emergency escape subs from their decades-old berths. One by one, rising gracefully like the bubbles themselves, the subs activated their engines and powered away, scattering in every direction. The space above the *Universalis* became an obstacle course of submarines, some fleeing, some chasing, some still intent on landing for their chance at the bounty.

At the same time, rising through the jagged rend in the hull above the flooded Garden, a long, bulky transport sub headed towards the n-pole. Then another, powering away quickly. Two more, then many more. Some turned to port, others to starboard, others around and away from the n-pole. The Garden had once given the people of the *Universalis* food that sustained them. Now it released those same people out into the world, its lifeless hold hiding their waiting submarines no longer. Hundreds burst from their hiding place. None wanted to leave, all knew they must go. There was nothing left of their home. Where their next home would be, none knew. In all directions they fled. Too many to pursue, not enough saved.

XIII

THE PANICKED MOB swarmed them. There was no common direction, people fled where others charged, the chaos building and building and building on itself. Screams and yells joined the din of gunfire, rending metal, and rushing water. Ralla tried to pull Thom, Dija, and Lo closer, to use the Lo as a sort of rock in the current. More of her soldiers pressed in, unsure of what to do. Ralla seemed to read the intention on Thom's face.

"We're not leaving. I'm not leaving," she shouted while being pushed from behind by the mob.

Thom looked up at Lo, his withered and hunched form still towering over them. Dija, crammed under Lo's good arm, stared unfocused at the deck. Lo looked back at Thom and answered the question unasked.

"I need to get her out of here," he shouted, his eyes darting to the top of Dija's head. Her sweat and his had matted her hair.

"Understood. Signal the *Runner*. Take as many as you can."

Lo's eyes darted to Ralla before giving Thom a questioning look.

"Go. I have to stay with her."

Lo nodded slowly, then straightened up the best he could, grimacing at the effort.

"It has been an honor, sir," he said.

For a moment, Thom looked about to cry, before choking it back.

"We'll see you up top," he said. "Di? Di, I need you to take care of him. Di?"

Dija's eyes remained unfocused on the deck. Her tiny hand held Lo's in a shaking, white-knuckled grip.

"We'll see you up on the ice. All right, Dija?" Thom said, leaning down to try to get into Dija's eye line. There was no reaction.

Ralla looked far up at Lo and placed her hand on his chest. He dipped his head in response.

"Go," she said.

As Lo turned, Thom reached up and squeezed his shoulder. Geran paused, as if to respond, then started with Dija toward the bow. It wasn't clear who was supporting who.

In a circle of injured troops, surrounded by thousands in a terror-stricken stampede, Ralla smiled weakly at Thom. "A moment ago you said to give up, now you want to stay and fight?"

"I fight with you, Ralla Gattley."

She kissed him as the world disintegrated.

—--

Geran Lo, beneath the edginess of fear and adrenalin, felt life slipping from under him. He stumbled more than walked, almost entirely on autopilot, toward the stairs that led to the last working lock on the *Universalis*. It didn't matter that its location had been kept secret, the people around him were fleeing anywhere *up*. The were no signs of water on the floor of the Basket yet, as if that mattered to the people of Tent City. Anywhere was better than where they were, and in that, Lo had to agree. Each person who brushed past his damaged arm caused a white spike of pain to shoot into his graying vision. That, at least, was keeping him conscious. Step, step, step, one leg at a time. The stairs loomed ahead, where he knew his and Dija's progress would be even slower. Worse, he knew he'd cause a jam on the small stairwell. For a brief moment, he considered sitting down, right there, and letting nature take its course. Let these other people flee.

He hadn't noticed he'd stopped. Dija wasn't pushing him on. She shook against him, gripping him against the force of the people shoving past them. Her shaking is what did it. Every part of him ached. Somehow the gunshot had made all his other pangs and pains worse. His arm had subsided to an agonizing ache, but his legs and chest throbbed with each heartbeat. He shuffled forward. So much pain. Dija moved with him.

"Di, I'm going to need your help on the stairs."

She remained silent, but gripped him tighter as they entered the dark, crowded stairwell.

Her shaking increased.

———

Thom pulled himself onto the roof of a shack that was, by some extension, eventually connected to the Terraces. He helped pull Ralla up using his good arm, while some of the healthier soldiers pushed from below. They knew they had to get off the Basket floor, and this was the most immediate way. From here they could climb toward the source of the water. Thom had no illusions; there was nothing they could do, but for now, he was following Ralla's lead.

The tiers of makeshift housing had always been rickety, shacks on top of shacks. Now, with the riot covering nearly the entire floor of the Basket, people bumped into supports and walls, which sent unsettling vibrations throughout the interconnected structure. Thom and Ralla climbed some broken planks that functioned as stairs to move up to the next level.

"This whole thing is shaking, right? It's not just me?" Ralla asked.

"It's not just you," Thom answered, scanning ahead carefully. Behind them, the dozen soldiers able to fight and climb were following the best they could. Thom and Ralla moved to the next level, via a ladder lashed to the structure, and stood on a tiny landing near the lip of the bow of the fallen cruise ship.

"Well, at least the pirates seem to be retreating," Thom said sardonically. Ralla didn't bother with a response. Above them and aftward, the gushing water made it hard to hear. Little streams poured down the tiers of the Terraces and into the Canyon. Others spilled onto the roofs of the shacks above Thom and Ralla, making the surfaces wet and slippery.

"I can smell the fire now," Ralla said, continuing upwards. Thom knew better than to ask if she had a plan for how they were going to stop the water. He realized he didn't want to find out if she didn't.

—-—

The moment Lo and Dija stepped out of the stairwell and onto the landing, it was as if they'd opened a valve. Hundreds of people exploded past them on their way upwards. He assumed it was instinctual, up, towards the surface. Or at least, up, away from the water and the panic below.

"This is Lo," he said into his comm. "Are you in position?"

"Roger, Lieutenant. We sustained some damage, but we're holding station and can still get you out."

"We're on our way." He looked down at Dija. "Just a bit more." He stumbled forward, feeling weaker than he'd ever felt before. His feet dragged on the tattered carpet. Ahead, he saw with some relief that their subterfuge had worked. The lock had been decorated to look like a barricade. Beyond, he knew, was the recently repaired opening that had once held a restaurant. He had watched too many people die that day, and he found no comfort in the fact that the same opening had let thousands escape. A secret kept from nearly the entire ship. A quiet partial evacuation.

Lo gently shook his head. His mind was wandering and his pace had again slowed to nearly nothing. With significant effort, he willed his legs to keep moving. He'd lost a lot of weight since his injury, but with it, a lot of muscle. Dija hanging on him certainly wasn't helping. His mind wandered again toward the different ways he could be carrying her instead that would have been easier. By the time he groggily focused back to reality, they were at the door. Hidden among the layers of paneling was a flat metal bar that looked like a brace. Lo leaned his weight on it. He heard the catch release almost exactly the same time his brain registered the voices. For a moment, fatigue took him, and he wanted to shout them away. He was going to get Dija off this dying ship. Everyone else could fend for themselves, and fend somewhere *else*.

Lo turned enough so he could see behind him. Gathered in the hallway were forty or fifty civilians, looking as frayed as their clothing. Some eyed him with hope, others concern.

"Is that a way out?"

"Do you know a way out?"

"Do you need help?"

With some difficulty, Lo stood up straight, looking over the heads of the crowd. It extended all the way to the stairwell, but he could see others inspect the crowd as they passed and continue up without stopping.

"Help me with this door," he said. His voice was so weak, he was surprised anyone heard him. A middle-aged man, limping himself, stepped forward and gave the heavy lock a tug. Lo looked down the revealed corridor, disturbingly unchanged since the incident with the restaurant. Minus, he thought grimly, the water and the bodies. It was dark, the only light came from a single open hatch, far down the hall, spilling a warm trapezoidal glow on the deck and wall. A silhouetted figure leaned part way out of the hatch.

"Lieutenant? What are all those people doing with you? We can't take them with us."

"They'll fit."

"It's not about the fit, sir, it's..."

"They'll fit, Sergeant, don't argue. Get down here and help me with Dija."

Lo had no idea if the people around him knew this was a lock, or knew that was a sub, but they started filing past him regardless. He could still see back toward the stairwell, and it seemed most people still followed the people in front of them, headed up the stairs. Few took notice of the group filing down a dark corridor.

But they all heard the sound at the same time. Gunfire, though Lo couldn't localize where. From the pace of the people on the stairs, and the shoving he could see, he guessed it was coming from below. The wiry, hirsute sergeant, having fought his way against the flow, arrived and tried unsuccessfully to pry Dija from under Lo's arm.

"Forget it," Lo said gruffly. "Close this door as soon as the last of these people are through. I can't stand here much longer, and I don't know if I have the strength to pull it closed."

"Sir, the sub can't handle this many people."

"Why."

"The main took damage on the way in. Most of the stern, really. We're maneuvering on thrusters, that's it. We barely got in here, never mind getting back out again."

Lo looked at the crowd of people, the crowd of weight, trying to cram through the tiny hatch of the sub. They all heard more gunfire, this time much closer. One problem at a time, Lo thought. The last of the people passed through the lock door, and the sergeant gave it a push. Lo didn't see the pirate reach the landing, but he heard the bullets impact the metal.

"There's a fusor on the *Runner*," the sergeant said.

"Get it. Quickly."

—-‑--

The shaking had gotten much worse. As people caught sight of Ralla, Thom, and the soldiers, they took it as a good idea, and started climbing themselves. The entire structure trembled. Thom could hear pieces falling off the shacks, crashing into lower levels, and eventually landing on the people below. Most looked like minor injuries, but Thom watched as one piece of corrugated metal fell straight down into a man's neck, erupting a geyser of blood and dropping him to the ground to be trampled. Thom looked away to find Ralla. She had climbed ahead, and was now searching for the best way to continue over to the Terraces.

The smoke had created a layer of haze along the ceiling, shifting the already dim light to a reddish-orange. It looked, to Thom, like the light from the sunset he'd seen with Ralla and Di on the *Runner*. It seemed so long ago. He focused back on the slowly accumulating smoke, and was surprised the ancient air scrubbers were handling it as well as they were. He grabbed the edge of a roof, stuck his foot in the opening that served as a window, and pulled himself up. His arms were so sore they'd started shaking, as if in sympathy to the shaking felt by his feet. With a hop on his good leg, he stood beside Ralla. There was a sizable gap between the rooftops, such as they were, and the listing bow of the cruise ship. Far below the two had connected, but somewhere along the way, the myriad builders gave up trying to secure the new structure to anything other than itself.

Ralla and Thom stared at the water gushing from the wall, nearly horizontal, as it arced down into the Terraces. Where it hit, it tore away at walls and plating like a cutting torch. The freed pieces joined the flow of water down into the Canyon. Though the floor of the Canyon was hidden from view by the lowest levels of the Terraces, they could see water seeping underneath the barricade on the forward end. They knew it wouldn't stop there. The pressure would let this new invader fill the Basket, and every open space left on the ship. Thom could feel some spray. It was painfully cold. He stepped closer to Ralla, letting their arms touch.

"We have to figure out a way to stop the water," she said, stepping away slightly.

"That much I gathered."

"Thom..." she said, turning to him. "I'm not trying to convince myself that if we stop the water we'll be safe. But if we *don't* stop the water, it will kill us all."

"I get it."

"I ask so much of everyone."

"Yeah, well. Someone has to."

"Thank you, Thom."

"I love you, Ralla. And I'm here for you. But I would love you a lot more on a warm shuttle driving hard away from here."

"I know..."

"Just saying."

Behind them, the soldiers had started joining them on the roof. One of them, seeing their situation, climbed back down and grabbed a ladder they'd passed. He handed it up, and the soldiers bridged the gap to the Terraces. Ralla was the first to cross, half hunched, her hand always close to the edges as she shuffled across. Thom turned to the six men as soon as she looked out of earshot. They looked terrified, and very young. Thom suddenly felt old.

"What if we can't stop the water?" one of the soldiers asked. "She seems like she wants to stay. I don't want to stay." Thom felt the all-too-familiar pulse of panic rise up and rush through him. Worryingly, as much as he pushed back, he couldn't get it to subside. He had nothing to say. They were right.

—ˉ‐‐

Once again Lo's ears filled with the sound of pounding on metal. The pirates must have sensed something important was behind the lock, and they were attempting to smash their way in. They'd have a tough go of that, he knew, but it was only a matter of time before they knocked away enough camouflage and figured out it was just a lock, like any other, that they could cut, pry, or otherwise easily open. He made his way, Dija still under his arm, to the other lock, and boarded the *Sealine Runner*. For a moment he was taken aback. He'd never seen it so crowded. From the hatch, all he could see was people; every seat taken, every aisle shoulder to shoulder with frightened, huddled, soon-to-be refugees. Well, that part remained to be seen, Lo thought fatalistically.

The hard seal around the hatch, the only physical contact the *Runner* had with the *Universalis*, dripped ominously.

Lo closed the lock and sub's hatch behind him. It didn't seem like much protection, if the pirates made it through the other lock, but it was something, he figured. People gave way the best they could, but even in his current state, his bulk was an issue. It took him a moment to get his bearings. They were on the top deck, the sub had turned around to line the hatch up to the lock, so at least they were facing the right way to escape the Garden. He made a guttural sound at a man in the closest seat, who promptly got up. The best he could, Lo removed Dija from his person, gently placing her into the seat like he'd break her. She immediately drew her knees up and buried her face in her legs.

"Lieutenant," the pilot said from behind Lo, an urgency in his voice. Lo turned, giving the pilot full view of Lo's blood-coated arm and gray, gaunt face. The pilot recoiled slightly. "I... we have no supplies. I mean there might be a medkit..."

"Find it."

The man Lo scared from his seat, slightly heavyset with gray hair at the temples, offered to find the medkit. The pilot pointed toward the bridge. Lo braced himself on the back of the seat and noticed all eyes were on him.

"Why aren't we leaving?"

"Sir," the pilot said, leaning in conspiratorially. "We can't. We took damage to the main. We got here on thrusters, and that should have been enough to get us back out, but now, with all these people the thrusters are at 100 percent just keeping us buoyant. This sub wasn't made to transport this many people. We've dropped all the ballast and we're still too heavy. If we try to move forward, we'll drop to the bottom. At this point, I don't think we can get higher than we are now, never mind clearing the entrance. Honestly, I'm pretty certain if we separate from the lock, we'll sink."

Lo felt nothing beyond the exhaustion. His muddled brain ran the scenarios, as if to verify what the pilot was telling him. The thrusters and the lock were barely keeping them afloat. If they released from the

Uni, they'd drop to the bottom of the Garden. The unarmored hull would take damage, or crush under the weight, and either way flood the interior.

The only choice was removing enough passengers so the rest could survive. Lo looked around, all the faces looking at his. Those nearest showed a fearful understanding of what the pilot had just said. Stepping off the sub wasn't a guaranteed death sentence... but they'd *think* it was, which was worse. Then there were the pirates, who after breaking through one door, certainly wouldn't stop at another.

Lo wanted to sit down, then realized the edges of his vision were disappearing and he was falling.

—ˉ--

The water shot overhead like a bizarre horizontal waterfall. The Terraces were soaking wet, puddles flowed into streams, which flowed through the gaps in the new floors, to run down the angled old floors, down to lower levels, and eventually into the ever-growing pool of water on the floor of the Basket. They could see now where the water was coming from, having been hidden behind the layers of makeshift bulkheads that made up most of the Terraces. Those had been torn away. They had to shout to be heard.

"I think that connects to a stairwell," one of the soldiers shouted. There was no way to tell what had been where the water was now bursting, but it looked too narrow to have been a ship. Ralla turned to Thom, her face terrified and showing something else Thom couldn't identify.

"What?" he asked, instinctually reaching for her arm.

"It is a stairwell. It goes all the way to the top. The top level," she repeated. "Access to the Spine."

Thom's face dropped as he understood what she was saying. The breach they'd used to slow the invaders, and thought they'd contained, was now flooding the ship. She didn't want to say it, but he could see it in her face. We caused this, or as Thom was sure she thought, *she'd* caused this. The doors had been sealed, it should not have been possible for water to force its way through. Someone must have done something to the doors, he figured. The bulkheads on each floor would have sealed at the first sense of water, but down here, who knows what had been done while building the Terraces. A door welded open, a bulkhead used for scrap, there were too many possibilities, and none of them mattered now. There was a clear shot for the sea, and the sea needed no additional invitation.

Her eyes unfocused, face slack, Ralla turned back toward the flow and sank to her knees in a puddle of water. Thom's heart ached seeing her in such distress. He didn't know why, of all the things that had happened, this had affected her so deeply, but her shoulders sagged as she knelt there, broken.

He wanted to drop to the deck and hold her, as much for his support as hers. As soon as he moved to do it, the white-hot ball swelled in his chest. He was going to have to take charge. They had to get out of here. He turned to the soldiers, who didn't seem to understand what had happened. He began to lose the fight against his fear all over again. But one look back at Ralla, her clothes soaked, blonde hair wet and matted, he snapped right back to the soldiers.

"I'm assuming command. We're crossing over to T-town. We'll climb up the Spire and if we're lucky, there are still some pirate shuttles up there. We are going to take one by force, is that understood?" The men nodded. "You are weapons-free. Fire on any hostiles."

Thom tugged repeatedly on Ralla's arm. She finally stood, but wouldn't look at him. Her eyes were puffy and red, her face wet, though he couldn't tell from what kind of salt water. She stared into the distance, or at the flow, Thom couldn't tell.

"I will carry you if I have to, but it will be a lot faster if I don't," he shouted over the roar. She didn't seem to hear him. He knew none of the usual platitudes about this not being her fault and having done better than anyone could have hoped, would do any good. "You saved thousands of people today, Ralla. We'd all be dead if it weren't for you. And right now, we're going to save eight more. Understood?"

She finally looked up at him, the fight gone from her face. Everything gone from her face.

"I love you, Thom Vargas," she said. The sadness in her tone tore at Thom's heart. Before he could respond, the loudest sound he'd ever heard hit them all like a hammer.

__-__

Lo opened his eyes and saw carpet and feet. He'd just been somewhere else, but he couldn't remember where. He had been there for days, months maybe. It didn't make sense he could still be on the *Runner*. How many hours had passed since he was...

Dija, wide-eyed, dropped her head sideways into his field of view. Her hair, still vibrant despite the layers of dirt, fell in front of her face. She put her hand to his cheek. Lo wanted very much to be somewhere else with that hand on his cheek and the amazing, quirky, beautiful woman attached to it. She said something, or at least her mouth moved, but he couldn't make it out. She left his field of view. When he tried to follow her with his gaze he noticed the pain. A splitting, sharp pain in his head, like his brain was trying to push its way out. As he tried to breathe, his chest answered with its own dagger-like pain. It was odd that his arm, gunshot and all, was somehow the least painful of the painful. Why do my legs hurt, he thought.

"By boo my megs hurt?" he mumbled. The words sort of sounded right. Dija reappeared. This time he could understand her.

"We elevated your legs. There's a nurse downstairs who's coming up to patch your shoulder."

This didn't make sense to Lo. He'd been unconscious for hours, how could it have taken them that long to find a nurse?

"How wong was I..." the words trailed off. He was so tired. There didn't seem to be any reason not to take a nap. He was already on the floor. Lo closed his eyes.

__-__

It was an otherworldly sound, a horrifying cacophony of metal scraping against metal, of tearing and rending, of the snapping of unbreakable composites. Two cracks shot out from the center of the ceiling, their malevolent black forms snaking their way toward the bow and stern. Thom had heard similar sounds during his days on the ice, but this was louder and significantly more menacing. Particles of dust, paint, and shredded composites fell from the ceiling like snow, reflecting the light from the picosuns through haze and steam.

Thom pointed with three fingers at the awestruck soldiers.

"Three ahead, two behind. Ralla in the middle. Go. NOW."

Something about the directness of his order caused everyone to move. They climbed down the Terraces, constantly slipping and falling in the slick. Their course curved toward the bow to avoid having to deal with the cataract, but then they were quickly on one of the bridges high above the Canyon. Below, bodies floated in water black with shadow and blood.

The group wasted no time upon reaching the other side. Single-file they sprinted up the tanker into T-town. Thom had little choice but to limp as quickly as he could, following Ralla, who followed the soldiers in front of her without seeming to notice where the group was, or what else was going on.

The dark confines of T-town's corridors became an obstacle course of jagged walls, debris, and corpses. There was nothing to do but run. Stairs led them up and back, finally connecting with the Spire. The ladder slowed their process, but moved them quickly vertical. Within a few minutes, they climbed into the quasi-open of the unfinished floors. Through the horizontal slit afforded by the ceiling and floors, Thom could see massive slabs of ceiling fall past his view, then hear them crash out of sight. The humid air took on a foul stench and attacked their lungs, denying them deep breaths. Still he pushed his group to climb.

As they neared the top, a new sound reached their ears: a hiss, just barely audible over the roar of the distant water and the scattered screams of thousands. It took a moment for Thom to register what it was.

The soldier behind him, alarm in his voice, spoke aloud what they all were thinking.

"Do you think that's water hitting the picosun?"

Thom figured it was, but said nothing. It was the unmistakable sound of steam, and only a lot of water, hitting something huge and hot, could make that kind of noise. Soon their ears started popping. A pressure change that rapid, Thom realized, meant only one thing: This was about to get very bad.

XIV

"**OWWWW.**" Lo said groggily. "Did you hit me?"

"Lieutenant, I can't let you fall asleep. You might have a concussion." Lo wanted to say something in return, but couldn't focus enough to do so. Then, as he was lamenting that, his focus and vision suddenly snapped into place. The sergeant's face dropped level with Lo's eyeline. "Nurse Kera had medical supplies with her. You're lucky she didn't go with the rest of the Medbay staff. She's gone back down to treat some other wounded. She sewed up your shoulder and gave you a shot of something."

So he had been unconscious. A lot of good that slap did, then. His heart felt like it was trying to violently pump its way out of his chest. Lo tried to roll on his side, and got assistance to do so from the sergeant. Dija was back in her seat, looking at him over the tops of her knees. Lo tried to sit up, and got assistance for that, too. Had it really only been a few minutes? There was no banging on the hatch, so the pirates must still be outside the main lock.

"Can we repair the main?" Lo asked.

"I don't know. It was knocked out by a concussive blast, not a direct hit. Chewed up the stern pretty good, but the propeller is there. It spins when we move. I'm not sure if that's good or bad."

"Help me up."

The sergeant looked like he was about to argue, but thought better of it. Once on his feet, Lo swayed woozily. Whatever the nurse had given him was masking the pain, barely, and gave everything a vibrancy layered over fatigue and reality. Every movement still hurt though, every breath causing sharp pains in his chest and his head. Using the chairs and nearby people for support, Lo followed the sergeant a few steps aft to a trapdoor in the deck. People pushed back to clear enough space for him to open it. Lo looked down the laddered shaft to the engine nacelle, at least three body lengths below. He could see water glistening back up at him, but otherwise it was dark. If he'd tried, he could have fit his arm in the shaft, but not much else. He looked quickly at Dija, hoping she hadn't seen. From the way she was rocking back and forth, it was clear she had.

With his medically induced ultra-lucidity, Lo's brain skipped from option to option. He couldn't ask Dija to go down there. That was every one of her fears, embodied. But he'd seen too many people die to ask anyone on this sub to leave. He exhaled slowly as he came to the only logical option. He stumbled back toward the hatch, placing his bloodied hand against the bulkhead to steady himself. Pain shot up his arm, mixing and blending into an electric cocktail of agony. The clarity drained out of him, overwhelmed by his fatigue and wounds and the knowledge of what he had to do. Slowly, with much effort, he used his free hand to remove his pistol from its holster.

Lo cycled the hatch open, raining water down on his head as the *Runner* shifted against the seal. He was going to fight. It would be his last fight. He was going to fight and give these people a chance, somehow. That was the only choice. He marveled at how easily his brain slipped back into the comfort of violence, as if welcoming him back. This was what he could do. This was all he could do, all he'd ever done. It didn't matter that Dija would never forgive him. Geran Lo felt some small relief knowing he'd never have to see how badly he was about to let her down. How badly he was going to break her heart.

—ˉ--

It was like moving through a sauna, the steam wetting their skin and obscuring their vision. They'd reached the top of the Spire. Enveloped in steam and smoke, everything beyond the superstructure was fog. A narrow, handrail-less bridge, no more than a few planks, connected the top of the Spire to an opening cut in a yacht on the wall. Thom knew how close they were to the ceiling, knew they were over a dozen stories above the Basket floor, yet could see neither. Their clothes dripped with sweat and moisture. Inside the yacht the steam and smoke filled the open floor plan. The only way Thom could tell the lead soldier had opened the hatch to the hallway was the gunfire, and the yellow halo-like flashes around the soldier's body as the light from the muzzle refracted in the moisture in the air.

"Get out into the hall. Don't let them trap us in here," Thom yelled, pushing past Ralla to help with the assault.

—ˉ--

Dija rocked back and forth. As she tried to curl into herself, her thoughts overwhelmed her. I want to reach out to Geran, she thought. Want to be away with him. He needs my help. He likes my help. I like that he likes my help. I like him. I can't let myself fall into this trap. Not right now. He needs my help now. No, I can't. Too much. There are too many people and this sub is too small and it's getting smaller. We're trapped here. The sub isn't going anywhere. We're trapped here because the sub is too small and there are TOO MANY PEOPLE and they weigh too much and we're going to sink and crash and drown. The lights will go out. We'll drown in the dark. All these people will drown in the I'M GOING TO DROWN IN THE DARK. Geran let me go and I'm going to drown in the dark. He needs my help and he let me go. I can't help him if he lets me go. I'm not going into that hole. That space is even... it's even... it's even tinier than the sub. There's no way out. It's dark and it's tiny and I'm going to drown in the dark. Geran won't let me drown in the dark. He has to leave. He's leaving. He's leaving but he can't leave. Why is he leaving? Why is he leaving with a gun in his hand? He thinks he has to kill more people. Don't kill more people. I need you here. I need you because I don't want to drown in the — *stop thinking about drowning in the dark*. But I don't want to drown in the dark. Stop it. I don't want to drown in the dark. Lo doesn't want me to drown in the dark. He has to go kill people because he thinks he has to kill people because no one knows how to fix the engine. I bet I could fix the engine but I don't want to drown in the — STOP IT. Don't do this. Not now. Don't let this happen now. He's stepping outside with a gun and he can barely walk because I know how to fix the engine but I don't want — STOP IT — don't want to drown in the dark. I know how to fix the engine but I don't want to drown in the dark. I know how to fix the engine but I — STOP IT — don't want — STOP IT. Stop. Stop thinking about the dark, but I don't want to drown there but I can fix the engine. I can fix the engine. I can FIX THE ENGINE BUT I DON'T WANT TO DROWN IN THE —

"STOP!!" Dija screamed, louder than she ever had in her life. Everyone on the sub jumped. Through a narrow corridor of people and through the open hatch, Dija saw Geran Lo freeze and look back at her. For a moment, their eyes locked. "I can fix the engine. I can fix the engine. You don't have to kill anyone. I can fix the engine."

Dija leapt from her chair, shaking with nervous energy. The sergeant stepped over to the trapdoor, pushing people out of the way and opening it. Dija stared down the gaping maw, into the muck-coated black water at the bottom of the nacelle, and each of the slippery-looking rungs that led there.

"There's an emergency tool kit on the starboard bulkhead," the sergeant told her. She nodded and looked over her shoulder. Lo stood half in, half out of the hatch, the water soaking him. He looked at her questioningly. Sadly.

"I can do this," she said, loud enough for him to hear, not noticing anyone else in the sub. He looked both proud and concerned and stepped fully inside the *Runner*, sealing the lock and the hatch. *OK*, he mouthed silently. She gave him a half-crazed grin, the best she could muster with the dread and excitement mixing in her blood. She looked down again, terrified, but confident.

Dija descended into the nacelle, not breathing once.

—--

The fighting was surreal. Thom couldn't see anything, and neither could anyone else. When one from his side fired down the hallway, a fusillade from the enemy would erupt, targeting the flash. Then Thom's people would fire toward where they'd seen flashes. Scattered crates and furniture littered the corridor, offering excellent cover. Without being able to see past the edge of any crate or desk, it was impossible to judge if there was cover any closer to the enemy, preventing any rational advance.

Thom realized how untenable their situation was. At any moment, the pirates could hop back on their transport, pull away from the hull, and flood the corridor. He could feel the increasing pressure in the air and wondered if it was possible to blow the sub off just from that. A part of his brain told him this was going to end badly, but another part refused to let that be now.

"We three," Thom said, before realizing at this point only the soldier next to him could see him, "we three behind this, uh, desk, will lay down covering fire. You three over behind that whatever, you start crawling forward until you find cover, or them. If you find cover and can take a shot without us hitting you, do so. We'll keep our field of fire narrow. Got it?" Thom heard what sounded like six different confirmations. "GO!" The two soldiers to his left rotated up and started firing. But the pirates were waiting for them, immediately returning fire and riddling the soldiers with bullets. The offensive stopped before it had begun. Thom sat back down, with his back against the desk.

All Thom could see was the closest foot of the dead soldier next to him, the air so thick with steam that anything past that was obscured. Suddenly, there wasn't anything else. Not the steam, not the fighting, not the ship around him. Just the foot. The foot connected to a dead solider. He had just gotten that man killed. He had killed that person, and he didn't even know his name. Thom's body went rigid, his mind unable to focus on anything but the foot. He couldn't move, and it seemed, he couldn't breathe.

Abruptly, Ralla was in front of him, her face nearly touching his, but still completely stoic. She placed a hand on his knee, but reached past him, her head disappearing in the haze. When she returned, she had the soldier's pistol in her hand. He felt guilty not offering her one before. Of course she was trained to use it, had fired one on many occasions. She deserved to fight as much as...

Ralla stood up.

Thom reached out frantically for her legs to pull her back down, but she stepped out of his grasp and immediately toward the enemy.

"Ralla, NO!" he half whispered, half shouted. He watched her disappear into the mist. He hoped his momentary pause was shock and not cowardice, but he finally rolled out into the open corridor and crouch-walked toward the enemy. No sooner had he gotten a few steps before shots rang out. It was semiautomatic, a pistol, three shots in quick succession, then two more together, then three more.

"Clear!" he heard Ralla shout. He leapt up, ignoring the pain in his leg, and half-hopped, half-ran down the corridor. What he saw left him speechless. Ralla stood beside a makeshift bunker of crates and composite shielding in the center of the corridor, gun still outstretched. Inside the bunker lay the corpses of four pirates. He looked up, and saw two more hanging lifelessly out of a jagged hole they'd cut in the ceiling leading to their sub. Several had multiple visible wounds. Ralla's face showed no emotion.

Dija landed in a nacelle filled waist-high with freezing, brackish, oily water. Emergency lights glared harshly, reflecting off the shimmering black surface. Not much higher than she was tall, the nacelle was nearly filled by the long motor, itself similar in shape to the streamlined nacelle. It didn't take long for Dija to find the tool kit, which was missing half its tools. The portable handheld diagnostics tool looked older than she was, its tiny screen cracked but working. Away from the crowd above, Dija could hear the thrusters straining to keep them all afloat. The sound was oddly comforting. Already her legs felt sharp pains from the cold water. She jabbed the diag into the port on the front of the motor. Nothing. That isn't good, Dija thought. She began to click through her usual checklist, making her way around to the back of the motor.

With almost clinical interest, she observed water spraying into the nacelle from the joint where prop shaft led to the propeller. She grabbed the prop shaft and tried to rotate it manually. It was cold and wet, causing her hands to slip, but it turned slowly. The leak, water, and shaft now checked off on her mental list, they ceased to exist in her mind.

She started from the end and methodically went through each step. The propeller was attached, or so they'd said. The stuffing box was damaged, but holding. The prop shaft turned. This brought her back to the motor. The motor was dead. Why was the motor dead? The ship had power. Did the motor have power?

"How's it going, Di?" Lo yelled down from the cabin. Dija snapped back to reality, suddenly very cold and wet. She noticed there was commotion coming from above. She played back in her head what she'd just heard. He sounded anxious.

"Still checking," was all she could think to reply. She sloshed over to a grime-covered wall panel and wiped it partially clean with her hand.

—-—

The pirates pounded on the outer lock, upsetting the passengers. Lo could see out through the porthole in the hatch and then through the even smaller porthole on the lock, at a handful of men determined to get at the *Runner* while it was still there. Lo couldn't understand their insanity. As far as they knew, the sub could pull away from the ship at any moment. Unless... unless they didn't know it was a sub. They probably think this is just some other part of the ship, he realized. If so, they probably hadn't followed the procedures they'd known since childhood: to secure any lock adjoining external access. So if they managed to open the lock attached to the *Runner*, and the *Runner* pulled away, with the far lock still open, they'd flood the *Universalis*. Well, flood it faster. Lo hung his head, overwhelmed by hopelessness.

He caught something out of the corner of his eye. Looking back through the porthole, he came face-to-face with the frenzied visage of one of the pirates. Except, it wasn't the intense look of a crazed looter. As best Lo could figure, the dirty, sweating face looking back at him was one of absolute terrified desperation.

—⁻--

Ralla was banging on hatches. That's all Thom could tell. She had disappeared into the haze within moments of his arrival. When a shape resolved in the fog, he'd assumed it was her. It wasn't. The elderly matriarch of a small family approached and asked for him by name.

"I'm Thom Vargas."

"Proctor Gattley told us you'd help us evacuate," the strength of the woman's voice belied the obvious frailty of her body. Behind her, a middle-aged couple stood beside a son just old enough not to make the evacuation cut. Thom turned to the four remaining soldiers. One hung half out of the hatch in the ceiling, paused midaction, pulling a second soldier up to the transport. All four looked at him, and he shrugged.

"Let's help them aboard. Quickly," he ordered. Thom didn't wait for thanks, setting off after Ralla down the corridor. His eyes were really feeling the pressure in the air. He could feel it on his skin. A different anxiety started to well up inside him. Its logic a harsh change. Not nerves, but dread. They needed to get off the ship, *now*.

He passed seven more families before he found Ralla, her face showing a wild intensity he'd never seen before. She showed no signs of stopping.

—-—

The pirates had broken the lock's porthole and were now shouting at Lo. He could barely make out their muffled voices, but it was clear they wanted in, and were threatening all manner of violence to get it. Lo could imagine there was some type of person who would take pity on these obviously terrified men. He wasn't one of them. He turned and made his way over to the access tube that had swallowed his girlfriend. That was the first time he'd thought of her with that word, he realized. It gave him little comfort or amusement in that moment.

"Di?" he yelled down.

"Soon!" he heard back immediately.

—-—

Dija, long wrench in both hands, struck the motor repeatedly with all her strength. Each metallic clang reverberated around the nacelle so perfectly, it was still ringing when she made the next hit. She leaned back, slapped a button on the wall panel. It glowed orange. She tried striking a different part of the motor. Again, she pressed the wall panel button. Again, it glowed orange.

She went through her checklist. Propeller OK. Stuffing box OK. Prop shaft OK. The nacelle was getting power. The engine could pass current, or at least wasn't shorted out, which was all she could test. Why wasn't it working? In her mind she imagined the inside of the motor. There had to be something different about this one, she figured. What would be different about a motor on a submarine than the submarine motors re-tasked for use in her dome growing up? The motors were the same. What could be different? Standing still, reasoning through the problem, Dija realized she had been shivering badly, and she wasn't sure for how long. Her brain, still in logic mode, reasoned this out, too. Why would I be shivering? she thought. Because I'm standing up to my belly in freezing ocean water.

The water.

It came to her in a flash. Having been so resolutely ignoring the water, she hadn't even considered it as the problem. The engine was sealed, of course, but there'd be some sort of fail-safe against any other wiring short or damage. They hadn't needed anything like that in her dome. She couldn't help but take a moment to be pleased she'd just fixed her first submarine.

"Di, I need to know if you can fix it. There's a... I just need to know," Lo shouted down. Dija heard some screams coming from the cabin.

"I figured out what's wrong. I think I can fix it," she shouted back. "Give me another minute."

_---

Lo looked from the access tube to the hatch, where he could see the jabs of the pirates through the broken porthole. Their strikes against the hatch echoed throughout the *Runner*, amongst the scattered screams.

XV

RALLA HAD WORKED her way back by the time Thom reached her.

"The corridor's blocked," she said as if it surprised her.

"Can we get back to the transport then? Please?" Thom asked. She nodded without looking at him and started walking. He set out after her at a hopping jog. Every part of his leg hurt. Worse, a headache had started a few moments earlier and had escalated nearly to the point of nausea. He reached the transport, shocked at how many people were there. It looked to be more than thirty, of all ages. The soldiers had fashioned partial stairs out of the barricade. Three of them now hung from the hole in the ceiling to pull the evacuees up into the transport. Thom couldn't see the other, and in looking for him, one of the soldiers motioned with his head.

"Jepin is getting the engines spooled up," the soldier said as he pulled an old lady up by the arms. There was some jostling for position around the barricade/stairs, but it seemed orderly. Orderly, but too slow. Ralla pushed her way through the crowd, Thom close behind, and both climbed the barricade to help. With each person he tried to lift, he felt something pull a little further in his arms and legs. The pain escalated quickly, and soon each partial lift felt like he was tearing the insides of his arms and jabbing knives into his legs. He looked around, eyes burning from the pressure and steam, and through the haze all he could see was more people, swarming toward him.

—-‑--

Dija confidently shoved the circuit breaker closed. Smiling, she hit the button on the wall panel. It glowed orange. The smile fell from her face. The breaker box was nearly hidden under the motor's front casing, dangerously close to the lapping water. It was rimmed with huge red letters warning against operating the motor while submerged. The wording wasn't clear, but Dija assumed it meant if the *motor* was submerged, not if the submarine was. The single large circuit breaker, wider than her hand, was covered in its own warnings. Most spoke of all the dangers of bypassing said circuit breaker.

She pulled it open again with a heavy click, then shoved it closed again. The wall button still glowed orange. She hit it again with her fist. Still orange. She resisted the urge to scream at it. This was it. She *knew* this was it. This had to be the problem, because if it wasn't, it wasn't something she could fix. She'd never interacted with a machine she couldn't fix. If she couldn't fix it, they'd all die. She'd die in the dark. She'd drown in the...

Dija shook her head violently, trying to stop the slide.

"Dija!" Lo yelled. She could hear the strain in his voice.

—-‑--

They surged toward him, not quite pushing each other away, but close.

"How many more?" one of the soldiers yelled from above. Thom couldn't think through the pain to count.

"Just a few more," Ralla yelled back. Sweat streaked her face, and her clothes stuck wetly to her skin.

"Ralla, I can't do this much longer. We have to get on board the sub."

"No."

"Ralla..."

"I CAN SAVE THESE PEOPLE," she shouted. Thom saw in her face, her eyes, so much agony and so much fury. Something in her had broken. Maybe everything. The ache returned to clench his heart. Instinctually he reached out for her but she slapped his hand away with contempt. She pushed around him, avoiding his gaze, and continued to help people up into the waiting arms of those already in the sub.

Thom stood in shock, his mind unable to focus through the physical pain he'd already been feeling, and now the shock at Ralla's palpable change. People shoved him around now that he was merely in the way. He looked down at the blood streaking his clothes, unsure if it was his. He tried to help a lift a gray-haired man, and couldn't budge him from the barricade.

There were still over a dozen civilians left when they heard the sound. Heard, and felt. It was a screech far worse than what they'd heard before. Slower, rising in pitch. They could hear deep popping and snapping sounds. Ralla and the others stared off down the corridor the way they'd come, as if they could see what was happening.

—¯--

Dija removed the circuit breaker with a combination of screwdrivers, a wrench, and the blunt end of a hammer. Before her lay the bare terminals, exposed to the air and the moisture. The water lapped at the bottom of the metal casing of the motor, nearly touching the terminals.

"Di!" Lo screamed.

The pirates wedged the sharpened edge of a long metal pipe into the bottom seam of the hatch, and were pulling on the far end. Their efforts, and the rocking of the *Runner*, caused water to gush in along the bottom of the sub's hatch. One good pull, and they'd snap the safety and the hatch would open. Lo couldn't wait any longer, he took out his pistol and aimed it at the hatch.

"I'm sorry, Dija," he said, but no one was listening.

—-—

"Ralla..." Thom pleaded, his voice weak, his body spent. If she'd heard him, he couldn't tell. The next civilian got pulled aboard. "Ralla, *please.*" Ralla pushed a woman up toward the sub, the soldiers grabbing her. The noise had risen even further in pitch, impossibly high, impossibly loud. The woman was halfway into the transport, when suddenly, the entire *Universalis* lurched, knocking them all off their feet.

—-—

The jolt dropped Dija to her knees, submerging her in the frigid dark water. Drown in the dark. Drown in the dark. Drown in the DARK. Dija snapped up, trying to jump out of the water completely. Drown. Drowning. *I'm going to drown in the dark.* The water sloshed side to side. Why was it shifting? They were sinking. They were all going to drown in the dark.

Dija's eyes focused on the tool kit and a single shining wrench. She grabbed it, then slammed it across both exposed contacts causing a violent spray of sparks.

"Not going to drown in the dark."

The button turned green.

—-—

Thom felt everything inside him get replaced by fear, both from the real danger of what was happening to the *Universalis* and the imminent need for action. He'd tried to take charge today, and he had killed the men, the boys, in his command. The world receded from his view, the pain a protective outer shell. People stepped past him on the barricade, still trying to get up to the transport. Ralla stood there, tirelessly helping to lift them. Her injured arm dripped with blood. He tried to think of something to do. That was it. He needed to get her off the ship. She wasn't going to do it. She was going to die here trying to save these people. He needed to... The sphere expanded to consume him, paralyze him. He dropped to one knee, unable to catch his breath.

Then they heard it, and it took their breath away. The sound was physical in its power, more deafening and forceful than anything they'd ever heard. A roar so impossibly loud it could only signify one thing. Instantly, his fear was gone. The sphere was gone. It was as if some primal force drove Thom upward, grabbing Ralla by the waist and hoisting her skyward. He felt muscles tear at the exertion, pain shooting up his arms and down his legs, but his brain blocked it all. He could feel her screaming, but could hear nothing but the roar. She kicked at him, struck at his head and back as he heaved her upwards. He didn't register anything as she struggled to free herself. He felt Ralla get pulled from his grasp, and saw her, still thrashing, as she rose away from him, into the safety of the sub.

Like a switch, the energy left him. The pain roared in. His arms dropped first, then his legs. But his eyes stayed locked on Ralla as he fell to his knees, her face crimson from anger and betrayal. The sound was overwhelming, the last death throes of the great citysub *Universalis*. The end would be quick, as instant an end as the lives he'd taken from mariners across the sea.

Suddenly, he felt himself being lifted up. While the others around him reached for life aboard the transport, one man lifted Thom up. Enough to get grabbed by the soldiers, and hoisted aboard. He tried to look back to see the man's face, but the hatch slammed shut.

Thom, in a haze of pain and exhaustion, only registered what felt like the transport getting picked up, shaken, and tossed into infinity.

_—"--

Unable to contain the rising pressure caused by the relentless buildup of steam, the outer hull of the *Universalis* bulged past the point of structural integrity, splitting along its length. Water burst inward, rushing between the eviscerated outer and inner hulls. Where there was no clear path, it hunted transversely between supports and bulkheads. The rend expanded lengthwise and branched out horizontally, finding cracks that led out into the Basket. Only slightly above freezing, the high-pressure water hit the steam, condensing it instantly back to water. The immediate drop in pressure imploded the hull as if smashed by a massive hammer. The remaining air found release as giant bubbles floating toward the surface.

—ᵗ--

"Go!" Dija screamed.

"Go!" Lo yelled from the cabin above. The *Runner* shot forward. In the nacelle, Dija struggled to remain on her feet as all the water surged aftward. She scrambled for the ladder, electrocution firmly on her mind.

"Tell them they can't stop till they reach the surface. If they slow down the engine will short out," Dija said as she emerged from the tube. Lo wrapped his arms around her, and remained stationary as the sub jostled beneath them.

"I'll tell them," the sergeant said, working his way forward. Dija gripped Lo even tighter than he was holding her.

The *Sealine Runner*, heavily laden, fled down the length of the Garden, shooting up and out through the tear in the hull and into the open sea. Those closest to the windows cried out in horror.

Lo and Dija returned to her former seat and leaned toward the porthole. Dija squeezed Lo's hand painfully tight.

The hulk of the *Universalis*, dark and crumpled, no longer resembled a citysub, but a tube crushed by a giant's fist. The concave and torn hull looked like an ancient shattered derelict.

XVI

ONE BY ONE, like metallic bubbles, submarines broke the surface of the sea. Hatches opened. Faces appeared. They converged on the shore: a foreign, snowy plain. There they found others. Subs were pulled ashore, moved together. Tunnels were dug in the ice. Some survivors found shelter in the towering remains of their enemy's former home.

On a high drift, above the growing town, Thom, Dija, and Lo stood, shivering despite the disappearing sliver of sun on their faces.

"We should start planning what we're going to do with the three months of partial power Koin has rigged up for us here," Dija said, her pale face reflecting the sun's meager orange glow. Koin had also told them the sun wasn't going to be coming back up for several months, not this close to the pole. So she wanted to absorb as much of it as she could, while she was still able. It was going to get dark. And cold. She nestled in against Lo for warmth.

"It's just an estimate, but I'm sure he's right, " Thom replied. He looked back at their growing settlement: circles of transports, their hatches in close proximity, already partially covered in snow. Channels dug between them offered little protection from the icy, cutting wind. In preparation for the coming darkness, tiny lights had been strung along the walkways. There were enough transports that their city extended from the shore back toward the *Population*, now some distance away. The icecap was growing, though now as they all knew, far too slowly to do anything meaningful in their lifetime.

Thom wasn't sure what to make of the scene before him. Koin and Ralla's secret project would keep those who had made it here alive, for now. But had they survived this long just to die on the surface? Was this stark, frigid landscape the new beginning they'd hoped for? These questions faded from his mind quickly, as they had many times over the previous days. His friends were alive, he was alive, and Ralla...

Dija seemed to read his thoughts and squeezed his hand. No patronizing optimism from Dija, Thom thought. They both knew what Ralla thought about what he'd done. Or at least, they assumed. She hadn't spoken to any of them since the escape. He turned back to face the sunset, with the vivid memory of the look Ralla had given him when they'd made it to the surface. It wasn't anger, it was contempt. He couldn't see her forgiving him; there was too much hatred in her eyes.

Lo reached over Dija's head and put his hand on his friend's shoulder. Dija wrapped her arms around the waists of both men and pulled them closer.

Together they squinted and watched as the deep orange-red slice of sun dipped below the horizon, enveloping them in a murky twilight.

Then darkness.

—-‑--

The ocean lapped at the ice, freezing some, taking some. The wind shifted directions, unsure in the fading light. The waves, just ripples when looked at from above, continued outwards in every direction. Every direction was away from the pole. Away from the Fountain. Away from the ice. At a distance the Fountain was but a black aberration on a darkening sky. At a distance, the curve of the world swallowed it up.

Out there, nothing but water.

Out there, swells and sea.

Away from the Fountain and down.

Farther and farther down.

Daylight again. The sun's heat warms the air, the wind pulls at the sea, taunting and teasing it, pulling waves higher and higher. Swells of enormous size, travelling the world, combining with others, rounding up, rolling beasts of tremendous power.

South, farther and farther south. The sun high above, evaporating the water, beating down the sea, building storms. Still the swells come, they come from hemispheres away, unable to stop, nothing to stop them. Finally, their power unleashed in a fraction of a moment. Rising up, peaking, reaching for the sky and the sun, before falling over, crashing down,

...on land.

ACKNOWLEDGEMENTS

To Dennis, Karen, and my beta readers Phil, Brent, Carrie, Sara, and Chris. This was a long time coming, I know. Your help and insight have been invaluable.

And of course to Mom and Dad. Thanks for always reading.

ABOUT THE AUTHOR

Geoffrey Morrison is a privateer writer and editor based in Los Angeles. You can find out more about him and his writing at geoffreymorrison.com, or follow him on Twitter @techwritergeoff.

The cover was designed and illustrated by the brilliant Clara Moon.

The sans-sarif font used on the cover, title page, headers, and elsewhere, is called TELEGRAFICO and was designed by Ficod, ficod.deviantart.com.